WHO DO YOU THINK YOU ARE, MAGGIE PINK?

JANET HOGGARTH

Boldwood

First published in Great Britain in 2022 by Boldwood Books Ltd.

Copyright © Janet Hoggarth, 2022

Cover Design by Alice Moore Design

Cover Photography: Shutterstock

A CIP catalogue record for this book is available from the British Library.

Paperback ISBN 978-1-80162-737-5

Large Print ISBN 978-1-80162-733-7

Hardback ISBN 978-1-80162-732-0

Ebook ISBN 978-1-80162-730-6

Kindle ISBN 978-1-80162-731-3

Audio CD ISBN 978-1-80162-731-3

MP3 CD ISBN 978-1-80162-735-1

Digital audio download ISBN 978-1-80162-729-0

Boldwood Books Ltd
23 Bowerdean Street
London SW6 3TN
www.boldwoodbooks.com

For my mum, Jean Roberts, who was named Glenys Wynne-Jones for six weeks before her birth mother, Mair Wynne-Jones, was forced to give her away. For Mair Wynne-Jones, who had no choice in the matter, and for Gladys Beatrice MacDonald, who was a wonderful mum and nana: I still miss you.

PROLOGUE

'She wants to breastfeed,' Fiona snapped at the midwife, 'why won't you let her?'

'She's not the baby's mother.'

'Of course she is!'

'This baby's going to the nursery. A nurse'll give her a bottle.'

'Let Morag do the bottle!'

Bone-weary, I gazed down at Shona swaddled in a scratchy towel, her perfect rosebud mouth pursed, blowing me a kiss, eyes squeezed shut like a sleeping mouse. They hadn't wanted me to hold her, but Fiona had forced them. They said I was shivering too much, I might drop her.

'I'll sit right there, she won't drop her!' Fiona had said calmly. I'd never witnessed this side of my sister before. She toed the line, crossed her Ts and dotted her Is, didn't step on the pavement cracks and never ever challenged the status quo. She wasn't a pushover, she just did was what expected. But not today. In lieu of a maternal figure, she had stepped into the shoes and admirably filled them. 'She's just been through birth, if you won't let her hold her baby, you're animals.' The older midwife had practically had steam blasting out of her ears and puffed up her chest to reply, but the younger-looking one had touched her arm, a warning gesture.

'I'd like to give her a bottle, please.' I drew on the last breath of fire in my belly. 'I'm not going to see her again, it's the least you can do.'

Five minutes later, after barely checking I was in one piece, the old bitch of a midwife thrust a bottle in my face, no demonstration of how to encourage Shona to 'latch on', the term I had gleaned from the library book Rita had borrowed for me.

'You better hurry up, she needs to have a bath and go to the nursery. This room needs cleaning.'

The younger midwife had already been called away to another birth, the yelling echoing down the hallway outside.

'Fine, we'll sit in the corridor!' Fiona spat at her. 'Don't mind that she's fifteen, scared, and has no idea what she's doing or feeling, you get your bloody Shake n' Vac out.'

'She can't take that baby anywhere.'

'Then give us five minutes.' Fiona stood up, like a boxer itching to start the fight. If she had gloves on, she would have been tapping them together in anticipation.

'Five minutes!' The midwife left, no doubt checking her watch so as not to give us a minute more.

'Quick, get yer boob out!' Fiona instructed.

'What?!'

'Breastfeed while she's not here. Give me that.'

I handed her the bottle and she put it on the floor.

'I brought this too.' She pulled a yellow blankie out of her handbag. 'Shall we wrap her?'

While I fumbled with the hospital gown, wearing a bulky sanitary pad harness under paper pants, Fiona clumsily wrapped Shona over the top of the towel in the blankie she had knitted for her. She looked like a plump sausage roll from Ruby's bakery in Tain.

'What do I do?' I hissed. 'I can't remember anything from those books, my brain's not right.'

'There's nothing wrong with your brain, you're just exhausted,' Fiona said. 'I read that the earlier you get them to latch on the better. Something about the initial milk having more goodness in it. Put her on your nipple.' Any other time, this would have been excruciating and hilarious – my sister prodding my boobs with her bare hands. We hadn't seen each other starkers since we'd been wee nippers, and all of a sudden she'd seen me wide open, naked, giving birth – my body public property, a birthing machine. She caught my eye and laughed. 'Sorry. I think she needs to sniff your milk, I read that in a book too.'

'It's like bloody David Attenborough!' But I did as she said.

Shona roused slightly from her post-birth slumber, eyes still closed, her mouth opening like a baby bird.

'Shove her on!' Fiona cried.

Shona couldn't latch on and started greeting, squeaks really.

'Here, squeeze your nipple, see if anything comes out.'

'Jesus, Fiona, I'm not a bloody cow.'

'Do you want to feed her or not?'

'Aye.' I squeezed with my thumb and forefinger, and a blob of fluid appeared like glistening mercury in a school science experiment. I tried Shona again and this time she attached herself and started sucking.

'You did it! How does it feel?' Fiona asked.

'Odd, tickly, stingy.' I stroked Shona's head while she fed. She kept falling asleep and I had to blow on her face several times startling her.

Fiona got her camera out.

'No, not while she's feeding. After.'

Both of us stared in disbelief at Shona, like we'd just spotted JR Ewing in the Co-op buying milk. Only yesterday she'd been wedged inside me.

'We could run away with her,' Fiona said desperately. 'I could get a job to support us.'

'You wally, you need to finish college.'

'I could do it after, when she's older.'

'What if we get caught? How'll we leave the hospital, where'll we go?' More than anything in the world, I wanted to agree to this daft plan. 'You've no money. I've none. We're buggered.'

'I could tell Da and he could send us cash behind Maw's back.' The more she travelled into the fantasy future, the less real it felt. 'We could rent a cottage near Loch Ness. Remember you've always loved it there, especially in the winter when the trees are bare and the tourists have trickled away. I could work in the visitor centre or a café, then you could work there too once she's at school...'

I looked at my sister, tears silently sliding down her cheeks.

'Yes, I could work shifts and we could take it in turns picking her up from school. Do you think she'd like going to gymnastics after, like you used to? Or guitar lessons, like me?'

I grabbed her hand and she squeezed it hard.

'Maybe she'll like something different, that's just for her...' Fiona kissed Shona's head as the door opened and the fantasy burst all over us.

'You've actually had six minutes!' the midwife said, then noticed what was going on. 'What did I say?! The bottle only!' She strode towards me and for one crazed moment I thought she was going to wallop me across the soulless room. 'Give her to me.'

'She's still feeding,' I replied, cradling her head, protecting her.

'She can go onto a bottle now. Hand her over.'

'Two minutes,' Fiona bartered.

'You've got one. You two'll be the death of me...'

When my time was up, Shona was asleep again and I tightened my grip. The midwife bent down to take her, but I wouldn't surrender my precious daughter. She sighed heavily, glancing at me, her eyes holding my gaze for longer than necessary.

'I've a granddaughter your age. Do myself a mischief if this was her... Tell you what, I'll put her in the nursery with a name tag on, near the door, make it easier for you to see her.'

'I don't want her to go,' I cried, my heart flooded with panic.

'You can see her in the nursery, I promise. She isn't going anywhere for a while. I'll keep her in the shawl.'

She attempted to prise my fingers from around the blanket. But I just held on.

'Listen, hen, we can do this the easy way, or the hard way. I don't think you want the hard way, do you?'

'We'll see her in the nursery,' Fiona cajoled me. 'Won't we? We'll go visit, take pictures.'

'Aye, she'll be waiting for you in there all clean like a new penny. Maybe you can give her another bottle.'

I looked at the midwife, now on her knees in front of me, her mascara flaking onto her blotchy cheeks, the powder worn away.

'What's the hard way?' I sobbed. 'It can't be harder than this.'

'Just give me the baby, hen. Rip that plaster off.'

I let my body go limp and howled like a wounded animal. The midwife swept Shona up from my lap and headed to the door, turning before she left.

'I've set you up in a private room. Stacey will be here in a minute to take you.'

'So, the old bitch has a heart,' Fiona whispered as I collapsed into her arms, my left breast leaking milk onto my gown.

1

Margaret Pink, Maggie for short, was forty-three, and well aware she could have survived the Blitz saddled with that moniker. She'd googled 'name change deed poll' a trillion times before she'd reached twenty-one, but gently grew into the name 'Maggie' like it was a pair of school shoes presciently bought a size too big, safe in the knowledge she would eventually fill them. Her gradual acceptance was also aided and abetted by *The Simpsons*, a programme her parents didn't approve of, but appreciated children might enjoy, even if the English spoken didn't resemble their boomer comedic favourites, *Monty Python* or *Faulty Towers*.

Her parents had always been old as far as Maggie could remember. They'd been lawyers dealing with dull local disputes, party wall wranglings and personal injury claims. The most thrilling case ever to embroil them was Totty v. Cadbury. Kevin Totty, a selection-box line worker, almost lost his hand in an unfortunate wrapping incident at the Hoylake Milk Tray factory. Pinks made the front of the *Liverpool Echo* when they succeeded to win their client a generous out-of-court settlement. Maggie had no idea you could put a price on two fingers and a thumb tip. Apparently enough for Kevin (forever known as Cadbury's Fingers) to live his best life in a footballer's mansion in Caldy... Even after the infamous victory, Maggie couldn't be lured to the dizzy heights of malpractice suits and lost income claims due to wonky paving slabs. Mum and Dad had promised her the office with its own handbasin next to the kitchen. Not even that luxury was enough, so when she graduated with her law degree, she immediately escaped to the bright lights of London like a character in a Beatles song.

Callow and sheltered though she was, Maggie was concrete in her conviction that the legal world was not for her. What on earth she actually wanted was less certain. The one thing that she'd really loved hadn't been overly encouraged, finding itself consigned to the back-burner. Of course, her parents humoured her with singing lessons and supported her through choir practice, both immensely proud when she was chosen to sing the Christmas carol solo at Liverpool Cathedral for the district schools service. However, they made it abundantly clear only a select few made a real living from singing. Why not pursue it as a hobby – there's always law, *the practice can be yours one day...*

Meanwhile, Nisha, her best friend from home, had offered Maggie the spare room in her poky Camberwell flat – no other medical students would take it. Maggie sold it to herself that she was getting unparalleled life experience in one of the most exciting (and expensive) cities on the planet while she decided what to do for the rest of her existence. In reality, she hardly saw Nisha and the box room she sublet had been an airing cupboard in a previous life, the pipes not rerouted, so turning over in bed could result in third-degree burns. And to add insult to injury, the rent ate up most of Maggie's waitressing wages. The lure of law and the safety net of living at home while she qualified almost claimed her. The day before she was going to throw in the towel, Nisha had rescued her from party wall oblivion by dragging her out to a bash at a karaoke bar in town. One bottle of Merlot in, Maggie wowed Eva, the birthday girl, with a rendition of 'Get the Party Started', waking the following morning with a grade four hangover, a pipe burn on her foot and a shoo-in of an interview at a city-based marketing firm. Who said you couldn't make money from singing?

The majority of Maggie's first day at Foster and Aden was spent fielding questions about her northern accent and lineage rather than finding out which was the temperamental photocopier, and what director to avoid in the lift. 'So you're from Liverpool!' everyone had crowed after each introduction as soon as she'd opened her mouth. A crass impersonation of her vocal calling card had swiftly followed, with these theatrical flourishes varying in accuracy from offensive to downright racist. Maggie soon grew tired of explaining she was in fact from the Wirral, and just nodded along when they mentioned the Beatles and the defunct TV soap, *Brookside*.

The Wirral was posh Liverpool, but not *actual* Liverpool. A cheap ferry ride across the river Mersey where all the footballers live. That fact alone should have been enough to pinpoint its whereabouts, though not many had heard of it at her fancy new London job, being south of Watford Gap services. Maggie wasn't even from the Wirral, she was technically Scottish, but that complication wasn't something she talked about...

As she deliberated whether to apply her usual eye make-up, Maggie reflected on her impetuous flight from West Kirby twenty years ago. Where would she be now if she'd not accepted that job at Foster and Aden? Deciding against mascara, Maggie smudged her lips with reliable Pillow Talk and blotted. Even if she'd remained in West Kirby, nothing could change where she found herself right now. Today was the funeral of Iris Pink, her mum. Maggie couldn't muster the appropriate breast-beating anguish in keeping with the death of a parent and for that she was riddled with guilt. Of course she was devastated, but the sadness was being power-hosed to smithereens by the undulating excitement and expectation of what was going to happen next. Maggie was about to discover Who She Really Was. But first she had to stand graveside in her Zara black dress and sunglasses and dutifully wave Iris off on her journey to reunite with Jonathan, her husband and Maggie's dad, who had died five years previously.

Of course she cried, her pinkie grazing Adam's thumb as he tried and failed to clasp her hand, either for show or for himself. Roxie stood next to him, typically avoiding any contact with her mother. Maggie stole a look at her in her navy H&M tea dress and Doc Martens, hastily cleaned with a make-up wipe just before the hearse had arrived. Roxie was trying not to cry, her knuckles yellow starbursts from the effort of squeezing them to keep the tears at bay. Roxie never cried. Unless Adam did, and then it was like the Rivers of Babylon. Her dad always her weak spot.

Returning to her childhood home where her past and future pulsed away in the back office, Maggie did the rounds, offering plat-ters of Marks & Spencer's finest. She politely talked to neighbours, including beloved Mr May and Harriet, the Granger family – the new owners of Pinks Solicitors, Nisha and her mum, Heema. Her much older cousins lived in Canada and hadn't flown over. If Mum and Dad had conveniently arranged to die at the same time, they would have coughed up for the flights.

When everyone had finally drifted off, leaving a graveyard of egg and cress, and Adam and Roxie were stationed in front of the TV, catching up on one of their interminable box sets, Maggie crept up the stairs. She stood hesitantly outside the home office, where her parents had stashed all her glowing school reports; graduation certificate; every single school photo with varying degrees of wonky bowl cuts; childhood drawings: a total curation of their love and hope for her, their only daughter. She touched the familiar brass doorknob, and breathed in the opposing smells of the house: polish and dust. This was it, the moment she had been unconsciously waiting for her whole adult life. Her heart throbbed in her throat as she opened the door...

2

The office was half empty, the shelves swept of books. The few Maggie had filched were stashed in the boot of her car, the rest living out their days at the Cancer Research shop, along with a forest of knick-knacks and bags of clothes soon to be catnip to hipsters everywhere.

Maggie had refrained from delving into the filing cabinet before now. It felt like a huge betrayal while Iris was above ground, like her comatose soul would rally the minute she opened the drawer, infuriated Maggie hadn't the manners to wait until she'd logged off. However, in reality, Maggie had actually invented that reason for leaving it until now, not wishing to unpack the myriad motives and emotions attached to an occasion like this.

Iris and Jonathan had always been very open with Maggie about the fact she was adopted and it was brought up periodically in conversations throughout her life. The last time had been before her mum had got sick. Iris had mentioned on the phone that Inverness had been in the news that day, a world record for the largest haggis having just been broken there. 'I wish I'd tried proper haggis when we came to collect you. It's supposed to be better than the ones in Morrisons...' Maggie had suggested trying MacAndrew and Sons in West Kirby next time she had a penchant for haggis. She was sure they'd knock one up for her...

Maggie had been in West Kirby 'working from home' since the call from Sheltering Arms nursing home over two weeks ago. 'I'm sorry, Maggie, she's probably got forty-eight hours at the most. I'd get here as soon as you can.' Even though it was expected, the call was still a shock and represented the culmination of toing and froing up the motorway every two weeks.

Maggie had sat with her mum until she died, holding her papery hand, returning to the empty house and an M&S microwave meal for one that was still there at breakfast. Maggie couldn't admit it was a relief when she eventually died, but she hadn't seen Iris Pink since she went missing in action sixth months previously, gradually drowning under a sea of diamorphine. Like the tortoise, the cancer had finally overtaken the dozing hare.

Maggie knelt down and dragged open the grey metal cabinet, everything arranged in impeccable alphabetical order, naturally. She pulled out the file that read *Margaret Adoption* in her mum's sloping script.

She could still recall the day they'd told her like it had happened five minutes ago. Other childhood memories had faded into ghosts of days out and generic holidays by the sea. This one remained in sharp focus.

'Margaret, we have something to tell you.'

Maggie had been wearing a red puff ball skirt, reluctantly allowed for her sixth birthday. They were ubiquitous vile marshmallow creations – a skirt and a cushion rolled into one. She could remember sitting on the chocolate-brown sofa in the living room, the plush velvet tickling the back of her legs, and that she'd eaten egg sandwiches for lunch with Walkers roast chicken crisps. She'd been looking through her mum's *Life Goes to the Movies*, her favourite go-to book ahead of a Barbie marathon. It was a cumbersome hardback coffee-table book depicting the lives and films of movie stars long past their sell-by date: Marilyn Monroe, Marlon Brando, Cary Grant, Paul Newman and many more cohorts. Maggie had loved turning the outsized pages almost as big as her, and pressing her nose against the glossy paper, inhaling the almondy-vanilla smell. She adored the glamour and pored over the old-fashioned dresses and behind-the-scenes pictures searching for inspiration for a particularly meaty Barbie storyline to act out with Nisha.

Her dad had opened the conversation while her mum stretched it out like one of Jimmy Stewart's famous monologues.

'You know that we love you very much and that all we want is the best for you.' Peculiar words for a six-year-old to receive, but her parents were used to dealing with adults. She remembered wondering when she could go out and play with Nisha because she had a new Barbie and they were going to introduce her to her Sophia Loren Barbie, and possibly Ken (Rock Hudson), if Maggie could find his check slacks (Iris called them that). 'Mummy and I need you to know that we weren't your first mummy and daddy.' Which was a bit of a surprise...

'Where are they?'

'Well, your first mummy is in Scotland, where we adopted you.'

'What's adopted?'

'It means we took you home and you became our daughter.'

'Why?'

'Because we wanted to have a child to look after and care for.'

'Where's my first daddy?'

'We don't know. Your first mummy didn't say.'

'Have you met my first mummy?'

'No. We know her name, but we never met her. Her name is Morag.'

'Why didn't she want me?'

There had been a long pause after that question.

'She was too young to look after you properly, so we helped.'

'Can I show her Sophia Loren Barbie?'

'Maybe one day.'

'Can I play with Nisha now?'

Morag had been steamrollered in favour of Barbie. In Maggie's young eyes, it was a worthy putdown, not able to articulate the slight at having been so heavily rejected.

'Can Morag ever find me?' she asked her mum one wet Sunday afternoon when she was about ten. She'd been watching *Annie* and it had sparked an avalanche of anxiety. Eponymous heroine Annie had been dragged from Daddy Warbucks' mansion by her 'real' parents, away from her charmed life.

'Your adoption was closed,' her mum had explained. 'That means Morag doesn't know who adopted you, or where you live. She has no way of contacting you. But if you want to trace her once you reach eighteen, you are allowed. Her details may be on file if she wants to be found. We've been sending a yearly photo to the agency as agreed, but all she knows is your first name.'

Maggie swung between total curiosity and complete and utter contempt for being carelessly thrown away like a broken toy. If she thought about Morag, especially when the teenage years hit, she tried to imagine giving away something she cherished (Snoopy circa 1986 who followed her to university and beyond, still rammed under her pillow to this day minus eyes and ears). Maybe Morag had never loved her. And when she'd reached fifteen, the age she'd learned Morag had been when she was born, the thought of being a mum seemed so far out of reach that Maggie kind of sympathised. Morag wouldn't have been able to go to discos, snog boys, buy clothes, have parties – she would have been looking after her. Not that Maggie was living the wild party life of an American teenage movie heroine, but it was nice to have aspirations.

As she approached adulthood, she realised Iris and Jonathan had not arrived at adoption via a smooth path. The fact that they had reached as far as Scotland in order to procure her spoke volumes. To safely preserve her cosy family in aspic, Maggie decided she'd leave Pandora's Box unopened then. However, she *was* curious.

From an early age, Maggie had been plagued by a constant sense of otherness. As well as her innate musicality, over the years another quiddity sprouted from nowhere. Iris and Jonathan sat at the sensible end of life's varied spectrum. Brown sofas, beige walls, practical shoes, taking their teeth out before bed. They had not abided by superstitions. Both parents would easily ignore a single magpie, happily open an umbrella indoors and often make a point of walking under ladders, setting Maggie's teeth on edge. Maggie, on the other hand, was drawn to these old wives' tales like a magpie to a sparkly ring. She'd heard Heema, Nisha's mum, bang on about Karma and not crossing on the stairs and she'd been hooked. Even now, if she forgot to salute a single magpie she lived in fear of a plane's frozen toilet waste falling from the sky and flattening her in the middle of Peckham Rye.

As time passed, the initial anger at her birth mother shrank and Maggie came to a decision she'd look for her when it felt right. Maybe Morag could provide answers to why her right thumb resembled a toe, while the left one was completely normal; and why her ridiculously wiry hair snapped off if she washed it more than once a week but smelled like a sheep if she didn't. Yet Maggie's own life ultimately became so all-consuming, the mere thought of embarking on an intense liminal journey with no guaranteed happy ending stalled her. Even when her mum and dad encouraged her, she still worried Morag might have a whole new life and a family who knew nothing of her existence. She didn't want to be that interloper barging in and bruising a perfect nuclear family. But the boiled-down reality was the tacit fear that Morag might want nothing to do with her at all; a second rejection would have been crushing. Nevertheless, by the time Iris was in the Grim Reaper's waiting room, a switch had flicked as if Maggie had been waiting for it the entire time. With both parents dead, there really was nothing standing in her way. Rejection now could feel no worse than this.

The manila file was rather flimsy and Maggie opened it, her hand shaking. The original birth certificate was present, along with all the information she already knew, Morag's age when she'd had her – Roxie's age. Roxie could scarcely put a mug in the dishwasher, or pick up her three-day knickers from under the bed with her balled-up socks. The idea of her making up bottles and rising before midday to do anything other than sit on her arse mainlining TikTok was laughable. Once more, Maggie tried not to blame Morag. Experience had taught Maggie that Morag had probably had to choose herself over her child. And what teenager wouldn't do that? After all, they were children themselves and prone to solipsism. But sometimes, if she dug a little deeper, that hurt she'd felt aged six, when she'd discovered she wasn't who she thought she was, floated to the surface like a protective life raft and she'd cling to it.

Maggie picked out a never-seen-before photo of herself in a yellow shawl, eyes firmly closed against the world. Something slipped out onto the floor: a plastic birth tag with a name written on: Shona MacDowell. The adoption certificate cited everyone's ages, occupations. Morag was a student.

Maggie flipped open her laptop on the desk, the form already waiting. She filled in the missing details and pressed send before fear ground her to a standstill. She had lasted forty-three years without knowing who Morag was and was certain she could wait a few more months. There were more pressing matters to deal with.

Endings were never easy, whether it be a family bag of crisps or the end of a relationship. The crumbs still went everywhere…

'What are you watching?' Roxie and Adam sat squashed together on the small faux Louis XIV sofa, sharing a bag of posh tortilla chips left over from the wake.

'*Ozark.*'

Maggie knew what it was, she just needed an opening. Fancy that – needing an opening with your own family.

'Are you both packed?' Maggie wanted to smack herself in the face for asking such inane questions but couldn't stop talking.

Roxie just rolled her eyes. Of course they'd not unpacked. They'd only come up for the funeral and they were all driving back tomorrow morning, together…

* * *

Once home, the following evening, Adam slowly cleared away the remnants of their takeaway, dragging time out like a dead man walking, whilst Roxie retrieved her phone from her pocket.

'No phone this evening, Rox,' Maggie said.

'What? We're not doing anything. Ash's FaceTiming in ten.'

'We're going to sit here a while longer.'

'I'm busy.'

'Rox,' Adam said in a warning tone like a teen whisperer.

'But, Dad…?'

'No, Mum's right. No phone for now. We need to chat.'

Playing to the gallery, Roxie made a meal out of shoving her phone back in her pocket. Sighing like a water buffalo finished off the performance nicely.

'What?!' If defiance were a person, it would be Roxie.

Adam sat next to her like they had planned, with Maggie opposite, girding herself for the vitriol. She had pondered opening with a preamble, but she guessed she'd be derided for not getting to the point.

'I'm really sorry, Roxie, but Dad and I are splitting up.'

Silence.

Adam glanced sideways at an expressionless Roxie.

'Do you understand, Roxie?' Maggie tried again.

'That's it, no easing me in gently? No, it's not you, it's us. We're useless twats who can't pretend like everyone else's parents.'

'Roxie!' Maggie couldn't fucking win!

'Roxie, we're sorry,' Adam said.

'Don't you mean Mum should be sorry. Do *you* want to split up, Dad?'

Maggie had no idea where this strength of her own convictions originated.

'I don't think anyone ever wants to split up, Roxie,' Adam finally managed. 'Otherwise why would people get married? It just happens.'

'So you and Mum *just happened*? Out of the blue? I'm not stupid, I can see what goes on!'

'Look—' Maggie began.

'NO! This isn't even fair. You get what you want and me and Dad have to put up with it. You've been like this ever since...' Roxie's voice faded like someone jumping off a cliff, hovering momentarily before plunging head-first into the abyss.

'Roxie, if you were little, I'd send you to your room – now,' Adam said quietly.

'Don't worry, I'm going.' She pushed her chair back, the legs scraping the floor like unoiled brakes.

Maggie studied her hands until she could be sure Roxie was in her room. The slamming of the door and the maxed-out volume of The Cure her sign to talk.

'That went well.'

'You think?' Adam sighed and shook his head.

'I was being facetious.'

'Wrong time and place. She just needs time to adjust. I need to move my things into the spare room.'

'Adam, I can move to the spare room. I said I would.'

'No. I can't bear to be in that bed on my own. You keep it.'

He stood and walked up the stairs, while Maggie sat at the table, guts swilling with adrenaline, but also something else: relief. Her phone pinged.

How did it go?

Nisha checking in.

Roxie's fuming. Adam's moving his things now.

Are you OK?

Shaky but OK. It's been a long time coming.

Love you. I'll ring at the weekend. But if you need me before, let me know.

Nisha was Maggie's chosen family, her personal curator who knew the parts of her Maggie had long since forgotten. She wished they lived nearer each other.

Suddenly, all hell broke out upstairs.

'Dad! *She* should move in here, not you!'

Maggie ran up the stairs two at a time, meeting a seething Roxie on the landing outside the spare room.

'Roxie, I *want* to sleep in here.'

'Only because she made you. Dad, grow some!'

'Roxie, stop! This is bad enough without you making judgements on stuff you know nothing about.' Adam rarely lost his cool, but his twitching eye was winking disconcertingly.

Roxie thundered back to her room and banged the door – a historic crack zigzagged from the frame all the way up to the ceiling. Years of Roxie's protests were evident everywhere. Most doors had various screw holes splattered around the handles where repeated slamming had caused the handle to work loose only to be reattached somewhere else.

'She's going to hate me for ever.' Maggie longed for Roxie's pudgy toddler hand in hers, but even that seemed like a dream now. 'I'm going to bed. I've had enough of today. Hope you get some sleep.'

* * *

That first week of living together apart was fraught with niceties. Suddenly there were cups of tea every five minutes, offers of dinners to be cooked from both parties and you have the telly, no *you* have the telly waved like olive branches across the living room. Maggie almost joked they should split up more often, but stopped herself in time...

Among the upheaval, the thought of a reply from Morag kept her adrenaline fermenting, bulwarking her from the reality of feeling rootless and alone, an orphan at forty-three yet no different to a young girl who had lost both parents.

Maggie had become adept at checking emails in meetings, utilising her well-worn poker face. By Friday, she'd given up and stopped looking every five minutes. As long as there was no news, there was still hope that Morag was out there somewhere, waiting to meet her.

On Friday evening, at five o'clock, she made one final sweep of personal emails, and was surprised by two messages. One from the Adoption Tracing Agency and one from the estate agent in West Kirby. She stared for a whole minute, unable to decide which one to open first.

She clicked the estate agent one: Iris's house had a buyer. There was no chain and Crystal was hoping it would all complete like clockwork by the autumn. Maggie's childhood home going, going, gone. She felt unexpectedly usurped. Someone else would sleep in her apricot bedroom with the crack on the ceiling shaped like Italy's boot. Someone else was going to live next door to crazy Mr May and Harriet, his tap-dancing wife. Someone else's car would drive daily over the barely visible blue E painted on the road by a drunk Mr May, the remaining vestiges of glorious Everton daubed the night they won the 1985 European Cup. A warning and an order to repaint the road black by the policeman, luckily a Toffee supporter himself, saved Mr May from a night in the cells. Her parents had dined out on the story for decades... Countless memories silted in the walls of her old home that she had to stop right there or she'd be trapped in her office for ever...

Maggie's cursor hovered over the other email.

'Just do it,' she muttered.

Click...

3

Dear Ms Pink,

Thank you for your recent enquiry about your adoption in 1979. I can confirm we found details of your birth mother, Morag MacDowell, on file. I am terribly sorry to inform you, but Morag died recently.

The screen blurred into a white smudge while questions chattered in an orderly line at the back of Maggie's mind.

'Shhhhhhh, give me a minute.'

How could she be dead? Why hadn't Maggie tried sooner? What had she been afraid of?

A surge of raw grief slammed into her, nothing protecting her from the onslaught now. She huddled over her desk howling. As she heaved up great sobs, her shoulders shaking, disparate images flickered in her head: her mum holding her hand as Maggie queued for ice cream on New Brighton prom; Mum reading The Church Mice books while she pointed at pictures; Mum crying into her cup of tea in the kitchen after Nana Hilton died; Mum and Dad insisting on driving her to her Durham University interview, subsequently splurging on fish and chips, then allowing her a glass of wine; Mum holding her after Kieran, her first boyfriend, dumped her, the pain unbearable; her parents' faces when Maggie said she wasn't going to be a lawyer, that she was going to live in London, hundreds of miles away... She was never going to see Iris again. Ever. There was nothing for it but to come undone, something she found deeply unacceptable. But the tide was too strong to fight it. The difference from ten years ago when everything had spun out of control was she knew she could ring-fence this surge.

A soft knock on her office door startled her.

'Maggie—Oh my God, what's happened? Are you OK?' Izayah, her assistant, ran to her side, but then had no idea how to deal with her.

'It's OK, I think I'm just having a moment about Mum...'

He patted her shoulder as she tried to wipe her face without a tissue. He pulled a pristine packet out of his back pocket, glad to have a solution.

'You're like a Boy Scout, always prepared.'

'They taught us well... Why don't you go home? Don't worry about anything until Monday. I can look over the screenshots for the earthquake appeal.'

* * *

Maggie walked into the house to be greeted by music and chatting voices wafting down the stairs, evidence both Adam and Roxie were home. She closed the door quietly, wanting to be alone for a while longer. Too late, floorboards squeaked on the landing and Maggie actually prayed it was Adam rather than Roxie.

'Hey, you're home. Do we need to talk about estate agents?'

Maggie couldn't reply.

'Oh shit. What's happened?' Adam rushed from the bottom of the stairs to meet her on the sofa. 'Is it your mum?'

'Which one?' Adam frowned. 'I decided to look for Morag.'

'Ahh... And?'

'She's dead.'

'Shit. I'm so sorry.'

Maggie burst into tears again.

Adam grabbed her hands, it was the most they'd touched for months. 'Can I do anything? I know it's awkward, but do you want a hug?'

Maggie was struck by how alienated they'd become that he had to get permission to offer comfort. *What did that say about her?*

She nodded. Adam drew her in as she bawled into his Nivea Sport armpit.

'Do you want to talk about it?'

Maggie pulled herself upright, rubbing her eyes.

'I got an email from the adoption tracing people. They said she was dead.'

'Did they say anything else?'

'I stopped reading after that, I couldn't face it. It was probably just niceties.'

'Don't you want to check? Just in case you missed something?'

'What like – ta-da! Just kidding, she's really alive!'

'No! What if there's someone else you can contact? Your dad?'

'Oh yeah, I suppose I should.'

Maggie grabbed her laptop out of her bag and opened the email, reading it out loud:

'Dear Ms Pink, thank you for your recent enquiry about your adoption in 1979. I can confirm we found details of your birth mother, Morag MacDowell, on file. I am terribly sorry to inform you, but Morag died recently. Her sister, Fiona, had been asked by Morag to act in her place should you contact her posthumously. She has given the number of a solicitor in Inverness should you want to get in touch so the enquiry can proceed through a third party. You will find the number and contact at the end of the email.'

Adam had the grace not to say, 'I told you so...'

* * *

On Monday morning, after a weekend of imagined conversations and practice introductions, Maggie rang the solicitor as soon as she closed her office door.

'Hello, er, I wonder if you can help me? I need to speak to Catriona Watson.'

'Can I ask what it's concerning?'

'I was given this number and Ms Watson's name by the Adoption Tracing Agency. My name is Margaret Pink. I think she may be expecting my call.'

Maggie was put on hold, accompanied by some unexpected jazz piano; she'd been anticipating Scottish folk music. She idly doodled an eye on her notebook, ready to record any important details.

'Ms Pink, it's Catriona Watson. How may I help you?' She knew exactly why Maggie had called so this little charade was odd.

'Hello, I believe you were put in place as a go-between should I ever get in touch about Morag MacDowell.'

'Ah yes, her sister requested it on her behalf. I need to know what it is you want.'

Rude!

'If you'll excuse me, I don't really know what it is I want. I wanted to meet Morag but have since found out she died.'

This was the point Catriona could have interjected with, 'I'm sorry that must be upsetting.' Stony silence prevailed.

'Her sister Fiona made a point of standing in for Morag posthumously and I wondered if that meant something?'

'Fiona did indeed put herself in place at the request of Morag. I think to carry on Morag's dying wish.'

'Which was?' Catriona's obliqueness could certainly give Roxie a run for her money.

'I'm not at liberty to say.'

'You do know I'm her daughter that she gave away forty-three years ago?'

'Aye. It just seems a trifle puzzling that you would get in touch now after so long. Especially after she died.'

'I didn't know she'd died. Hence ringing here to find out about her.' Maggie wasn't sure what transgression she'd committed to ruffle Catriona's feathers.

'OK, well, Fiona said I was to contact her if you got in touch. We just weren't expecting it after all this time.'

'Did Fiona say she would be interested in speaking to me?'

'Aye. She's given me permission to ask for your mobile number if you want her to call you.'

'Of course!' Maggie's tummy sank; what if Fiona was a battleaxe too?

* * *   '

After a few days of such ceaseless phone checking that it became a tic, Maggie finally received a text.

Hello, it's Fiona, Morag's sister. I wondered when was a good time to ring you?

Now!

She'd squandered so much time already. None the less, her ringtone still managed to startle her.

'Hello, is that Margaret?' She had a very soft Scottish accent.

'It's Maggie, yes. Hello, Fiona.'

'I can't believe I'm talking to you… Baby Shona.'

'I found my name tag at Mum's house after her funeral a few weeks ago. That was when I realised I had another name.'

'Aye, Morag was told you'd been named Margaret after the adoption. So sorry about your mum. They sent a picture of you with your parents after they took you home. Morag had always wanted to call you Shona. But Maggie's nice.'

'When did Morag die?'

'Eight weeks ago…' Fiona gasped. 'I'm sorry, I still can't get used to it.'

'Don't apologise, I understand completely. Mum has only been gone a month. Grief's a total rollercoaster.'

'You poor thing, both mums gone. Did you wait until your parents had died before tracing Morag?'

'I suppose so, yes. They never hid it from me, but I dunno, it always felt easier this way. I thought I'd a good few years because Morag was so young… I've wasted all that time.'

'Aye, the timing's all to cock for sure… Listen, is there anything you want to ask me about Morag?'

'Gosh, so many things and in the same breath no idea. It's so overwhelming.'

'I can only imagine. Where do you live, Maggie?'

'London.'

'Have you ever been to Scotland before?'

* * *

'Uh-uh. No way. I'm not coming,' Roxie protested.

'Where are you going to stay then?' Maggie could have chiselled the script in stone and read it out loud word for word. *Every fucking time...*

'Here. I'm fifteen, I can stay home – alone.'

'Not for a week!' Maggie cried.

'Roxie, it's seven days of your life. You're going to meet family you didn't know you had. It'll be interesting if nothing else.' Maggie thought Adam wasn't exactly selling it, possibly because the only gatherings his family had were funerals. 'Or you can go and stay with Granny Slater in Watford.' Adam's mum inhabited a world where she watched soaps from when she woke at 10 a.m., until she went to bed at 1 a.m., with four bottles of sherry sprinkled like fairy dust across the week. Last year, she'd sent Roxie a birthday card for a ten-year-old. She showed more interest in the dirt she scraped from her nails while she gorged on the fabricated lives of dubious characters from across the globe.

'Dad, I know you'd never make me go there! I can stay with Ash.'

'Ash? I doubt it. We're into school holiday territory now. Ash's parents won't want to cater for an extra person morning noon and night. You're going with your mother.'

Adam had to interview some precocious up-and-coming techno DJ at a Berlin festival and would be away five days. Maggie had managed to take compassionate leave with some extra days tagged on. Roxie would be with her a week, then Adam would come and rescue her. She even argued about that. 'I'm not a kid, I can get on a plane by myself!' But Adam and Maggie were a united front.

After Fiona had tentatively invited Maggie to Scotland, she suggested she stay in Inverness, to give Roxie access to shops. 'I know what teenagers are like. It wasn't so long ago that I had two at home.' They were to meet in Catriona's Inverness legal practice. 'It keeps everything above board...'

The week before the trip elevated the atmosphere at home to

Game of Thrones levels of insurrection, minus grisly carnage. If walls were living things, blood would have been haemorrhaging from them.

'You've stolen my civil liberties!' BANG! A hairline crack slammed into existence on the kitchen wall.

'You're as bad as her now. I hate you both!' BANG! Plaster fell from the already loose patch of ceiling below Roxie's bedroom door.

'I'm never speaking to either of you again. I'm going to divorce *you*!' BANG! Books tumbled from the downstairs picture rail shelf, taking down an innocent vase and a key tray below.

'You're both fucking idiots. You deserve to die alone eaten by cats.' BANG! Roxie's door frame was shaken loose and at risk of falling off, a latticework of plaster cracks splintering outwards like a bomb blast.

Maggie and Adam attempted to reprimand her, but it was impossible to reason with, let alone censure, someone who just didn't give a fuck.

Maggie wasn't keen on Roxie accompanying her, but there was nowhere else she could go. She'd even considered postponing a few months, but she wasn't free of major work commitments again until October. Time felt like it was slipping away; she'd waited long enough. Maggie truly believed Roxie would come round, but she grossly underestimated the strength of pathological teenage brinkmanship.

'Roxie, we're leaving!' Adam called up the stairs on the Friday morning. The day was newly hatched; honeyed light streamed in through the kitchen windows.

Maggie held her coffee in a death grip waiting for Roxie to appear on time. There had been no movement since Adam had woken her at five, enough time to trowel on her pallor-inducing make-up. Maggie's foot tapped out an SOS on the floor, the table shaking in harmony. She and Adam both knew there was no point in trying to drag her out by force. Roxie would protest until the eleventh hour like a criminal futilely claiming their innocence on the steps to the gallows. All they could do was wait.

Adam joined her at the table and topped up his coffee. 'This is ridiculous. If you or I had acted like this when we were her age, we'd have been in the shit for years and clipped round the ear.'

'I actually don't know what to do. I've tried asking her quietly how I can help, that I'm sorry this impacts her, but it's not like I'm sending her to a gulag. It's a jolly, admittedly for me, but she's acting like it's torture. She only responds to you, but you can't play that card now.'

'My dad would have dragged me out by my hair and shoved me in the car with no clothes on. I remember once shouting at him I'd ring Childline and he started dialling it for me. He was a hard wanker.'

Maggie smiled ruefully at the well-worn story of Adam's tough-love household. In comparison, hers had been like an Enid Blyton novel.

'Right, I'm going to get her.' Just as Adam stood up, a door slammed above and insolent footsteps stomped down the stairs.

Roxie appeared in the doorway, dressed entirely in black, her face expertly made up to look like a doll. Protest make-up implying she was just a possession or some such diatribe. Right there, right then, Maggie didn't give a flying fuck, she just wanted to get on that plane.

4

Maggie's mum and dad had never visited Scotland, apart from to collect her, therefore she'd not been either. In hindsight, they were probably terrified Morag might spring from behind a shaggy Highland cow and steal Maggie away. Even though they had officially adopted her, the implicit fear was Morag would be hovering with a giant net and a bag of chocolate-covered raisins, Maggie's childhood snack du jour. Blood trumps water after all.

Well, it was supposed to, Maggie's own flesh and blood was doing a good impression of ghosting her. Not even chocolate could tease Roxie out of the doomscrolling black hole she'd forcibly locked herself in.

Maggie gave up and sat out the journey in her own bubble of anxiety.

Inverness Airport looked as if it had been airdropped in the middle of a field, like a glorified milking shed. The subsequent car journey led them through verdant fields populated by cows and into the city centre ten minutes away. It wasn't a conurbation like Liverpool or London with sprawling suburbs gradually bleeding into the surrounding greenery. One minute you were in the coun-tryside, the next you were absorbed into an abrupt cityscape.

Maggie expected an ardent protest about the fact they had to share a room in their city-centre hotel. Instead she was met with weighted silence. She glanced at Roxie, her nose pressed against her phone waiting for Maggie to finish unpacking (Roxie hadn't bothered). Maggie was certain an entire generation of kids would need counselling should they ever find themselves without adequate distraction for all of two minutes. Fuck knows how they would have coped in the nineties with Snake and a Discman that jumped every time you breathed. Maggie had no idea what Roxie was gawking at, some inane TikTok twat in a V-necked tight T, singing about baked beans most likely. *How was this OK?* No wonder that tangerine tit had made it to the Whitehouse.

Maggie procured an on-the-go Marks & Spencer meal deal so they didn't have to acknowledge the chasm between them. In a few hours, Maggie was going to meet her mother's sister, a genuine blood relative. She wanted to shake Roxie into understanding the enormity of it, but she was so far down the rabbit hole of My Mum's a Bitch, it seemed pointless.

As the hour loomed, Maggie steered them away from the shops towards the lawyer's office plonked between the shopping centre and a butcher's claiming to be purveyors of Inverness's most deco-rated, award-winning haggis.

'Hello, you must be Margaret,' the receptionist greeted them as they walked into the cosy waiting area. 'Please take a seat. I'll just check with Catriona.'

Maggie sat gingerly on the edge of one of the comfy bucket chairs, ready to jump up at any given moment while Roxie flopped into one as if she'd just hiked all the way from London. Maggie eyed the small coffee table loaded with magazines and leaflets:

'Family Law', 'How to Divorce Amicably', 'Will and Probate: a Guide'. They needed to up their leaflet game, there wasn't one on how to deal with sulky teenagers...

'Ms Pink, hello!' A short woman with salt-and-pepper hair bustled in wearing a smart navy suit, a whiff of school uniform about it, and a beige blouse the same colour as the hotel bathroom. She smiled and proffered her hand. A very different fish to the Catriona Maggie had been expecting. She wondered if she just had a terrible phone manner, or if in fact she'd initially been suspicious Maggie had her eye on the family silver...

Maggie stood, wiping her palm on her leg before offering it up.

'I'm Catriona, Fiona's waiting in my office.'

For the first time in years, Maggie wished Adam were here holding her hand, pressing his thumb reassuringly into her palm. That had worked in the distant past, but this yearning now felt incidental. She pushed it away with a 'Nice to meet you,' and turned to Roxie.

'You coming?'

Her daughter sighed like the very thought of standing was going to kill her.

Maggie glanced at Catriona, who smirked. Either she was relating to the couched parental-teenage tension or for the millionth time she was thinking thank fuck I don't have kids. Either way, Roxie stood up like her puppeteer had had a heart attack and slouched after them.

Catriona strode towards her desk set in front of a French door leading to a small outside courtyard. A petite woman sat with her back to the door and, at the sound of everyone trooping in, stood up – almost pirouetting to face them. She stared at Maggie for a second, then her face split into a wide smile, tears glistening in her eyes.

'Maggie!' She stepped forward to grab her hands. It was clear

Fiona's hair had once been as vibrant as Maggie's own much-maligned auburn glory. As she clasped her icy hands, the tight knot of anxiety loitering in Maggie's throat edged up and dissolved into tears. 'I'm sorry, that's my fault. I set you off!'

Fiona flustered around her pockets searching for a tissue and produced a pack before Catriona could reach over with the box from her desk.

'Please, sit yourself down.' Catriona ran and grabbed a spare chair by the door for Roxie. Roxie appeared to be as caught up in the drama as they all were and for once sat without a fuss.

Fiona glanced at Maggie again, almost holding her breath. 'I'm sorry, Maggie, it's just that you look so much like Morag, it's hard not to gape.'

'I'm so glad you said that!' Catriona said in relief. 'I've no idea what the protocol is for an event like this. But, yes, you look so like Morag!'

'I don't know what she looked like though,' Maggie said, longing to be in on the act.

'Let me show you.' Fiona ferreted about in her handbag and retrieved her phone, scrolling before handing it over. 'This is Morag two years ago, at Countryfest, compering the folk stage. Look through, you'll see a few of her.'

Maggie had previously declined Fiona's kind offer of sending photos before she travelled up. It felt a bit like googling the menu before going to a restaurant, hence dampening the thrill of antici-pation. But Maggie took the phone now and stared at the woman with the untamed red hair, obviously dyed to hold back the tide of time. Roxie stretched her neck to have a look, so Maggie shared the phone with her.

'Wow, Mum, you really do look like her,' Roxie breathed in disbelief. Maggie found it so discombobulating when Roxie behaved 'normal'.

Maggie studied Morag's face. Her brim-full of mischief eyes, the turn of her mouth as she confidently held the microphone, waving her arms towards an act just out of shot. She wore an exquisite purple African-print jumpsuit and a glut of jangling multicoloured bangles. The red sequinned feather earrings were unidentifiable to ornithologists everywhere.

'She's got better teeth than you though.' Back-of-the-net insult – Maggie almost congratulated her daughter and automatically pressed her hand against her lips, as if that could camouflage the gap between her front teeth. She loathed that gap and for a time had mildly hated her parents for refusing to pay for a brace. They'd insisted it gave her face character and she'd be grateful one day. She was still awaiting gratefulness, though Adam had said that was the first thing he noticed about her, apart from her beautiful singing voice. He'd said it was sexy. Maggie did get pregnant about five minutes after meeting him...

When Maggie had spoken to Fiona on the phone, she had briefly explained parts of Morag's life and what she had been up to in the last few years before her untimely death at the hands of breast cancer. There had been too much to absorb that being here felt like the best option. Just seeing the pictures of Morag on stage involved in music had germinated a bud of familial recognition that Maggie had longed for.

'She loved the festival,' Fiona said as Maggie swiped through the pictures, Morag bursting with energy in every single one. 'It became the focal point of her life over the last twenty years. It's also the biggest tourist draw for Benlachie. People book the hotels and campsites a year in advance for the four days no matter what the weather. Those weeks straddling the festival are enough for us to keep going through the winter months when less footfall passes through. Morag is—was a cornerstone of the village.'

'Who's looking after the festival now?' Maggie asked.

'That's what we're sorting out,' Catriona piped up. 'I'm a friend as well as Morag's lawyer. I draw up the artists' contracts. We're all stepping in until we find someone suitable who shares Morag's vision.'

'How about coming to dinner in Benlachie this evening?' Fiona impulsively offered. 'I know you've so many things you want to ask. You could follow me over there now in the car, have a look around? It's only twenty minutes away and it stays light until late at night, so you wouldn't be driving back in the dark...'

* * *

'Benlachie's a horseshoe shape. We're in the centre here – this road joins the other parallel one through there.' Fiona pointed towards the left of the car park at the road disappearing round a slight bend. Squat grey stone cottages on either side butted straight up to the pavement with no front gardens. Nets hung in some windows keeping rubberneckers at bay. 'Our pub's on the corner by the seafront, I thought we could have dinner there later. I have to dash back to do the banking before five and a few other bits. I wasn't expecting to drag you here...' She smiled at them. 'Och, I don't know what I was expecting, to be honest. Expect the unexpected, I think!'

'We can explore, don't worry. We'll meet you there, when?'

'Five thirty?'

Fiona rushed off in a cloud of apologies, leaving Roxie and Maggie wandering aimlessly towards the seafront. Maggie was grateful to have an hour or so to ingest the afternoon's events and inspect Morag's stomping ground for herself. As well as Fiona's general air of calmness, she also seemed genuinely pleased to meet Maggie, soothing her previous trepidation. Maggie breathed a sigh

of relief as gulls screeched overhead, synchronising with Maggie's
phone pinging in her pocket. Adam.

How did your meeting go? Hope you're OK.

Maggie found this pre-divorce no-person's land peculiar. Were
they friends? She didn't know. She *did* know Adam wanted to
remain together, though God knows why – they hadn't had sex
since she'd last waxed. And that exact date escaped her. Her mum's
death had been a line in the sand for so many events, the numbness
curiously safeguarded her from weathering heartbreak's storm:
losing weight while mainlining Aldi's finest rosé. Or sobbing at
every single advert on TV, especially those portraying a relationship, be it romantic or with a pet. This break-up felt different;
Maggie didn't yearn for everything to go back to how it was. They'd
tried that and it hadn't worked. Not the pretend dates, not the new
clothes, not the desperate weekends away to *talk things through*.
NOT the fucking painful as birth Brazilian. This split wasn't
sudden, so no one could accuse anyone of being surprised. Instead
it was rather like being slowly boiled alive.

'You and Adam were madly in love. Madly!' Nisha had lamented
when Maggie had first vocalised her desire to leave. 'Where does
that love go?'

'I don't know, Nish. But I can't find it.'

'You sure? I know you guys have been through the wringer,
especially you, but you were *so* good together, until, you know...
Everyone cried at your wedding because it was like True Love's Kiss
in *Shrek*. You'd found each other and had little Roxie.'

'Are you implying I'm Princess Fiona?'

'I mean you were meant to be together. I've been to so many
weddings where you're thinking, I give this two years max, or not
even that. Sometimes one or both of them have shagged other

people in the run-up. You and Adam weren't like that. It was refreshing.'

Nisha's reaction hadn't swayed her decision. Adam never knew about Maggie's initial confession to Nisha, because before she could pin him down, Iris rang. She had stage four bladder cancer. Caring for her hundreds of miles away became the convenient excuse for pretty much everything over the next two years. But as the chemo stopped slowing the inevitable, Adam and Maggie hit a wall. Maggie just couldn't see the point of staying and it became increasingly difficult to hide her irritation at his mere presence. He'd not done anything wrong, not then, anyway, it was all her...

Once Iris was in steady decline, Maggie had set the wheels in motion. Her skin itched at the thought of having to fake any more holidays, any more Christmases, any more birthdays. So she'd pulled the plug before she could back out with another excuse, hands shaking, palms sweating.

'I need to leave, Adam.' Roxie had been at Ash's house for a sleepover; Adam was chopping onions for the spag bol. He'd stopped chopping and turned to look at her, knife in hand.

'As in, leave leave? Not popping to the Co-op leave?'

'Yes. Proper leave. I'm really sorry.'

'Oh.' He'd put the knife down and considered it for a moment, his shoulders slumping.

Please don't cry, please don't cry...

'Ewwwww! A seagull just shat on my shoulder!' Roxie yelped, snapping Maggie back to the present, all thoughts of a vapid text reply to Adam lost.

'Didn't you know that's good luck?' Maggie rooted around in her bag for tissues and handed her one. Trying to help her wipe it would result in flinching and yells of 'Geroff!'

'Did you make that one up or is it a real superstition?' Roxie mocked her.

Roxie clearly hadn't inherited Maggie's irrational obsession with unexplained folklore. 'It's real... You shouldn't really wipe it off.'

Roxie rolled her eyes and immediately rubbed it off her black sweatshirt, leaving behind a pale streak.

The road to the seafront charmed Maggie, with renegade cobbles rupturing the tarmac and repurposed stone horse troughs overflowing with starbursts of buttery pansies and hot pink geraniums. Skew-whiff Disney-fied cottages fronted by dinky fairy-tale doors painted baby pink, lemon yellow and azure blue lined the street: Snow White's uniform. Roses climbed heroically from narrow raised beds set boldly on the pavement and sprawled up the trellised doorways, splashes of colour punctuating the grey stone facades. The odd pebble-dashed or brick building disturbed the uniformity and, as they approached the front, palm trees with whitewashed trunks stood to attention in several front gardens. A snap glance at them evoked a memory of Adam and Roxie dressed as mummies for Halloween years ago, both wrapped in a month's supply of loo roll. *Daddy and Roxie...*

A fair few tourists wandered lazily with ice creams, gulping down the sea air like landed fish on a quay. Years ago, Maggie would have automatically held Roxie's hand as they walked anywhere, even when everything was shit and she'd stumble zombified on a day trip. Roxie would always cry and demand Daddy too, so she would end up between them both, Maggie clinging on for dear life and Adam swinging her, keeping their family together on a wing and a prayer. But Adam wasn't there any more.

Turning the corner, the presence of the ocean smacked them in the face. The solid sea wall anchored the endless sky and scuttering clouds while the fierce salty breeze swiped their breath. They crossed the road to peer over the wall and discovered a perfectly white sandy beach, a few brave families holding down towels with stones and sandals. The tide was halfway up the long stretch of sand and a couple of kids chased the choppy waves as they broke. Maggie pulled the hood of her sweatshirt over her head to prevent her hair taking her eye out.

A flotilla of small vessels bobbed in the small marina, flags and poles viciously flapping, rammed in like sardines. A few weathered boards advertised day trips to the 'Famous Caves of Benlachie' and fishing trips for tourists wanting to catch a 'tiddler for tea'. Impressive sand dunes stretched far into the distance from the beach along the coast to the right, way past the village. It was simply stunning. This was where Morag had lived, she had breathed this air and had walked these streets.

Behind them, a row of shops curved round the seafront and joined the parallel road Fiona had pointed out. The Sea Shanty Tavern was perched on the furthest part of the bend at the bottom of the other street. It reminded Maggie of the stern of an ancient wooden sailing ship, crisscrossed windows spread along the outside and hanging baskets swung perilously either side of the heavy slate grey door, their floral passengers stoically withstanding the gale. It was still too early to meet Fiona, but a walk on the blustery beach would certainly inflict sand burn.

'Shall we get a drink from that shop there?'

Roxie nodded and they headed over the road to Trading Post. It appeared to multitask as a post office plus deli/café cum tourist trap selling postcards, dubious exotic shells and ubiquitous Scottish tablet. An old-fashioned bell tinkled as Maggie pushed the door – quite at odds with the old-school rave playing at the back of the shop behind the counter. Not very seaside.

A statuesque woman with braids tied up in a pink and yellow headscarf unpacked a box on the counter, bangles jangling on her wrist. Maggie coveted her yellow African-print top dotted with royal blue stars and red cherries; it reminded her of all the colourful material shops in Peckham where you could buy a ream of cloth for a tenner.

The woman glanced up from her task and, as Maggie peeled off her hood, she suddenly baulked before shrieking,

'Oh my God, a ghost!'

5

Roxie hadn't always hated her mum. 'Hate's a strong word,' Maggie bleated whenever Roxie declared she hated the next thing lining up for her hard-won derision. What was wrong with hating anything? There were so many things to hate. Obviously all the big stuff, like racism, sexism, war, abuse, rape, climate change, murder – all worthy of the strong emotion: hate. Small things shouldn't miss out either: fake pockets, Tiana Fucking Twatface, all of Year Twelve, the school's mashed potato (was it even potato?), those trainers with toes, February, Mr Harris, hairless cats (eewww), dark chocolate, pink, hummus, periods, getting roasted, feeling stupid, being publicly shamed, school – this list could probably stretch to three pages. Quit while you're ahead (another aphorism Roxie hated from Mother Dearest during arguments).

Also, what was it about her mum's ridiculous preoccupation with magpies, crossed cutlery and all the other oddball superstitions? There seemed to be something new each week. Roxie had no idea why her dad had put up with her for so long. They didn't exactly argue, but they never held hands or acted like they *used* to hold hands, or have sex. Roxie couldn't even entertain the notion of the latter because it made her stomach lurch like a tilting ship.

Mum always seemed to be on the verge of rolling her eyes; getting cross; snapping about the smallest things; didn't listen to her; never understood anything cool; patronised her by asking if she was OK. All. The. Time – *I'm alive, aren't I*; made her leave her room and 'join in'; talked to strangers like they were her best friends but didn't talk to her dad like she meant it. Admittedly, none of these were hanging offences, but for as long as she'd had cogent memories, Roxie felt her mum was 'other'. Aloof, that's what she was. Like she was better than them. As if someone else meant more to her than they did...

Roxie thought her dad was cool, as far as dads went. Obviously he was still old, right? But he knew some stuff, he was fun, always kind, told terrible jokes, was good at explaining things, apparently a DILF (puke in mouth), and he could parp out 'Jingle Bells' by squeezing his hand in his armpit.

Roxie had felt sad for her mum when Nana died, she wasn't a *complete* monster. She'd loved Nana – well, she had no choice, her other grandparent was an absolute twat. How had Granny Slater managed to deliver Adam into the world when she was like something from *Hoarders* on Sky? She was also Not Nice. It was a miracle she remembered Roxie's name half the time. Adam went once every six weeks to check she hadn't got rats (again), or that she hadn't died (here's hoping). She had no friends. Grandad Slater had been wiped from history when he eventually walked out, leaving Adam the man of the house. Roxie was convinced Granny had actually killed and buried him in the garden like a Netflix Scandi murder show. Anyway, Adam never talked about it, and that was all Roxie could garner from loitering behind doors listening while people were on the phone.

She couldn't believe her mum was behaving like the whole

'let's separate' was a mutual decision. The look on her dad's face told her everything she needed to know. Why couldn't they just stay together and carry on the charade until she'd left home? But why did she want them to stay together if she found her mum *so* annoying, and potentially hated her on occasions? *Interesting question.* The answer was twofold really. Firstly, she didn't want to live in two houses, dragging stuff from A to B all the time, having to spend time with her mum On Her Own. And secondly, whatever her mum's peccadillos, she was still her mum, and her dad was her dad and their job was to be her parents in the same fricking house. Otherwise, what was the point of having kids? Roxie knew it wasn't as simple as that, though for now, that's how she chose to view it. It made it easier than thinking about the truth, the past, about her parents as people with their own wishes and broken dreams...

As Roxie hovered next to her mum in the small shop in Benlachie and the beautiful-looking lady screamed at her, Roxie wanted the ground to open and swallow her whole. Drawing unwanted attention should actually be number one on the hate list before fake pockets.

It took her mum a minute to realise the woman was speaking to her. They weren't the only ones in the shop after all. The other customers turned to stare at her like a traffic accident, then, when they realised there was no ghost, returned to raking through the shell boxes or browsing the fancy biscuit shelf.

The woman grasped her mouth in horror, at the ghost or her outburst, Roxie wasn't sure. Her mum grabbed a couple of Cokes from the fridge and approached the counter, while Roxie cringed, knowing what was next: Talking to Strangers. Added to the list after Tiana Fucking Twatface. *I can't even...*

'Hello, I'm so sorry, I didn't mean to scare you.'

'No, *I'm* sorry,' the lady said, clearly embarrassed. 'You look so like a friend. It's uncanny.' Her eyes flicked away, but she couldn't help herself.

'Sorry about your friend... The ghost kind of gave it away.'

Stop it, Roxie wanted to yell, remaining as silent as a grave.

'She died a few months ago. I really miss her,' the woman continued.

'Did she live round here?' her mum asked.

'Aye, above the main pub.'

'The Sea Shanty?'

Roxie poked her mum in the arm. *Don't say anything else!*

'Aye, she did. Morag MacDowell. D'you know her? I mean, you could be related...'

Roxie poked Maggie again, so she shot her a sideways glance and received a death stare.

'No, I didn't know her.'

'Well, I bet I won't be the last person to say you look like her. Are you staying in Benlachie?'

'No, Inverness. Not far. We're here visiting. I better pay for these.'

'Have them on the house.'

'No, don't be silly, let me pay.'

'Och, I couldn't possibly, after I screamed at you.'

'Honestly, it's fine!' She pushed a two-pound coin towards the woman, but she wouldn't take it. There was an Alzheimer's charity money box next to the till so she posted it in there instead. The nice lady smiled. One of the shell seekers behind Roxie was clinking their quarry itching to pay. 'Thank you, nice to meet you.'

'Aye, and you. Pop in again.'

'Oh my God, Mum, I thought you were going to tell her,' Roxie burst out as soon as they were in the street.

'Is that what the poke was?'

'Dur.'

'Thought it best not to say. What if no one's supposed to know?'

'That's what I was trying to tell you.'

'Well, it's good we agree on one thing then.'

Roxie narrowed her eyes – she'd been tricked into talking. She loathed it when her mum drew parallels between them. She was NOTHING like her. She didn't even look like her. Everyone said how much she resembled her dad.

They wandered past The Sea Shanty silently sipping their drinks, nosing in shop windows. Roxie spotted a quirky-looking gift shop further up and strode ahead, stopping in front of the window. Something caught her eye; it wasn't merchandise. It was a boy behaving in a nefarious manner, something she knew all about. In January, Tiana Kaplinsky had tried to force her to shoplift a bra from Victoria's Secret in town. Roxie had never liked her, and this proved it all along – Tiana was a scrape. Tiana skirted the edges of friendship groups trying to fit in but never did. She didn't fit in because she tried too hard. And bitched ALL THE TIME.

'Get that one,' Tiana had urged Ash, Roxie's best friend.

'Er, no. I don't shoplift,' Ash had said. 'And I only wear crop top ones. If you want it, you get it. Leave me out of it.'

'How about you,' she'd tried Roxie.

'No chance.'

'You're all too scared. It's easy.' As they'd watched her stalk her prey – a pink and white stripy boob-busting lacy job – a blanket of doom had draped over Roxie. She knew what was going to happen – she would get blamed, it happened *all* the time. 'It's your resting bitch face,' Ash had joked once when Roxie had been accused by Mr Harris of smashing a box of new test tubes. 'You should smile more. Makes you look less aggy.' Roxie hated smiling when she wasn't in the mood. Fake shit wound her up. *Just be real...* Tiana had sidled up to the bra and moved other bras around to make it appear like she was considering them, then walked off round the other side. Roxie didn't want to be a part of it, and marched off, intent on leaving the shop. But as she had walked out of the door, the alarms exploded like bombs in a dick flick. What followed was the most humiliating few hours ever. Someone had rammed a bra in Roxie's bag without her noticing. And it didn't matter what she said, no one believed her. Tiana had fled, with or without the bra, Roxie never found out. Ash had stayed and faithfully relayed what had happened, that Roxie hadn't done it, that they had been with her the whole time. Obviously no one cared about checking the CCTV to see if Roxie was innocent. Her mum had been called and Roxie had been given a warning and barred from Victoria's Secret. Her face was pinned on the staffroom wall so people would recognise her as enemy number one.

'I can't believe you got yourself dragged in to something like that,' her mum had fired off, furious at being hauled out of a meeting.

'I didn't do it! It wasn't me!'

'You made the choice to hang out with this Tiana girl even though you don't like her.'

'I didn't have a choice, she followed us into town.'

'There's always a choice, Roxie. Next time, do yourself a favour and think first.'

'I did! I didn't do anything wrong!' But it didn't matter what she said, her mum wasn't on her side.

Roxie shivered at the memory as she watched the boy through the shopfront set up his lift: an expensive-looking leather notebook in a box. She checked the convex mirror up above him, he wasn't even trying to hide it.

'Do you want to go in?' her mum asked when she caught up with her.

'Maybe.'

Her mum headed to the door and pushed through, holding it

for Roxie. She followed and stationed herself opposite the boy, pretending to look at some cutesy china mugs in pantone colours and garden lanterns made from recycled tin cans.

The boy looked up, catching her eye. Roxie held his gaze and shook her head, then motioned to the mirror above him. He stared blankly at her, giving nothing away. He looked a similar age to Roxie, maybe a year older. His wiry black hair was cut close to the nape of his neck with the top springing free in black curls, one of which he pushed away from his forehead as he brought the notebook up towards his open coat. Roxie shook her head again, but he ignored her and slipped the book inside his jacket, turned on his heel and strolled towards the door without a care in the world. About ten seconds later, a large woman in a red dress sprinted past the display, through the shop door and after the boy.

'What's going on?' her mum asked, tipping a lantern so the candle almost fell out.

'No idea. I was checking out the mugs. Can we go?'

'I just want to look a bit more. I won't be a sec.'

Roxie walked towards the door to leave, but just at that moment the woman in the red dress paraded the boy inside, careful not to knock any of the displays, his arm in a vice-like grip. Roxie just happened to be standing right in their path. She kept her head down, not wanting to get in the way and flattened herself against the table.

'Thank you, lassie,' the woman said. Then she called to the man behind the desk, 'Can you ring Issy, he's done it again.'

'It's all go here, isn't it?' her mum said brightly. 'Maybe we should go somewhere else.'

Roxie couldn't get out of there quick enough. Before she left, she couldn't resist one last look at the boy before he was no doubt taken out the back and his parents called. But he was one step ahead of her. Standing at the till, his shoulders squared, back to the shopkeeper, he was ready for her. The minute Roxie rolled out her affected not looking but I am looking glance, he pierced her with his stone-cold eyes, lifted his hand up to his neck and drew it across executioner style. His message was loud and clear.

Roxie turned and fled, her mum calling out after her as she ran into the wind. Why did things *always* happen to her?

6

'It's a cute pub,' Maggie enthused, not even having to lie.

'Thank you,' Fiona said appreciatively. 'Morag and I put together the... look.'

The copper-wrapped bar governed from the centre of the room, below a low uneven beamed ceiling, while deep aubergine walls zipped up the space in a Stygian cocoon. Maggie imagined settling down next to the open wood fire as a storm battered the outside, a glass of Merlot in hand. Beautiful framed woodcuts of fishing boats, photos of stark black and white beaches and modernist paintings of the harbour and sand dunes hung on the walls, interspersed with posters from Countryfest's past festivals. She'd noticed a horseshoe hung upwards above the main entrance, an unmistakable talisman for good luck. Maggie had begged Adam for one when they moved into the Peckham house, but he'd complained it was an invitation for trouble and could be used to smash in a window. He'd bought a burglar alarm instead.

'I thought we could sit here so we have a bit more room.' Fiona motioned to a weathered table in the farthest corner. It was wedged up against a window seat, where they dumped their bags. Roxie chose to sit on the window seat and leaned into the bank of colourful cushions, the world passing by in the street behind. As soon as they sat down, a young girl approached with menus.

'Hi, there. Welcome to The Sea Shanty Tavern. The specials are on the board by the bar.' As she handed Maggie the menu, her mouth dropped open and she looked away, quickly handing Roxie hers.

'Thanks, Iona.' Fiona smiled. When Iona had walked off, she turned to Maggie. 'You're going to have to get used to that. I don't think you realise how alike you and Morag are.'

'The woman in the post office thought I was a ghost. She screamed!'

Fiona laughed. 'Issy, I bet she did. She and Morag were as thick as thieves.'

Maggie felt a pang of irrational jealousy that she would never know what it was like to have experienced Morag in her life, unlike everyone else here. Instead, she said, 'I've never looked like anyone in my family before.'

Fiona's eyes darted from her to Roxie and nodded. 'You look alike round the mouth.'

Roxie stiffened.

'She's her dad all over.'

'Let's choose our food and then we can chat properly. I always find I can't concentrate on anything until I know for sure some food is coming.'

After everyone had ordered and the small talk petered out, Fiona leaned forward and steepled her fingers.

'So, what did you want to ask me?'

'Who was my father?' Maggie's hand automatically covered her mouth. It had slipped out unguarded – she'd meant to ask if Morag had any other children, had she married, did anyone else know about her...

'I should have expected that one, shouldn't I?' Fiona laughed nervously.

'Sorry, you don't have to say. I don't know why I asked.'

'No, it's right that you asked...' Fiona took a sip of her wine. 'We don't know who your father is. Morag wouldn't tell us.'

'Wow, that's peak,' Roxie said clearly intrigued. 'Did you honestly not know?'

'She didn't want to tell us, flatly refused. When my parents went on at her, it made her more determined to keep him a secret. Even as an adult, she never talked about it and in the end I stopped asking. Our family... wasn't a chatty sort of family. Was finding out about your father something you wanted to do?'

'Up until it came out of my mouth, no. I'd always focused on Morag because I knew no father was listed on my birth certificate.'

Fiona nodded. 'I'm sorry I can't help you.'

Maggie didn't understand how no one even had a suspicion. There was something that felt forbidden to ask. *Had it been consensual?* What if she'd been the result of a rape? She wouldn't want to meet *that* man.

'I can tell you that Morag hadn't wanted to give you away.' Fiona looked directly at Maggie, then glanced at Roxie. When she returned her gaze to Maggie, her eyes were moist. 'Maw, our mum, pushed her into it.'

'Why?' Maggie asked, suddenly incensed, having to dig her nails into her palms.

Fiona sighed, covering her mouth, like her own words alarmed her.

'I'm sorry. Is this too much? We can talk about something else. Or continue through a mediator?' Maggie had read about those online, lawyers acting as a neutral moderator, allowing both parties to ask reasonable questions in a safe environment. Adam and she would need one eventually, *going forward* with the divorce... 'Going forward' – Maggie detested that phrase. Other offenders: 'Put some water between it' and 'Keep the lines of communication open'. She knew where she'd like to ram those sayings...

'No, I'm OK, really. It's just dredged up a lot of things that I haven't spoken about for years.'

'If you're sure?'

Fiona leaned over and grabbed Maggie's hand. 'I want to do this, I promise you. I owe it to Morag. And I owe it to myself. It was her dying wish that you knew you were loved, that she would have kept you... if she could.'

Maggie's eyes stung.

'So why did *your* mum make Morag give *my* mum away?' Roxie swooped in, rescuing her. Maggie wanted to kiss her, but still wanted to live, so didn't.

'That is a good question...' Fiona rubbed her face again. 'I don't know the real reason, is the answer to that. But my da wanted you to stay. As did I.'

'Why did no one fight for me, then?'

'Maw was a tough woman. She put her foot down and that was that. I tried to persuade her by saying I would defer college, so Morag could go on and finish high school. But she wouldn't hear of it. She kept saying the baby would ruin Morag's life, all her plans, everything she ever wanted would disappear. She didn't want that for Morag.'

'Surely it should have been up to Morag whether she kept the baby or not?' Roxie asked.

'Having a baby as a teenager back then was even harder than it is now. Morag wouldn't have been allowed to stay on at school if she'd been a single mum. They sent you away as soon as you started to show and you had to give birth alone...'

'Oh Jesus – how barbaric!' Maggie cried.

'I think if Maw had followed the social worker's advice, then I would have adopted you myself. Da forced a compromise. Morag stayed on at school so she had a better chance later on. But Maw wouldn't give in and let her keep the baby.'

'What about alternatives?' Maggie asked, cautious of saying the divisive word out loud. 'Obviously I'm glad she didn't or I wouldn't be here!'

'By the time Morag told us she was pregnant, it was too late for an abortion.'

'I don't know how your mum lived with herself seeing the major trauma she was causing.' The second the words flew from Maggie's mouth, Roxie's head snapped towards her, an accusatory glare singeing her skin.

By sheer chance, Iona chose that moment to deliver the food.

'Does anyone else know about me?' Maggie asked, attacking her melt-in-the-mouth halibut once Iona had gone.

'Yes. Most people round here know she gave up a baby girl for adoption, just because it came up in conversation.'

'She never had any more children?'

Fiona shook her head. 'Morag left home as soon as possible. Eighteen, she was off travelling, working across the world, singing in bars. She reinvented herself as Lonestar, a country singer. After you, music was her one true love.'

Tingling spread throughout Maggie's belly as a sun rose in her chest. *So that's where it came from...*

'Once she was up and running properly with a band, she toured Europe and parts of Australia. She was pretty successful in a jobbing-musician kind of way – they were always busy. She signed to a minor country label in London and put a few EPs out. They did OK, but didn't get the airplay she'd hoped for. They had a basic website and stuff for a few years, so if you'd googled her way back, you may have come across it. Country music just wasn't as big in the early nineties in the UK as it is now.' Roxie leaned in to the table, her towering burger forgotten. 'She had a few love affairs, one big one, and then, in 1997, she said she was coming home for a year, just to recharge. She left Casey in Germany. He was her beau at the time.'

Maggie's stomach plunged, her shoulders curving. Fiona looked like she was chewing a lump of gristle she couldn't spit out.

'Just say it.' A baffled Roxie glanced between Maggie and her great-aunt.

Maggie's body tensed, sensing the crossroads where she could have changed history.

'She came home to wait, though she never explicitly said that. She'd made enough money from touring to buy a very small house in Benlachie near where Gordon and I had settled. She wanted to be near her family and she adored my girls. Spoiled them rotten. She worked in this very pub behind the bar, just to pay bills, and performed solo at weekends for extra money. Touring was on hold for the time being. She'd always thought she would go back on the road once she *knew*.'

'Knew what?' Roxie asked.

'When she was going to see me,' Maggie almost whispered.

'But why would she see you?'

'Because I was eighteen.' Maggie's voice broke and she reached for water. 'The age I could legally search for her.'

'Oh.'

'Did she not think of looking for me?' Maggie wondered. 'I know there are ways round the system.'

'She tried, registered with so many adoption tracing agencies, but because it was a closed adoption, it was always a dead end. There had been talk of hiring a private detective to see what they could uncover, but then the fear kicked in.'

'Fear?'

'That after everything, maybe you wouldn't want to be found.

That she would be ruining your life by turning up in it. She loved you and didn't want to cause you any distress.'

Maggie sighed, wondering how she would have felt had Morag appeared out of the blue? Maybe she wouldn't be in this mess now if she had...

'Was she OK after my birth?' Maggie asked, her hands trembling.

Fiona smiled sadly, tears in her eyes.

'Your parents came and took you a day or two after the birth, while Morag was sent to a convalescent home. She never saw you again.'

Fiona stopped and breathed deeply. Her voice more hushed, controlled after she picked the tale back up.

'When she returned from the convalescent home, she defiantly put your baby picture in a frame on our mantelpiece. Maw never tried to remove it – that was a battle she could never win. Every year, the agency sent a photo – that was what had been agreed. It was very rare, but your parents granted it, I still don't know who asked for it. When Morag was on tour, I had all her post redirected to me, so I would send on the photos wherever she was. The only trouble with receiving the photos was she had this innate belief that you would find her the minute you were able to. I tried to reason with her so many times that you might not, that you may choose never to seek your roots, but she said why send photos? Your adopted parents would want you to engage in your Scottish heritage. She was rock-solid certain of it. The photos were a link back to you.'

'Of course there would be no more photos once I was eighteen?'

Fiona shook her head.

'I feel awful.'

'Don't. You did nothing wrong,' Fiona insisted.

'What happened when she realised Mum wasn't going to contact her?' Roxie asked.

Fiona flubbered her lips.

'It's OK, I don't want to know,' Maggie said, anxiety prowling like a caged animal.

'You sure? I don't mind telling you. You're not responsible in any way, Maggie. You should know that. Morag wouldn't want you to be upset or take it on; it was her battle. Anyway, it's all in the past.'

'I think maybe I'll be ready for more tomorrow, if you can spare the time? I wasn't expecting it to be so... I don't know... I feel so linked to her already, and I'll never meet her...'

'Why don't you come tomorrow and stay? The flat upstairs is empty. We own— *owned* the pub together. It's where she lived for the last eighteen years.'

Roxie flinched next to her.

'I really couldn't, it's such an imposition.'

'I insist. It's what Morag would have wanted, so you can't say no!'

'If you're sure? You don't know us from...' 'Adam' almost tripped off Maggie's tongue. She didn't need to remind Roxie about anything.

'From what I've seen you both seem perfectly normal. And it would be a pleasure to help you. This way you can immerse yourself in life here and get a real feel for the place and what Morag was like.'

Roxie started yawning, provoking Maggie, and soon they both couldn't stop.

With tomorrow's times and place arranged, Maggie stepped out of the relative darkness into the bright evening sunlight, finding herself temporarily blinded. She didn't see the woman turn the corner and bashed straight into her shoulder.

'Oh shit, I'm so sorry!' Maggie yelped, rapidly blinking her eyes to adjust to the glare.

'It's OK. I'll live. Oh, hello, it's you!' It was the screaming woman from the post office. A boy loitered awkwardly by her side. Maggie thought he looked implausibly familiar.

'Yes. Hi.'

'Hi, Fiona.'

Fiona reciprocated the greeting as the woman, whose name she failed to recall, darted her eyes enquiringly between Fiona and Maggie. Roxie inexplicably jumped behind her mum's back.

The woman looked at Maggie. 'I'm sorry to be so forward, but can I ask something?'

Maggie nodded.

'Are you Morag's daughter?'

7

Maggie glanced at Fiona, almost to get her permission, this new protocol a minefield. Fiona nodded like a farmer to her faithful collie, *Go on, gal.*

'I am.'

The woman's face split into a meaningful smile, as if recalling some covert mischief she and Morag had cooked up. 'Oh, how amazing. So this is a family reunion?' People were stepping round them into the road. The boy stared at the ground, his hands stuffed in his jean pockets, hostility pulsing off him in waves.

'Kind of. I met Fiona for the first time today.'

'Well, I trust it's been OK?' She looked hopeful.

Maggie glanced at Fiona.

'It's been lovely,' Fiona replied. 'Like having a small piece of Morag come to visit.'

'And this is your daughter?'

Maggie wasn't used to the natural inquisitive nature of people outside London. In London, you could be chatting to an acquaintance for half an hour and neither of you would acknowledge the silent husband/wife/child/friend/person with a bleeding wound standing next to you waiting for the ground to swallow them. However, should you have a dog, it was a totally different ball game. Everyone always asked how they were and what was their name, whilst still ignoring the person bleeding out on the pavement. Maggie wanted to be a dog in her next life.

'Yes, this is Roxie.' She was past that age where Maggie had to goad her to say hello, but she thought she was going to have to. Maggie stepped sideways, exposing Roxie; she blanched and was soundlessly nodding.

'Pleased to meet you, Roxie. This is Angus. I'm Issy. A friend of your grandma's.'

'Hi,' Roxie mumbled.

Angus looked up from studying the floor just as Roxie's eyes dived back down. Angus didn't even say hello. He just lifted his chin in some kind of tribal greeting. Maggie held phones responsible – they'd robbed kids of their manners as well as tolerance for awkward empty space. Studies would be done in a thousand years' time when the world had returned to cave dwelling because the planet had been ransacked. Phones would be obsolete and everyone would have to embrace writing with pens again. She sighed...

'Do you live in Benlachie?' she asked Issy. Maggie had liked her the minute they'd chatted in the shop, pretty certain she'd experienced a seismic tumble from life's high wire. A fellow circus performer always recognised another.

'Aye, at the top near the car park. If you're coming back tomorrow, pop into the shop, have a coffee. I've got a new blend from a small roasting house in Inverness. It's lovely. I need guinea pigs to try it before I sell it in the shop. I have all the milks you can think of.' She winked.

'Of course. Thank you.'

'Enjoy your evening.' Issy fanned her hand across her face in a wave and pointed her head at Angus to follow her up the hill home.

'So, you know how to get back to the hotel?' Fiona asked.

'Left at the top and all the way to Inverness, through the town and round the back somewhere. I'll find it.'

'You're just like Morag. She was born with a compass in her head. I get lost going to the toilet.' Fiona grabbed her hand and leaned in to kiss her. 'It was so lovely to finally meet you both.' She kissed Roxie too, who surprisingly let her.

* * *

'It'll be nice to stay in Morag's flat,' Maggie said as she pulled out of the car park.

'I don't see why we can't stay in Inverness.'

'Because Fiona offered, and it'll be lovely to actually be here, live like Morag.'

Roxie groaned. 'It's peak. There's nothing to do. At least there's stuff in Inverness...'

'You mean shops?'

'No. Stuff.'

'What stuff?'

'Just stuff!' Roxie cried, exasperated. 'It's not a lame village. It's a town...'

'A city actually.'

'Whatever.'

Maggie wasn't in the mood to fight and they drove in silence for the remainder of the journey.

That evening, too exhausted to sleep, Maggie's burning legs twitched stay awake, stay awake, stay awake, like a rumbling train. Roxie lay with her back to her in the small adjacent single bed, teenage surliness wafting off her. Maggie imagined a different version of her life when she had found Morag at eighteen. Where they became friends, she attended her wedding, met Roxie, and they'd embraced a whole Scottish family that tripled Maggie's otherwise narrow only-child existence. In this fantasy, Morag didn't die of breast cancer...

* * *

'I thought you might like a minute to settle in, then maybe we could grab a coffee with Gordon, my husband? That's if you don't mind. He's dying to meet you too.'

Fiona guided Maggie and Roxie through the pub towards the stairwell at the back by the toilets. Stale beer and pine disinfectant competed for her attention. Two turns up the stairs, past a storage room and staffroom, a red front door waited at the top on a tight landing, another upturned horseshoe positioned above the frame. A dark wood-turned umbrella stand rested against the wall, a lone green golfing umbrella stuffed in there with a pair of dusty navy Hunter wellies squeezed in beside it.

Fiona looked at her before she turned the key. Maggie realised she hadn't answered her half-posed question, her mind preoccupied with staying in Morag's own home.

'Yes of course we can get coffee. We'd like to meet Gordon too.'

Her heart lodged in her throat as Fiona opened the door and stepped across the threshold. The first thing she noticed was the smell.

'Lemongrass always reminds me of Morag,' Fiona said, smiling. 'She loved it, said it impregnated the air in Thailand. She hid little wooden lemons all around the flat infused with the oil. I keep thinking she's secretly topping them up because the smell still hasn't faded...'

Fiona walked ahead and Maggie and Roxie followed her down

the narrow pale pink hallway hung with a few framed black and white seascapes and doors leading to other rooms. The original floorboards creaked beneath their feet like the deck of a timber sailing ship in high seas. Fiona made a beeline for the light wooden door ajar at the end.

'Wow!' Roxie uttered her first word since devouring her all-you-can eat breakfast buffet earlier, stuffing napkin-wrapped croissants into her pockets for elevenses.

They walked into a glorious living room studded with lead-framed glass windows curving round the outside wall, identical to the nautical ones downstairs. Dust motes danced in sunbeams slicing across the room like mini searchlights catching the thick red and blue brocade curtains hanging at each window. One half of the space was painted baby pink and the other sea green with brazen jungle wallpaper covering the chimney breast. The entire place was festooned with artefacts from countries across the globe: silk wall hangings, bright ceramics, Indian glass cabinets crammed with evidence of a curious mind and artistic nature. Books toppled on shelves, and paintings similar to the ones downstairs hung in heavy gilt frames, while a vintage teak turntable cabinet stood proudly next to an extensive collection of vinyl; Maggie wondered if Morag's records lived amongst them.

Roxie plucked the strings of the two guitars hanging in the corner by the piano draped in a mustard yellow mirrored sari, a stained-glass art deco lamp resting on top. Maggie loved the leather chesterfield sofa piled with mirrored cushions where two battered armchairs cosied up to a low mahogany coffee table flecked with red wine spirograph roulettes. She saw herself drinking Merlot and chatting to Morag about her life while the candles flickered on the table beside them. Maggie missed this room before she even knew of its existence, though imagined it was a bloody pain in the arse to clean. She felt like she'd stumbled across an artists' café where like-minded people gathered to debate politics, music, art and literature. It spoke to her dusty corporate heart, filling her bones with a feeling of finally belonging.

'I love all the cushions and throws. So unusual,' Maggie said, stroking a multicoloured, delicately embroidered blanket draped over an armchair.

'Aye, they're unique. Issy made most of the soft furnishings in here.'

'Really? As well as running the post office?'

'Before she worked there; she doesn't do it any more.'

'What a shame, she's obviously very talented.'

Maggie's eyes were drawn to the well-used fireplace in the centre of the chimney breast where various framed pictures of her ascending ages were displayed along the mantelpiece. She walked over to inspect, noting an optimistic wedding invite for next month pressed into the corner of the gold baroque mirror.

This moment felt so big and yet it was just a room. How could a room sway a person's foundations so they thought everything they'd done, everywhere they'd been before this had been a sham?

'If walls could talk, eh?' Fiona said.

Maggie picked up the same baby picture that she'd found in the adoption file.

'I knitted that shawl for you,' Fiona said behind her. 'Maw wouldn't knit for you, said she hated knitting, so I did. Morag was no fan either; she always dropped too many stitches.'

Maggie was beginning to dislike Maw but kept it to herself. *One shouldn't speak ill of the dead...*

'Thank you.'

Fiona touched her shoulder.

Maggie could literally see herself mature before her eyes, the gap in her teeth carefully hidden with tightly zipped lips and a mandatory smile. There were no official photos after about sixteen.

Instead, there were a few pictures of Maggie in bad nineties get-ups, hair too big to be out on its own, dressed to kill (and possibly blind) in purple dungarees and camo trousers.

'You've got blonde streaks in your hair!' Roxie scoffed, sneaking up behind her, happy to ignore Maggie, but if an opportunity knocked to mock, she was first in line. 'You look like a skunk.'

'That was all the rage, I seem to remember,' Fiona said. 'Spice Girls started it all. Morag was very proud of your independent spirit.'

'What happened when I never contacted her?' Maggie's heart fluttered in her throat. Surely this was the home of someone who transformed life's lemons into lemonade?

Fiona picked up a small golden Buddha, inspecting him intently, rolling him round her palms.

'She became withdrawn, quite low, but carried on working here to keep money coming in. We didn't own the pub then, the McAllisters did. Her old flat was above the card shop further up the hill. Casey came and stayed, in between touring, and persuaded her to come back on the road, rent out her place. But then she got sick...'

'What was wrong with her?' Roxie asked.

Fiona paused before she spoke.

'She got breast cancer. She was only thirty-four.'

'Oh God. She had it a long time,' Maggie said, her mouth suddenly parched. *Was that my fault too...?*

'This was the first time. It wasn't aggressive and they caught it before it spread. But she wouldn't have a mastectomy. Chemo had already robbed her hair, she didn't want it to rob her boobs. I persuaded her to harvest eggs for future children, but when they attempted it, the eggs were of such poor quality, they said it wasn't worth it.'

Maggie's palms started sweating and she yanked at her sweat-shirt; it was sticking to her back and neck.

'She'd been through so much that this felt like a real kick in the teeth.'

'So she went through the menopause at thirty-four?' Maggie sat heavily on the sofa, her legs liquefying. 'Could I please have some water?'

Breathe, Maggie, breathe it away. A swell of anxiety was building. *She'd caused this. This was why she'd been punished...*

'Of course. Are you OK?'

Maggie nodded.

Fiona sprang up and through a door she'd not spotted because it was camouflaged the same green as the wall. Maggie glanced through the doorway and into the large light-filled kitchen, which looked as eclectic and noteworthy as the living room.

Maggie lay against the cushions, resting her head on the back of the sofa.

'Mum. You've gone white. Are you OK?' Not even Roxie's implacable concern registered.

Maggie continued with her mindful breathing as Fiona handed her a glass of water.

'What's going on, Maggie? You're clammy. Do you need me to help you to the bathroom?'

She shook her head, thankful the cool water staunched the fire within. 'I'm having a hot flush. I have them every now and then,' she said, telling a half-truth.

'You're very young to be having them. I didn't have the change until I was about fifty-two.'

In for four, hold for four, out for four, hold for four.

'I've been through the menopause, also very young like Morag.'

'I'm so sorry to hear that. You have my full sympathy. I hated it. I'm still on HRT now because every time I try to come off it, the roundabout of hell restarts and Gordon thinks a harpy's stolen his wife.'

'Yeah, me too. Been on it for almost ten years.' Maggie finished the water, the tide of anxiety receding, leaving behind damp rings beneath each armpit.

'When you're ready, I can show you how the kitchen works and you can dump your things in the bedrooms. Gordon will be at Trading Post in about ten minutes. Do you think you'd mind watering the plants? There's rather a lot of them...'

* * *

A well-preserved man in his sixties reading the *Scotsman* sat at one of the four small tables shoehorned in by the door near the shells.

'I'll be over in a jiffy,' Issy called from the back, the bell alerting her.

'Gordon, this is Maggie and Roxie,' Fiona announced.

Gordon folded up his newspaper and stood up. He was a head taller than Fiona, with receding once black hair and a palpably gentle manner despite his bone-crusher handshake.

'So pleased to meet you. How d'you like the flat?'

'It's amazing,' Roxie said before Maggie could speak. 'Where's all that stuff from?'

'Morag collected it from her travels and touring. She had the big items shipped to us until she returned. Did you like the elephants in the kitchen?'

The elephants lived in the corner below a mint green glass and metal cabinet stocked with herbs and spices. The hot pink mother elephant was adorned with jewels, mirrors and carvings. The baby was mustard yellow and vermillion with similar embellishments, but only reached Maggie's knee while the mum reached her thigh. The mother and child symbolism wasn't lost on Maggie. Elephants never forget...

Roxie nodded. 'I like the idea of making every room a talking point. That's what a home should be.'

Maggie thought of their house with its bland hessian-coloured walls and cream carpets fraying round the edges from lack of love. The spare room was also painted a necessary neutral. No wonder Roxie's walls were plastered in Blu-Tacked pictures cut from magazines and printed off the internet like a post-modernist mosaic. She needed to make her mark in a house her parents had long given up on.

'Morag certainly knew how to put together a look,' Fiona said fondly. 'She just wanted to make visitors feel welcome, but also live somewhere that was a sanctuary where she could retreat to…' Fiona stopped abruptly and wiped her eyes. 'I'm sorry…'

Gordon grabbed her hand.

'Oh no, I feel like I'm making things worse…' Maggie said, guilt flaring up again.

'No! You and Roxie are a bright spark in a dark time. You *should* be here. It's just overwhelming thinking about her flat. I mean, it's part of the pub, and we're still running it.' Gordon nodded. 'But it's empty and yet so full of life, even after her death. Dismantling it feels wrong. I'd obviously take her plants, she loved those bloody things, talked to them like people…'

'Then don't sell. Why can't you keep it? Rent it out?' Maggie suggested.

'I don't know. We're not going to run the pub for ever. And when we sell, the flat goes too.'

'Are you selling?'

'Not yet. But Morag was going to take over our part of the business, we have a smaller stake, and then it would've all been hers and we were going to find a bigger house just outside Benlachie. Somewhere for the grandkids to run around, more bedrooms for them to stay, maybe Airbnb. Not immediately, but in the next few years. Now if we sell, her flat will die with the sale.'

'You can take the things, can't you?' Roxie asked.

'Yes, of course, but it's not just that. It'll dismantle her completely. When I can't cope not seeing her again, I just let myself into the flat and it's like she's there, in another room. I don't feel like she's...' Her eyes filled again and tears fell. 'I'm being silly.'

'You're not!' Maggie insisted. 'I understand. I felt like she was there and I've never met her. That flat is unique... and in the present moment, it remains. Yesterday is history, tomorrow is a mystery, today is a gift, that's why it's called the present.'

Fiona's face crumpled. Gordon passed her a paper napkin to mop up.

'That's uncanny,' Gordon explained, rubbing his wife's arm. 'Morag used that quote all the time.'

'Oh crap, I'm putting my foot in everything today.' Maggie paused. 'It reminds me not to worry about stuff I can't control.'

'It's from *King Fu Panda*,' Roxie interjected.

'It's actually Eleanor Roosevelt, I think, or Winnie the Pooh,' Fiona said, smiling through her tears. 'I used to want to wallop her whenever she said it because she was always right. I tend to catastrophise and she didn't, and I'd no idea how she managed to keep sane after everything she'd been through.'

'Some people can. I'm not one of them either...' Maggie admitted.

'So, what can we get you all?' Issy had sneaked up with her pad in hand, her son lingering at her shoulder. 'Angus is helping out today. I'll get him to bring over your orders in a bit. Angus, remember Roxie and Maggie from yesterday?'

He nodded and that was when Maggie noticed his pin badge on his T-shirt. *Hello, I don't speak.*

8

Roxie had made a pact: she would be polite, muster up an effort, *try* not to roll her eyes, BUT, only if the gods one hundred per cent protected her from the fierce twat boy who wanted to kill her. Why he thought getting caught was *her* fault, she'd no idea. She couldn't even imagine the punishment he thought appropriate but was pretty sure he wouldn't commit murder for such a slight. It left you nowhere to go if you genuinely wanted to punish something deeply offensive... This predicament was one reason why she didn't want to stay in Benlachie. Though Morag's flat was cool, the village's quaint vibe didn't grab her like it did her mum. She would be dragging her round dead churches next or lame garden centres. What was it with old people and garden centres? How was she going to stand a whole week here? Thank fuck for the internet...

Yesterday, when they'd been talking about Morag being forced to give up Maggie as a baby, Roxie had felt sorry for her mum, but then she'd ranted on about Morag's mum not understanding about the hurt she'd caused. Talk about not reading her audience. Leaving Dad was hurting him and going to one hundred per cent ruin everything. Moving house, two places to live, separate holidays. How was

that not seeing what was in front of her? Of course, parents were
people with their own worries, just like teachers (did teachers have
lives though? And did they ever get drunk or smoke weed?).

The one thing that had properly upended Roxie was her mum's
funny turn earlier. Her mum never let on any more if things were
tough or if she felt rough, apart from when she was hung-over,
which only led Roxie to believe her mum's heart had curled up and
died years ago. It would explain why she was callously swanning off
to live her best life. But earlier in Morag's flat, she'd almost fainted.
Roxie intuited there was something else at play that had rocked her
mum to the core, dredging up long-repressed and forgotten feelings
of her own from that time her mum disappeared from view. But
she'd brutally shoved them away like she did every other time...

Roxie pretended to read the menu, the words smudging on the
page, her face burning, anxiety churning as the boy hovered. She
hated being a teenager. Things were so much simpler in Year Five
when all she had to worry about was whether her Hama Beads had
been ironed in time for show-and-tell. No one had ever threatened
to kill her in Year Five.

'Roxie, do you know what you want?' her mum asked her, inter-
rupting a distracting daydream involving her biggest Hama Bead
creation ever: Totoro. She still had him somewhere, his loose head
taped to his rotund body like a cat flap...

None of them had studied the very basic menu, so why her
mum was asking her, she didn't know. She quickly focused and
hastily chose a pasty and a cup of tea. Her mum deliberated in her
usual infuriating way, changing her mind three times until she
settled on her original choice of carrot cake.

The boy took the menus and, as he bent over, Roxie noticed his
badge. It unnerved her. Was it real or the name of some über trendy
band she hadn't heard of? And please welcome to the stage, I Don't

Speak. How would she ask and find out? He wasn't going to tell her, that was for sure! She gave him the side-eye, but he caught her and, when no one was looking, silently snarled at her, making her knock her cutlery on the floor. Peak.

'Roxie!' her mum cried. 'Be careful.'

Roxie could feel her face smart; that was so not her fault.

Angus wordlessly brought her a new knife and fork. However, she couldn't bring herself to acknowledge him, setting off her mum again.

'You could have said thank you to him,' she hissed at her. 'I'm sure he's not deaf.'

Right then, she couldn't decide whom she hated more, her mum or the boy.

'I know I'm being nosy,' her mum began once Angus had retreated, 'I don't want to put my foot in it. Angus is wearing a badge...' She looked embarrassed to ask, but for once, Roxie was glad her mum had stuck her beak in.

Gordon and Fiona looked at each other as if weighing up who was going to explain.

'Yes,' Fiona answered. 'He doesn't speak.'

'Oh,' her mum replied, waiting for full disclosure. It never came because Gordon asked Roxie about school, something Roxie loathed talking about, but a reliable subject every single grown-up defaulted to when they had no idea what else to say.

* * *

'Did Angus give you all the right orders?' Issy asked at the end of the meal.

Everyone nodded.

Roxie had fully expected to choke on broken glass inside her pasty and had cut it into such small pieces it had taken her twice as long to eat. She didn't trust that boy...

'I'm trying to keep him busy after the exams. His friends are off with their families in Spain or the west coast. He needs distraction... The shop isn't the best place for him.'

Everyone looked at Roxie. Oh no, she wasn't stepping in...

'He's got all his festival stuff to get on with, hasn't he?' Fiona asked. 'Morag set him up with it before she...'

'Yes, he's done most of it. Looks amazing. I just want him to get out, avoid hiding in his room with the door shut all summer...'

Maggie looked at Roxie and arched her eyebrows. Roxie glared and she backed down. NO WAY!

But Issy had already leaped ahead. 'Why don't you two come for dinner at ours tonight?'

Maggie glanced at Roxie and interpreted her silence as a yes.

'We'd love to, wouldn't we, Roxie?'

Roxie wanted to scream. THIS was why she hated being a teenager. You literally had no say, and if you explained why you didn't want to do something, either you were exaggerating or got accused of crimes such as being selfish, insular, unadventurous, screen-obsessed, et cetera. Roxie knew her own mind and her mind was telling her NO!

'I thought we were going to get fish and chips?' she sulked.

'We can get them if you like?' Issy suggested. 'Angus will be pleased.'

Roxie couldn't imagine Angus being pleased about anything. Maybe he'd raise a smile whilst sawing off her head...

Thankfully, Angus didn't appear at their table again and they left a for a walk along the beach out towards the sand dunes.

'Morag used to sit for hours and draw here,' Fiona said. 'The pictures in the pub are hers. So are the ones in the kitchen and the living room at the flat.'

'Wow, she painted too? Those pictures are amazing! Roxie paints, don't you? She's doing GCSE Art. I always wondered where she got her artistic talent from because it wasn't me or Adam.'

'Now you know. What do you paint?' Gordon asked Roxie.

'Large canvases and illustrations.'

'I'd love to see them,' Fiona said.

'She has pictures on her iPad,' her mum offered. 'We can show you later.'

What was she, a performing monkey?

'Mum almost went on *The X Factor*,' Roxie burst out. Maggie glared at her.

Now you know how it feels...

'What?!' Fiona cried. 'Would we have seen you on there?'

'No. I didn't make it to the show itself.'

'You have to explain now,' Fiona cried.

Her mum's cheeks blazed. Roxie knew she hated talking about it. *Good!*

'I... er, well, it was Adam's idea really. He knew a guy on the show, they were looking for a story. Someone who wasn't a singer, that kind of thing.'

'So you can't sing? That's why you were cut out?' Gordon asked, obviously confused.

'I can sing, kind of, it's how Adam and I met. I was belting out "I Will Survive" at a karaoke bar in London when he turned up to review it for his newspaper. He thought I was a singer and asked me out. Originally I wasn't up for *X Factor*, but eventually thought sod it, just have a go, never expecting to get chosen.'

'And what happened?' Fiona was intrigued now, Roxie could tell.

Her mum sighed, a strange look glazed over her eyes like she had to dragoon the troops. 'Well, you know all those sob stories are researched and planted in the queue. I'd had to send an audition tape, just to wait in line like a lemon until I was "discovered" on camera, but on the day, I came down with something. What I didn't know was I was already pregnant with Roxie. I'd thought the puking was nerves...'

'Did they offer another date?'

Roxie laughed inside. It was amazing how people got sucked in.

'No, I was so sick, I just couldn't do it. All day puking for the first sixteen weeks, so bad work let me stay at home three days a week and work from there. Adam and I had only been going out four months, so it was a bit of a whirlwind. Being on *The X Factor* just didn't feel like a priority. The producers said I could fast-track the next year if I wanted, but I never did.'

'Well, look at you two – both of you inherited Morag's talents. She'd be so proud!' Fiona beamed.

Roxie wanted to reveal her mum's singing voice was purely mythical, having never heard her sing, and that her one true talent appeared to be her home-wrecking ability, but she remained tight lipped.

* * *

'Is it plugged in?' Maggie asked Roxie.

She crawled on her hands and knees and shone her phone at the socket underneath the record player, shoving the plug in.

'It is now.'

Her mum had leafed through Morag's records and found her EPs hiding among a varied collection that included the Carpenters, AC/DC, Duran Duran, Arcade Fire, Dolly Parton, Patsy Cline, Tammy Wynette, Dusty Springfield, The Cure (Roxie was particularly happy about that), First Aid Kit, Johnny Cash, Chet Baker and many more besides.

'Lonestar,' her mum murmured. 'I wonder which one is the

most recent?' She picked one with a picture of Morag and her band on the front sitting in a wreckers' yard on battered oil drums and threadbare car seats. It was called *The Heart Wants*. They'd worked out from previous annotated pictures that Casey was the good-looking taller man with dark hair curling round his ears and a strong chin.

Her mum edged the record out of its sleeve and placed it on the turntable. Roxie knew all about turntables. Her dad was a vinyl obsessive, with a panoply of records reaching into the thousands. His collection snaked along the narrow hallway and round into the living room, curated in alphabetical order within musical genres. It was her dad who had shown her how to put a needle on a record, listening to the crackle before the track launched. It was a kind of sacred ritual, very different to pressing play on a CD player or, indeed, asking Alexa to spin your latest whim.

Roxie and her mum both held their breath as the cabinet's built-in speakers sputtered. A guitar strummed and a woman's melodious voice began singing, sweet and pure, waxing lyrical about travelling all over and never finding a cure for her loss.

Her mum turned the volume up and walked over to the window and stared out, her back to Roxie. Morag's heart-rending voice filled the room, warbling in places like a traditional country singer, though Roxie's knowledge on the category was patchy. Country wasn't a genre her dad stockpiled at home. However, Dolly Parton and Patsy Cline had made the cut, along with Johnny Cash, in the truncated country section in the hallway.

Roxie read the sleeve notes. The tracks had been written by Morag and Casey. This one was called 'The Cure', which felt quite coincidental. But according to her mum, there was no such thing as coincidence...

'She had a beautiful voice,' her mum said when the track ended before the new one launched.

'She did. We should look on Spotify and see she if she's on there.'

Her mum nodded just as the next song began, a rambunctious tune with Casey and Morag duetting, riffing off each other about who stayed out later and closed the door.

'Does your voice sound like hers?'

Her mum turned the volume down, her face pensive.

'I don't know, Roxie. I can't remember what my voice sounds like any more.'

Surfing a headrush, Roxie asked her mum a virtually forbidden question.

'Don't you miss singing? I mean... what if you'd won *X Factor*? You might be singing now instead of working in marketing...'

Her mum pursed her lips, before forming an answer.

'A, I couldn't do *X Factor* because I couldn't stop puking, and B, life just... got in the way. I was never meant to be a singer.'

'But you could sing because you enjoy it.'

'I...' Her mum didn't have an answer. 'I'm just going to have a shower. You carry on listening.'

Roxie couldn't work her out. Morag's music had clearly upset her mum, and that was understandable. She was singing about her loss and her mum was obviously attributing it to her. But it might not be about that; it could be anything. All music grew out of love and loss and similar emotions... Roxie had trouble believing her mum could have ever performed live, having no recollection of her ever doing so. She just wasn't interested. If you had a gift, wouldn't you want to share it, keep doing it no matter what?

Morag's voice accompanied Roxie as she assiduously inspected the room, browsing objects and leafing through books. She wandered over to the piano and crudely bashed out 'Chopsticks' when her phone began ringing on top of the instrument where she'd left it. Instead of grabbing it, she accidentally knocked it into the slim gap between the piano and the wall. She bent her arm down, her face pressed into the side of the piano, when her fingers grazed what felt like a doorknob before locating the phone. She had a missed call from her dad, but she was more interested in the mystery doorknob. She peered into the space, picking out a tiny door set into the wall, invisible to the eyes because the piano completely blocked it. Roxie's natural nosiness took over and she tried to the move the piano, but it was too heavy.

'Roxie – your dad's ringing you?' her mum called from the bedroom. 'Can you pick up please. We're going in ten minutes…'

She'd look later when she had time. Why was the door there? What was it hiding?

* * *

'Welcome to my wee humble abode.' Issy opened her front door and Maggie and Roxie stepped straight from the street and into her front room. Her home was a chocolate-box cottage up near the car park, the pale pink pebble-dashed exterior laced with trellis round the windows and door frames upon which drowsy yellow roses flopped in the breeze. Inside, Issy's head almost grazed the low-beamed ceiling. The antiquated exterior belied the cornucopia of incongruous tastes and clashing patterns within the snug space. Decorative rugs and equally well-travelled ornaments comple-mented vividly framed mirrors lining the walls, whilst hot pink and yellow African-print cushions rejuvenated the weary navy sofa. Roxie's anxiety about Angus momentarily dissipated, hoodwinked by the assault on her senses.

'I love your house,' she gasped, awestruck. 'It's so like Morag's place.'

'Yes, I can see why you two were friends,' her mum agreed, handing over a bottle of red wine.

'Aye, Morag and I were great pals for sure. When I moved in here, she helped with the painting and planning.'

'Where's Angus?' her mum asked, looking round the room, peering into the kitchen beyond.

'Ah, yes. He isn't here. We had a bit of a, erm, spat.'

Roxie's shoulders dropped, unaware they'd been touching her earlobes.

'Oh no. I'm sorry. Is there anything we can do to help? Leave?' her mum asked, half serious.

Issy blew her lips out and shook her head. 'I don't know if anyone *can* help, you know. It is what it is.' But what 'it' was, she didn't elaborate. 'Let me get you some drinks...'

While the mums disappeared into a sotto-voce mum-zone conversation, the occasional words catching her attention (*trauma, angry, unresolved issues*), Roxie perched next to the open fireplace and gazed at photos on shelves in and around the hole in the wall. Several pictures of Angus as a younger child, less awkward and angular, round cheeks and gappy smiles, stared back at her. A large family portrait on the bookcase intrigued her and she stood up to get a better look. Issy was laughing, her head thrown back. She had her arms round a little girl who looked a bit like Angus while Angus was leaning into a man with a generous smile and glasses. The dad? The sister? Where were they?

'Do you guys want to come down and choose your supper from the Cod Father? My treat. We can eat it back here. It's the best chippy in Benlachie.'

* * *

'Do you want to watch TV, Roxie? It can't be any fun listening to us oldies witter on about boring stuff.' Roxie wasn't sure if that was a question or demand. Issy smiled at her as she stuffed the chip wrappers into the brown paper bag and cleared up. The intoxicating smell of vinegar and delicious deep-fried beer batter still hung in the air.

Roxie had a better idea. She looked at the almost finished bottle of wine and the mums' red-stained lips. They'd settled in for the night.

'Do you mind if I go back to the flat? I can watch TV there and chill.'

'That sounds like a sensible plan,' her mum answered. 'As long as you go straight back to the flat. No wandering off...'

It was still light outside, not burning midnight sun; it was only nine o'clock. An uncanny late-afternoon vibe filled the air as people meandered towards the seafront. In London, it would be heading towards sunset by now.

As Roxie hit the corner where The Sea Shanty perched, she spotted him leaning over the sea wall, with his back to her, his height and hair a dead giveaway. She hovered next to the outside tables behind a family of four eating burgers and chips until they noticed, making huffy noises. She dodged across the street and crouched behind one of the flowering horse troughs. Roxie could see now he was on his phone, not looking at the view at all. He suddenly rammed his phone in his back pocket and strode off.

She wasn't following him. Not at all. She just happened to be walking in a similar direction. Before she knew it, her feet hit the sand, slowing her right down. She found herself retracing the trail she'd taken earlier with Fiona and Gordon into the dunes. So far, Angus hadn't looked back and she kept well enough behind that she could turn round and pretend to be walking in the opposite direction if he did.

Angus ploughed on and people, dog walkers, life, slipped behind her, a good four hundred metres away. What if he was luring her to some kind of grisly human sacrifice for the cult he was obviously a member of...?

They were deep in the dunes now, their undulation an exaggerated simulacrum of the sea. The sun was fading over the horizon, still not yet sizzling in the water; it would be light for a while longer. Roxie had kicked off her trainers and carried them in her hand. She'd almost forgotten what she was doing when she stumbled into a hillock of tufty lyme grass atop a steep ridge and found herself surprised at nearly careering down the sheer sandy bank into Angus. He'd stopped in the dip below and from what she could tell, it was 'his spot'. He lowered himself to the floor, where evidence of past fires blotted the pale sand like crusty chickenpox.

She flopped down on her stomach, the grass screening her. Angus shifted onto one bum cheek and pulled a small scruffy tin out of his back pocket. He retrieved a pre-rolled joint, lit it and started to smoke, the recognisable smell eventually drifting towards Roxie. Guilt prickled down her spine and she edged backwards intending to leave. She couldn't imagine what would happen if he spotted her spying. He was fucking scary, like the turf-war maniacs at school. They looked like they crunched on live gerbils as snacks.

Angus suddenly pulled himself to his full height, and yelled from the belly of his lungs. Jesus, maybe he was capable of eating a whole chinchilla. Dropping her trainers, she watched horrified as one of them tumbled down the sand dune, leaving a puckered trail behind it as it bounced, coming to a standstill just before the first fire remnants. Angus looked up as Roxie dived for cover behind the grass. She snatched up her remaining trainer and barrelled downhill, falling twice in her bid to escape. Once she reached the solid damp sand, she sprinted towards the town, only once glancing over her shoulder in a panic, convinced she spotted him standing on top of the dune, observing her erratic flight. She was going to have to stay inside for the rest of the visit until Dad came to rescue her...

9

Maggie hadn't noticed the family pictures when they'd arrived at Issy's, she'd been too busy talking. But they were obvious now they had moved to the living room. She sat down on the sofa and drained the wine, feeling curiously out of her depth.

'Roxie's a sweet girl,' Issy said as she sat opposite Maggie in an armchair, the leather creaking as she got comfortable.

'She can be when it suits her.' Why had she said that? It was true, of course, and most parents divulged indiscreet snippets like that constantly, but Roxie and she didn't have that kind of relationship. There wasn't patient fond eye-rolling at her moody teenage crap. Instead, a gulf existed between them that housed a multitude of skeletons whose femurs could have built a bridge.

'I think that's all children. Angus still manages to press buttons and get his point across without words or noises.'

'It must be so hard he doesn't talk.'

Issy laughed and Maggie worried she'd said something inappropriately amusing.

'Och, sorry, your face. I know you're a northerner, but you've been Londonised.'

'You're not the first person to say that.' Maggie smiled, still unsure what she'd done.

'Nice middle-class people from London would never dream of asking why Angus doesn't speak. The same as they wouldn't ask why you only have one child or no child. Everyone's life is public knowledge here, and if it isn't, someone somewhere probes until it is.'

'That must be difficult.'

'Aye. But also not. It's how it is. You can't expect total privacy if you live in a small place. Most people already know you're Morag's daughter...'

'Blimey! What if you don't want to talk about it?'

'Och, that's fine – they just talk behind your back instead, filling in the gaps until their version of the truth lands at your door and you're forced to tell the actual truth. Or not and you accept the warped version if it takes your fancy.'

'Wow.'

'I know, but I also wouldn't be anywhere else.'

'Have you always lived here?'

'No. I used to live just outside Nairn – not far from here. I'm originally from Glasgow. My dad's from Trinidad, came to work on the docks, met my mum before he left, she arrived after, had me and my brother.'

'Are your parents still in Glasgow?'

'Aye, they're not together. Dad decided marriage wasn't for him pretty early on. Mum's with someone else now – Ken, he's nice, treats her like a queen.'

'When did you move here then?' Maggie asked.

Issy nodded towards the nearest picture frame where a mystery man and young girl smiled for the camera. 'A year after Francis and Ginny died, so five years ago.'

'Oh Jesus, I'm so sorry.'

'Don't worry, it's always a conversational hand grenade.'

Maggie glanced again at the family photos squeezed between books and candles along the sideboard and mantelpiece.

'Francis was taking the kids to get school shoes at the end of the summer holidays. He collided with a tractor after another car overtook it not looking ahead. Angus survived pretty unscathed.'

'Did he lose his voice in the accident?'

Issy shook her head and smiled sadly. 'No, it's a choice not to speak.'

'Since the accident?'

'Aye. He just refused. We've seen every doctor you can think of. I decided not to address it for about a year because I was too broken. Mum pushed for it in the end. So by the time he was getting proper help, the habit was entrenched. Ergo, my fault.'

'Not your fault at all!'

Issy shrugged and poured herself another glass of wine.

'How have you coped with everything?' Maggie asked, her own crumbling marriage a stroll in the park in comparison.

'Morag suggested I moved to Benlachie when this house became available.'

'How do... did you know her?'

'Francis was a musician. Everyone knows Morag from the folk and country circuit. He played guitar and drums. His band used to fill in at the festival on the sea wall front stage. They weren't huge or anything, they all had day jobs. Francis was a music teacher so being in a band was an extension of that.'

'And it's helped, being here?'

'Aye. I know I said everyone loves a gossip, but they mostly have hearts of gold. Nosy as fuck, but they're grand. They let me play house music in the post office, the oldies quite like it, says it energises them.' She laughed. 'This cottage was the postmistress' house and when she retired, Morag earmarked it for me, along with the job. Said it would get me out, seeing people. And it did. I haven't done as much sewing since taking on the post office.'

'Fiona said you made a lot of things in Morag's flat.'

'Aye, I make clothes too, as well as soft furnishings and accessories. I used to sell through Etsy, and a few local shops also stocked my stuff.'

'Was that your job before the accident?'

'Yes. I loved it, but it was quite solitary. At the post office I was able to step out of the darkness, interact with people. I stopped sewing completely after the crash, couldn't face it. I keep meaning to get back to it in the evenings, I have the spare room all set up with my machines, but I need a good stretch of time to make anything, and putting myself back out there feels too much, even now.'

'I think you're amazing doing what you're doing. Dealing with Angus and your own grief must be so hard.'

'Morag helped with Angus. She got him involved with social media for the festival. Making posters, sending out reminders, posts, info. She paid him and it gave him something to do. He's been in a bad place since Morag died. They used to jam in the flat – she encouraged his music after Francis died. Francis had been teaching him guitar, he's pretty good. He's angry, that's why he disappeared. I said you were coming and he just took off.'

'He knows I'm her daughter, right?'

'Aye. I don't understand what's going on. He'll come back when he's ready. He's... och, I don't know, trying things out, pressing my bloody buttons. Boys and their mums...'

'I'm so sorry for your loss, Issy. Grief is a hideous thing.'

'It is. But life goes on around it, trying to fill the holes in your heart. And then it doubles back and snaps at you again... It's like the fucking bear hunt – you can't go over it, you can't get round it, you have to go through it...'

Maggie nodded.

'How about you? How's it being here, meeting family for the first time?'

'Good. Odd. Not sure how it will be now I'm too late...'

'As in Morag's passed?'

Maggie nodded.

'Maybe this is the time you were supposed to come?' Issy suggested.

When Maggie left at midnight, Issy and she had just emerged from a clubbing wormhole circa the late nineties. They'd both loved the same DJs, she'd been down to London and they'd worked out they'd attended the same festivals. A bottle of wine each plus a Limoncello nightcap had pulled the rug. Maggie briefly skated across the subject of her impending divorce. Life was shit enough without unpacking her disasters like a car-boot stall.

A loud crash jolted Maggie away from a comforting dream about Iris. She sat bolt upright in the bed, sunlight streaming in through the glass, the undrawn curtains hanging limply either side. She wanted to dive back into her dream and swim in a sea of memories, the pit in her chest aching with loss. But the sudden noise and pulsing in her temples put paid to that. She had no memory of climbing into bed last night, a shadowy recollection of swaying down the hill to the flat, then oblivion. She must have been really drunk because her earplugs were still on the bedside table. Maggie usually liked to lie in bed with her earplugs in her hands and listen to the world for a few minutes before she snuffed it out in preparation for sleep. She discovered she'd slept in her clothes when she heaved off the duvet, her chest tacky with night sweat, hair rinsed through at the base of her skull.

Being a woman was a gift and a joy. What did men have? Receding hair, droopy cocks (Viagra their silver bullet) and fear of death (sports cars assuage that), but apparently menopausal women were already dead, if you believed the hype. They were the invisible spectres who minister aging parents, grumpyfuck teenagers and spin a thousand plates while navigating vaginal atrophy (yes, it is a thing!), insomnia, rage, anxiety, burning limbs, burning mouth, brain fog, hangovers even when sober, dizziness – the list was inexhaustible. Maggie believed that men didn't know they were born.

As her hangover tightened its grip, her mood plummeted further. Why had she thought Limoncello was a good idea? A sudden memory of Adam trying to drag her out of a bar when the DJ was spinning proper handbag house overwhelmed her. She'd never known when to give up the ghost...

Parched, she padded to the kitchen via the living room, her eyes itching from crusty day-old mascara.

'It was an accident!' Roxie squawked defensively as she walked into the room, spooking her. In her jaded state, the source of her rude awakening had rapidly slipped Maggie's mind. 'I knocked over a vase.' Roxie was in the middle of clearing up shards of red smoked glass.

'What happened?'

'I fell over backwards into it moving the piano.'

'Why? What are you even doing awake before eleven?'

'I couldn't sleep.'

Maggie gazed past her to a box on the floor, its lid carpeted with dust. Beyond that, a small door lay wide open adjacent to where the piano had been standing yesterday. A proper hiding place.

'We're guests and shouldn't be poking around or moving furniture,' Maggie snapped. 'What if you'd broken the piano as well?'

'I'm not a baby!' Roxie stridently retaliated, switching gear from nought to sixty. 'God, Mum. Stop acting like I'm a complete idiot. How would I have broken it?'

An important detail caught Maggie's eye, derailing her pithy riposte.

'Oh my God! Shona's on the side of the box!' she cried breathlessly deciphering the black scrawl.

'Jesus – why d'you think I pulled it out? Duuuh!' Roxie rolled her eyes like her mum had just graduated the Fuckwit Academy. Maggie chose to ignore the blatant invitation for a fight.

'Let's clear up the mess and then look at this,' she said instead.

Roxie appeared momentarily startled, as if she'd been expecting to go into battle, before resuming picking up the smashed vase.

Ten minutes later, they sat on the kitchen floor sipping scalding tea and crunching thick slabs of buttered toast, the box resting between them, its contents brewing anxiety and excitement in equal measure. Maggie brushed crumbs off her fingers and wiped away the dust with some kitchen roll. She looked at Roxie who was holding her breath mid bite. She eased off the lid, carefully placing it on the floor behind her and peered in. A layer of tissue paper protected the contents.

'It's like a sarcophagus, without the body!' Roxie exclaimed.

The paper crinkled as Maggie peeled it up like a layer of sunburnt skin. Inside were several notebooks, a Boots photo envelope, Jiffy bags, a Boots plastic bag and a sentimental teddy bear holding a squashy heart.

'Do you think Fiona knows about the box?' Roxie asked.

'I would say no. The dust and the fact it was stashed in a hidden wall cavity. I bet no one knew it was there.'

'I wonder why Morag hid it? It wasn't like you were a secret.'

'No, but my father is.' The top of Maggie's head tingled, shooting shivers down her spine – someone had just walked over her grave in stilettos. 'Right, let's look in here.' She picked up the nearest Jiffy bag. Folded up inside was the yellow shawl that Fiona had knitted. She lay it on her knee, stroking it, trying to obtain a sense of feeling cocooned, loved and then lost, her eyes prickling.

'The notebooks have dates on them.' Roxie pointed out the top two unassuming brown school jotters.

Maggie picked up three in one go, all roughly in date order. The top of the pile was inscribed December 1978 in blue ballpoint pen, four months before she was born. Her birthday was April twenty-third, the same day as Shakespeare, controversially also St George's day. A soothsayer's sign of what was to come...

Maggie burped a cocktail of Limoncello and Marmite, frisking through one jotter for immediate clues. Each diary entry varied in length from one page of the notebook to three or four, with not every day accounted for. Morag's curlicued teenage writing neatly filled every line, as if she was conscious her words might be read by someone other than her one day.

Maggie gently closed the jotter, not quite ready for its revelations and set aside the three books. She grabbed the other Jiffy bags, handing two to Roxie while she took one and the photos.

'Ah, cute!' Roxie held up a tiny denim pair of Mothercare dungarees. 'They look like they'd fit a Build-A-Bear.' She handed them to her mum. They still had the label on them – two pounds and ninety-nine pence, the same price as a Costa. Yellow knitted booties followed and a white cardie with an intricate knitted pattern round the chest. A lump gathered in the base of Maggie's throat – she swallowed hard against it.

'Rox, will you look in this one. Think my hangover's kicking in.'

She nodded and dipped her hand inside, drawing out a pink rabbit babygrow with floppy ears attached.

Maggie's eyes pooled. She jumped up to grab more kitchen roll, her head throbbing.

'Mum?! Are you OK?'

'Yep, give me a minute. I'll be fine... Having some water.' She turned the tap and flipped the cupboard doors until she found the glasses. Standing at the sink gulping down water, her eyes traced over the windowsill's inhabitants. Amongst the terracotta jungle of house plants, one of the many brass Buddhas squatted beatifically next to a picture frame of Morag on stage singing her heart out. She was caught up in the moment, at one with the music. Between that frame and a blue glass bottle, a well-thumbed postcard rested against the glass. *Do not give the past the power to define your future.* She picked it up. The postmark was dated September 1999.

Dear Morag, I'm thinking of you. Having expectations of an outcome can ruin a person. Don't let it ruin us. I love you, Casey.

Maggie wondered what had happened to him. The postcard obviously meant a lot to Morag if it was still here all these years later.

'Do you want to look at these?' Roxie had snuck up on her, carrying the photo envelope.

Maggie leaned against the sink and took it from her. The first few pictures revealed a very young Morag at a party, friends mugging for the camera, big sweeping fringes solidified with an entire can of hairspray a piece. Morag's untameable hair had been fought into flicks down the sides of her face and her cheek high-lighter would have been visible from the moon. There was no sign of pregnancy.

'Those were the days, Rox, when you took a film to Boots and waited a few days for them to develop it for you. You'd no control over the quality of the pictures and quite often you'd have photos that were months apart because you didn't use all the film in one go. It was a photo lucky dip.'

The next few pictures were blurry, slapped with an edifying

bad-quality sticker from the film developer. The one of Fiona smiling holding a small brown terrier-type dog was in focus, then a time hop to Morag looking about seven months pregnant, her denim dungarees stretched to breaking point, huge white hoop earrings tangled in her wild hair, the flash sparking off a mirror hanging behind her on what looked her bedroom wall. Creased posters of Blondie and David Bowie as Ziggy Stardust pinned up next to the mirror. Morag's forced smile made Maggie wonder who had taken the picture. There were a few more of her in various maternity clothes, and then, bang, one of her holding Maggie wrapped in the yellow blanket, freshly out in the world. Morag's white face said it all: exhausted, traumatised, uncertain. Maggie felt it all holding that photo.

'She was your age. But she already looks older.'

Roxie took the photo and stared at it. 'I can't imagine giving birth. Getting out of bed in the morning's a struggle.'

They leafed through the rest. Pictures of Morag holding Maggie, half smiling, pictures of Fiona kissing her. A man Maggie assumed was Morag's dad, her grandfather, cradling her. What was he thinking? Why did he let her go? He didn't have red hair like Maggie, Morag and Fiona. She couldn't find any pictures of Morag's mum; did she even meet her? Did they get their hair from her?

'Is there anything else in the box?' Maggie asked.

A few baby bottles were in the Boots bag and a couple of white towels. The other Jiffy bags contained more clothes.

'It's so sad. It's like Morag buried a time capsule in the wall for you to find. Do you think your dad's identity's in the diaries?'

Maggie shrugged. Reading them would introduce her to her mother in an underhand way. She'd never read Roxie's diaries or anything private – she'd been burned before... There was a reason that box had been hidden and she felt permission was needed from someone closer to Morag before she peeked inside the jotters.

10

'We found a box of stuff, hidden in the wall...' Fiona had barely crossed the threshold, bringing bags of photos from home, before Maggie bombarded her.

'How did you find it?' Fiona's voice slipped into what Maggie used to call Iris's 'trying not to twat you' tone. The one specially reserved for admitting when she'd fucked up, but not to what extent, giving her mum's voice time to reach fever pitch once the unfolding crisis had escalated into its full glory...

'I found it,' Roxie piped up, embarrassed. 'I'm not gonna lie, I was nosing when I shouldn't have been...'

'Och, it's OK. Do you want to show me?'

Maggie stared open-mouthed at Roxie, taking it for the team. It was irrelevant that she'd been the one perpetrating the crime in question, the fact she admitted it was a bloody miracle.

Roxie explained everything as Fiona delved into the box on the living-room floor, hugging the yellow blanket to her chest, tears edging over her lids.

'I haven't seen this since you... left. I always thought your parents took it with them.'

'There are other clothes in there too, and all her diaries...'
Maggie pointed out.

'I got you those dungarees! I paid for them with my Saturday
job. Morag bought the rabbit babygrow. She believed if she dressed
you up in the cutest possible clothes that Maw would give in and let
you stay... I should have done more...'

'No, you were young too. You did what you could.'

'I always wondered if she'd kept those diaries. I safeguarded a
battered suitcase of hers for years in my loft while she travelled – it
must have had all this stuff in it. She probably threw it away – it
wouldn't have fitted in that tiny cupboard, would it?'

'But if she didn't want all this to be found, why have it at all?'
Child logic from Roxie.

'Sometimes, Roxie, things aren't as straightforward as that,'
Fiona explained. 'We may think we don't want things, but in fact we
do, just not to look at. There's something about just knowing they're
there...'

'Do you want the diaries?' Maggie asked Fiona.

She deliberated.

'Actually, I think you should have them. Unless you don't want
to...?'

'I want to read them, but surely you should first?'

'Och, I don't know if I could... yet. But *you* should.'

After coffee and Fiona's home-made shortbread, they rummaged in
the photo bags.

'So these albums are from when we were growing up, all the
baby photies, school dances, and then ones from Morag's life after
she left. Her travels, pictures with friends, her life on the move. Up
to about fifteen years ago really, when everything became digital.

All those are stored on her laptop, that's in there too with the password. You could log onto her Instagram page for recent stuff. We've kept it up. There isn't loads on there, mostly stuff about the festival, her artwork, that kind of thing. I can leave all this here for you to go through in your own time.'

'I'd rather look with you here. I won't know who anyone is, if that's OK?'

'Of course! She did also write a letter before she died...'

'For me?' Maggie gasped.

'Yes. Ever hopeful you would find her. It's in the other bag in a sealed envelope; it was for your eyes only. Catriona kept it in Morag's file at the office...'

'I'll read it later, once I've looked at the pictures.'

'Now, there aren't many pictures of either of us as babies. I just have what I took from home years ago. Maw kept the rest.'

The album pages creaked as Maggie turned them. Some of the pictures had slid down underneath the peel-back see-through plastic cover and remained trapped lopsided down a page, half covering another photo. She rearranged as she went, the sisters' black and white lives transforming into dayglo orange seventies pictures over time. Looking at Morag was like looking at her own baby pictures. Obviously others took family resemblance for granted, but for Maggie it was like a magic trick.

'Da was always taking the pictures, so there aren't many of him.'

Morag peered out from underneath a pile of curls sat on a woman's knee.

'That's Maw.'

Maggie studied her face – so like Fiona round the eyes, but she looked pinched. Like someone had stolen her joy.

'What was your mum like?'

Fiona remained silent for a moment.

'Like she'd expected something more from life. I know she

loved us in her own way, but a sheet of glass lay between us and her. Like she was observing rather than participating.'

'What happened after I was given to my parents?'

'Morag came home, as I said, she placed the picture of you on the mantelpiece, and I think everyone expected life to just return to how it was before. But it didn't. Morag was a strong person, but not even she could move on at the pace Maw wanted her to so we didn't have to be complicit in her pain. I left home in the August to start college, was back in the holidays, but the house felt dead. Morag was out as much as possible, Da was always at work and Maw lived in a world where she was so used to her life not being how she wanted it, it felt no different. That was my take on it, anyway.'

Maggie flicked through more pages – a Christmas photo when everyone looked super happy, the girls must have been about ten and thirteen. Morag wore a navy tank top and red shirt with collars you could land a plane on, while Fiona's green checked pinafore dress made her look like one of those Scottish dolls sold at the airport. Their dad peered from the photo, grinning. Maw was laughing, her head thrown back. Cappuccino-brown swirly carpets and bright orange curtains framed the scene, purple tinsel hung across the curtain pelmet like a drunk hairy caterpillar.

'Where's that?'

'Christmas at Uncle Keith and Aunty Lillian's. Dad's younger brother. Aunty's taking the photo.'

'It looks like you're all having a ball.'

'We always did when we visited them. They couldn't have children, so they doted on Morag and me. I loved Uncle Keith. Aunty Lillian was nice, but, I dunno, something not right there, maybe the whole kids thing. Maw always came alive when we visited, like she stored up all her energy for those times. Something about escaping Tain, getting to the city perhaps. I did wonder if she wished she'd lived there instead.'

'Did you ever ask her?'

'Jesus wept, no chance! Talking to Maw about feelings was like asking Boris Johnson to tell the truth. She shored up her own conscience with logic that Morag was better off without a child – that was all she kept saying. *Don't ruin your chances at happiness.* It all felt rather arbitrary. Maw colluded with social workers. I remember before the birth Morag had a visit from Mrs Meek, she was a hard woman, who explained to her she was too young to know what she was doing with a bairn and a nice couple who couldn't have children had already been promised her baby. It was a done deal. Maw was able to sign you over because Morag was a minor. It was all wrong.' Fiona breathed heavily and unclenched her fists.

'I'm sorry.'

'No, *I'm* sorry! Even now, it makes me so cross. And I shouldn't be. It's in the past, but sometimes it still feels like yesterday. Especially with you right in front of me. You could have been here the whole time...' Fiona gathered herself, brushing her face with her hands. 'Poor Morag, I never know how she coped with her own feelings... She and I couldn't talk about Maw without having an argument. I naively thought over time she'd forgive, but she wouldn't even talk to Maw at Da's funeral. That was the only time we properly fell out, and I hated it. So we agreed to never talk about her again, even to the point of Morag dying – it was like Maw didn't exist. Morag liked to compartmentalise her life... Gosh, Roxie – all this horrid talk, what must you think. Families drive you nuts!'

'One hundred per cent!'

'I think the guilt weighed heavy on Da, he couldn't persuade Maw. He died when he was only fifty – heart attack. I always wondered if you'd stayed, maybe he'd still be alive, or lived longer...'

'That must have been awful.' Maggie could feel the burden of her absence pressing on everyone, so much so she felt the onus lived with her instead of her dead granny. Rage brewed in her guts, if only she could give this evil pilch a proper dressing-down from baby Shona's point of view. Yet wading in with her grief at being given away felt spurious because Maggie hadn't had a terrible childhood, far from it. Baby Shona and Maggie were two completely different people. She was angry, but it was more a by-product of her own ill-timed response than anything else.

'It was awful when he died,' Fiona admitted. 'I was about to give birth. Maw changed afterwards, like she'd been waiting for him to go. She didn't cry, she just carried on, then went travelling for the first time ever, on her own. Visited Paris, came back and just hardened even more, then withdrew from everything. She wasn't hugely interested when Katie was born, didn't care for any of that granny stuff. So I stopped bothering. I asked her if she needed help with her grief, and she just said I had no idea what I was talking about.'

'That's heartbreaking... When did she die?'

Fiona blinked a moment.

'She hasn't.'

'Oh...' Maggie's faux pas set her cheeks aflame. 'I, er... assumed she had. Just the way you talk about her... like she isn't here any more.'

'She is and she isn't. I still visit regularly and at Christmas, her birthday. But it's ticking a box, more to stop me feeling like a bad person, a dreadful daughter, rather than any kind of family connection. She's in her seventies now, been alone for nearly thirty years. She had me when she was almost eighteen, just after she married Da.'

'Does she see your daughters?'

'They visit, and she's perfectly nice, but just not... invested.'

'Did Morag visit?'

'No. She went travelling, and then Da died. She returned for the funeral, but she and Maw only really spoke after she became ill the second time.'

Maggie recognised the familiar secrets, lies and misunderstandings that children half understood, then rewrote so they grew arms and legs, eventually turning into a monster...

'Have you ever asked her what's going on, why she's so distant? Maybe there's a simple explanation?'

'I don't want to, Maggie. I've given her ample opportunity and she always responds with "you have no idea". So, no, I don't have any idea what goes on in her head, and maybe that's best. I love my life, my husband, my girls, I just wish Morag was here.'

As Roxie flipped through more photos, they came across pictures of Casey on stage, his eyes always trained on Morag, their chemistry evident.

'Is that Glastonbury?' Maggie touched a picture of them jamming together in a small tent before a reasonably sized crowd stuck beneath a picture of the Pyramid stage in deep perspective.

'Yes, she used to go. Not every year. They played on one of the folk stages.'

Maggie clutched her cheeks. 'Do you know if she went in 2002?'

'Casey had left the band by then – he and Morag had split up, but Lonestar did a final tour without him in 2002 before calling it a day. I seem to remember they played Glastonbury one last time.'

'I was there too!' Maggie's heart practically burst from her throat.

'Did you go to the smaller tents? There are so many...'

'I think so. But we mostly stayed watching all the big bands. I remember Coldplay on the Pyramid stage. They were good.'

'Coldplay are dead...' Roxie muttered.

'I wonder if you walked past her at all,' Fiona said dreamily. 'Let's say that you did!'

'What happened with her and Casey?'

'Oh, that's a whole other story.'

'Sorry, I'm being too nosy.'

'You're not. Tell you what, why don't we go and stretch our legs. I can take you up over the cliffs and tell you about Casey. Then we could stop for lunch somewhere. Do you want to try outside of Benlachie?'

'Can I stay here?' Roxie asked stiffly. 'I don't feel like walking over cliffs.'

'It will do you good to get out,' Maggie insisted.

'I went out yesterday.'

'God forbid you get out again. You might fry to death in the sunlight.'

Roxie pulled a face and Maggie could feel irritation tickle her belly.

'You can come for lunch.'

'I could eat here.'

'No, we'll go for lunch together. Please.'

Roxie sighed and pursed her lips. It was a subdued Mexican stand-off because of Fiona's presence. Had she'd not been there, the gloves would have been off.

'It's OK,' Fiona said, refereeing. 'Let Roxie stay here if she wants. There's Lennie's Pizza Van in the cliff car park. You could meet us there later? They're proper sourdough ones – best for miles. Morag persuaded him to come from Inverness twice a week.'

'That sounds cool,' Roxie said.

Maggie had to dig her nails into her palms. Mary Mary, quite fucking contrary.

* * *

The wind had died down, which was a blessing – walking along the cliffs was precarious enough. In some places, the heather couldn't find much purchase and the edge dramatically cheese-wired away to a crippling drop. But the view over Benlachie and the coast beyond was spectacular. Fiona pointed out peregrine falcons hovering on thermals and jackdaws pecking at an abandoned sandwich. Maggie felt a calmness seep into her bones gazing down on the beach, the sea air cleansing parts of her no virtuous broccoli juice could reach.

'Afternoon, general,' she muttered, saluting a lone magpie strutting along the path in front.

'What did you just say?' Fiona barked.

'Oh, sorry, I'm just being silly. I always salute lone magpies. To be honest, I salute any number, just to be on the safe side.'

'Morag used to salute magpies as well – she even called them general! She loved a superstition.'

'Oh, me too! I'd rather risk getting run over than walk under a ladder on the pavement.'

'Morag was the same!'

'Did she have a fear of umbrellas being opened inside?'

'Well, you saw the umbrella stand on the landing, and horseshoes everywhere...'

'I had no idea stuff like this could be hereditary. It's probably coincidence.'

'Morag would have said there's no such thing as coincidence!'

'Oh my God! You beat me to it – I was just about to say that!' Maggie laughed.

They silently hiked up a precipitous slope that momentarily stole their voices. Maggie wondered what Morag would make of her cookie-cutter lifestyle, complete with stable job, snarky teen and upcoming divorce. Maggie realised she was a walking midlife cliché.

'Morag wasn't the marrying kind?' she asked once the terrain levelled out.

'I think it was more complicated than that. She never actually said. For all Morag's up-front honesty about your existence, she was a dark horse about everything else. All I knew was she turned Casey down, twice, and Casey wasn't the kind of man to ask three times. Though I do know, a few days before he married his wife, he came to see her. He was at the funeral too. It was lovely to see him. Even though it was packed – Morag had so many friends from so many places. Mostly because of the festival.'

'Why did Casey come before he married?'

'To let her know they were expecting a baby and he didn't want her hearing it on the grapevine, or over the phone. He knew what having a child meant to her. But she'd pushed him away.'

'How long were they together?' Maggie thought Casey sounded like a true old-fashioned gentleman, a rare breed.

'Nearly twelve years. They met in Thailand. He came with her to Da's funeral. He loved Benlachie. He's Canadian and I think the Highlands reminded him of British Columbia. That's quite mountainous too, I believe. He took Morag once and there was talk about her moving with him, but when she came back here to wait for you, I think it became a pipe dream she wouldn't commit to, just like she wouldn't commit to him in the end. He was a lovely man, kind and patient, and a gifted guitar player. Morag never really had anyone like him after. I know the early menopause messed with her and she said what was the point. Most men wanted to settle down and she couldn't offer him a family.'

'Gosh it must have been so frustrating watching her navigate life and being unable to help.'

'It was. And it all stemmed from that one decision Maw made all those years ago, all about you. Though the festival and her music was born out of all the grief. That was her baby in the end. And living here gave her the sense of belonging and roots that she craved. Now, of course, we don't know what would have happened if you'd stayed. Morag may well still have contracted cancer, she most likely would never have met Casey, might have had more children, become a teacher, travelled the world with you in a papoose, who knows. All because Maw thought you were going to ruin her life...'

'I think that says more about your mum than it does about anything else.'

'Yes. I've tried not to think about that. It feels like Maw never wanted children, looking back with hindsight and time and distance taking the sting out of it. When most grandparents are revelling in their grandchildren, she's shutting them out. And her great-granddaughter. It makes no sense.'

Fiona's phone started ringing.

'It's Issy. I better answer it.'

'Hi, Issy. Yes, she's here. What?! She's OK? Right, we'll come now.'

11

As her mum probed Fiona about Morag, the obvious parallels between this Maw character and Maggie began to grate. Roxie clenched and unclenched her fists. Her mother was apparently blind to their clanging similarities. Making decisions on behalf of others, ruining lives without seeming to give a shit. But then, on the other hand, her mum was exactly like Morag: chasing ghosts... Her poor dad. Roxie had wanted to throttle Maggie, scream the truth at Fiona, about how her mum didn't see her half the time, was always wishing someone else was there. Someone Roxie couldn't compete with...

Without any other footwear and the inability or energy to conjure up some convoluted lie, Roxie didn't have a choice but to seek her trainer out. The truth would have just led to yet another pointless argument. *Trainers don't grow on trees...* Dipping out of the cliff walk was the perfect chance. Hopefully a seagull hadn't already claimed it as a nest, or worse, started using it as a luxury toilet. She was confident Angus wouldn't have taken it, unless he had a creepy shoe fetish...

Roxie found boys to be a different species and always fancied quirkier types. Like Jamil at school, with his sick sideburns and round glasses who collected porcelain frogs and had three hamsters called Rod, Jane and Freddy. They had their own Instagram account and had appeared on some YouTuber's Who To Follow last year. He could get away with being that extra because he had the body and face of a *Love Island* contestant without the Kardashian sensibilities. He appeared to be gender fluid, but apparently was straighter than a ruler. He could also play football like a boss. Yeah – he had it all going on and the chances of him *ever* noticing her were below zero, unless of course she came to school dressed as a fucking frog. Roxie considered this a moment; would she do that? Where would she get a costume? Could she make one? Shit just got weird... For all her gobby frank talking, approaching a boy she deemed hench was like throwing yourself into a shark pool on your period. Social death. She'd yet to meet a boy she could talk to easily like she could to Ash or any of her other friends.

'You know Mum asked me while she was driving if I liked girls or boys yesterday,' Ash reported on Snapchat while Roxie rummaged through Maggie's suitcase looking for shoes. Ash had recently switched their pronoun to 'they', something their parents were struggling with. 'She didn't want to look at me, so I gave her something to think about. Told her I was an equal opportunities lover. She almost crashed into the back of a white van. I'm hoping she'll stop calling me Aisha now.'

Roxie snorted with laughter and wondered for the millionth time if there would ever be a boy she could connect with as fluidly as this. According to the *Don't Call Me A Teen* podcast, those types of boys existed, mostly travelled in pairs and drank coffee, but so far they were as rare as unicorn poo.

Roxie unearthed a pair of flip-flops whilst Ash said their good-byes. They were on their way to Camden with Robyn to try the ice-cream shop they'd seen on TikTok. Apparently Jamil was there too

– he was live streaming on Stories. Typical! She was trapped in the middle of nowhere with a psycho killer who wanted her scalp.

Roxie appreciated she was taking her life in her hands just leaving the flat on her own. What if he saw her? What if he'd really killed his sister and dad, the ones from the photos in his house? They were missing; no one had mentioned them. Perhaps he'd had them disappeared so he could be the golden child? She shivered. From the dead look in his eyes, she thought him capable of anything.

Once she hit the mostly empty beach, she kicked off the flip-flops and let her toes drag through the fine sugary sand, imagining starring in an indie film or a TV show all about her. The Cure's 'In Between Days' drilled into her head via her AirPods as she swung her legs in time to her very own theme tune, the camera panning overhead for the animated typography opening credits. She didn't see the smashed bottles as she reached the bottom of the dunes. But she felt one rip open her foot and slice through her tendon, blood splattering all over the sand.

'Argh, fuckkkkkkk!' Roxie fell to the ground, her hand grazing the other broken bottle, cutting the tops of her fingers. She landed next to a third one, narrowly missing being gouged in the arm. *Roxie's Teen Beach Movie* had morphed into *Saw – The Revenge*.

She lay momentarily in shock until the pain struck, then practically screamed her lungs out of her chest. From nowhere, a strong pair of hands slipped under her armpits and effortlessly scooped her off the sand. The Cure were still blasting inside her head, disorientating her further. Her first instinct was to kick her assailant, but at the same time her foot exploded in agony.

'Who is it? Who are you?' She twisted her head this way and that, trying to catch a glimpse, but they remained silent, letting their woody aftershave do the talking for them. Whoever it was strode away from the horror scene, blood dripping like machine gun fire behind them and lay her gently down on the ground. She looked up into Angus's concerned face, his mouth set in a determined grimace. He pulled off his T-shirt.

'What the fuck are you doing!? Nooooo!'

Ignoring her obvious distress, he tore his T-shirt into three shreds, holding up his hand in a calming gesture, motioning her foot. She made the fatal mistake of looking towards it: the gore was overwhelming. Darkness beckoned...

* * *

Roxie could hear shouting, a woman's voice escalating from far away. Was she underwater...?

'What happened?' the woman yelled. 'Is she OK?'

Roxie struggled to lift her head; her neck threatening to snap, eyes fluttering against the light. When she managed to open them fully, Issy was sitting next to her stroking her hand. Then the throbbing tore through her foot, fine needles of pain stinging her fingers.

'It hurts so much.' Her breath jolted as it escaped her lips, tears brimming, scalding panic surged through her chest.

'You poor wee thing. What a nasty shock! Would water help?'

She nodded and Issy helped her slowly sit up and offered her a glass bottle of posh mineral water, evidently liberated from the shop. The pain though! Roxie had never felt anything like it. She breathed deeply; she wanted her dad...

'Do you mind if I check out your foot?'

Roxie hadn't noticed the man; he'd been standing behind Angus like a faceless TV extra.

'This is Robbie, the lifeguard.' Issy continued to stroke her hand, which she realised was wrapped in Angus's T-shirt. 'Your foot's all covered, so you can't see it.'

Robbie was as handsome as Jamil from school. What if he also had a trio of performing hamsters? Wouldn't that be weird? She almost asked him in a fit of madness, but took a tentative peek at her foot instead. Angus had applied a tourniquet from his ripped T-shirt. It was soaked with blood, but that didn't bother her as much as seeing the shard of glass hanging out of her wound earlier. She nearly fainted again at the mere thought.

'I'm going to apply a pressure bandage over what's already there,' Robbie explained. 'I'm afraid it might hurt, then we need to get you to hospital.'

Angus watched silently, his eyes darting from Roxie's face to Robbie, wincing when Roxie cried out.

'Are you happy to drive her there? It'll be quicker than an ambulance. Needs to be soon though, Angus told me the wound was deep; it might have cut her tendon.' Robbie pulled the bandage further over her foot, the pain detonating once more. 'She'll need a cast if so.'

'Let me ring her mum first. Where is she, Roxie?' Issy asked

'With Fiona... on the cliffs.'

Issy tried three times, but her mum didn't pick up.

'I wonder if she doesn't have a signal? I'll try Fiona instead.'

* * *

Roxie sat in the back of Issy's car with her foot up on the seat. Her mum was meeting them in A&E. Angus had a pad and pen on him and briefly scribbled down all the drama like a war correspondent in a black and white film. She clocked that he was now wearing a *True Romance* T-shirt that looked convincingly vintage. The film had been on her watch list for a while... Angus explained in writing that he'd been walking along the beach when he heard her scream and belted over. He'd spotted the glass in her foot and recognised it had to come out, but didn't know how. Fortunately Roxie had fainted and he'd whipped it out safely with it being a clean cut. She was lucky he hadn't tried to vengefully garotte her while she was out cold.

The angst and sullenness had dissolved from his face, revealing a charming, engaging boy despite his lack of verbal communication. How would he ever save himself from drowning? she pondered. If he refused to scream for help.

Roxie had never broken a bone or seriously injured herself before. What were the chances that the one parent she desperately wanted wasn't able to show up? Nonetheless, her mum was unbelievably calm once she arrived ashen-faced in the half-empty waiting room after the nurse had established Roxie wasn't going to bleed out on the floor.

'Are you in pain? What can I do?' was the first thing her mum asked as she hurried into Children's A&E.

'Can you ring Dad?'

Her mum breathed in sharply, then leaned in to hug Roxie gently, not wanting to hurt her. 'Yes of course. I'll call him now.'

Roxie missed the sympathetic look that passed from Fiona to Maggie.

The minute her dad spoke, Roxie fell to pieces, her words caught in her throat. She returned the phone to her mum while Issy ran to the nurses' station to grab some tissues.

'What's going on?' her dad asked her mum. Roxie could hear his voice reedy and small in the mouthpiece.

'She's had an accident. We're just in hospital now, about to see a doctor. She cut her foot open on a bottle. It's fairly deep, will need stitches. Her hand also, but that's not as bad.'

Roxie couldn't decipher the rest because the tannoy interrupted, asking for Doctor McGinn to go to treatment room five. She motioned for her mum to hand her the phone.

'Dad, it's me. I'm OK. Issy gave me whisky for the shock before we came here.'

'Wow, you're a proper Scot now! Do you want me to come?'

Roxie hesitated. She really *did* want him to. But, also, interred in her heart lurked shame that she felt her mum wasn't enough. She caught her mum's eye and she smiled at her, guilt multiplying like fungus.

'No, Dad, I'm OK. Mum's here.'

* * *

Roxie felt sick, dread and anxiety swilling inside, aided by her throbbing foot. She wanted to kill her mum, signing her up for a fucking play date like she was five. Before Issy had dropped them home last night, Angus had handed Maggie a note in the car – Roxie had been half asleep, the painkillers washing her out. Apparently he'd asked if he could pop by to see how Roxie was.

'Oh, how sweet!' her mum had mortifyingly crowed. 'Of course you can come round!'

This made it impossible for Roxie to ultimately ghost him. Not only would he conclude she was as dull as fuck because she was only fifteen and he was the ripe old age of sixteen, but he might be a psycho. Age differences of over a year at school were calculated in dog years – you may as well be dating a suit with a car and two kids. Not that this was a date in any shape or form, or that he fancied her – in fact it was the complete opposite. He felt sorry for her because she was trapped inside for a few days and his visit could be his good deed for his boss, Beelzebub. At least she didn't have to worry about her missing trainer. She still had the right trainer, the left one was now lost in the dunes for sure. Her mum would never know...

If Roxie could have paced the living room, she would have. Her mum had left the door on the latch so Angus could let himself in.

She'd disappeared with Fiona on a trip to Fiona's childhood town... It was drizzling making staying inside a perfect choice. Roxie liked staying in, and her mum hated it. They spent school summer holidays at total loggerheads when her mum would ring from work and ask if she had left the house that day. Her dad would lie sometimes so Mum would get off her back. What was it with her? Staying in was great! So many shows to catch up on and YouTube Epic Fails to gloat over whilst feeling smug you'd never be such a loser.

The door knocked, jolting her out of her reverie. Tits, he was here. She wasn't mentally prepared for him to be on time; she was late for everything. Only psychopaths arrived on the dot; that proved it! She couldn't really run away on crutches...

'It's open! I'm in the lounge.' It was pointless hiding, every horror film she'd ever watched had put paid to that notion. Best get this over with...

Footsteps echoed towards her and the door swung open. She thought her heart was going to choke her before hurdling over her tonsils.

Get a grip!

Angus was taller than she'd remembered but that could be because she was sitting down. He waved and smiled. Smiled! How was this going to work? Did he communicate with sign language? She could just about remember 'toilet' and 'cheese' from Makaton Reception lessons. And for some reason 'racoon'. She didn't have the advanced skills to sign 'are you a psycho'?

Angus plonked himself on the leather chair opposite Roxie on the chesterfield. He placed a largish gift bag on the coffee table in front of her and motioned for her to look inside.

'Thank you.' What if it was a dead animal? She'd watched a programme on Netflix about how psychos initiated their killing journey by butchering small rodents or birds to hone their murdering technique.

She leaned over and pulled out her left trainer. Her face ignited. OMFG, she hadn't imagined him watching her run away.

'Oh...' She didn't dare look at him. He was shaming her before he killed her.

He knocked on the table to grab her attention. His eyes were sparkling and he was grinning at her. An assassin's smile, no doubt. He nodded his head – *there's more in the bag.*

Roxie peered in and discovered a box of Cadbury's Celebrations, and a DVD of *True Romance* with a Post-it note attached.

I thought we could watch this some time. You said you liked my T-shirt.

'I don't remember saying that.'

Angus whipped out his waiter's notebook from his back pocket.

You were spaced out after the gas and air for the pain. Said it was on your watch list.

'Oh, cringe. What else did I say when I was off my head?'

Something about Rod, Jane and Freddie. The rest you'll have to guess... He'd even written dot, dot, dot. Not the work of a murderer.

'Oh, peak... So, you found my trainer. I guess you spotted me in the sand dunes.'

He pulled an emoji wide-mouthed face, the tendons popping in his neck.

Roxie laughed, then spewed the word vomit. 'So, yeah, I was out and saw you on the beach so decided to see where you were off to. I was bored, Mum was drunk with your mum and so I was like, why not? I one hundred per cent swear I wasn't spying. I honestly wasn't. I was just bored. Oh, I already said that. Anyway, I climbed up the sand dune and my trainer fell out of my hand and that's when I ran off. I'm not gonna lie, I was totally morto. I was on my way to get it when you found me bleeding on the beach... Sorry about your T-shirt.' She took a breath as he started his reply. Did he suffer cramp with all this writing?

I was getting your trainer when you screamed. Rain was forecast. I wasn't sure you'd go back and get it in time. Thought I should – I didn't take it with me in the first place in case you came looking for it and it made it even more awks. Don't worry about the shirt, it was a shit one anyway.

'That's so kind of you. Thank you.'

He shrugged.

Are you from London?

'Yes. Peckham. Have you ever been to London?'

He shook his head.

I'd like to go. Morag told me all about it. She'd been loads, performed with her band there. She used to stay in Camden. Have you been there?

'Camden's sick. Lots of trendy shops that sell vintage clothes. I got an actual 1980s pair of Doc Martens from there... What else did you and Morag talk about? What was she like?' Roxie imagined Angus making the sound of a Morse code machine as he wrote. Would it be easier to sit there and text each other on phones? Why was she talking like it was a race?

She was pretty much the nicest person ever. She seemed a lot younger. Really good voice, and guitar skills. She told me about your mum.

'What did she say?'

He shrugged again.

I got the impression she was waiting for her, but also not.

'Also not?'

Getting on with life. The festival was her coping thing. Why did your mum wait so long?

'She didn't want to hurt her parents, so waited till they were both dead.'

He nodded.

I think she would still be alive if she'd come sooner.

Roxie felt unexpectedly torn. She'd started to like Angus, but he was dissing her mum. Not dissing, worse. Saying it was her fault

Morag was dead. Only *she* was allowed to throw shade on her mum.

'You don't know that. Surely it's Maw's fault.'

Maw?

'Morag's mum. She made her give my mum away. Look, can you grab those bags by the piano? There're photos in there.'

Angus shot up and heaved the bags onto the coffee table.

Why did you dob me in to Sue at the gift shop? You didn't have to do that. I normally get caught on my own without you helping it along.

'I didn't! I was warning you about the mirror above – it's how they spy on customers. That and CCTV. Why were you shoplifting?! Then threatening to kill me?'

He sighed, gazed right at her, then dived into the bag and pulled out one of Fiona's albums, but he also grabbed a handful of diaries. He gestured – *what are these?*

'Morag's teenage diaries, and from through her life, I think.'

He opened one.

'Don't read it! Mum hasn't looked at them yet.'

She was my friend too. I actually knew her. She taught me guitar and helped us when everything was shit.

'If you're going to do it, at least let me read them at the same time. Start at the beginning...'

He leafed through, finding the right one dated December 1978 and stood up to sit down right next to her. Goosebumps sprang up on her arms as his knee touched hers.

Read it out loud – it's easier.

So she did.

12

December 2nd 1978

I always wanted to write a diary, but nothing exciting's ever happened. Until now. Well, apart from that time Kevin Cunningham was in a drive-by scene when they were filming *Garnock Way*. We got bacon cobs from the catering van.

Exciting is probably the wrong word, more like pure mental. I'm up the duff! After all the snidey things people say about teenage mums, I've now joined that gang. I've not had any odd cravings like coal or soap, but the thought of cabbage makes me want to boak (nothing new there!), and I'm obsessed with spaghetti hoops, Findus Crispy Pancakes (cheese ones, not the mince ones) that fake Smash tatties with the Aliens, and cheese toasties. Can't get enough of them.

I'm almost five months and some people have started to notice. Sean Macalister said I looked fat the other day and Kev Stewart told him to shut it, that I was preggers. They were all laughing, not realising it was true. It'll be Chinese whispers soon. Knobs. The teachers know and I've not been doing Games for a while. They let me sit in the library like a right swot and do the work I won't have time for once the baby arrives. To be fair, it's a bleeding relief not to be doing cross-country. Everyone starts walking and smoking as soon as they get past Munro's main gate. It's the cold and mud I hate. I've been told to say I have a bad back.

I can't find a book in the school library about what's happening. Just stupid textbooks with the reproduction cycle and how the baby grows. Nothing about birth, nothing about why my mouth tastes like metal filings, what to look out for. I can't talk to Maw because she's acting like everything is normal, but it isn't normal. I'm not normal. The midwives treat me like a right eejit, think I shouldn't be in this mess. One of them handed me a leaflet as I was leaving a check-up, but said none of this applies because you won't be keeping the baby. It was all about how to change nappies, bottles, swaddle a newborn. I said I was keeping the bairn and she laughed!

They're all mean wifies, apart from this young one called Shona, she's been kind. She stood up to Maw and Mrs Meek when they were talking about adoption. Asked them if they had asked me what I wanted. They looked at her like she was mad. She can't look after a wee bairn, Mrs Meek said. She's a wee bairn herself. She's no idea what it entails. I had to look up 'entails' in the dictionary. I thought it meant animal guts. I couldn't have them thinking I'm even more of an eejit!

* * *

December 13th 1978

Maw asked me what I wanted for Christmas today. Did I need clothes? Or did I want stuff for after the baby's born so I've got something to look forward to. I asked if I could keep the baby, that would be the best present. I don't care about clothes right now.

One of the teachers at school whose daughter just had a bairn loaned me a load of maternity outfits. They're minging, like something out of the Ark. Horrible pink stuff with frills. They make me look like a marshmallow. Rita wet herself when she saw me in one of the dresses, like Pan's People gone wrong, said I looked a right dafty.

Obviously Maw ignored my asking to keep my own child, just said she'd have none of my lip. She'll give in eventually. This is just like that time she said we couldn't have a dog. Fiona and I wailed on and on until one day when we got back from school, Frankie was waiting for us. Now Maw loves that dog more than she ever loved us. He gets to sleep in bed with her and Da, and she even makes him a cake out of dog food on his birthday.

Fiona said she'll come round. I just have to be steady, grow the baby, work hard at school and Maw will see how grown up I am and let me keep the baby. I know she will too. Everyone loves babies, they're pure magic.

December 17th 1978

It was the school Christmas play's first night this evening. I was supposed to be the lead. Dorothy in the *Wizard of Oz*. The auditions were in September when I'd no idea I was pregnant – I just thought I had a dicky tummy. Once the school found out about the baby, they asked me to leave the play. Mrs Odell was sad, and hugged me. Said I was the best Dorothy she'd seen at this school, but I needed to rest, not throw myself across the stage. I had a baby to think of. I knew she really meant Dorothy was a virgin and even if I hardly showed, everyone would know. The school was embarrassed. I greeted for a week, but at least Rita was my replacement. I got to practise with her and show her the ropes. But even Rita knew I was a better Dorothy. Shit, the whole school knew I was a better Dorothy.

I hadn't seen R for ages either, but I saw him earlier. He was with his da in the middle rows watching Isla singing in the chorus. I wondered how I'd feel seeing him. I knew he might come, but not which night. I'd predicted the last night, but no. He looked at me and smiled, but never looked again. I wonder if he knows. I mean, not everyone does. And he's not at school, so maybe not.

When Maw asked me how the baby happened, who it happened with, I couldn't say. She was raging, pure mental. The name wouldn't come. I kept thinking Da would start trouble, say it was all his fault, lose his job if he battered him. Though, I'd never seen Da batter anyone before. Anyway, it wasn't R's fault. I mean I was there, I'd wanted to be there. R didn't force me like a lot of them do. Rita said she was jumped by Calvin at Rory's party in the woods. He followed her and pinned her to a tree, putting his hand down her jeans, trying to rip them off. She kneed him in the goolies and managed to run away. It wasn't like that. R was gentle and I fancied him. We'd been meeting for a few months ever since Jonny Mac's sixteenth, just for the craic. R had been in the ceilidh band and I'd asked about his guitar. I want one, Da won't let me. Said it'd get me in trouble – too late for that! R said I could try his, one thing led to another. Then at the summer marquee after his band finished, he asked if I was 'ready'. So I said yes, dazzled by his bloody guitar. He's not an obvious hunk like that Les from the Bay City Rollers. He's no Marc Bolan or David Bowie either. God, I love David Bowie. I want a guitar just like his.

R's da won't let him join a band full time, but he said he'll leave, go to London as soon as he's got enough money, so we kind of fizzled out. Then I realised what was going on, why I felt minging... I don't know how he'll be once he finds out, once the bairn is with me. I know a lot of girls want R for themselves, but I want this baby more. He's very shy really, hiding behind his guitar. I'm not in love with him. Aye, I fancied him, but love? I don't know what that feels like. Rita says she thinks it's when you feel sick and can't stop thinking about them and just want to be next to them. I felt like that about Frankie when we got him. I used to draw pictures of him in class. But I don't feel like that about R. I know I should, but I don't. I loved pulling him, and I loved 'the business' on the third try, first one not so much. But he didn't like talking and I do. I don't want to end up like Maw and Da, sitting in the same room, him behind a paper, her reading *Woman's Own*, not even looking at each other. I've never seen them hold hands and Maw acts like she'd rather be alone half the time.

I don't know if R will want to be a part of us, he can, but I'll be OK on my own. I'll tell him when I'm ready. Da said he'll find some extra money, says he'll talk Maw round – how though, they never talk!?

Rita was good as Dorothy in the end. I bought her a box of Milk Tray to say well done. I knew I was better though.

* * *

December 31st 1978

Goodbye old year. This is the year I'm a mammy. I can't wait. I'll still finish school. My exams start after the birth and it's all planned – I'll take them at school but will be at home the rest of the time. Maw said we have a meeting with Mrs Meek in January – I hate that ol' wifie, she's a face on her like a bulldog licking pee off a nettle.

When we went to Uncle Keith's for Boxing Day, Maw had a few sherries and laughed loads, I think she was pure dead steaming. She's always happier at their house. Da had to put her to bed when we got home. I went up and before she fell asleep, I asked her where the baby could stay – there's enough room, but I could move my wardrobe for the cot. She just laughed and said children ruin your life, you'll thank me in the end and to be glad I wasn't being sent away, like all the other unweds. Fiona was standing behind me. Give it time was all she kept saying.

She's always like this after Uncle Keith's. She thinks she's starring in bloody *Abigail's Party*. Starts off on a high and crashes when we get home. Fiona says Maw hates living in Tain. Always wanted to be a toonser. I said she never wanted us, that's what it sounded like.

I've been stashing things for the bairn under my bed. Rita got me some baby clothes from Woolworths. A wee yellow woollen hat and mittens. So cute! I want him or her to have a wee David Bowie T-shirt. I can feel the baby all the time now. Swimming around like a fish. At first it felt like butterflies but now there's bumps and jumps, especially at night if I lie really still. They're going to be a party animal – we can go dancing together when they're older. Maybe I'll take them to see Blondie or The Skids, show them all the things I missed while I grew them inside me.

* * *

January 19th 1979

I can barely hold a pen. I feel so sick to my stomach. Mrs Meek's found an English couple to take my bairn. It's happening. Maw was pleased, said the sooner this was all over, the sooner I could get back to my life. No one need ever know I'd had a baby. We could change schools for the Highers. There was a place in Inverness I could get the bus to where no one would know my story. I could start again. I screamed at them – I don't want to start again! This is my beginning. I ran out of the clinic, no idea where I was going when I bumped into Shona. She calmed me down, said I didn't have to give away the bairn if I didn't want to, that she would talk to my mother and Mrs Meek. Maw wouldn't speak to me all the way home.

I had spaghetti hoops on toast for tea and tried to watch *The*

Goodies. Bill Oddie always makes me laugh, but not today, I may as well have been watching the test card. Maw wouldn't even look at me apart from when she said I had no idea what I was doing, that she knew what was best for me and that I was just a bairn. I know more about this kind of thing than you will ever understand, was what she said. She never gave any of us away! I bet she wishes she had.

* * *

January 27th 1979

I can't write loads, I'm too sad. Shona's been 'moved' to another job. And unless I stop this havering and arguing, Maw will take me to a home for unwed mothers – she threatened me last night. Fiona's at college and doesn't hear half of it and Da seems scared of her. Did she ever love us? She's only ever clipped us round the lugs, so maybe. Rita's been battered round the noggin by her ma for pulling a boy before.

I saw R outside school – he was meeting Isla. He ignored me. He knows, I'm sure. I can't believe it. I'm not one of them, having a baby to trap him for his money, to be married. I NEVER want to get married. I want to take the bairn and we'll go away. Far away. I've seen programmes about Thailand and Australia on *The World About Us*. I want to fly there, it all looks so beautiful, pure mint. R can fuck off to London. Everything's shite.

I'll write more when I can face it. Fiona's coming back this weekend – she's bringing her new boyfriend. I hope she doesn't end up pregnant like this.

* * *

Roxie stopped reading. She looked at Angus who was biting his lip.

'That was traumatic to read. There's a load more, but I need a drink of water. How can someone make you give up a baby and not even care?'

The Morse code beeped in Roxie's head as Angus scrawled his reply before getting her a glass of water.

Sometimes people are blind to anyone else's feelings. They just think about how they believe they would feel in that moment. So apply that to the situation. It's messed up. Times were different then.

'I one hundred per cent get that, but when your own child's begging. And the baby's related to you, but also you want to send it away. I don't understand people... Shall I carry on?'

He nodded.

Maw had swiftly been added to the top of Roxie's hate list...

* * *

March 1st 1979

Dear Diary (isn't that what people say in books when they write in a diary?), sorry I haven't written for a while. Life's been too much. I feel like I'm carrying the weight of the world inside me. Rita asked me if I miss seeing people. The school have made me have lessons on my own, like pregnancy is catching. Aye, I miss being with people, but the teachers are being nice. Even that dour old jobby, Mr Keene. He's really explained how quadratic equations work. I've spent the last year totally in the dark and he showed me. He said I need to pass maths if I want to get on in the world. And Miss Mcloughlin said if I need help with references if I don't stay on, to make sure I come straight to her. But none of that matters. I want to have my baby AND stay on at school. Be the best I can be.

Even Fiona's stopped saying Maw will change her mind. She won't. My last hope is she'll see the bairn and be won over.

I'm massive now, like a bleeding Spacehopper. The baby feels like it's going to just fall out like a bowling ball. Little feet keep digging in my ribs – it's the strangest thing, doesn't listen to me asking it to budge up. I had to stop eating tea the other night because it felt like it was doing the pogo on my actual stomach. No one needed to see chewed-up Findus Crispy Pancakes.

* * *

March 25th 1979

I heard R escaped to London. He left last week, didn't tell his family. No one knows what he's doing or why he left. I do – he thinks I'll tell and his da'll make him take on the land to support me. But I'll never tell. I don't want him. I just want my baby. That's it. I hope he finds what he's looking for. Pretty sure the streets aren't paved with gold. Unless his da cuts him off, he can always come home. If he's on *Top of the Pops*, I'll eat my hat. I'll be raging if he meets Blondie before me – he'd not heard them until I taped them off the radio for him! That Debbie Harry is so cool. I want to be like her one day, forget being in Pan's People like Rita wants. Pan's People are for right wallies. Rita asked me the other day if I was a Sandy or a Rizzo. Well, Sandy wouldn't be up the duff, would she? Lousy with virginity! Rizzo it was. But to be fair, I'm a Rizzo to my bones, bairn or no bairn. Tell me about it, stud.

* * *

April 9th 1979

Baby day. Nothing's happening. Da has already done ten practice runs in the car to Inverness. He's got it down to twenty-two minutes. I went with him on one of them, in case he got stopped for speeding and we needed to use me as an excuse. He even made me wear a seat belt, though it only just fitted over my bump. He let me bring one of my mixtapes to play on the journey – told me I was honoured. I knew I was, no one's allowed to mess with the dial, let alone play a cassette. His car, his music, usually John Denver or Ricky Nelson. Da's into his country. Your ma won't change her mind, he said on the way back. She wants you to have a better life than she had. I couldn't believe he'd said it. I asked what was wrong with her life. He was silent for ages, then said it fell short. We all have dreams, Morag. And when they don't come true, it can be painful. But you learn to live with the outcome and make the best of it. Unfortunately, I don't think your ma feels like that. I'd no idea what he was havering on about, and he wouldn't give me any more clues. So we sat in silence for the rest of the journey home, pretending the baby wasn't the reason we were out in the car and that when we drive back from the hospital, it will just be me.

* * *

April 26th 1979

How am I supposed to live without baby Shona? She's so perfect, with pink lips like my old Tiny Tears. She smells warm and comforting, like a wee mouse. They won't let me have her. Even Maw cried. EVEN MAW!

And the lies, everyone lies about labour! Unless you've pooed a football, you won't have a clue. All the leaflets I was given never mentioned one thing about the pain. But if you think about it, a huge baby has to squeeze through a small hole – how is that ever not going to hurt? I can't think about it too much, flashbacks.

I was overdue, the midwives decided to induce me. I'd no idea what that meant and they didn't really explain, just said it would speed everything up and I wasn't to make a fuss. Unholy hell. They failed to say it would make everything hurt like being ripped in two.

Maw had asked if I wanted her there. I'd said yes, but the

hospital sent her home. Said they would ring when it was all over. At one point, I thought it would be better to die and wished Fiona had been there. Then suddenly she was. She forced her way in to the delivery suite! Da had rung her lodgings and told her what was happening, and she got a taxi straight here. As soon as I saw her, I started wailing. The midwives told me to shut ma puss, but Fiona grabbed my hand and suddenly baby Shona came out, just like that! Well, obviously not just like that. I think seeing Fiona made everything all right.

I thought I wanted to keep Shona before, now I know I do. A fire burst in my chest when I held her. Fiona asked for us to be alone and then I tried to breastfeed. I managed it before a midwife came in to clean the room. Then they took her away to the nursery. One midwife took pity and said I could see her in her cot.

Fiona had to help me walk – they wouldn't give us a wheelchair. I pressed my nose up against the glass and when no one was looking, Fiona marched in and took Shona and brought her to me in the corridor. I held her for ages. She was asleep, all swaddled up in Fiona's yellow blanket – she took pictures of us sat on the chairs outside. I want to keep her was all I could say. Tell them, Fiona. She said she would. But then it all went a bit blurry. Next thing, I'm in a normal hospital bed with Da and Maw sat next to me. Maw holding my hand. Did you see her? Did you? I asked. Da was greeting. He said he'd seen her. He'd asked if he could. Maw hadn't, she wouldn't look at her. Her eyes were red.

I wasn't allowed to hold Shona again. Her real parents were coming. After that, I was jabbed in the arm because I tried to run away, find her, take her somewhere, anywhere other than here. Last thing I remember is Fiona holding my hand sobbing, telling me it would be OK in the end. But it wouldn't. It never would again.

* * *

Angus sat back against the cushions. His face had contorted; he'd turned inward. Roxie closed the diary.

'Are you OK?'

He flinched, then seemed to shake himself whole again. He nodded.

'You sure?'

More Morse code.

How many books are there?

Roxie counted.

'Eleven. They get thicker; the others are proper notebooks.'

Do you want to read any more? We know how the story ends.

'No, you're right. I think we should leave them for Mum and Fiona. Perhaps we should watch an episode of *Peppa Pig* to cheer us up?'

Angus shot her a sardonic glance before loftily penning a reply. She had been joking. Kind of.

Adventure Time *is better.*

'I LOVE *Adventure Time*. No one else gets it. Ash does, but they get bored if I ask to have a binge. Does Morag have proper TV channels here?'

Angus heaved himself up, he knew exactly where to look for the remotes.

Morag liked Adventure Time *too.*

Roxie laughed and they settled down on the sofa, Angus sitting next to her, *Adventure Time* blaring out of the TV. Roxie sank into the cushions. She couldn't concentrate; it wasn't just because Angus's immediate proximity ignited her whole right side with furtive electricity. She couldn't stop thinking about 'R', her grandpa.

Do you want to do something once you can walk a bit more?

'Like what?'

Shoplift?

Roxie burst out laughing. 'I still don't know why you were shoplifting when you knew you'd get caught.'

He brooded for a few moments and she worried she'd knocked their friendship back to the start and he'd hate her all over again, but then he was scribbling again.

It's complicated. A game mostly, to remind Mum that Dad existed.

'Why wouldn't she remember your dad? What happened?' Roxie recalled the family photos on the shelves, the assumed mystery sister and dad.

My dad died with my sister Ginny in a car accident when I was ten.

'Oh shit, how awful, I'm so sorry.'

He shrugged.

'Why do you think your mum's forgotten about your dad?'

Morse code frenzy.

Because she goes on dates.

'That doesn't mean she's forgotten. Do you want her to be single for the rest of her life?'

I'm not talking about this any more.

Angus put his pad down and slipped the pencil into the little hook attached.

'So you're not going to talk at all now?'

He shook his head.

'Even if I rolled off my chair into a sinkhole and needed rescuing and you had to ask if I was OK, you wouldn't talk?'

He just stared at Roxie, but the corners of his mouth were fighting a smile.

'Even if you were trapped in the bathroom so had to slip a note under the door to tell me to open the window from the outside, you wouldn't talk?'

Another head shake.

'Even if you were sinking in quicksand and I was walking past so you had to pen a quick note before you drowned and fold it into a paper aeroplane and throw it my way, you wouldn't talk?'

Angus remained silent.

'Even if—'

Angus leaned over and kissed Roxie on the lips, taking her by total surprise.

There was nothing for it but to kiss him back. It was only her fourth kiss in her fifteen and a quarter revolutions around the sun. She'd snogged Frank Laithwaite last Christmas and that had been gross. He didn't even wait until he'd tried to feel her tits (zone one) and got the green light on that, he went straight for the knickers (zone three). Red light! She'd only ever let Jack down there and she'd been so tense because what if he told anyone? She'd wished he hadn't tried at all, it'd been so mechanical. Ash said it was always better to go with someone a bit older because they'd know what they were doing, but they'd also expect more... If Ash's parents ever found out about all the things they knew, Ash would be grounded well into their forties...

Stars dazzled behind Roxie's eyelids and her stomach flipped like she was flying high on a swing.

Angus pulled away, looking at her contemplatively.

'Even if you kissed me? You wouldn't say anything?'

I had to shut you up somehow. Can I kiss you again?

This time she didn't worry about her sweaty armpits like with Freddie, or her fajita breath like with Jack.

It was perfect, and he nibbled her lips, making her jump so she banged her bad foot and squeaked a bit like Ash's dwarf hamsters when they enthusiastically gobbled their food.

Sorry, did I hurt you?

'No, I'm OK.'

Morse code click click click.

I better go. Don't want to be here when your mum gets back, she might have an idea, you know... Can I get your Snapchat?

'I like that you write dot dot dot.'

He smiled as she showed him her username, then added her to his friends.

He jumped up and handed her a note, making her laugh.

Bye!

13

'I'm going to go in the car park round the back of the town. Maw doesn't know we're here.' The drive to Tain had been extremely pleasant, the open empty roads a joy compared to London's crawling traffic when two miles could take forty minutes.

'When was the last time you saw her?' Maggie asked Fiona.

'At the funeral and then last week. She was unusually upset for her. She came to the wake afterwards but didn't stay long. I don't think I properly spoke to her all day.'

'How is it when you see her?'

'Like I'm visiting someone's mum I used to know from school. Surreal. Och, I know she's *my* mum, but it feels like the thread connecting us severed a long time ago.'

Morag's letter remained in the bag of photos in the flat. Maggie had planned to read it the previous evening, but the day's events had overtaken her. The letter deserved her full attention, but on waking, familiar anxiety had stalked her. Seeing Roxie in hospital had fired up all her worst fears, her dread of loss and grief, of love having nowhere to go. Fiona had already suggested a trip to Tain, but Maggie didn't want to leave Roxie alone after the accident.

However, Roxie would explode with her there, asking if she was OK every five minutes, and she wouldn't be able to stop herself. So when Angus had suggested coming round, Maggie had jumped on it. They wouldn't be long, just enough time for her to clear her head, see Morag's childhood home, and return to read the letter.

Tain was much bigger than Benlachie, with a decent-sized high street and rows of independent shops. There were multiple offshoot streets and an imposing sheriff's court, lording it over the other buildings with its fancy intricate architecture. It even had a public rose garden opened in the seventies by the Queen Mother. Maw lived just off the main drag in an end-of-terrace solid sandstone flagged house. It wasn't grand like some of the others, but a more humble abode.

'My room was at the front, just there, and Morag's was at the back over the kitchen. Maw and Da were next to me. We had an outside toilet until 1980, but I'd already left home by then. They added a whole bathroom downstairs onto the utility room. Avocado, very eighties.' They stood on the opposite side of the street. Apparently the windows were no barrier against tittle-tattle.

'What did your dad do?'

'He was a ghillie for the local laird. In charge of the land and wildlife for the shooting and fishing seasons. We'd lived on the estate, but then Morag arrived and the house wasn't big enough, so we moved here. When Da died, old man Munro let Maw keep the house, on the proviso it returned to the estate on her death. He was good like that. No one else got that treatment. He could be a bit of an old bastard.'

'And your mum?'

'She took in sewing and mending to get extra cash, and then when Da died, she lived off his pension.' The permafrost was palpable.

They wandered round the streets in the rain, Fiona bumping

into a few people she knew locally. They nosed in shops, bought some crusty bread and coconut cakes from Ruby's bakery to take back for Roxie.

'Does Roxie have many friends at home?' Fiona asked.

'She has a handful, yes. Why?'

'Just thinking the divorce will be hard for her.'

Maggie's hackles stood to attention.

'Oh, I'm not judging you. No! Sorry. I was thinking back to my parents. They should have got divorced, but Maw was a Catholic. Anyway, I wasn't ever sure she wanted to get divorced. I think she wanted to be married, just not to my da. So Morag and I lived in a house where the two adults were wishing for a different life. I admire that you're not doing that, that you're following what you need. Children always know if the parents aren't happy. It makes for a confusing time.'

'I agree. Thank you. It wasn't an easy decision, and Adam and I tried for so long. Or rather we failed for a long time. I didn't set out to get divorced. No one does. A series of unfortunate events knocked us off course.'

'You loved Adam?'

'Madly. Crazy in love, like a couple of teenagers. Maybe we had extremely high expectations... And when we had Roxie, it was full on – we'd only been together just over a year when she was born. We still didn't really know each other. But we got through it and we were genuinely happy. But life got in the way...'

'Do you still sing?'

'Jesus, no. I can't remember when I last sang. It kind of died off when... when things went wrong. I know most people would tap into their passion then. I just squashed it. It felt easier.'

'We still have open-mic nights at The Sea Shanty. We've one on Thursday... Would you consider singing at it? This one's to raise money for Breast Cancer Awareness, something Morag wanted to support.'

Just below the searing panic that carved up her sternum, a bud of joy seeded beneath Maggie's belly button burst open. *Surely not...*

'No one wants to hear that.'

'I think people would be delighted to have Morag's daughter sing for them.'

'That's emotional blackmail!'

'Aye it is. Morag wasn't shy of using it herself... Think about it. Open mic's never set in stone. It can be last minute, fuelled by a glass of red wine. Roxie would love it.' She winked and Maggie gaped in open admiration at how she'd just been played.

'Fiona! You're a bad woman.'

'I try my best.'

They had completed a leisurely loop of the town centre and bathed in the heady scent of the famous rose garden when they ambled back to the car past a charity shop. A woman's voice suddenly called out from behind them.

'Fiona?'

They turned round and faced a small elderly lady with lived-in eyes, her lips strained into an equivocal smile. She pulled an Aran cardigan round her scant frame, her jeans nipped in at the waist, stylish navy penny loafers on her feet and a natty animal-print scarf tied round her delicate neck. She was patting her halo of white hair as if that would protect it from the foul weather.

'Maw! Where did you spring from?'

Holy fuck, Maggie thought. *The antichrist.* She seemed so trifling and harmless, but then the devil needs to be in order to make an unobtrusive entrance. Fire and brimstone were so passé.

'I didn't know you were coming today, you should have rung.'

'It was a bit of a last-minute thing.'

Both women stood staring at each other.

'Come in the shop and say hello.' She motioned to the Cancer Research charity shop behind her.

Fiona dithered for a moment, then nodded.

'OK, we can't stay long. We were just on our way back.'

'I'm sure your friend won't mind you saying hello to your old ma for five minutes...' Up until that point, Maw had only deigned to give Maggie a cursory glance. Maggie held her breath, not wanting to draw attention to herself. Maw's eyes flicked from Fiona to her; if she noticed anything, she concealed it well.

'I don't mind at all,' Maggie replied. She wanted to hate her, this woman who had stripped away Morag's motherhood, who had banished Maggie to an alternative life, for better or worse was irrelevant. Morag had had no choice, like Maggie had no say in being born. But standing in front of her in the drizzle, Maggie just felt hollow where the rage should have been.

They followed her into the shop and she motioned she'd be a minute to the other older lady behind the counter. They stood by the front window like shop mannequins, next to the ladies trousers, or slacks as Iris used to call them. The air smelled of mothballs and that used-clothes smell that all vintage or charity shops seemed to secrete. Roxie's blasé attitude to second-hand clothes constantly perplexed Maggie – she wore them immediately without washing, the smell compressed between the fibres. What if someone had died in them?

'Do you work here?' Fiona asked obviously puzzled.

'I volunteer, aye. I've been doing it for a few months. It gets me out of the house.'

'Why haven't you mentioned it before?'

Maw shrugged.

'If you want to get out, you can ring me. You can come to the pub for meals. I've said it before.'

'I don't want to get in the way, be a bother... Anyway, I enjoy it here. Meeting people. Lots of teenagers coming in for the latest thing, not that we have any of what they're looking for. They like to up-thingy, now – what's the word...?' Her brows knitted together while she tried to summon the correct term.

'Upcycle?' Maggie offered.

'Aye! That's what they do. Thank you ...?' She waited for Maggie to fill in the gap.

'Maggie.'

'Maggie...?' She drifted off.

'Anyway, Maw, how've you been? Any news?'

Maw snapped to attention and regaled Fiona with the latest death toll of friends and acquaintances as elderly folk like to do, her eyes constantly flicking in Maggie's direction. *Was Maw putting two and two together?*

Maggie decided to look away and provide her racing mind with something to latch on to, distract her from the building anxiety of an impromptu 'big reveal'. Her eye caught a heavy hardback book on one of the shelves: *Sex in the Middle Ages*. Middle ages as in a middle-aged person, or in feudal times? Her brain gratefully jump-started on the topic of sex. It had been so long that she wondered if parts had retreated, grown over; maybe she was a born-again virgin? She fondly thought of her sex drive as an old familiar friend she'd lost touch with but would love to become reacquainted with again, especially when she remembered all the fun they'd had...

She and Adam had enjoyed a thrilling sex life, shagging almost everywhere at the beginning. It became a personal quest to find the most outrageous spot they could and claim it with a 'done it here' flag. Her favourite had been Stockwell underground station after a wine-fuelled night in Soho. The cluttered janitor cupboard squeezed between the Victoria and Northern Lines walkway sufficed as their unlikely clandestine passion palace. They could have been arrested.

Maggie suddenly felt the unmistakable yet unforeseen twitch of desire – what a turn-up for the books. She made a move to grab the hardback when Maw spoke.

'Maggie? Why do I think I know you? Have we met before?'

'No. I'm here on holiday with my daughter. But she's back at, er… Benlachie. She couldn't come…'

'Maw, we better go. As Maggie said, her daughter's on her own. We said we wouldn't be long. Give me a ring if you want to come over. Gordon or I can come and get you.' Fiona leaned in for a dry kiss on the cheek and Maggie forced a smile as they left the shop.

Before they turned the corner, Maggie glanced back. Maw was watching from the window, a puzzled look on her face. Her grandmother. Her actual goddamn granny. But she'd given Maggie away. *How could she?* A gut punch whoofed her in the belly as she remembered Iris's mum, Nana, reading her stories, making shortbread biscuits at Christmas and then decorating them with those tiny silver baubles that wreck your teeth. She had all the time in the world for Maggie. She'd nip into Boots and sniff the Max Factor face powder and sprayed lily of the valley perfume to conjure up Nana's face. Her favourite saying had been 'Don't tell your mum' before slipping Maggie some bonfire toffee or Blackpool rock when they'd been to watch the illuminations. Nana felt a world away from Maw, who appeared to flout her granny badge when most grandparents wore them with pride.

'I thought she was going to clock who you were for a moment. I'm sorry, I couldn't deal with it,' Fiona apologised.

'Me too, I completely understand. Did she ever know anything about what happened to me afterwards?'

'Only what we all knew initially: that you'd been adopted by an English couple and that you were called Margaret.'

'Did she ever ask you about me as a baby?'

'Even if she wanted to, I don't think she knew how. She's so buttoned up.'

'I think she was wondering who I was. I could feel the cogs turning.'

'Aye, I think you're right. Why d'you think I hotfooted it out of there?'

* * *

'How was Angus?' Roxie was alone when Maggie arrived back. Fiona had to run off to prepare for evening service. Apparently the meat delivery had been short of eight chicken breasts, causing a last-minute menu revision.

'Good.' Blood from a stone.

'Why's your trainer on the table?' Maggie snapped. 'You know you shouldn't put shoes on a table – it's a harbinger of death!'

Roxie just rolled her eyes.

Maggie's core tensed. Why couldn't she just answer properly? Shoes on the table made her stomach turn inside out. She snatched the solitary trainer up before anything bad could happen, breathing deeply, changing the subject.

'Do you need anything? I thought I could make some dinner later, go and grab some bits from a shop.'

'Sounds good.' Roxie wouldn't look at her mum.

Maggie noticed the photo bags were stuffed under the coffee table.

'Were you looking at photos?'

She nodded.

'Anything good in there?'

She didn't answer for ages.

'What's wrong? Are you in pain? Do you want some Nurofen?'

'Your dad's in the book!' Roxie looked stricken.

'What?'

'I read Morag's diary, the first few months when she was pregnant with you. She mentions your dad.'

14

The breath wouldn't come. Maggie sat down and pinched the hollow at the base of her throat, coaxing it out by force.

'Mum, I'm sorry! I wasn't going to. It's just that... Angus wanted to see photos. We didn't look at anything else. I promise.'

'My father?' she whispered. 'His name's in there?'

'Not his name. Just his initial. But I reckon Fiona would know who he was. There were a lot of clues...'

'Fuck. OK. I'm not cross. Can you show me?'

Roxie scrambled with the bag and pulled out the first school jotter.

'There's nothing in the end of this book after your birth. Mum, it's awful...' She uncharacteristically wrung her hands after Maggie took it from her.

'I'll read it now. Do I need a cup of tea first?'

'Wine I would think.'

'It's a bit early. Tea'll do, do you want one?'

Roxie nodded.

Five minutes later, Maggie sat on the sofa next to Roxie, mugs of tea on the coffee table, the book on her lap. She stared at it warily for a few moments before she turned the front cover and began to read.

Roxie kept glancing at her nervously. 'Mum, are you OK?'

Morag's pain seeped into Maggie's blood. Maybe it had always been there, passed from mother to child like dairy intolerance or hair colour. A woman's eggs formed as a four-month-old foetus inside her mother's womb and were in fact fizzing in the blood of her own mother whilst inside the womb of *her* mother. Maggie had read about it on *Huffington Post*. She was part of Maw too; there was no escaping that connection, Fiona must know that deep down.

'I need to read something positive. Something where Morag isn't feeling like she wants to die. That can't be where this ends today.'

'Did you read about your dad? Surely that's a positive?'

'Yes, but all the other stuff kind of shits all over it. I feel a bit meh about him right this second. Not because of how he behaved, which is totally understandable, but more because the other stuff is so much worse.'

Roxie rooted inside the bags and retrieved a handful of books, fanning them across the coffee table croupier-style. The dates ranged from a year after Maggie's birth to the last ten years. 'Which one?' she asked. 'What about something a year after, see how she's doing? Will you read them all eventually?'

'Yes. But not now.'

Maggie fingered the books, pulling one from the selection like picking a tarot card. It was dated January 1981.

* * *

January 24th 1981

We're going to Uncle Keith's for Sunday lunch tomorrow, Fiona said she'd meet us there. I want to see her engagement ring. Apparently Gordon spent a month's wages on it. Decent. I got Fiona a linen spray for her bottom drawer as a joke – they're all the rage if you're going to be a housewife. Fiona said she was going to keep working and that Gordon could stuff his crumpled shirts up his arse. Good for her. Maw had her hair done today while Da's been out all day on the estate. They're digging ditches or something. Maw never gets her hair done.

* * *

January 25th 1981

Jesus Fucked. I can say that because no one will ever read this. Apart from me when I'm ancient and have travelled all over the world. I'll sit back and look at these words I wrote and it'll all seem pathetic because I'll have visited the Sydney Opera House and the Pyramids of Giza. I'll have a good old laugh at all the shite I used to rage on about because my family is pure mental.

Maw's in her room and won't come out. I'm the only person who knows why. We got back from Uncle Keith's two hours ago and she's been in there ever since. Uncle Keith has a bigger house than us. Even though it's just him and Aunty Lillian – it's like bloody *Rentaghost*.

We'd all been admiring Fiona's ring, and Aunty Lillian got out a bottle of Asti and we had Twiglets – which are apparently only for special occasions and Christmas. I was allowed a sip of Asti – it tasted shite, like sickly lemonade. Gordon brought proper champagne. He'd proposed on the beach at Benlachie when they'd gone for a drive. I know it's all romantic and everything, but I never want to get married. I don't get why anyone does. I hate cleaning, cooking, being 'nice', and when Mrs Pickford gave a career talk, she said the best I could hope for was a job as a secretary. I know Fiona's a secretary, but I don't want to type. I want to busk, I want to play, I want to feel foreign lands under my feet and I want to fly in an aeroplane halfway around the world until it's time to come home. Until I see Shona again. One day.

I love the photos. Shona looks so cheeky now. She's got the same hair as me. So glad you can't see R in her. He's come back with his tail between his legs. Never made it in London. I want to beat that. I want to be a success. Da was showing him how to manage the pheasants, how to dig ditches – the old man wants him to know what he's doing so that when it's his turn, he can do it properly. Isla would be better. She likes the country ways. R hates it. Why can't the girls be the boss? Why are men allowed to do everything? Joan Jett gets to play guitar.

Anyway, we were celebrating Fiona and Gordon and I nipped off to the loo. Uncle Keith has a new one now, they put it in the bedroom! All pink and fancy. So I'm in the cludgie, checking out what he has in his cupboards when I look out the window and see Uncle Keith talking to Maw, who's gone out for a ciggie down by the apple tree. She doesn't know we all know she smokes. Next minute she's hugging him, it looked like they were going to kiss. I dropped the posh Imperial Leather soap down the pan in shock.

I ran downstairs and slipped out the back door to see what was what. Maybe it wasn't Uncle Keith. Maybe it was Da. He and Uncle Keith sometimes look alike, but I've never seen Maw and Da hug before. I was stealthy, like the Milk Tray Man, and parked myself behind the potting shed. I couldn't hear them at first, they were whispering. Then Keith was saying he couldn't ever leave Lillian, not after everything. Maw said she felt so bad, she wished things could be different, but they'd done the right thing, even if he didn't feel it at the time, it wouldn't have been fair on anyone. Uncle Keith said he wished he'd not cared about his brother's feelings in the long run and none of this would've happened at all.

I could feel my blood boil like jam in a pan. I wanted to hurt her, but I didn't know how. All the pain, all the tears, all the RAGE exploded in my head. I stepped on a twig backing away from them. They heard and Maw ran after me, grabbing my hand. What you doing out here? she asked. I said nothing. You been spying? Uncle Keith came up next to her, all in my face. She didn't hear anything, did you, Morag? You're together, I said. Believe me, we're not, she said. You want to be. I heard you. After everything you did. After all the things you said to me, about how I'd regret my life with Shona in it. Now I know why. You wished you were with him all along! Did you get pregnant with Fiona before you could marry him instead? Maw slapped me across the face. I tried to run off, but she grabbed my hands, the light went on in the kitchen and I saw Aunty Lillian walk in with a tray of empty drinks. You never saw us out here and this never happened, did it? Did it, Morag? She was spitting. I could tell Da. Why would you do that? Uncle Keith asked. That'd just hurt him for no reason. There's nothing going on with me and your ma. She's just a wee bit blootered out here and I was making sure she's OK. Why would you tell your da something that isn't what you think it is. It's nothing. When I got back inside, Maw asked if we could go. Aunty Lillian asked who had thrown the soap down the toilet. I'd clean forgot all about it.

* * *

'Fuck!'

'What?' Roxie had been Snapchatting Ash with her AirPods in.

'Read that.' Maggie handed her the journal. The transcribed events and conversations downloaded into her head, patiently digesting like slow-release carbs. A web of lies so heavy they could have supported an elephant driving a tank. She wasn't sure if it was best practice to inform your teenage daughter about her great-grandmother's scandal, but Maggie was past caring. She needed someone else to immediately bear witness and hash this over with.

'So, Maw was having an affair with this Uncle Keith bloke? Who was he again?'

'Her husband's younger brother. I'm not entirely sure it was an affair.'

'Will you tell Fiona?'

'I think I need to read more first. This feels so underhand. I understand why Morag hid everything now.'

'Why didn't she just burn them?'

'Like Fiona said, she wanted them near. It's quite hard to let go of things sometimes...'

* * *

January 30th 1981

Maw finally got out of bed this evening before I went to guitar. She looked like she'd been to hell and back. I checked to see if I felt sorry for her. I didn't. I'm not sure I'll ever feel anything for her again, apart from rage. I keep it in, biding my time. I've almost a grand now, saved up. Fiona's helping me with the passport too, not long till school's out. Said Gordon will verify my photo.

I saw Mrs Meek on the street today when I was leaving college. She was going into the post office opposite the college gates. The urge to batter her was overwhelming. Minty old fud. No man would ever get her up the duff. Unless they were blind. She looked up from checking inside her handbag and right at me. I felt a twist of a knife and could tell she felt nothing. She didn't even recognise me. Or maybe she did and her conscience wouldn't let her in on it. The last thing she ever said to me was I'd get over it eventually, I had my whole life ahead of me and that she was just doing her job protecting me and the baby – we'd both be better off in the end.

Like I was going to be the world's shittest mother. That title's already been taken.

When Maw started making tea this evening, she acted like nothing had happened. Like she hadn't been in bed for five days solid sneaking down to watch *Take the High Road* when no one's looking. Da's been sleeping in Fiona's room. I heard him creep out of their room and into hers, thinking I wouldn't notice. Da wasn't home from work yet. I flicked the kettle and asked if she wanted a cuppa before I went out. The kitchen was the warmest part of the house usually, but the frost coming off her was Baltic. She didn't answer me at first. She was just chopping up some veg. I asked again and she shook her head. Maw, what's going on? Never you mind, she said. You go off and have your lesson. She spat it out, like she was jealous or something. I'm having a tea first, I said. See, you're doing what you want. You got your life back. I couldn't believe what she was saying. I never lost my life, I said. But you would have, she replied. Why? I asked. She stopped chopping and looked at me then, pain etched across her face. When you're a mum that's all you are. It's different for men. They can do what they like. She wasn't wrong on that one. I would have gone to school and been a mum, I argued. How would you have done that? she asked. I didn't have an answer. You'll understand one day, Morag. I did the right thing by you. You'll be happy, meet a husband, have kids. You won't be trapped after a mistake. Shona wasn't a mistake! I raged. How can you say that? I miss her every day. I wonder what she's doing. If they love her enough. If they play with her like I would. How can you miss what you never had? she asked like she really meant it. You do! I'd poked the bear, and it was out of its cage. Uncle Keith's more important than us, I said. Always has been. I thought she was going to clout me again. Poke poke. You never wanted us, and you thought I'd be the same. But I'm not you. I'll never be you. Shona was more important than her father. I want nothing from him, ever. She laughed, bitterly. Oh Morag, you think you know everything about life, about me. You've no idea. You think I chose to be nothing? You have the chance to be something. Take it! You have a choice. I had NO choice! I screamed and I walked out of the door with my guitar. I left the cup of tea. Da was walking up the road – how did he not know? How did he stay?

* * *

February 14th 1981

I saw R in the offie after my shift at three. He saw me and waved. He actually sodding waved. I ignored him, bloody Valentine's Day and all, no chance, pal. I've managed to get through the past few years never seeing him. I got all the way to Mackinlay's before I heard footsteps. Did you not hear me? he asked. Nope. What you upty? The cheek! I wanted to boak, standing next to him. Not how I used to feel. Your da said you're terrific on the guitar. Which one do you have? No mention of where's the baby? Maybe he thought it wasn't his. Fucking taking the biscuit! I made my excuses, something about having to be back and legged it. I couldn't do it.

I was going to Rita's later. We were looking at brochures for going abroad in the summer. Difference was, I wasn't coming back. She was going to technical college in Inverness to do hairdressing, but wanted to go Interrailing. It was what all the rich kids did, and Rita was after having a rich man all to herself, and living in that world. So we'd been saving up for the tickets.

The atmosphere at home was strange. Da kept asking how things were, Maw ignored me most of the time. Apart from to give me my tea, or brekkie. I didn't care any more. Da asked me yesterday what was going on. And I said nothing. I haven't changed. But when Uncle Keith and Aunty Lillian came over for tea last weekend, I made sure I had a shift at the Grand and stayed out until I knew they'd left.

Then, Jesus H Christ, something happened. There was a knock at the door during *Minder*. It was pishing down when I opened it. On the doorstep was a guitar case. Da was like after breathing down my neck. What's this? I didn't have a clue. Was it even for me? I opened it – inside was a Gibson guitar, with an envelope slipped in between the strings. Maw and Da left me to it in the kitchen. The guitar was beautiful, must have cost a bomb. I couldn't believe it. Someone had left it there? No one was in the street outside, I'd checked.

I opened the letter.

(Morag had stuck the letter in between the pages.)

Dear Morag

I think you'll get more use out of this than I will. I think about you and wonder how you're getting on. Your da's been keeping me posted recently. But I didn't know what happened with the bairn. I ran away, I'm sorry for being such a wally. I know this won't make up for that, but I want you to know, if you'd wanted to keep the bairn, I would have supported you. Why did you never tell me? I am assuming the bairn was mine. You never said. Running away seemed like a good idea at the time. Not just from you, from here. London didn't work out for me. Camden is dead brilliant, pure bloody scary and crazy, and the pub we played in, The Dublin Castle, always has spots for up-and-coming acts. Maybe you'll go there one day. Anyway, the guitar is all yours. You deserve it. I will always regret disappearing, but I'm glad you're doing OK. If you ever want to jam, let me know. I kept a Fender.

Robert The Bruce

Roxie had been reading over her mum's shoulder.

'Robert the Bruce?'

'I think he was a King of Scotland. I'll have to google.'

'Blimey, so he gave Morag his guitar. Do you think they ended up together in the end?'

'No. From what she said in that entry, she'd moved on from that part of her life.'

Roxie sat back and looked at Maggie.

'You still have the letter. When you going to read it?'

'My head feels spangled. We know things about Fiona's mother that she's no idea about. I'm not sure I can cope with unlocking any more secrets.'

Roxie shrugged, puzzled. 'Everything's already weird. How can it get any weirder?'

Maggie nodded, Roxie's logic actually making sense... She reached into the bag and claimed the envelope with her name on the front. Even though she'd waited all this time for words from her mother, dread swamped her like a damp towel.

Dear Margaret (You will always be Shona to me),

If you're reading this, then I am dead. I have always wanted to write something dramatic like that! Sorry, I need to have something to laugh at during these last weeks.

I have approximately four months of life left in me. I can feel it struggling to stay. Things have been hard the last few years after the diagnosis, but I'm not here to talk about that. I want to give you information that might prove useful should you ever come across this letter. I want you to know I never 'gave you away'. I was forced to. It was the worst day of my life and also the best day when you were born. I've never again felt love like I felt holding you after you slipped into the world to meet me and your Aunty Fiona. Your aunty has instructions to be there in my place, answer all questions she can, and if she can't, there is this letter.

Where to start? In lieu of myself being in your life, you may wish to know who your father is. He doesn't know about you. Well, he does, he just doesn't know for sure. I never told him, or indeed anybody. I'm afraid I couldn't – it felt better that way. Then, over the years, it seemed pointless rehashing it all and revealing his name like the plot of a bad soap opera. Let sleeping dogs lie – but now feels right. Possibly cowardly because I won't have to answer any nosy questions!

William Munro was a decent man, conflicted, trapped in a life he didn't want. Unfortunately, he doesn't live in Scotland any more. The last I heard he had emigrated to Canada. I don't know where. We didn't really keep in touch, but I have a feeling he would be OK if you wanted to contact him. His sister is the local landowner. Her name is Isla Ross, though she may also not know where he is. He left on bad terms. Fiona should be able to point you in the right direction.

Getting the yearly photos from your parents was a small act of redemption and very important to me. I looked forward to them every year. I think you were lucky having your parents adopt you. I came to realise over the years that they were decent folk. It was rare to keep in contact with the birth mother. I found out years later that my own mother had organised that.

I don't know what kind of life I could have offered you as a sixteen-year-old. I imagined taking you on my travels all over the world, you asleep in a wee bed next to me. But, in reality, I know that wouldn't have happened. You needed stability, not the life of a nomadic musician. I would have stayed home and had a different life with you. That would have been my choice, but the alternative ended up being an adventure that I'm glad I experienced.

I think about you every day. Have you children of your own? Did you ever marry, or are you an eternal adventurer? I wonder if your hair sets the world on fire like mine used to. Do you love what you do? Can you sing as well? Singing and performing helped me get on with my life. They became my joy, as well as my nieces, Fiona and friends.

I need you to understand your grandmother is not an evil person. I made my peace with her recently. She came to visit and her life after you were taken has been her penance. She doesn't believe she is worthy of love, my words not hers. She would never have the self-awareness to realise this is how she feels, she is very shut down, which comes across as frostiness, though through our recent chats, she surprised me with her insights. She has borne the weight of her betrayal of you and I for long enough. I am not asking you to visit her. I'm just asking you to keep an open mind about it all. People can do terrible things when they think it's for the greater good. I realised my hating her was making me ill. She did what she did to spare me what she thought was going to be a lifetime of regrets. Hard as it was to hear, I understood. Dying makes you realise hating is futile.

My sister is the kindest person on the planet and she will look out for you no matter what. She keeps up her relationship with Maw even though Maw pushes her away. This is how kind she is. I know you will love her. She has always loved you.

Whatever you have done in your life and wherever you are, I hope you are happy. I hope you know love, and if you don't, know that I will always love you, from the stars and beyond.

With all my love,

Morag, your mother

Maggie handed Roxie the letter and walked into the kitchen, ransacking the cupboards until she found the whisky, downing two straight shots. Unfortunately her hands still wouldn't stop their shaking. Situations flashed in her head: her own life, a mirror, like *Alice Through the Looking Glass*, but she'd been older and wiser and hadn't been forced to give her baby away... Maggie hadn't expected the letter to floor her like it had. Of course Morag was still dead, no amount of words could make up for that, and uncovering her father was exciting. However, the abiding maternal grief she shared with her mother poked at wounds that had never fully healed.

'Mum? Are you OK?'

The flashbacks were too visceral, her words trapped elsewhere.

'Mum!' Roxie's voice was tarred with panic. 'Shall I get Fiona?'

'No, I'll be OK. I'm fine. Just a shock, that's all. I don't know what I was expecting... I'm just going to lie down. Sorry, I'll be right as rain in a bit.'

As soon as Maggie shut the door to her bedroom, she smashed her face into a pillow and sobbed. She wanted someone to obliterate the pain, she just wasn't sure who that someone was.

15

Roxie grabbed her crutches and hopped to her mum's shut door and listened, unmistakable sounds of muffled crying seeping through the crack. When she'd been younger, she'd eavesdrop at doors to glean information littered behind hushed talking, secrets and uncertainty that had tainted her early childhood. She'd overheard unfathomable conversations about post-traumatic stress disorder, flashbacks, depression, grief, psychosis. One thing she had understood at the time was that her mum was unlike normal mums.

What was she like now? They bickered mostly, and her mum's glib treatment of her dad drove Roxie bonkers. Apart from that, she didn't really know her, other than she worked long hours, liked red wine and had once almost been on *The X Factor*. The finer details had been lost in the resin of time...

The stand-alone fact was Mum rarely cried any more, and this secret display heralded something inexorable coming on the wind. Roxie couldn't handle a nervous breakdown – she needed back-up, so she broke into Maggie's phone. It wasn't challenging – her code was Roxie's birthday.

Relief flooded her veins like cheap vodka at the park when Fiona swept into the flat ten minutes later.

'Thank you for coming,' Roxie whispered in the hallway.

'Why are we whispering?'

'Mum doesn't know you're here.'

'Is that wise?'

'I can hear you!' her mum called from the bedroom. 'At least whisper properly.'

Roxie smiled. If her mum was being bossy then she was feeling better...

* * *

'Am I ruining your early-evening prep?' Maggie asked anxiously later in the kitchen. 'I told Roxie not to bother you.'

'No. Gordon's whizzed down. He still works outside the business but is always on hand when needs be...' Fiona smiled encouragingly. 'Roxie was worried...'

'Yes, sorry, Rox. That letter, I dunno, it triggered me. My own stuff, Mum dying, Morag not being here, how she never got to see me... All the stuff in the diaries too – it's too much. There're things you need to know, Fiona...'

Fiona was silent for more than a moment.

Roxie held her breath. She wished she'd never found that time capsule in the hidey-hole. Why was she such a nosy parker? But she was Roxie, she picked scabs, followed people on beaches, and spied from behind closed doors. It was what she'd always done because no one ever told her the whole truth.

'I see. What kind of stuff?'

'Things about Maw. And Morag told me who my father is...'

'Jings, that's huge.'

'I don't think it's meant to be a secret any more. William Munro?'

Fiona blinked, then cleared her throat.

'Och, OK. I didn't expect it to be him... Back then, he was *the* most eligible bachelor, son of the laird whom our father worked for. No wonder she kept that quiet. Da would've gone mad about it.'

'Was he not nice?'

'No, he was decent, quiet, not one for playing the field. Just that he was older than Morag, my age, and Da worked for his da. And, if I remember rightly, he ran away to London for a while, causing an uproar.'

'Morag said he emigrated to Canada?'

'Aye, he ran away again. There were rumours. His da's dead now, so the land's passed on to Isla. She stayed here, got married, had some kids, runs everything. Has some Airbnbs on her estate for the hunting/shooting/fishing crowd.'

'So Mum's the daughter of a laird?' Roxie liked the sound of this. 'I'm a granddaughter of one? Would we inherit the land?'

'Sadly, he was disinherited. So no. You'd have to go through the courts if you wanted to. But I wouldn't recommend it.'

'Roxie! I'm not after their land. It would just be good to see a picture of him.'

'There must be some in the ones I brought round. Let me see.'

Fiona disappeared to the living room and brought the pile back in, dumping it on the floor before rummaging. She pulled out an old Boots envelope and started flicking.

'Here, this is him at a marquee.'

'Isn't that a tent?' Roxie asked.

'Yes, but also a twice-yearly fete that goes on for three or four days, with traditional dancing, discos, tombolas, that sort of thing. Most villages hold them in the Highlands. They can get a bit raucous, and people have been known to get into fights. Always the same families...' Fiona rolled her eyes. 'It never seems to skip a generation.'

Fiona handed Maggie the picture. She scrutinised it, then kept glancing over at Roxie.

'I think I see a likeness in Roxie, but not me.'

'No, you're one hundred per cent Morag. Let me see again?'

Fiona followed suit with squinting and comparing.

'Aye, it's there all right. The same hair, build, shaped face.'

'Though he does look very similar to Adam, so it could be that.'

'Please can I see?' As soon as she looked at the man, boy really, Roxie's skin bristled like she'd walked past an open freezer. He marginally resembled her own dad, but maybe that was an inherited longing in her mother from *her* mother. He was holding a guitar but posing for the camera and grinning – his lopsided smile was her genetic trademark. 'Hello, Robert the Bruce.'

'Oh my lord!'

'What?' Roxie and her mum both cried.

'Maw would always ask Morag who're you off meeting and she would say Robert the Bruce. We thought it was a joke that she was with Rita, or one of the other lassies. Morag wasn't that interested in boys back then, or rather she was secretive about them, about lots of things as it turns out...' Fiona teared up. 'Sorry, I don't know why I'm upset.'

'Because nothing about this is typical, is it?' her mum said, patting Fiona's hand. 'Maybe you shouldn't read the diaries.'

'Ah, red rag to a bull. Point me in the right direction. I'll take them home and read them after work.'

'What were the rumours about William?' Roxie asked.

Fiona sighed and drooped her shoulders.

'That bad?' her mum asked.

'No, not at all. Just gossip. You know how things get blown out of proportion in small villages and towns, especially round here where there isn't loads going on like the city.' She paused. 'I don't know whether I'm adding to the rumour mill. Apparently his da caught him with another man and threw him out. I'm not sure how the rumour started, but being gay round here in the eighties and nineties with all the doom-mongering about HIV and AIDS was akin to being a social pariah. That's not how *I* felt, but a lot of people felt – *still* feel – like that.'

'But if he was gay, how come he and Morag, you know...?' Roxie quizzed Fiona.

'Experimentation? I don't know. He never married and when Da was training him up and showing him the ropes, he never had a girlfriend. Whether the rumour was true or not, he definitely left in the mid-nineties under a cloud and Isla inherited his role, which was unheard of round here at the time.'

'And he can't return?' Roxie wondered.

'I don't know, love. Maybe he never wants to set foot in Scotland again. He might have met a nice chap and they live happily ever after in Canada together. He was always into music. Da said he wasn't a natural with the way of the land. He was going through the motions. Music was his real passion, so I guess that explains his connection with Morag. I can tell you this, he was a gentle soul, kind and always up for a party. Very like Morag in that respect.'

'Will you try to find him now, Mum?'

Her mum sat staring at the picture of her father, a look on her face that unleashed unease inside Roxie.

'It feels like I have more than enough to discover in Benlachie this week.'

'Let me know and I can set you in touch with Isla. She's the only one who might have William's details. She's Maw's landlady, so we have dealings with her...'

Roxie didn't want this new quest to happen while she was here. What if William were dead too? She couldn't deal with her mum on her own if that were the case. This was why she needed two parents. The seeds of a plan began sprouting inside her head...

16

Maggie perched on the sea wall with Fiona and Issy watching the sun slowly slip-slide into the sea. She could almost hear hissing. Angus and Roxie were holed up in Morag's flat demolishing the ice cream Fiona had brought up once the rush was over, before collecting Issy and Maggie for an al fresco bottle (or two) of wine. The waves breaking on the beach reminded Maggie of the perpetual motorised purr in London after most birds had nested for the night, the ebb and flow like the ceaseless acoustics of breaking water.

'So, how long do you think you'll stay?' Fiona asked, handing Maggie a glass of wine. 'Not that I am turfing you out any time soon. I just wondered.'

'Initially I'd been planning on two weeks because I also wanted to tour round the area from the hotel base. Adam's coming to take Roxie home at the weekend, but now I don't know.'

'As in you might stay longer?' Issy asked hopefully.

'Maybe. Reading all the diaries, finding out about everything, makes me feel I need to go home and digest it all, especially now

Roxie's injured. I feel bad leaving her with Adam when he'll have to work.'

'She could stay here with you?' Issy suggested. 'She and Angus seem to be getting on. Believe me, if Angus didn't want to hang out with Roxie, he wouldn't. Stay!'

Maggie pulled her hoodie over her head as the wind picked up, gulls circling, airborne ice-cream predators.

'I'm finding this all a bit too close to the bone, reading Morag's letter, the diaries, the grief and the loss...' The gulls swooped and squawked, people laughed, their voices rose, the wind catching their words, whipping them away into a void, this infinitesimal space where silence reigned for a moment and the truth spilled out... 'I lost a baby too. My son... Louis.'

The world continued spinning, no one fell off the sea wall and, more importantly, Maggie didn't crumble into dust.

'I knew something deeply upsetting had happened,' Issy said quietly. 'I could just tell. Obviously losing two mothers in the space of a month is horrific, this felt more profound...'

'I'm so sorry, Maggie,' Fiona added, touching her hand. 'You and Morag have so much in common.'

'The loss was never my war cry, or a tool I used to identify with others, though I know a lot of people do that and it's OK, whatever helps. I just felt I had no point of reference, no idea how to navigate the situation...' Maggie breathed deeply, the words she'd corralled into a corner of her mind fought to get out. 'After it happened, the person I was before Louis died, died with him. I was left being someone I didn't know, *still* don't really know. Someone who blamed themselves.'

'But how was it your fault?' Fiona asked gently. 'I'm sure you weren't to blame.'

'Louis... died during labour...' Maggie's eyes stung; ten years on and the hole in her heart could still pulse louder and harder than the rest of her. 'The cord was wrapped round his neck... three times and he got stuck, then I had to have an emergency C-section that ended up in a hysterectomy...'

Issy handed her a tissue from one of her cleverly hidden pockets.

'Thanks... I seldom cry, I spent so long crying that I hate it now. But I've cried more times in the last few weeks than I care to remember.'

'But it's our body's way of letting go. It's cathartic,' Issy sighed.

'I guess... I lay in bed for months, life ticked on. It was dark, I was so lost, I felt I must have done something wrong somewhere along the way. I'd always toed the line, saluted all the fucking magpies, never walked under ladders, uncrossed whole sets of cutlery, constantly been the good girl, forever doing what my parents wanted me to, even not contacting Morag because I thought it would hurt them... But I'd felt suffocated in West Kirby, I didn't want to be a lawyer. I wanted to be somewhere exciting, do something exciting, *become* someone exciting after so long being square... So I ran away to London.'

'Were the streets paved with gold like you thought?' Fiona asked.

'No, but it was fun, then I met Adam. Having Roxie solidified us, we were together just over a year when she was born. The five-year gap between her and Louis was intentional. We needed a breather, got married, got pregnant with Louis, then got hit by a truck. That's when I started looking for clues. How it was my fault because the guilt weighed me down. I started seeing people in trees and bushes, they would whisper I'd caused it. I know now they were psychotic episodes brought on by the trauma and being thrown into the menopause at thirty-three. The entire time this was happening, Adam was getting on with life, looking after Roxie. He hadn't had his identity and insides ripped apart – and that made me resentful too. He'd lost a son, but he hadn't also lost himself... My dad sat me down one day and told me all the tears in the world wouldn't bring Louis back, I had a daughter who needed me... When I started to come out of the fog, she'd fully attached to Adam, and it felt wrong muscling in, so I hung back. And it's been like that ever since. I've tried, and I've failed. Roxie pushed me away. Adam and I fought about it, and he said I needed to give it time, but... this is the thing, I was so terrified of fully loving her... in case she was taken too. I couldn't cope with it again. It was safer to not engage... Then Adam and I imploded, limping along until now...' A sob wound its way through her chest. 'I can't talk to her about it, it's been so long. I don't know how to, how to be a mum to someone who won't let me.'

'I think you do a good job from what I've seen,' Fiona said. 'Being a mum isn't a set of rules. Roxie's OK, she's here with you, isn't she?'

'Only because Adam forced her. Everything's a fight. I know that's also teenagers, but it's been like this for years, and if I cry or have a flashback, it freaks her out, so I try to press everything down. I think it reminds her of how shit things used to be. She knows Louis died, we haven't hidden that from her, but I've hidden so much else. She's angry with me for everything.'

'Do you have PTSD?' Issy asked.

'Yes, I'm not sure today was that, it was pretty mild. Just horrors of Louis dying.' Maggie inhaled a massive glug of wine. 'I could feel how I'd felt, but it eased off.'

'That sounds like a PTSD flashback to me,' Issy said. 'You don't have to play them down. It's OK. Maybe Roxie needs to see you have one and that you're OK afterwards? Hiding things never works out in the long run. Angus had PTSD after the accident. Night terrors. He would scream, but afterwards refuse to talk.'

'A letter can trigger something like that?' Fiona asked, genuinely astounded.

'Aye,' Issy said. 'Anything can.'

'I have it here, do you want to read it?' Maggie asked them.

'No, it's yours,' Issy said.

'There's nothing in there you don't already know…'

She refilled her glass while Fiona and Issy huddled over the letter reading it.

'Fuck! Sorry, just… bloody hell, what a story!' Issy exclaimed when she'd finished, shaking her head, handing back the letter after Maggie had surmised the potted family history. 'No wonder the letter sent you into a spin. You both lost babies…'

'Aye, you did. But I do think Morag found some kind of acceptance before she died,' Fiona admitted.

'She didn't blame me then?' It slipped out, unannounced…

'What? I told you before, how can anything be your fault?' Fiona gasped. 'You were taken away.'

'But I took too long to look for her… She'd still be alive if I'd found her quicker.' It was no good, the little demons scratched inside her, wanting airtime.

'Maggie, you can't blame yourself for this.'

'It was the first thing I did when I heard her story.' For someone who hated crying, Maggie was flouting her own rules spectacularly. Issy rubbed her back. 'It suddenly all made sense…' She choked on a sob, tensing her stomach not much help. 'I've always tried to reason why I lost Louis. I just couldn't accept it was one of those things. But now, it kind of adds up. Karma is a thing, right? This is mine…'

'No, no, NO!' Fiona cried and jumped off the wall. 'Look at me!' Maggie turned round to face her. 'Morag didn't get cancer because you didn't contact her. And the universe did not snatch away Louis because you waited to get in touch when it was right for you to do so. These events are not connected in the way you might think they are. They are connected in the fact that you are Morag's daughter and experienced a one-in-a-million similar situation to her, you both lost a child, as did our Issy here.'

'But people can die of a broken heart.'

'They can, but Morag mended hers, eventually. She found solace in music, her friends and family – she said so in the letter. The festival is... was her child. Music was her happy place.'

'I just wish I knew her...' Maggie slipped away, overwhelmed by a longing she never knew existed. 'How does it hurt so much? I can't believe I can feel this sad about someone I never met.'

Fiona took her in her arms while she sobbed into her hair. 'Because, dear girl, she was your mother. And she was a legend whose love for you was undimmed. Somehow, that love trickled into your life, your heart, without you ever realising. And now she's gone, your heart knows it. But you know what, you have me. I'm so happy you're here. I've missed you. I never realised how much until now, until you opened up, showed yourself to me. You are so like your mum, a hard nut to crack, but when you do, it's worth it. I loved your mum so much. And always will.'

'I need a hug! I need to join in!' Issy cried, tears streaming down her face.

The trio stood next to the sea wall, a statuesque Amazonian cradling two flame-haired kinswomen.

'So now you've made us all cry and ruined the evening, what are you going to do to make it up to us?' Fiona laughed at Maggie.

'What would you like me to do?'

'Well, there's one thing... Something Morag would LOVE...'

'Oh no, not that...'

'What? What?' Issy cried. 'Tell me!'

'It's a surprise...' Fiona gloated at Maggie.

'Don't look like that because I haven't said yes.'

'Yet...'

17

Fuck being an invalid, Roxie only liked lying down and doing nothing on *her* terms. Tomorrow she was allowed to walk on her cast with her crutches and hop about the place, maybe make it to the seafront, go shoplifting... She'd tried to get into a pair of baggy jeans earlier but had to abandon them; they didn't fit over the unwieldy cast. It would have to be her mum's denim nineties wannabees shorts again, and they were cringe. Mid-nineties was sick, everyone agreed, but Roxie was more of a not-following-trend person. She preferred to walk her own path, without realising many souls had trodden the well-worn 'I want to be different' path before her.

Roxie had yet to learn nothing was ever truly unprecedented in the world. Someone somewhere would always have identical experiences, the same thoughts and opinions, similar feelings about peanut butter that you do (it's claggy paste and brings nothing to the world, unlike Marmite). And when you met that person, it felt like you never existed before they air-dropped fully formed into your life as your soulmate. But what Roxie didn't know (couldn't know at fifteen and a smidge) was that maybe there would be more than one soulmate on your 'I want to be different' path.

As she huffed about having to wear the shorts *again*, Roxie felt sick. Sick, sick, sick. Angus was on his way and she despised that she liked him. Roxie prided herself on not getting fully sucked in to any boy's vortex. But she found herself agonising over slathering on her lip-plumping lip gloss, or if that was too obvious, *or* if there was even any point because nothing might happen *ever again*. It wasn't exactly a date, and their mums would be hovering like staid Jane Austen chaperones, peering over their knitting, making sure no one was revealing an ankle or, God forbid, looking directly into each other's eyes without wearing a condom. Angus hadn't Snapchatted since she'd last seen him, admittedly that had only been earlier in the day, but the thought of this dwindling into the abyss made her feel sick sick sick, once more. Every kiss she'd ever experienced had been a one-hit wonder. The vortex was winning.

She was supposed to return home that weekend, but she was hoping things would change since she'd set the wheels of her evil plan in motion. Both outcomes would benefit her doubly; it was a win-win situ. As she turned this way and that in Morag's beautifully carved mirror, she wanted to punch her reflection.

'Be chill,' she whispered to herself. 'Morag wouldn't stress like this!'

Roxie couldn't look directly at Angus when he arrived with Issy for the dinner that he was going to prepare. The fact that he could cook elevated him above everyone she had ever crushed on. She made a bet Jamil couldn't cook... When Angus smiled, it wasn't a clandestine one that told her he hadn't stopped ruminating about their kiss earlier. It was infuriatingly inclusive of everyone in the room, even her mum's various incarnations on the mantelpiece. Roxie pinched herself – if Ash could hear her thoughts, they would be rolling on the floor laughing. *You want to marry him! You love him!* Pull yourself together, Roxanne, he's just a boy, is what they'd eventually command before blowing a giant bubble as was their wont, sucking it back into their mouth and repeating the process all over again. Ash punctuated most serious conversations with the smacking of gum against their lips.

Roxie had played and replayed an opener to accompany the unlikely situation of finding themselves on their own this evening. She wasn't sure she'd even manage to speak, though had joined in over dinner on such topics as ice-cream flavours, worst ever attack by a seagull, bitchy girls at school, and who would win in a fight: Black Widow or Wonder Woman?

The stars aligned in her favour when the mums headed out to meet Fiona towards the end of supper, saying they'd be back later. They left Angus stationed at the sink finishing off the washing up, which seemed grossly unfair after he'd cooked a tasty seafood risotto. Roxie eventually found the silence unbearable as he clanked dishes in the sink, his back to her... She abandoned the allegedly witty (passive-aggressive, let's be honest) 'cat got your tongue', for a more beige icebreaker.

'Thank you for cooking. Where did you learn to make proper food like that? I can just about heat up beans in the microwave...'

Angus wiped his hands on a tea towel and slipped his pad out from his back pocket.

From books and YouTube. Mum isn't massively into cooking. And Morag. She showed me loads too.

'You said she taught you guitar as well. Do you still play?'

He nodded.

'What kind of stuff?' They'd already covered musical tastes and discovered lots of similarities knotted amongst their two lists.

Thankfully Angus loved The Cure – a deal-breaker in Roxie's eyes.

Angus walked over to the acoustic guitar hanging on the wall by the piano in the next room, and lifted it off the hanger. He sat on the kitchen stool by the window and tuned the guitar, blowing dust off its glossy neck so the motes danced in the evening sunlight. He looked right at her and then began playing. She recognised it from her childhood, one of her dad's favourite songs. He glanced at the strings, recalling the chords from memory, his hands sliding down the frets. He was very good. Roxie clapped when he'd finished.

'The Beatles, right?'

He nodded.

'Are they your favourite?'

He shook his head, rehung the guitar and joined her at the kitchen table, his pad out.

'Blackbird' was the first song my dad taught me once I'd mastered the basics.

'That sounded so difficult to play. My dad loves music. He has all the Beatles albums on vinyl at home. He used to take me to record fairs and shops years ago, before it was trendy.'

Your dad sounds cool.

'Yeah, he is. You'll get to meet him when he comes to take me home.'

Angus smiled and started another missive.

Do you want to go somewhere tomorrow?

'Yes! I can walk with my crutches or stick by then, but I can't go for miles.'

I thought you might want to see the famous caves.

'How would that work? Don't we have to walk along the beach?'

There's a raised path underneath the cliffs. I could give you a piggy-back for some of it? Take it really slow, get a picnic?

Despite her nerves, Roxie burst out laughing.

What?

'I'm a lot heavier than I look.'

I'm a lot stronger than I look.

'OK...' Roxie could feel her breath catch in her throat. She smiled and that was when he threw her a bone.

How long do you think they'll be gone?

'Well, it could be anything from ten minutes to two hours – it's a pub downstairs. That's adult Disneyland.'

He smiled.

Time enough to kiss you again?

Roxie nodded while trying to quell the swooshing butterflies and other creatures surfing the waves of nausea. He leaned over the table and brushed her lips with his, sending shocks across her entire body. She had yearned for this, but not expected it in the slightest.

Do you want to sit on the sofa?

She nodded again and he walked round, confidently scooping her up like she was in a film. Not the ones she usually starred in, they were predictably dark and revolved around anti-establishment behaviour or being in a band and ruling the world. This time (small puke in mouth), Roxie was showcasing her talents in a tawdry romcom.

Surely he was going to clip her head on the door frame as they walked through it? No, he executed it perfectly, turning sideways. He lay her gently on the sofa and slid in next to her. His eyes were so intense she could barely hold his gaze. Why was he looking at her like that? *Oh... no...*

'I don't want to have sex with you.'

Angus jumped like she'd zapped him with a cattle prod. There was no unsaying it now; it was out there like a wrecking ball... Angus shot his hands up, then scrabbled around for his notepad.

What made you say that?

'I don't know. I just freaked out, that's all.'

If I gave you that impression, I'm sorry. Maybe I should go?

'No, please don't. I don't know why I said it. It just came out. It was my evil twin, I promise!'

He lay back against the sofa cushions and rubbed his face with both his hands.

Incoming Morse code, Roxie's anticipation topped out. Why wouldn't he just fucking talk?

I really like you. I know it's hard that I don't talk and miscommunication is one of my biggest problems, but they do say most communication is non-verbal anyway.

'Do you think you'll ever talk?'

That's not something I want to talk about.

'What happened then? Why'd you decide not to? You never said earlier.'

Angus sighed and covered his mouth with a clenched fist. What was he hiding? Scribble scribble...

You tell me something first. Something you've never told anyone.

'I secretly like Coldplay.'

He smiled.

Something real. No one likes Coldplay.

'They clearly do.'

He gave her a Paddington Bear stare.

'Something I've never told anyone before...?'

He nodded.

'OK, here goes. I can't believe I'm actually saying this out loud...' She flubbered her lips. She tried to recall the last time she'd consciously spoken about this. Maybe it was when she'd told Ash after they'd met in Year Seven. 'When I was nearly five, my parents told me I was going to have a baby brother or sister. I wondered if they'd buy the baby from a shop, would I get to choose what type? I'm not gonna lie, I don't remember being happy about the whole experience, most likely I'd have preferred dwarf hamsters like my friend Ash. Or a dog. I bloody wanted a dog. Dogs are way more interesting. And you can teach them to do tricks. Babies just lay around. Rather dull mostly.'

Angus nodded in agreement.

'Anyway, the spare room had been painted, things were put in there ready and waiting. But something went wrong, even now I still don't fully understand what. I was told various versions as I got older and I googled once I could. But by then, I didn't need to know, or want to, because googling was making an effort with something I could never compete with... Louis can never disappoint anyone, he has nothing to live up to. He's his own legend ... and he also caused my parents' split. They've been a nightmare for years, secrets, not really talking, fake everything. Mum's always cross about some-thing: Dad's breathing, the way he eats crisps, you name it, he's annoying to her and I don't get why – he adores her, it's obvious. I think he's amazing, funny, kind, a good cook and she just doesn't see it. It's like there's some kind of barrier up around her. She talks to me as if I'm an idiot, and it feels like it's me and Dad in one corner and her in the other. She just wishes Louis was here and that's all she cares about... It feels like Louis still takes over even when he's dead. Now Mum has two dead mothers and one mother also lost her baby. It just feels like everything's fucked, a chain of pain.'

Angus leaped up and strode into the kitchen, coming back with the kitchen roll and ripped off a piece, handing it to her.

'What a loser, not you, *me*. I can't believe I'm crying about *this*.' Roxie was angry with herself. She'd ruined potentially the most exciting night of her small life so far by churning up the past and then bawling about it like a twat. There was also her #metoo blurt at Angus to consider. She should be frogmarched to a Coldplay concert front row and made to listen without ear defenders...

I think it's OK to be upset about that. You've a lot going on in your head. Having a dead brother is very sad, and then your parents splitting up because of it. It sucks. Are you sure they're getting divorced because of your brother?

Roxie paused, not used to the bat back. Ash had just agreed with her: the ghost of Louis does it again...

'What else could it be?'

So many things. Adults are a mystery to me. My mum dated fugly Denis who runs the gift shop. Why?

'Maybe Tinder was empty? It's kind of remote round here... Is that why you shoplifted?'

Angus nodded.

'How'd that work out for you?'

She went nuts and said her love life was none of my business. But it is if she's with someone unworthy. I don't want them in my space. I'm not playing fucking happy families with a numpty. But I have no say.

'Yeah, I get that... If Louis isn't the problem for my parents, then I've no idea what is. It feels like they've never been quite right. It's such a head fuck. I just wish they'd stay together so I don't have all that hideous dating parents shit to deal with.'

Have you asked them why they're splitting up?

'No. Are you mad? What if it's something even worse than Louis?'

Though she struggled to think of a worse situation than a dead baby...

He nodded and Roxie let the absence of a reply wash over them. She shot forward in time and imagined her and Angus together – would it work, him not speaking...

'So... I shared my innermost secret...'

And?

'It's your turn now! Why don't you speak?'

I never said I'd tell you, you just assumed.

'Wow, you're annoying.'

Fine. Have you got the patience to wait while I write an essay?

'Maybe, but wouldn't it be easier if you just spoke and told me out loud?'

Yeah, funny. I'm not falling for that trick.

'OK. Tell me, in your own time…'

He headed over to Morag's desk and pulled out drawers until he found a large pad. He sat down next to Roxie and started scribbling. Her phone pinged with a Snapchat alert, but she controversially ignored it (a world's first for her), staring at the ceiling instead for a few minutes before watching him work, his hand racing across the page, the velocity rendering the scrawl almost illegible. She had no idea what he was going to come out with. But she found herself relaxing into the sofa, the earlier anxiety having dissipated. She could almost be sitting with Ash in their bedroom (minus the dwarf hamsters). She felt she could tell Angus anything and he wouldn't laugh at her, or tell her she was stupid. Or flyer the whole school announcing she was frigid because she'd freaked out about sex. Angus was just … kind of normal in a fit boy sort of way.

He looked up and caught her staring, she felt her cheeks redden, but he just smiled, making her heart burst into a million tiny shards. *Oh no…*

When he'd finished, he handed her the pad and got up to sit on the piano stool, spinning it round until it was the right height.

The morning of Ginny and Dad's death was a normal day. Dad and Mum had had yet another argument in the garage. Ginny had followed to listen and I tried to drag her away. I heard Mum shout at him she may as well be a single mum, I'd never seen her that crazy before. She said he could take us shoe shopping – she was on strike. So we went in the car. Ginny was being a pain in the arse. She kept asking why they'd been fighting, why Mum was angry. Dad kept telling her it was nothing, but she wouldn't shut up. In the end, he shouted at her, making her cry. I felt bad for her, but then she said she was going to tell Mum he'd shouted at her. I told her to shut up, she tried to hit me, God, she could be a little shit. I told her if she ever hit me, I'd kill her. So she started goading me, trying to hit me, I said I wished she'd just die. Dad turned round to tell me off, then I woke up in hospital. I don't remember the accident. I was trapped in the wreckage for an hour while they tried to save Ginny and Dad – they were on the side of the impact. I was in a weird shell-like protection where nothing got me. But I was knocked out. I remember Mum asking me what had happened. She was a mess. All I could remember was the last conversation, or rather fight, I had with Ginny, wishing she would die. I decided it was safer if I never spoke again because look what happened when I did.

'None of that's your fault, you know that, don't you?'

He shrugged.

'Does your mum know *why* you don't speak?'

He shook his head.

'Do you think she feels bad about the argument? I know I would.'

Angus stood and rejoined her on the sofa to pen a reply.

I don't know. The whole year after the accident was a blur. My granny stayed with us. Then we moved here. Might seem unfair, but I felt if she hadn't had the row, everything would be OK.

'Yes. Is that *actually* why you don't speak? Because you're really punishing her?'

Angus stared at Roxie, then squinted like he was thinking.

Maybe.

Roxie changed tack. 'What would you do if you needed to speak or you wouldn't get the job of your dreams?'

Then it wouldn't be the job of my dreams.

Roxie could tell this was an argument she was never going to win.

He bent over his pad and started scribbling again.

What time shall I come and get you tomorrow?

'Seriously? We're going to the caves?'

We don't have to, but I can bring some food from the shop. You could wrap a bin bag round your cast to keep the water from it. It's up to you. It'll be a braw day out.

'Braw?'

Nice day out. You need to learn Scottish. I can teach you some on the date.

'Is it a date?' She smirked uncertainly at him.

That depends.

'On what?'

If I'm allowed to look at you.

'I'm sorry about earlier. I just... don't... you know. Argh-I-haven't-kissed-loads-of-boys.' Roxie rushed the last sentence, her neck burning as the words fell over each other to escape her indignity. She would never ever EVER admit something as deeply excruciating as that to a real boy at school.

Don't worry, I haven't kissed loads of boys either.

She laughed out loud.

It's not a competition. No one usually wants to know me because I don't talk.

'Well, I never usually like anyone...'

He smiled. *So it's a date?*

She nodded imperceptibly, nerves gripping her once more. She knew *she* would have to kiss him after what had happened...

18

The room was spinning gently off its axis. For a moment, Fiona wondered where she was, before a hazy memory floated into view of Gordon making her drink water before she climbed into bed. She had a hangover – that could only mean one thing: Issy had been involved.

Gordon was up already, the covers pushed back on the bed, the pillow still dented where his head had rested. A cup of tea sat on the bedside table, steam wafting off it. Fiona sat up slowly, assessing the level of hangover. Not quite a two – five being the worst. Perhaps one and a half. Nothing a slab-like bacon piece and this tea wouldn't remedy.

Fiona wasn't a big drinker, but the last year had been her bête noire, and she'd found herself reaching for the Rioja at the end of a shift, or whenever her anxiety threatened to conquer what little equilibrium remained. The warm buzz as it filtered through the swirling pool of unfettered worries was an instant panacea that sleep alone usually managed. The constant state of apprehension meant she'd lost a bit of weight too. That was never to be sniffed at, but at sixty-one you were thrown into Sophie's Choice about what was more important. The size of your arse or the hollows of your cheeks. Face won at this age – not many people noticed your arse any more; menopausal women were mostly invisible. Unless you looked like J-Lo or the *Friends* cast, which Fiona clearly didn't. Yep, being in your sixties was like running through sniper's alley, she just hoped she'd manage to dodge dowager's hump...

There had been a time when she could have rivalled some minor celebrities with her fiery mane of hair and nipped-in waist (courtesy of the grapefruit and egg diet – all the rage in the eighties). Gordon had said he'd asked her out because she reminded him of Sue Ellen from *Dallas*. At the time, she'd have preferred to have been wholesome Pam Ewing and not JR's alcoholic wife.

Fiona couldn't bring herself to do her roots at the moment. The grey was creeping down her crown and she hadn't the emotional energy to visit Trish in Inverness and have it blasted away on a sea of ammonia. It had been at least six months since she'd set foot in Head Masters.

Morag had been fastidious about her appearance, religiously getting the dull tell-tale roots fired up, nails were always short and red, Gucci Goldie Red lipstick non-negotiable. Morag had been the ebullient sun they'd all revolved around. She'd possessed the energy of two livewire women in their twenties. Even in the last few ghastly months, she'd been organising, getting everyone involved in making sure Countryfest would seamlessly carry on without her.

But what about Fiona? There'd been no plan in place for how *she* was supposed to carry on once Morag had slipped away... Of course she had Gordon, her daughters and now granddaughter – but they were miles away in Edinburgh. Gordon was a huge support, and she wished a Gordon on everyone who got married because that's how it should be and often wasn't. But Morag had been her cheerleader, her best friend, the oil on her creaky wheels, her sounding board, her little sister whose battle scars would throw most people under the bus. She was part of her, she'd lived in the weird shadowland that had been their childhood. Now there was no one connected to that time, apart from Maw...

Fiona heaved herself up, sat on the edge of the bed and sipped her tea. She spotted her bag on the floor, the diaries peeking out. She'd taken most of the day off but still checked the time on the alarm clock – eight fifteen. She had a couple of hours before she needed to pop into The Sea Shanty, get the orders in for Monday deliveries. She'd wanted to try a new ice-cream supplier and had samples arriving this morning. Wayne had been primed to put them in the freezer until she got in.

Fiona spread the books out on the duvet and started with the earliest one. She sat back against the pillows, sipping her tea, and got sucked into her formative years but from an alternative perspective. Gordon arrived with his rescue remedy – a BLT – and left her reading, disbelief at what she'd missed being away at college. This is what Maggie had meant when she said there were things she needed to see. Maw had been embroiled in what looked like an affair with Uncle Keith. Maybe she was mistaken? Morag couldn't have made that up? Why hadn't she told her? While Fiona stared into space, reflecting on something concealed in plain sight, a monstrous thought landed like a bird on a lake. Fiona suddenly understood why Morag had buried these diaries... What if her da wasn't her real father? What if Uncle Keith was? Could that be the reason Maw was so unhappy – she'd wanted to marry Keith, but for whatever reason, he couldn't marry her or never knew he was her father? Uncle Keith and Aunty Lillian had been infertile – make that just Aunty Lillian then... Thus, over the years, Maw and Keith kept their love in the shadows so as not to hurt everyone, like Morag had alluded to in these very pages.

Fiona sought the words again, rereading them for a different meaning, but found them lacking: '*Maw said she felt so bad, she wished things could be different but they'd done the right thing, even if he didn't feel it at the time, it wouldn't have been fair on anyone.'* Fiona almost laughed at the sheer audacity of her imagination – no, that was madness, the stuff of soap operas, not her actual life. Who her father was had never been in question – why would it be? But once things had come into focus that had previously been blurred, it made perfect sense that he might *not* be her dad. She couldn't unthink it now... Maw's actions became slightly more understandable, but still reprehensible in Fiona's eyes. Fiona would take to her grave that she suspected cancer might never have taken hold had Maggie contacted Morag once she turned eighteen. Though there was no guarantee with the big C – that broken heart could have been brewing trouble from the minute Shona was snatched out of Morag's arms in Inverness hospital.

Fiona would never forget Da calling her in the lodgings. Old Mrs Donaldson hovering by the phone, earwigging, making sure it was actually her father and not a fancy man on the end of the line. Men were forbidden to cross the threshold! She'd used her last ten pence to ring for a taxi; Morag needed her. The dash from the hospital drop-off to the labour ward had been like an Olympic trial. With the wrong shoes on (stilettos) and a stupidly tight skirt, she'd had to kick the heels off, laddering her tights, arriving at the delivery suite with them in her hands. Morag had been screaming – she could hear her down the endless corridor. Years later, she would think of that corridor like the one from *The Shining*.

One of the midwives was engrossed in telling Morag off for making too much noise. Fiona, not one to cause a scene, told her not to speak to her little sister like that, she was just a wee bairn. Morag's face had lit up and she'd reached out for her sister. As soon as Fiona had grabbed her sweaty hand in her own, Morag had let out a keening sound like one of the cows birthing on the croft up behind the town. She'd seen it once, Da had had to jump over the fence and pull the calf out with his bare hands. The bloody thing staggered up after about two minutes like it had just been down the pub for two pints, its bantling legs a tad wobbly.

'The baby's coming!' Morag had shouted.

'I don't think so, we'll tell you when the baby's coming!' the old boot had cried.

'If she says it's coming, it's coming!' Fiona had snapped. And, sure enough, Shona's head began to crown. The minute Morag rolled onto her side, Shona shot out like a bullet from a gun. Fiona caught her, all those years as netball captain came in handy after all.

Fiona shook herself, the memory as fresh as if she'd just handed Morag her baby... How happy Morag would be to know her daughter and granddaughter were staying in her home. Fiona recalled the conversation they'd had on the seafront, about Maggie's tragedy, about all the secrets people hide and the festering damage they cause. Morag had never kept Maggie a secret, nor her love for her, but there were a lot of secrets she had harboured, all locked away between the pages of these diaries.

Why had Maw asked for yearly photos to be sent? Why hadn't she just stopped the adoption instead? Those pictures were false hope, like a slow torture – look what might have been... Morag had explained in her letter that Maw didn't think she was worthy of love. From whom? Uncle Keith? Her own daughters? Her husband? Da had clearly loved Maw or he wouldn't have stayed. But, again, back then in small towns ruled by the church, divorce was seen as a huge failure of character or a crime against God rather than something that just happened. People genuinely stuck to their marriage vows. Till death us do part was surely *the* most depressing line in the whole charade? But it never stopped the infidelity or unhappiness or spousal violence, just drove it all underground.

Fiona sighed, she had been lucky. Gordon was a good man and

she had detected that the minute she locked eyes with him over the pickled eggs at the Castle pub on a girls' night. He'd smiled and nodded at the eggs. 'Fancy one of those fellas, do you? Let me treat you...' When he'd asked her to marry him, he'd produced a pickled egg out of nowhere on Benlachie beach, the ring proudly poking out of the top, the perfect display cushion as he got down on one knee in the damp sand.

Fiona smiled fondly. Yes, Gordon was a good egg! But her father had been a good man too. If he was indeed her father? Was Uncle Keith a good man?

Fiona rarely delved into these old wounds because she'd always believed it had been solely Morag's story. But it had been *all* their stories. When a child was taken or sent away, it not only affected the mother, it corroded the bedrock of what family meant. Seeing her sister sown inside Maggie, her progeny carrying on her legacy with Roxie, bringing her to the place she held most dear in the entire world, it filled Fiona with the kind of joy she hadn't experienced for a long time. But Maggie wouldn't stay for ever; her London life would soon beckon. Fiona wanted to spend as much time with her as possible. She'd rung her own daughters, Katie and Laura, and they were both coming to visit this weekend to meet their cousin.

Her phone pinged. It was Maggie.

Thank you for last night. I have a sore head this morning. Do you still want to meet for coffee like we planned? M xx

Fiona smiled, just like she'd received a text from Morag. Maybe Roxie would come too now she could walk on her cast. That girl was a sweetie, Fiona could see the soft centre she fought to disguise with teenage ennui and moodiness. Fiona wouldn't go back to being a teenager again even if lured with ten million pounds, a tummy tuck and Botox for life. However, thirty-five was a different matter...

Her phone pinged again. This time it was Maw.

Hello Fiona. It was nice to see you the other day. Something has been troubling me. Your friend, Maggie. How do you know her? Wasn't Morag's daughter called Margaret?

19

Agnes stared out of the Cancer Research shop window onto Tain High Street. It had been raining earlier and a few kids had popped in seeking cheap brollies. She'd unearthed three next to the wellie boots at the back near the walking sticks. How people managed to keep brollies alive long enough to donate to a charity shop was a mystery to her. Every one she had ever owned had died a sudden death in a storm, or its spindly framework snapped from being closed too sharply on a full moon after she'd looked in the mirror and turned in a circle three times while chanting the *Lord's Prayer*. Bloody contrary things had a mind of their own. She didn't rely on them any more to protect her hair – she had a nana hat – a see-through rain hood she tied under her chin like the rain protectors on a baby's pram. She'd sworn she would never buy one, but mother of invention became necessity in the face of feeble brollies in inclement Highland weather.

She'd sent the text two hours ago and Fiona still hadn't replied.

The door tinkled and Agnes smiled at a woman bringing in a black bin bag of donations.

'Just leave it by the desk, hen,' she said. She'd look through it if Sandy didn't. She quite liked nosing inside the bags. Mostly it was tat, but occasionally she exhumed a jewel: a decent leather hand-bag, or a lovely scarf, just like the one she'd been wearing the other day when she'd bumped into Fiona. She'd rescued that one from a bag brought in by Rose Paisley, who had been sorting out her daughter's room after she'd finally moved out. Agnes was wearing one of Skye Paisley's jumpers today. Pink and blue stripes, some trademark of a cool trendy teenage shop Skye had long grown out of.

Agnes liked clothes, and looking after herself; fashion still inter-ested her even now, and she'd scour the *Scotsman on Sunday* supple-ments for the latest trends and then search for cast-offs in the black bin bags. She always paid for them, it was just good to be front row at the Cancer Research fashion parade. She couldn't get over the amount of bras donated. Of course they couldn't sell them! So she kept those for free if there were any in her size. Perks of the job.

Like her daughters, Agnes's hair had been her outstanding feature but was now reduced to thinning white fluff that she had smoothed into obedient waves every month in Tain. She laughed at those daft buggers who continued to dye their hair well into their seventies. Like it magically erased wrinkles and bald patches? Ridiculous. But yes, if there was one thing she missed, it was her hair. Apart from that, she still felt the same in herself, notwithstanding a niggly bladder and sleeping a lot less. Her knees needed oiling and her right hip was tricky in the damp, but her mind hadn't started to pack up and she could still climb the stairs if she gripped the bannisters for leverage. Seventy-nine wasn't an age she'd expected to reach. It had seemed ancient to her when she'd been fifty, let alone in her thirties when all the trouble had kicked off...

Agnes didn't, or rather wouldn't, identify as a cauliflower head –
the group noun she bestowed upon the elderly. She saw them
doddering round town in their polyester slacks and plaid skirts, or
grossly overweight riding mobility scooters, their shopping
rammed so high in the front basket they couldn't see over it, often
running people over. No, she was different. She kept herself young
and fit walking everywhere, nails painted, cheeks rouged, two litres
of water a day and a mostly vegetarian diet. Though she did love
the occasional pork pie and bottle of Asti.

Agnes checked her phone again; no message.

Maggie had felt familiar from the minute she'd turned round in
the street. Agnes had tried not to stare, so had made a conscious
effort to look away. But her face… she so resembled Morag it made
it virtually impossible. She must be the same Margaret, she would
be around the right age. She could have been one of Fiona's daughters, she looked particularly like the younger one, Laura. Genetics
were difficult to outrun. Agnes had half expected baby Shona to
turn up one day, but as the decades rolled by, the possibility of such
an encounter had waned.

Agnes clenched her fists as a deeply buried maelstrom of
emotions began to paw at her insides. She wasn't sure she'd ever
been fully prepared for this eventuality, if indeed Maggie actually
was Shona. It was essential to keep busy, less time to torment
herself: the devil makes use of idle hands. She decided to tidy the
men's shirts, they were looking particularly unkempt. She had
colour-coded them last week and customers had mixed up the
greens with the stripes and contaminated the blues with whites. As
she rearranged hangers, she was shot through with a memory from
a time before life became so complicated. Keith wearing a blue shirt
standing in the kitchen doorway at his parents' house while she
waited for Lachlan to get changed after work.

'Are you Agnes?' Keith had asked, his face showing interest in his big brother's new girlfriend.

'Aye. You're Keith? The wee brother?'

'Less of the wee. I'm older than you!'

She'd laughed and felt her cheeks flush. At nineteen, Keith was nearer her age at seventeen than Lachlan at twenty-one, yet he was as urbane as a toonser, something outside of Lachlan's reach. He even smoked in a sophisticated manner.

'I hear you want to be a teacher in the city,' Keith had said, sounding impressed, offering her a cigarette. She took one and he lit it for her by striking a match off the mantelpiece.

'Aye. Art. I need to do a foundation course, hopefully at Glasgow. Then training college after.' She had sounded more confident than she'd felt. No one in their little town had escaped to Glasgow School of Art before. Her ma had thought she was ridiculous.

'Art, Agnes? What good will that do you when you have a wee bairn to look after and a husband to cook for. How's art going to help with that? Who'll pay for it all?'

'I'm never getting married, and I'm NEVER having children!' she'd cried at her frustrated mother. 'I'm going to be an art teacher, escape the bloody sticks! I want a career!'

'Really? I'd like to see you try! You never finish anything!'

'Lachlan'll have his work cut out on trains up and down visiting you when you go,' Keith had said with raised eyebrows.

She'd shrugged. Bagging a trainee ghillie was seen as a smart move in her group of friends. Eventually you got given a house, and had a man in work indefinitely. No factory closures or gruelling hours away in a lorry. A ghillie would be home after the shoot had wound up and always near at hand. Fresh game whenever they fancied it and sweeteners with a car too. But Lachlan wasn't her endgame. He was fine while she was finishing school, someone to cut her teeth on, take her virginity so she wasn't some backwater Lizzie when she made it to Glasgow School of Art where they all wore black turtle necks and smoked Gauloises cigarettes. You couldn't buy them in Tain, she'd tried. Apparently there were places in Inverness that sold them.

'Oh, playing it cool, are you?' Keith had teased.

'No, just not thinking that far ahead.'

'Poor Lachlan, he's hook, line and sinker for you already. Though you probably know that.'

'Och, Keith, don't be giving your brother's secrets away!' Marion, their ma, had called through from the small kitchen behind him. 'He won't be a minute, hen, I'm just finishing off his shirt.' The hiss of the iron had drowned out Keith's chuckle.

Agnes couldn't remember what shirt Lachlan had ended up wearing, or even where they went out, but she could recall the mischievous glint in Keith's eyes as he teased her about his brother, well aware she was going to break his heart. But it was Keith who'd made her feel like *he* was the one she wished she was going on a date with...

She reached for the blue shirt now and carefully moved it to the right side of the clothes rail with the other blues, her breath catching at the back of her throat with the effort of the stretch. The age spots on her hands always startled her when they caught her off guard – in her head, she was twenty some days, thirty-odd on others. Keith wouldn't talk to her now. Not that she'd tried him since Lillian had passed. In some ways, it was just easier being on her own. The toilet seat was always down and she hadn't missed sex now for at least ten years. Maybe longer. She could watch what she wanted to on the box and regularly amused herself reimagining *Love Island* for cauliflower heads. Would they all be visiting churches and ancient ruins, sweating in their polyester?

Agnes's phone beeped and she feverishly checked it: the opticians reminding her about this week's eye test. Hurry up, Fiona.

Why wasn't she texting back? What if that Maggie was *the* Maggie? Would she want to see her? Would she be angry? She'd probably had a great life down in England, anything was better than being stuck with Morag in this dead-end town. Morag would probably have never made anything of herself being encumbered with a baby at fifteen. Children held you back, just look at her, she'd never done anything of note in her life, trapped with Fiona at eighteen. Dreams of Glasgow shattered. Marriage to Lachlan a compromise to her raging parents who threatened to throw her out if he didn't slip a ring on her finger. She'd never seen that side of her father before, belting her across the face with the back of his hand.

'What in the name of God have you done? Bringing shame on our family, your mother's a mess.'

Her mother had turned the other cheek to her husband's fury until Agnes had walked down the aisle in her hastily bought ill-fitting white satin dress. 'You'll need a size bigger so no one can see your belly,' her mum had said at the time, then she acted like there'd been no shotgun wedding, bustling with excitement for the new arrival. Happy her only daughter wasn't escaping to Glasgow to live in digs and carouse with beatniks and scallies, indulging in alcohol, sex out of wedlock (though that boat had already sailed), and wasting her life as an artistic type instead of settling down like she had and bringing up a family. There was nothing wrong with having a job before you got married, but a career – what was that? She didn't care what women were doing elsewhere.

But would Agnes *really* have gone all the way to Glasgow? At seventeen, it had still felt far enough in the future to not be frightening. If Keith had lived up to his promise of the good life in Inverness, an accountant, big house, flash car, everything she could wish for and more, did she really *need* to go to scary Glasgow? Was Agnes a classic case of all talk and no trousers? Could she see what she was? Did anyone else see what she was? A fake hiding behind her domesticity. Women were off conquering the world whilst raising a family. Lachlan had never stopped her... It was too late now anyway.

Agnes shook her head, this wasn't like her. Introspection wasn't something she indulged in. But bumping into Fiona and seeing Maggie, now that had put the cat among the pigeons. Whether she was Shona or not almost didn't matter. The simple posing of the question opened up a portal into a time of her life she tried hard not to look at. But the scab was itching, so she'd sent the text. Just to see. If she wasn't who she thought she was, Agnes could ignore everything and go back to her small life in Tain and shuffle off this mortal coil without ever having to explain herself to anyone. Fiona certainly wouldn't broach the subject.

The dark truth was, Agnes had never wanted children. That was one thing she'd been certain of. Finding out she was pregnant had been the biggest blow she could imagine. Her monthly curse had always been erratic to say the least, so it had appeared she was more pregnant than she thought she was. Her breasts had already been swelling and her nausea wasn't caused by the tricky predicament she'd found herself in: caught between two brothers.

Nancy, her oldest friend, knew of a woman in Dingwall who could get rid of it for you. She wasn't a doctor, just some old wifie women went to when they 'got in trouble'. Nancy said she'd come with her on the bus because she shouldn't be on her own, 'in case anything went wrong'. Neither of them understood how an abortion was performed, they just knew it cost ten guineas – money neither of them had. There had been gory tales about knitting needles, but they couldn't be sure. Agnes had managed to tap some money off Lachlan, lying that she needed it for the travel costs and materials for the upcoming interview at Glasgow School of Art, that her parents wouldn't pay for (that part was not a lie).

On the day itself, Nancy had packed them lunch of a Sandwich

Spread piece and a bag of salted crisps each, though the smell of the Sandwich Spread made Agnes's mouth water and not in a good way. The bus ride was a challenge, Nancy had gripped Agnes's hand the whole way.

'What if I die, Nance?' she'd kept repeating. That was the rumour anyway, that women went to their death after an abortion, either struck down by God or infection.

Once they'd reached the wifie's house on a side street down from the imposingly fearful courthouse, Nancy had to drag Agnes inside the black front door, the wifie practically pulling them in before anyone could wonder what the greeting girl and her friend were about.

The front room had nets up and Agnes could remember that she'd wanted to run away from the brown velveteen sofa with its intricate cream laced antimacassars and the vague smell of boiled cabbage mingled with disinfectant hanging in the air. She'd suppressed the retch that was fighting hard to surface. *Music While You Work*, her ma's favourite programme, burbled on the radio somewhere downstairs, possibly out the back in the kitchen, and Agnes could just about hear the house band belting out 'Cheek to Cheek'. Even sixty years later if she heard that tune she'd be right back there in that dingy house in Dingwall, cold fear roasting the base of her throat.

'Have you the money, hen?' the wifie had asked, her face as unreadable as a slab of Scottish sandstone. She'd looked like someone's granny, but not the sweet kind, the kind that would clip you round the lugholes for having your elbows on the table and forgetting to say grace before a bloody cup of tea.

Nancy had handed it over and as the wifie had reached out for it, Agnes had spotted the knitting needles sticking out of a ball of yellow wool on the sideboard, next to a wedding photo in a pewter frame and a carriage clock stuck on eight twenty-five. She had jumped up.

'I can't. I've got to go. Sorry.'

Nancy had gawped at her, shaking her head. The wifie had seen it all before and didn't move a muscle. Agnes ran to the front door, the chain was on, her hands shaking she managed to undo it, turn the handle and run out into the overcast afternoon, almost getting run over by a post van in the process. Nancy had joined her moments later.

'What are you playing at?' Nancy had cried.

'I saw the needles. She might kill me.'

Nancy had hugged her.

'I'm sorry, Nancy.'

'Och, don't apologise. It's you that's up shit creek. I grabbed the money out of the old boot's fist before she could say a word. We can still try the old-fashioned way before we get home, have some fun as well? You need a fag.'

So before getting the bus home to Tain, the girls went to the Caledonian Arms and downed as many gins as they could before they ran out of money. Agnes didn't remember getting home. Or being sick on the bus into the empty paper sandwich bag. She awoke the next day to a blazing headache and throbbing tits, knowing she was still pregnant and mother's ruin hadn't been the embrocation she'd hoped for. Giving birth had been easy compared to the rest of it. Living a life she hadn't wanted and then being vilified for trying to prevent it happening again to Morag. Kids, they trapped you, but you got used to it in the end. She loved the girls, for sure. That crept up on her over years. She'd initially felt mild dislike, followed by huge dislike, then it thawed and suddenly she was pregnant again. Morag arrived with lukewarm acceptance and eventually love blossomed like the poppies in Flanders fields.

Before she knew it, Agnes was faced with her own past, except this time, Morag thought she knew what was best...

Her phone pinged in her pocket.

Hi Maw. Yes, Maggie is Morag's daughter. There's something I need to talk to you about. Are you in tomorrow?

20

'So you'll do it?' Fiona looked at Maggie, anticipation glinting in her eyes. 'We have two days to rehearse if you, you know... want to.'

'We?'

'Well, *you* have two days to rehearse. I have two days to help you where I can.'

Maggie and Fiona sat in Trading Post while Issy weighed parcels and sold late-morning ice creams to parents eager to start the day off right. Maggie nursed a mild headache, along with a strong coffee Issy assured her would shoo away cobwebs and lethargy. Fiona kept yawning.

'Look, I know we were joking about it last night, all three of us saying we should do an ABBA tribute act, but me on my own?' Maggie sipped her coffee. 'It's not karaoke, it's a proper open-mic night, real performers with something to say. Some of them write their own stuff. I know how these events work. It's a showcase for most people...'

'Aye, it's semi-serious, we don't tend to get people belting out disco classics or Madonna. But you don't have to perform your own stuff, you can do covers.'

'More than one song?' She shook her head. 'I can't play an instrument.'

'Angus could accompany you – he's amazing, and quick at picking things up. Morag taught him well.'

Maggie wondered when was the last time she'd sung? For joy, for the hell of it, for an audience? Someone's birthday, before Louis...

'Fiona, I haven't sung for so long. I don't even know if I still can.' Her shoulders slumped. How would it feel? Just to try... Just to see if her lungs still worked underneath the baggage, the judgement. 'Is there somewhere we can go where I can have some privacy? I'm not doing anything in front of Roxie.'

'Really?'

Maggie nodded uncertainly, unsure what she was agreeing to.

'Give me two minutes.'

Fiona jumped up and weaved her way over to the counter and interrupted Issy.

'Issy said we can use her house. Apparently Angus is on his way over to take Roxie out.'

'Ah yes, she was raging about having no clothes this morning. I wonder if she has a crush on him...?'

'Issy said she has an Alexa in the kitchen,' Fiona said, peering at the shelves. 'Do you need to do voice warm-ups?'

'Jesus Christ! No! Just shout Alexa, she'll tell you where she is.'

'Alexa, what time is it?' Fiona asked timidly, like she was scared of disturbing her tea break.

'The time is 11.41 a.m.'

'She's there, on the top shelf with the mixing bowls. What do you want to sing?'

'The Carpenters.'

'Oh, I love them! Which one?'

'"Close to You".'

The door abruptly burst open and Issy fell into the front room.

'Have I missed the audition?'

'It's not an audition!' Maggie cried.

'What are you doing here? Who's looking after the post office?' Fiona asked.

'Mrs Strachan said she'd hold the fort for half an hour.'

'Doesn't she have a hearing aid?' Fiona questioned.

'Aye, but I told her to get people to write shit down if she can't understand them. I've a million pads because of Angus. So...?'

'She's about to go.'

'I'm still here! I'm not hearing-impaired!'

'Sorry, hen. You instruct Alexa when you're ready,' Fiona said, winking at her.

'Sorry, I didn't catch what you said,' Alexa piped up.

'Bloody Alexa,' Issy muttered quietly under Alexa's radar.

Maggie walked over to the sink, cleared her throat several times, grabbed a glass off the draining board, filled it from the tap and gargled with water, refilled and downed a whole glass. She could feel two sets of eyes boring into her back while she googled the words as a prompt on her phone.

'Alexa, play karaoke version of "Close to You" by the Carpenters.'

'Playing karaoke version of "Close to You" by the Carpenters.'

Maggie turned round during the short intro, but glancing at Fiona's expectant face and Issy with her hands covering her mouth hiding her nerves totally put her off, so she missed her mark, crashing badly.

'Sorry, can I start again?'

'Yes! Pretend we're not here.'

'I can't, you're looking right at me.'

'Come on, Issy, let's go into the lounge, leave Maggie to it.'

She waited for them to leave and settle before instructing Alexa. As soon as the intro dropped into the vocal section, Maggie planted herself in the melody. Her throat initially protested, but she ignored it and engaged with the lyrics on the phone screen. She recalled Adam and her driving through northern France in an open-top car à la *Bridget Jones* (without the hurricane hair), but he wasn't cunty Hugh Grant. They'd visited France very early in their relationship and decided on a weekend break taking a hire car through the Channel Tunnel. They'd had amazing sex in a lay-by just outside of Calais before driving to Le Touquet, a Gallic version of a traditional south coast seaside town where a lot of original period architecture had been flattened in the war and replaced with brutalist tower blocks facing out to sea. They'd stayed in a cheap faceless hotel, and consequently fallen through the middle of the two single beds pushed together mid-shag after several carafes of red wine. Maggie had banged her chin on the unforgiving tiled floor. 'Close to You' had been playing on the hotel radio as her teeth bit into her tongue, the taste of blood sobering her up immediately.

'Close to You' was Maggie's favourite Carpenters tune because just about anyone with a half-decent voice could get away with it. Obviously it was hard to compete with Karen's caramel-infused vocals, but she gave it her best shot. As the music petered out and the close to yous receded into the mixing bowl on the shelf above her head, she opened her eyes, not realising they'd been closed, the googled lyrics semi-redundant.

Fiona and Issy stood in the living room. Before she'd closed her eyes, they'd been balanced on the edge of the sofa. Fiona was openly weeping. Issy's hands sprawled across her face, her eyes wide.

'What?!' she squawked.

Fiona walked through to where Maggie stood in the kitchen.

'Darling girl, that was the most beautiful rendition of "Close to You" I have ever heard.'

'Fucking hell!' Issy screeched. 'Where have you been hiding that voice?' She ran over and started lifting up Maggie's top, jokingly looking for it. 'Your mum would have wet herself. Pure class!'

'Really? I kind of went off somewhere. It hurt to sing. My throat's aching.'

'You're not used to it, that's all. Honey and lemon's what you need. Morag swore by it. Issy?'

'Already on it.'

Before Maggie knew what was happening, a remedial concoction was thrust into her hands.

'Right, so we've established you can sing. What's it going to be?' Fiona enthused.

'What's what going to be?'

'What songs are you going to sing on Thursday?'

'I don't know if I can...'

'Look, everyone will just be so happy to see you perform,' Fiona attempted to reason. 'Your voice is a gift, like your mother's, and it's there to be shared. Honestly, you have no idea the size of a hole Morag's passing has left in Benlachie. We wouldn't throw you under the bus, Maggie. You have the talent, but you don't need anyone telling you that, it's something you must believe inside yourself. If you don't want to do it, that's completely OK. We shouldn't be on at you. You think about it.'

'Is this the pep talk you give to all artists when they have stage fright?'

'No! That was Morag's job.' Fiona smiled at her.

'I understand the nerves,' Issy said, making cups of tea. 'You haven't properly performed before, have you?'

'She has...' Fiona said, a cheeky glint in her eyes. Maggie glared at her. 'Well, you have to tell her now!'

'I almost made it on to *The X Factor*.'

'What? When? Would I have seen you?' Issy's hand suspended mid-air, dripping a sodden teabag all over the counter.

'No.'

'To be truthful, I've never seen it. I can't bear those kinds of shows. It's all a set-up anyway.'

'Well, funny you should say that...' Fiona winked at her. 'How did it happen, Maggie?'

Maggie relayed her curtailed *X Factor* journey to an open-mouthed Issy, while Fiona finished off making the tea.

'So is that why've you never sung since?' Issy asked.

'It was always a hobby that wasn't nurtured by my parents. They'd never seen the point if I wasn't going to be Madonna, so I guess I never took it seriously either... Then Louis... and any kind of musical attachment just withered and died with him. I ran from stuff that made me happy. It was easier just to go to work.'

'Maybe it's about time you stopped running?' Fiona said.

'Yes!' Issy cried. 'If you do this, I'll properly start sewing again. I could make you an outfit for Thursday night! Won't take me long, I have a few quick patterns I can adapt. I could take your measurements now. Would you be happy to hand me over complete creative control if I show you my ideas?'

'So...?' Fiona asked.

'I think that's enough emotional blackmail for one day,' Maggie said, smiling.

* * *

That afternoon after Issy had measured every part of Maggie, including the insides of her arms to her wrists, she and Fiona settled in Morag's living room scouring through her record collection for inspiration. They'd pulled out Fleetwood Mac, The Carpenters, Dolly Parton, Emmylou Harris, Annie Lennox...

'I don't know what else to sing,' Maggie fretted.

'What brings you joy – that would be a good place to start.'

'It's been so long, it's like I've forgotten what I really like.'

'OK, well let's practise "Close to You", get it as good as we can, and then sort the other song later.'

Without a bottle of wine and a karaoke screen to bolster her, Maggie was petrified of standing up and clean forgetting the words, like that mortifying time at the Save the Children conference when she delivered the wrong information with the right slide. She'd muddled up her flash cards and sweated through her blouse until it was see-through. She'd been wearing her manky yellowing sports bra too because her other ones had been in the wash. The last thing she wanted was to flash her bra to an entire pub. She couldn't let the stage fright win...

21

'How long will it take to get there?' Roxie asked, trying not to sound like a petulant child in the back of a car. Angus and she were standing on the back steps of The Sea Shanty assessing the weather. Rain wasn't threatening yet, but she'd learned that what her phone predicted and what the weather in Benlachie actually was were two completely different outcomes.

She'd taped two bin bags over her cast to protect it from a potential drenching, and also to hide her disgustingly filthy toes that she'd hurriedly cleaned with a make-up wipe before Angus had arrived. *So, can you put weight on it?* Angus had asked Roxie in a prewritten note. He'd appeared at her door about ten minutes ago with a bag containing a fresh sliced loaf from Trading Post, some fancy deli ham, cucumber, cream cheese, an enormous family bag of posh crisps that would cost the same as a one-bedroom flat in London, and two flapjacks. He handed her another slip of paper: *Everyone loves a flapjack, right?* He'd smirked while she'd poked around at the goodies before he stuffed the booty in his rucksack.

Since last night, Roxie's cinematic mind had constantly

replayed the evening's events, the projector evidently trapped in a loop. Contrary to her erstwhile belief, she felt worse now she'd spent another evening fooling around with Angus at her behest. Worse being an umbrella term covering all variations of anxiety rolling along the conveyor belt. She'd expected to relax into it, he seemed interested, and after she'd kissed him last night and they'd explored each other a bit more, she'd hoped to take her foot off the proverbial emotional rollercoaster pedal. But she couldn't. ARGH! How did anyone ever get past this awkward getting-to-know-you stage and arrive at normality? Or did people just spend their entire life in a perpetual state of apprehension about relationships? Not that this was a relationship. She'd class it as a friendship, with initial roots as enemies (like all the great romances), subsequently leaking into snogging and zone one and two (bum) touching. Before leaving last night, Angus gave her a slightly chaste brush of his lips, barely grazing her own after chewing her face off earlier. But when he'd arrived this morning, there had been no kiss. Should there be? Was she overthinking it?

Angus thrust a note at her, preventing any more agonising.

It takes about twenty minutes to get to the caves from here without an injury. So it will take as long as it takes.

Roxie nodded and tentatively stepped down onto the pavement, ailing foot first. Angus held her hand to help her and didn't let go. She'd brought a walking stick instead of her crutches and was using that whilst leaning on Angus. His hand gripped hers hard, sending more shocks to her core; he turned and smiled at her. Anyone looking would surely mistake them for boyfriend and girlfriend...

However, it soon became evident that venturing outside was drastically different to a cosy hang in Morag's flat. There was no easy banter, chit-chat, teasing, flirting – all of those needed flowing conversation or a readily available notebook and a quick draw pen.

They wouldn't get anywhere if they were stopping every minute so Angus could scribble a witty repartee in response to anything that left Roxie's Glossier painted lips. A mother wouldn't be too worried about the relentless incommunicado having lived with it for some time, but someone with an alternative agenda could theoretically find the wall of silence a hindrance...

Once they reached the rocky path along the bottom of the cliffs, Angus stopped and drew out his pad.

Do you want me to give you a piggyback?

'I'm fine for now. Maybe if it's too wet and slippy.'

There would definitely be lack of communication with her on his back! However, as they trudged along the path her foot began to throb and she was forced to slow down. She stopped to find her painkillers.

Right that's it, I'm carrying you.

Angus lowered himself so she could climb on before standing up and, with her arms hooked under his armpits, she leaned her full weight on his back. He was strong and that made her like him even more, in a pathetic, stereotypical way. That and his woody scent she gulped down; she had to restrain herself from licking his neck.

Angus strode over the uneven ground while Roxie relaxed, breathing in the dramatic scenery of swooping gulls and sky-scraping cliffs rising from the pebbles as far as the eye could see. Small day-tripper boats tagged alongside further out, also heading to the caves.

Angus suddenly stopped and dropped for her to get down. He scribbled...

They're just round this bend, but you'll need to climb a bit because it's too dangerous with you on my back. It's quicker if I lower you off the big rock rather than walk to the end and across the rock pools.

Conquering the substantial boulder with footholds worn into its surface they continued the walk holding hands. Roxie's tummy fizzed – what were they going to do once they reached the caves? Was it a snogging palace where kids smoked weed, hung out in packs like the Dawson Heights Estate back home? Most evenings, even in winter, the grassy slope overlooking the twinkling cityscape was rammed with stoners and kids necking cheap vodka or Bulmers, making out in the bushes, listening to music until they'd overstepped their curfew. It was an adult no-go zone, plus it was pretty, the tower blocks sparkling like dystopian palaces in the distant land of Zone One. Zone Two Peckham and Dulwich were practically the countryside by comparison.

As they rounded the cliff, the cave's baronial entrance greeted Roxie, crapping all over the view from Dawson Heights. She'd barely spoken since they'd left the flat. Roxie hadn't fancied chatting into a void; it did nothing to calm her second-guessing chaotic mind. So she let rip with verbal diarrhoea.

'Wow! When you said caves, I thought you meant something small, like a pothole. This is seriously impressive, like St Paul's Cathedral. I went there once on a school trip – it's amazing. Can we go to the back? Where does it go? Have you ever gone far in there? Do they have a name? It's magical!'

Angus smiled at her verbosity and scratched out a reply.

I come here a lot, mostly on my own. Legend says the tunnel at the back leads all the way to the top of the cliffs – or that's what Morag always used to say. It was used by smugglers. They're called the Uamhs of Benlachie. You say uamhs like oo-av – it's Gaelic for cave.

It was more of a grand ballroom than a cave, graduating from an under-cliff hollow stretching deep into the landmass behind it, pounded out by the toiling sea. With the tide out, they were able to walk down to the shoreline, where Angus offered to pick her up again and carry her over into the mouth of the cave. It had started to drizzle and they found protection under the natural roof while they ate their food. A few people like themselves had walked and were pitching up for picnics further back from them. Not a stoner in sight.

It's better for boat trips a bit later on when the tide is higher. But the idiot tourists still sign up for them, not realising you can't get near them until then. It's free to walk here. The tide turned about half an hour ago, we have a while before we'll head back.

Roxie shouted hello and the walls doubled her efforts, the acoustics bouncing her words around until they absorbed into the rocks. She giggled like a little girl, her face lighting up at a memory. This place reminded her of a fairy land she'd read about in a tatty library book her mum used to read to her. She couldn't remember the book's title but could still conjure up the enchanted land where the fairies had lived, enthralled by the delicate illustrations. She'd always wanted to visit somewhere like it, convinced that the fairies and their dell had been real. Even now, having left that side of her behind with the Build-A-Bears and Playmobil people, the magic of the fairy land book prevailed.

Golden shafts of light beamed down like messengers from the gods, hitting the rock pools, splintering into star-filled underworlds where creatures talked and secret treasure lay stashed beneath a seaweed forest. Roxie's heart filled with an innocent wonder, reconnecting with the part of her that didn't want to grow up and accept that the book had been make-believe all along. Being here now was proof that it *was* genuine, and that instilled hope – maybe anything was possible...

'It's so dreamy,' she breathed, inhaling the briny air. 'It's like my favourite childhood book. I could live here...'

I think that too. It's like something from another world. I never get bored of it.

The echoes of gulls reverberated like the horn section of an orchestra, while the distant crashing waves accompanied them as rolling cymbals.

Angus unpacked the food and they assembled their own sandwiches perched on a flat rock next to a small pool. He'd even brought a knife for spreading the cream cheese. After they'd eaten everything in silence (hard to write and eat at the same time), she spoke before checking herself.

'Thank you for bringing me here... Is this one of your places you come to scream?'

Angus opened his mouth in shock. Now she'd really thrown the gulls among the sandwiches. Morse code...

You heard me in the dunes then?

'Yes. Why do you do it? I saw you smoking weed too.'

Everyone smokes weed round here. My mum does – she's no idea that I know.

'So why the screaming?'

He shrugged.

'You don't know? You must do. You just don't want to say.'

He stared out to sea as if taking strength from the tidal pull.

It relieves the pressure of not speaking. I never say actual words.

'But if you need to do that, surely it would be better to speak? Do you say stuff just to yourself when you're alone?'

He shook his head.

'So how does not speaking make life better?' Roxie felt irritated, not something she'd anticipated after so looking forward to this outing.

I don't expect you to understand.

'But I want to.'

Angus took a deep breath and started packing up the bits of uneaten food before the gulls launched an aerial attack. Once he'd finished, he wrote a reply.

It's been six years, I can't remember what it's like to speak. This is who I am, speaking would stop me being me. It started off as one thing and became something else.

'You're who you are because of lots of things, not because you don't speak. Some people don't have a choice in not speaking. Have you not thought about sign language – you'd be speaking but still silent.'

He fired off a rapid reply as her irritation gathered momentum.

For a start, I'm not deaf, it would be appropriation. I told you, I don't expect you to understand. No one does in the end. It's better that way.

'What do you mean?'

Angus swept everything into his backpack he'd hung on his front so he could carry Roxie.

'So you're just going to ignore me? Not tell me?'

He shook his head, slowly retrieving his notebook from his back pocket. He shoved it under her nose when he'd finished.

What if I told you your anger at your mum was ridiculous. That all you had to do was ask her about your brother, ask her why she's down on your dad all the time? Ask her what's really going on, why she let your brother's death ruin the family. What would you do?

'I'd rather eat shit than do that.'

You have your answer then. Speaking opens up stuff you don't always want to hear the answers to. This way everything is on my terms. And that's how I want it.

'But what about other people? What about what they want? Doesn't it push people away?'

It's how it is. My friends are OK with it, Mum accepts it. The right people stay around.

He wasn't her boyfriend and he lived a million miles away. Why did she care if he never spoke again?

You'll either get used to it or you won't. You're going home at the weekend anyway.

'What's that supposed to mean?' Roxie bristled.

There's no point me breaking this for you.

'Thanks!' She heaved herself up with her walking stick. 'I'm going back.' She turned round while he was writing a note. Yep, she was done with this. It was too weird. He was hot, his kisses made her head spin and she'd wanted to get beyond zone three touching, but even if this panned out over the rest of the week, what was the point? He was in control, all the time. And he was right, though she hated to admit it, why would he break it for her? Her mum put Louis before her, why would it be any different with anyone else. Her dad was the only one who really looked out for her and he was going to be here as soon as he could.

Angus tapped her on the shoulder and handed her a note.

I'm sorry, that came out wrong.

'It's OK... It's your life. You do what you want. Sorry I made it weird. Come on.'

She could feel her shutters coming down. She'd been crazy for him earlier and now she couldn't get away quick enough, which, annoyingly, wasn't very quick at all.

Traipsing back was beyond awkward. Roxie refused his offer to carry her and insisted on hobbling over rocks the long way round while the incoming tide chased their heels. She trailed behind him as the terrain smoothed out and the sea wall came into view. She had no idea what to say once they reached Morag's flat. She didn't want him to come in and felt guilty and awkward about everything. She knew she might get used to his lack of communication over time, but unfortunately time wasn't on her side.

'So, I better get back upstairs. Mum's sent me a few texts.' (She hadn't.) Roxie stretched her cheeks, offering up a toothless smile. God, she wanted to just disappear. 'Thank you so much for taking me to the caves. I loved them.'

He nodded and raised his hand in a half-hearted greeting, then loped off up the hill towards his house. What a wet fart ending.

Roxie pushed open the flat door and limped down the pink corridor. It sounded like Mum was listening to Morag's records again. The record player wasn't on; the voice was floating towards her from the kitchen. She wound her way through the living room and stood in the doorway to find Fiona listening to her mum sing. Fucking hell!

'What are you doing?' Roxie asked her startled mum.

'Rehearsing. I wasn't expecting you back so soon. Is Angus with you?'

'No. He went home.'

'Oh. Is everything OK?'

'Yes, why wouldn't it be?'

'I just thought you were going out for the whole day.'

'I wanted to come home.' She wouldn't look at her mum. 'Why are you rehearsing?'

'I've asked your mum to take part in the charity open mic night on Thursday. She has a beautiful voice,' Fiona explained.

Roxie remained silent for a moment or two. Her mum could actually sing like a boss, rendering Roxie genuinely awestruck. They were definitely getting on better, but she wasn't ready to surrender her disdain just yet...

'You can't play an instrument though. What will you use as a backing track?'

'We were hoping Angus would accompany me,' her mum said. 'Do you think he would agree to it?'

'Why would I know?'

'You seem pretty friendly.'

'Well, we're not.'

'Let me talk to him,' Fiona said. 'We just need to find another song.'

'I can help with that. I know more about music than Mum does!'

Roxie laughed at her mum's indignant face. It was true though,

Adam had passed on his enthusiasm like a revered stamp collection or favourite book.

'OK, what genre are we thinking?' Fiona said, obviously pleased Roxie was joining in.

'Country of course! I think I know which track...'

22

Angus stormed up the street towards home, his brain trying to untangle the muddle it had got itself into. This was *exactly* why he didn't engage with girls: they *always* blew hot and cold. Life was so much easier without them in it. Kai and Ali were reliable; he could trust them to be the same every time he saw them. If they had a row with their parents or anyone else, they didn't drag the vibe to the table; they parked it at home or got over it in record time. No analytics or excessive overthinking with a cortege of friends re-enacting said spat in its full glory.

Ali, Kai and Angus could 'talk' for hours about nothing (Clarkson on the *Grand Tour*: dinosaur anti-woke twat or petrolhead hero) and everything (could they invent something bigger than Minecraft? How to access porn without parents copping on, though that had been a fairly half-hearted phase). To be fair, his mum had read the riot act about porn when he turned thirteen and scared the crap out of him with her honesty. What he couldn't admit was porn made him feel peculiar, and he knew he was in a minority there. Maybe it was because he'd stumbled across a hardcore site when he'd just been looking for some tits. But if you wanted to join in the

school banter, you had to agree it was amazing. But Angus couldn't
fake shit if he tried – he was glad Ali and Kai preferred Minecraft.
He never had to worry if they were going to judge him, like some
people did, about his lack of speech or refusing to toe the laddish
line.

He'd known Kai since primary school and just over a year to the
day after the crash they'd walked into Nairn Academy and bumped
into Ali. He'd recently moved from Birmingham and had never
known Angus to talk out loud so took it all in his stride. Everyone at
Angus's old primary had known his story but no one talked about
it, the teachers treated him with kid gloves and he couldn't wait to
leave by the end of Year Six because he just wanted to be Angus
who could play guitar and didn't speak.

Unfortunately, his fretting mother had insisted on taking him to
a lady called Anita to 'open up'. Her office was perched at the back
of Nairn community centre next to the toilets and always smelled of
lemon bleach with a hint of arse, while Anita smelled of lavender à
la cigarettes and had this odd way of rolling her tongue when she
was thinking. Angus would spend the whole time waiting for her to
do it. They'd all expected him to resume talking after a few
sessions, but Angus knew otherwise. The more Anita asked him to
draw his feelings, the more he wanted to bed down in silence and
be left alone. He couldn't be fixed, and Anita told his mum he
would talk when he was ready. Money well spent.

The older he got, the harder it became to be someone who
chose muteness. It crashed into everything. His little sojourns into
the dunes to let off steam were becoming more and more frequent,
and his conversation with Roxie had rubbed him up the wrong way.
He couldn't break the silence now, not while she was here. Then
she would be right. He would just look like a numpty. He didn't
want to look a numpty in front of her. Not after the way she'd

feigned her acceptance of his silence when she clearly hadn't accepted it at all.

Kai had only ever asked him once why he didn't speak. They'd been having a sleepover in Year Seven during the Easter holidays and Kai asked him with the lights out if he would ever speak and then flicked the light on for the answer. Teenagehood was beckoning and Kai had possibly foreseen a blighted future.

'What will you do when you need a job? How will you do it? Aren't you scared?'

If he was being really honest, Angus never thought further than the next week in relation to anything in his life. His mum had always said they'd figure it out and Morag had taken him under her wing at that point, helping him hone his guitar skills.

'I don't care if you speak or not,' she'd told him when she'd first started hanging out with his mum more. 'As long as you get on, and don't let it hold you back, you'll always be grand. Your guitar can do the talking for you.' Another time, she'd said: 'It shows commitment to not talk for this long. So that should ideally go in your favour in the future – strong principles and strict adherence to methodology.'

He missed Morag. He'd loved her, she'd really looked out for him and Issy and she never ever treated him like a kid or made out not speaking was a 'thing'. After she'd died, Fiona had let him sit in the flat and play Morag's guitars when she was downstairs during dinner service. He'd once asked Morag about the pictures on the mantelpiece.

'She's my daughter. I had to give her away at birth; I wasn't allowed to keep her.' She'd said it pragmatically, not an ounce of self-pity. Morag fully understood awful things happening to you as a kid... Something about her transcended her age. Her spirit was for ever young, that was why people gravitated towards her. He couldn't believe she wasn't here any more. And now her grand-daughter was messing with his head.

With nothing to do in the Highlands other than smoke weed and drink Buckfast in the dunes, perfecting your catalogue of getting-off manoeuvres was something everyone was desperate to constantly upgrade. Angus had only ever kissed a few girls. They'd not really been on his radar until he hit fifteen. He'd historically found them puzzling and hard to relate to. When he was still up to his eyeballs in Minecraft, they'd been obsessing over YouTubers, Influencers, TikTok twats and screeching (or crying), or so it appeared to him. He tried not to take any notice and they certainly paid him no attention. He preferred Ali and Kai and being part of Morag's army of behind-the-scenes elves who launched Country-fest out into the public domain. But after a party that Ali had dragged him to, he realised girls could be fun, and spent an hour communicating with Beth MacAulay at the bottom of the garden. She liked Minecraft and vodka and they ended up snogging by the compost heap. But on the Monday at school, she'd ghosted him. Like he gave five fucks, but still, whatever.

He'd had lame crushes, a few snogs, not graduating much further than a bit of tit action and one proper fanny grope after Christmas, which he was puzzled about because neither of them seemed to get anything out of it. He'd had an expert hand job from Fazza McGeown in the sixth form when she'd been at her brother's birthday party in February and was shitted on Bucky. That had been revelatory, but he'd yet to repeat the thrill with a partner. Everything was about research, observation and development, a bit like being lab rats. No one was really interested in going out with him. He knew he was a bit of a freak show in that respect – *try the silent boy, see what he's got in his bag of tricks.*

While Kai was terrified of girls (Angus had his own thoughts about that, wondering if Kai would *ever* like them) and Ali was embroiled in an on-off friends-with-benefits arrangement with Sunita from his Chemistry class, Angus never really liked anyone, properly. So it was a surprise to him that he was taken with the funny girl with the crazy make-up and black clothes who'd dobbed him in for shoplifting. She was tough, for sure; her accident had been horrific. It was a good job *Saw* and all its million sequels hadn't stalked his dreamscape, water off a duck's back. Pulling out that shard of glass had given him some kind of perverse pleasure, like the *Sword in the Stone*, or (and this he couldn't admit to) a hero rescuing someone in a cheesy film. He didn't shine the spotlight on it too brightly. He'd bet that Anita with the lizard tongue would attribute it to his survivor's guilt, or whatever the fuck she was trying to brand him with. No matter, he'd stepped over the line now and realised he liked Roxie more than he usually allowed. It could be because he knew she was leaving, so it was almost easier to get close, open up, feel connected when the investment had a short shelf life...

As Angus ploughed up the hill, something Morag had said to him before she died popped into his head. She'd been in the hospice; Issy hadn't wanted him to see her like that, but Morag had said it was OK. 'Angus needs to know, so he can live life to the full.' She'd been real to the very end. Her egg-yolk yellow room had been jammed full of bouquets of flowers from fellow musicians, friends, business colleagues, while the Bluetooth speaker played country music softly in the background. He'd never seen her looking fragile before. Issy had nipped out to get a coffee from the machine and Fiona wasn't arriving until later. It was just Angus and Morag. She was in and out of sleep, drugged up to her eyeballs with diamorphine. Sometimes she was lucid, other times not so much. Angus had got up and was reading the cards. Why did people send cards when you were dying? You couldn't take them with you.

'Hey, Angus.' He'd turned round. Morag's eyes were open and

she was looking at him clearly, not through a haze of painkillers. 'Shouldn't you be at school?' Her voice cracked with the effort. He'd whipped out his notebook. 'Hey, I haven't time for you to write. Speak to me.'

He shook his head and penned a reply.

It's Saturday, no school. How you feeling?

'I'm dying, so I feel great obviously.'

He'd frowned. How do you reply to something like that?

'Come here.' She'd patted the bed and he'd sat on the edge, trying not to squash her. She took up very little room. 'Don't die on that hill.' He had no idea what she meant, and quizzically shook his head. 'I admire you for your tenacity with the silence, but one day you'll meet someone and you'll grapple with this decision...'

I'm OK so far.

'Because you haven't met them.'

The right person will accept it.

'At first, yes. But this is a choice you're making, for whatever reason... What if they change their mind? People do, all the time. It's what makes us human.'

Then they're not the right person.

'As I said, don't die on that hill.' She'd squeezed his hand hard, impressive for someone with so little life left inside them. 'I lost someone because I chose to die on a hill. Stubbornness is great and also a curse in equal measure.' Morag kept having to stop, or close her eyes. The painkillers needed topping up.

Casey?

She nodded, grimacing, whether in pain, or through remembering what she'd let go.

'He's coming to visit. Saturday today, you say?'

He nodded.

'Maybe tomorrow. I dunno. But he's coming. Final goodbye.'

As Angus turned the key in the front door, he recalled Casey at the funeral, bawling his eyes out, shoulders shaking, crammed in at the back of the crematorium, his duet with Morag accompanying her on her final journey as she slid between the velvet purple curtains. He closed the door just as his phone pinged with a text. It was Fiona.

Hi! I have a massive favour to ask…

23

Issy logged everything carefully into the computer for the end-of-day cashing-up, still not quite believing she ran a successful business that involved cash flow, profit and loss, as well as coffee tasting and artisanal biscuit purchasing. She poured herself a wine from one of the bribery sample bottles she regularly got sent. She read the label: a new full-bodied red, biodynamic, meaning the grapes were picked under a sodding full moon by French wood nymphs or some other gobshite marketing ploy they'd coughed up in a brainstorming meeting. She didn't care if angels had farted it out, it was wine and it was free. She took a sip.

'Jesus Christ and all the saints!' If embalming fluid and battery acid produced a baby, this wine was it. Maybe the first mouthful paved the way. She took a second sip, bracing herself for her mouth to shed its lining. It wasn't as bad. The trouble with these biodynamic wines (most of them without sulphites) was they tasted pure boak. The sulphites were there for a reason – they kept it fresh. She never understood the whole 'natural' wine phenomenon. It was the emperor's new clothes dreamed up by health freaks. Where were all the mass graves piled high with bodies poisoned by sulphites? If you were imbibing wine, there was no way your body was a temple; that horse had already bolted.

The final post collection had been an hour ago. Bernie had swung by with his bag, the van kerb-mounted outside, hazards flashing. 'You got anything extra for me, Issy, darling?' he'd said with a wink. Bernie was scraping seventy and should have hung up his post bag a few years back, but he loved his job and often said they'd be sending him home in a box before he took his last pay cheque. He brushed over #metoo or derogatory labelling with his cheeky-chappie demeanour. Women were 'darling', 'love' or 'her indoors'. Issy always laughed and didn't take any of it personally; her age (forty-five) and her lack of giving a shit prevented her from stepping on a soap box. Bernie and his ilk's days would soon be numbered when the next generation of women were running the world, busting balls. Oh, she couldn't say that either, it was pejorative too.

She'd handed Bernie the last few pastries she hadn't managed to shift and a loaf of bread relegated for toasting.

'You're a cracker, you know that!' Bernie had said. 'Thank you. Her indoors will love the apple turnover. See yous tomorrow!'

Issy's indifference was born out of myriad abuse over the years in Glasgow and beyond, casual and outright racism, sometimes it was hard to distinguish between the two. Her mum, Beatrice, had borne the brunt of it during the seventies and eighties, turned down for cleaning jobs or sacked for no reason (once from the public library for being caught reading Caryl Phillips while she was 'supposed to be dusting the shelves', the head librarian not looking her in the eyes as she was issued marching orders). She'd been on a tea break but that fact had been conveniently glossed over. It was a common trope that persisted beyond its decreed sell-by date of so-called 'racial equality'.

But in Benlachie, Issy had forgotten to keep her guard up

against the inevitable racial profiling. Instead she'd blown in on a shitstorm, not seeking anything other than a safe harbour and a place that didn't remind her of her loss every time she turned a corner. She'd remained unprotected and her neighbours and customers had crept softly in, welcoming her in a way that she'd not formerly experienced. She was too much of a shambles to be aware of anything other than breathing and putting one foot in front of the other, getting through the day with Angus. It wasn't until one of her Glasgow friends made her watch *Brigadoon* that she briefly thought maybe she'd fallen into a mythical village that was untouched by the realities and prejudices of life as she knew it, a vanguard for the new dawn. Whatever it was, she felt supported and safe, and living in Brigadoon was facilitating some kind of emotional rehabilitation.

Before she moved to Benlachie, the life insurance had paid off the mortgage and Francis' pension provided a necessary safety net, but she couldn't stay home for ever, sleeping in Ginny's room among her cuddlies and cushions, watching the dawn break underneath the crack at the bottom of the pink butterfly blind. She felt like Dorian Gray as her body continued about its business while her soul withered away.

Morag had started dropping by a few months after the accident, cognisant of the drill. People can't get enough of fresh trauma, circling unintentionally like vultures, popping in with cakes, roasts, or a whole Tesco shop. The drama hooked them in. Then puff, they were gone, reabsorbed by their own lives, the tedious everyday grief too much to bear alongside their own crap. They weren't to blame, they were just grief tourists, existing in blissful ignorance that the reaper would grace their lives one day.

Morag had sat with Issy in silence, making cup of tea after cup of tea, holding her hand when she thought she would float off this earth and into the sky to join their wandering souls. Along with a select few, Morag had been an anchor, keeping her in the here and now, reminding her Angus needed her without actually saying it. Morag would take him off to Benlachie when all Issy could do was lie in a dark room and howl into a pillow. When Morag suggested the postmistress job that came with the small cottage a year after the accident, Issy had initially said no.

'You gonna sit here every day and snub the world?' Morag had asked her.

'I go walking! I get out.'

'Aye, by yourself. I don't think you see a soul. I know you won't believe me, but being with people will dilute the despair. Just try. Why don't you come and do a shift with Jenny? She's got six weeks before she leaves. The post office said if no one fills the role they'll close it. I'm doing this for entirely selfish reasons – I don't want to drive miles to post stuff.' She'd winked at Issy. 'You'd be saving a community hub.'

'If it means you'll stop nagging me about getting out, then OK. But I'm not promising to take the job. Och, I might be shit at it.'

So she'd driven over on a late-August morning, clouds hanging low in the sky, much like the dreich weather on the day of the accident. Jenny had shown her the basics and said if she was keen, she could train her up so that by the time she retired, Issy would be a dab hand. Issy didn't have time to think about anything other than trying to process what Jenny had just shown her. Customers had greeted her like a long-lost friend, and asked her advice about what cards to buy for a teenager, whether she could look up postcodes for them and how was she finding Benlachie. When she'd explained she was only on trial, they'd expressed a hope that she would take the job, nudging Jenny who stood over her like a benevolent aunt at the counter. 'It's about time we had fresh blood here.'

By the time Morag had turned up with Angus in tow, she'd

spent an entire day not thinking about Ginny or Francis, then immediately felt guilty because she hadn't. She couldn't win!

'How'd she do?' Morag had asked Jenny.

'She's a complete natural with the customers.'

Issy had glowed inside, like she'd just received a shining school report.

'Everything else I can teach her, but you can't teach that.'

Morag had raised her eyebrows at Issy.

'Yes, you were right,' Issy had reluctantly admitted. 'But how will I do this with Angus?'

'I told you, the job comes with the cottage,' Morag had explained. 'I can collect him until you find a permanent solution. Set him up with a table and he can do his homework. Surely there's clubs and things he can do in the holidays, or help in here? He can get involved with Countryfest. We'll find a way.'

The following morning, Issy had woken feeling inexplicably hopeful, her elegiacal disposition in abeyance. The physical pain remained, but there was a cushion beneath it. She'd said yes to the postmistress job and so began the next chapter of her life...

Issy missed her friend, Morag had joined the hole in her chest where Francis and Ginny lived. How she longed to pinch Ginny's cheeks – they'd been like little chipmunk pouches full of kibble and irresistible at bedtime when she'd been tucking her in. Ginny would ham it up. 'Don't bite them, Mummy!' she'd beg and screech theatrically whilst presenting her cheeks to be nibbled.

Issy sipped her biodynamic wine, her stomach clenched against the memory. It took her sixth months before she put Ginny's bedside water glass in the dishwasher. Those smeared fingerprints and lip marks were evidence she'd been alive. Some days she would look at videos of Ginny stored on her phone and the gut punch would knock her sideways. She'd hoped over time it would lessen, but seeing Morag deal with the grief of losing her daughter, she realised she would just have to learn to live alongside it.

However, Francis' presence in her life hadn't been born from her loins – she'd chosen him. And yes it was fucking awful when he'd died so suddenly, and of course if she hadn't been such a whingy bitch that day, all of them would still be alive. Morag had taught her one thing: self-blame was the path to an unproductive life. Every now and then, she liked a pity party where she accused herself of their deaths, but she didn't outstay her welcome. She always left early, never brought a bottle, not revisiting it for a long time.

Even now she still slept with Ginny's two favourite Build-A-Bears: Autumn and Rainbow. If she ever met anyone else, they would have to fight for space on the bed. How on earth did you meet anyone though? Endless doomscrolling on dating apps was like living your own death sentence and attractive customers were either married or just passing through.

Issy hadn't fancied Denis at all. He was her age, divorced, ran the gift shop with his ex-wife, so it was all a bit *Modern Family*. They seemed to get on and Sue didn't mind when he'd asked Issy out for a drink in Nairn. Sue popped in to get change regularly and they chatted. In fact, it was Sue who'd suggested Denis ask her out in the first place. Issy had been on a few dates with Denis and they'd had a laugh, but she couldn't get past his height, or lack of it, making dating him feel like she was supervising a school trip. She wasn't heightist – Francis had been just the same height as her in flats. She'd towered over him in heels. It was the size of Denis's hands – they were like a child's. She was a feminist; she didn't need a man for anything, she'd proven it so far, nevertheless if she was going to hook up with someone, she wanted to feel equal, not like she was going to crush their fingers holding hands to cross the road. There would be no date three, but it appeared Angus hadn't received the same memo. Issy understood – whomever she dated was going to impact her son, especially if they didn't get on. But Issy also appreciated it wouldn't matter if she chose the coolest, wokest man in the universe, Angus would still probably hate him. He wasn't his dad.

And that was the problem for her too. No one was Francis. For the last three years before the accident, their relationship had felt like a constant tennis match, batting questions between them regarding the house, the kids, work or arguments about whether they should get a dog. She'd missed their carefree days of sex on a rainy afternoon, watching films with a hangover. It had been Francis who'd wanted kids, and she was glad he'd pushed for it, but for a while it had felt like an incessant uphill slog with two raging Wookiees strapped to her back. They'd never made it through to the sacrosanct other side that people blissfully talked about, reaching marriage nirvana, proving the one in three wrong.

After conversing with people all day at work, she didn't mind the silence at home so much, but not hearing Angus's voice since he'd been ten still crushed her heart. Surely it would have broken by now. Maybe it hadn't if he'd not used his vocal cords? What if it they'd atrophied, like all the google wormholes had suggested? She could feel a pity party gathering. Bawbags – it was because she'd started on the angel fart wine. She was very much aware that she possibly drank too much, it was her way of blocking out these thoughts. She also knew she could stop it if she wanted to.

She turned up the music on the CD player she kept behind the counter. An old Space Ibiza compilation blasted out, the bass rumbled through her chest, scattering the pity.

Earlier, when Maggie had been singing in her small kitchen, she'd conjured up Morag on the sea wall stage at the festival, performing the pared-back set she always sang on the last day just after lunch. She couldn't wait to get stuck in creating Maggie's dress for the open-mic night and had already sketched some ideas on one of Angus's pads by the till. This was exactly the kick up the arse she needed – just the thought of delving into her sewing room rekindled a flame inside her. Maggie reminded her so much of her dear friend; she was going to miss her terribly when she returned to London. It felt like they'd known each other their entire lives when they'd only just met.

'That would be a soul connection then,' Morag's voice echoed inside her head.

'Aye.' Issy toasted the air with her wine. 'It sure is.'

Maggie had repressed her beautiful singing voice for years; Issy wondered what else she might be hiding? There was something, she just couldn't put her finger on it.

24

Fiona's stomach churned all the way to Tain in the car, future conversations nattering away inside her brain. 'Hello, Maw, I've read Morag's diaries and she says you had an affair with Keith.' 'Can I ask you something? Did you even want children? Also, is Uncle Keith my real dad?' 'Maw, did you ever love us?' 'Did Da know about the affair?' Fiona pondered whether answers were actually going to change anything or just tie her life up in bigger knots...

She'd left Maggie and Angus rehearsing in Morag's kitchen, Roxie in charge of quality control. As Fiona pulled up outside the small house, her home until she was eighteen, her eyes were drawn to the faded plastic guttering which was leaning away from the wall and needed fixing. She made a mental note that she knew she'd instantly forget and backed it up with yet another memo on her phone. There were currently about twenty-five, none of them actioned.

She looked up as the front door opened. Maw was poised in the frame, her hair groomed into place, her dapper scarf twisted at a jaunty angle and her pink gansey wrapped around her, insulating against the brisk wind. Fiona didn't even have enough time to gather her thoughts as she climbed out of the car, Maw watching her every move.

'Where is she?' Maw called out before Fiona had even slammed the car door shut.

'Who?' Fiona asked, knowing full well who she meant.

'Maggie?'

Fiona could feel herself stiffening internally. Did Maw think she was bringing her? *Really?*

'She's at the flat.'

Maw's face fell – she'd clearly been gearing up for this since she'd bumped into them.

'Afraid you'll have to make do with just me.'

Fiona followed her mother into the gloomy interior and through to the 'decent' front room that had historically just been used for receiving guests. In recent years, it had been demoted to the TV room and hadn't been updated as far as Fiona could recall. The ancient three-piece suite would outlive them all. Maw had bought new stretchy plain grey covers for it about ten years ago, permanently embalming the hideous brown mid-eighties crushed-velvet flower pattern. The powder-pink and gold standard lamp was enjoying a renaissance, as was the red leather pouf where Maw always rested her feet clad in animal-print slippers. Tired framed pictures of Monet's *Water Lilies* and Van Gogh's *Sunflowers* hung too high on the wall behind the sofa, while Tina the Spanish lady (also having an ironic rebirth) reigned above the fireplace, her spindly gilt frame showing signs of patina on the corners. Various Lladro-type ornaments acted out scenes along the mantelpiece and a gold carriage clock (a gift from one of Da's regular guests on an estate shoot) stood pride of place bang in the centre, its ticking cutting through the weighted silence. Fiona could hear the radio babbling in the kitchen out the back.

'I made tea,' Maw said, pointing to the navy tray balanced on the red pouf. What looked like a Dundee cake on a 'special' plate sat next to the good teapot, milk jug and three bone-china cups and saucers.

'Maw, I never said Maggie was coming. You never asked, did you? You didn't make that cake?'

Maw almost laughed. When had anyone known her to make a cake?

'No, I got it from Ruby's. It's the best Dundee for miles around.' That was certainly true. 'Shall I be mother?' Maw asked, the irony almost curdling the milk.

'Sure. Do you want me to cut the cake?'

Maw nodded. 'None for me, I'm watching my figure...'

Fiona inwardly rolled her eyes. Maw had been watching her figure for their entire lives, surely she could retire at seventy-nine? Fiona had retired years ago; life was too short to live without cake. Was Maw still resisting for herself or for someone else?

Fiona plunged the knife in between two almonds and cut herself the thinnest slice possible, levering it onto a china flowery plate stacked under the saucers. She sat on the settee with her cup and plate and leaned back against the cushions.

'So, does Maggie know who I am?' Maw asked first.

'Aye.'

'Was she cross?'

'Och, I don't know, Maw. I don't think so.' Fiona was astounded her mother was asking questions pointing a veiled finger of blame towards herself. A first if ever there was one.

'She looks just like Morag, don't you think?'

'Aye, the spit.'

Maw sipped her tea, her hawk eyes studying Fiona as she bit into the cake. It was perfectly spiced and moist but absorbed all the moisture from her mouth like a thick wad of felt. She swallowed loudly and took in a mouthful of tea to help wash it down.

'What was it you wanted to ask me?' Maw began, blinking.

Fiona took another sip of tea and then cleared her throat.

'Maggie's daughter Roxie found a hidden box in Morag's flat. There were diaries in there, as well as old baby stuff.'

'What was Roxie doing rooting around the flat?'

'I don't know, Maw! Being nosy like all teenagers. That part doesn't matter. What's important is that Morag's diaries date from when she was first pregnant and then through the years that followed.' Fiona was certain Maw had paled underneath her rouge.

'Full of stuff and nonsense I presume?' Maw asked, her voice catching slightly.

'Full of secrets.'

Fiona let that settle, sipping her tea. She wasn't conscious of wanting to force Maw onto the ropes; it gave her no pleasure – this was as uncomfortable for her as it clearly was for Maw. But she couldn't bring herself to be bold and ask immediately. She wanted to offer the chance for the truth to unfold naturally without Maw being press-ganged into it.

Maw fiddled with her gold chain bracelet Fiona had given her for her seventieth birthday. 'What kind of secrets?'

'The name of Maggie's father amongst others...'

'Who was it?' Maw's voice cracked as she leaned forward in her chair.

Fiona considered her stance.

'Why don't I tell you after you tell me who *my* father was?'

The ticking of the carriage clock slowed down, drawing Fiona's attention to the beating of her own heart in her throat.

Maw blinked again, her brows dipping in bafflement. 'Your da is your father.'

'I don't believe you.'

'Well, it's the truth.' Maw shuffled back against the cushion.

'What about Uncle Keith?'

'What about him?'

'I think he's my da.'

Maw burst out laughing.

'It's not funny, Maw!'

'It is. I don't know what young Morag wrote in her diaries, but it couldn't have been that Uncle Keith was your da.'

'She implied it.'

'How?'

'She said you were in love with him.'

'That doesn't mean he's your father. You da was your father. End of story.'

Maw's reaction certainly lent credence to her answers.

'Is it true you had an affair with Uncle Keith?'

Maw eyed her carefully. 'What are you hoping to gain from this, Fiona? Making me out to be even more evil than you already think I was for making Morag give Shona away? Let me tell you, nothing you can point at me will ever make me feel more dreadful than I already do. I was hoping to live out the last few years without having to think about it. But Morag's untimely death and now the re-emergence of Shona have brought it all rushing back. Morag and I made our peace before she died...'

'I just want to know why you did it, why you made Morag give Shona away,' Fiona's hands shook, the teaspoon tinkling on the saucer. 'I know it was something to do with how you felt about Uncle Keith and my birth.'

Maw placed her teacup down on the tray and straightened her slacks, pushing an imaginary wisp of hair behind her ear. She sighed heavily, expelling all the air from her lungs and inhaling another huge breath.

'OK... I'll tell you, but I don't expect you to understand. It won't be easy to hear. Somehow the truth never is. If you want to try, imagine a time when abortion was illegal. Look at those poor women in Texas – some man's ruled that if there's a heartbeat at six weeks, regardless of circumstances, a woman has to give birth, even if her father raped her. Men don't have to carry a baby, so why should they decide anything? They've returned to the dark ages and, back then, that was unfortunately how it was unless you had access to a crate of money. Which the majority didn't. So women took matters into their own hands, often with tragic results...'

While Maw painfully explained her own dalliance with the abandoned abortion in Dingwall, Fiona realised she was now knee-deep in virgin territory as Maw cracked open her past with a mallet. She wasn't entirely sure she could bear witness, but Maw proved unstoppable once the truth began spilling out...

An hour and half later, Fiona drove away to meet Maggie and Roxie for lunch in Dingwall, leaving Maw waving her off on the doorstep. How had she lived with such a hefty ballast and not told a soul? Fiona needed to sit with it awhile before telling Maggie. Just when the past couldn't feel any more confounding, in flew the facts and blew all the lies out of the water.

25

'Ladies and gentlemen, please give a big round of applause to Dillon McCrae and the Southside Crew.' Fiona hovered, bingo caller-like, in front of the main fireplace where the 'stage' was set up. Two top-heavy speakers on spindly-looking stands flanked her, while a low table was set with a water jug and a stack of glasses ready to whet rusty larynxes.

'How are you feeling?' Roxie asked as Maggie peered out from the back table she'd secured by the toilets before the crowds had commandeered all the space. With the low ceiling and the unexpected crush in the bar, the atmosphere had been nudged from cosy to claustrophobic.

'Like a turkey on December the first.'

'You're going to be great.' Roxie smiled. For the first time since toddlerhood, it felt like they were on the same team. Roxie had been able to walk more confidently in the last day. The crutches had been left in the flat and she was able to put weight on the cast without worrying about falling over. Angus still hadn't arrived, but Maggie wasn't on for at least half an hour.

Roxie's phone rang and she dived on it before it fulfilled its complete fanfare.

'Hey! Yes, hang on, I can't hear you, I'll go somewhere quieter.'

Roxie disappeared back up the stairs towards the flat as Dillon and his crew kicked off their three-song set. There were so many band members that they'd moved the table and formed two rows to fit the cramped space.

Sweat pooled under Maggie's armpits; she was going to have to stuff paper towels under them at this rate. She didn't want to ruin Issy's beautiful piece of handiwork she had gifted her that morning. She'd been astounded that in between working at the post office, she'd miraculously knocked up a stunning wrap dress out of seemingly thin air. The African fabric glowed with burnt oranges and deep blues, transforming her into a firework that would hopefully distract from the nerves threatening to overthrow her voice.

As she sipped the warm honey and lemon tincture Fiona had forced upon her earlier, she was thrust back to 2006 and the morning when she was due to be planted in *The X Factor* queue. With calescent panic mounting, she'd run to the toilets. She'd never been hamstrung with stage fright before, having always self-anaesthetised with red wine at karaoke. Of course, the puking had undoubtedly been a budding Roxie, but it hadn't detracted from the frayed nerves, the shaking, the imminent feeling of it being over better than any orgasm a girl could experience.

Vanquished by the invidious fear of forgetting the words, of feeling exposed before the entire Sea Shanty Tavern, Maggie shot up from the table just as Issy, shoulder-height above the crowd, forced her way through the buzzing throng. Angus trailed behind her using his guitar case like Moses to part the hordes. She made it to the surprisingly empty toilet before the remnants of lunch hit the bowl, her hair plastered to her scalp. But as Maggie glanced up seeking loo roll, she plunged into a murky abyss, silence ringing in her ears.

'*I always puked before a gig in the early days,*' a soft Scottish voice whispered. '*The boys used to put a bucket by the stage as a joke. Casey got me a special tartan one. I ended up using it as a beer cooler in the end... Know that the whole pub wants you to succeed. I have every faith, my darling wee girl...*'

'Maggie? You in here? Oh fuck!'

The floor shifted beneath her as Issy gently rolled her into the recovery position, the cold tiled floor slapping her cheek. She tried to speak without success. Issy jumped up, the toilet door swinging, fanning the music into the cubicle.

'Here, try this.' She'd returned, Fiona with her this time. 'Can you sit up?'

Maggie nodded, her vision sharpening. Fiona offered her a pint of water, condensation streaked down the sides.

'Oh, Maggie, I feel terrible. Are you OK?' Fiona's voice cracked with emotion. They both sat on the floor with her. 'We need to get you out of here and into bed.'

'No!' she croaked. 'It's just stage fright. I'll be OK.'

'You might have banged your head!' Issy cried.

'I didn't. I just puked, then blacked out.'

'Jesus Christ and all the saints,' Issy muttered.

'The show must go on. Morag would expect it,' Maggie said, not quite believing she'd spurned her Get Out of Jail Free card.

'You don't have to. You *never* had to,' Fiona replied. 'It was just a daft idea I got into my head.'

'You told everyone, though, didn't you?'

Fiona pulled a remorseful face.

'It's OK.'

'Aye, everyone's here,' Issy agreed. 'Not had a crowd like this for a long while.'

'Do they know who I am?' Maggie realised she sounded like a Z-lister ducking under the velvet rope.

'If they don't now, they will when you've finished, *if* you finish,' Issy said cheerfully. 'We need to sort out your make-up and your hair. It's gone south. You sure you're up for it? No one will mind if you say no.'

Maggie hesitated before nodding.

'Morag suffered with terrible stage fright for years,' Fiona said, hauling her up with Issy's help. 'Steady now... Casey even—'

'Got her a tartan bucket,' Maggie butted in, Fiona's mouth agape. 'I know. Come on! Let's get this show on the road!'

* * *

Break a leg. Morag would be proud.

Angus handed Maggie the note just as Fiona stepped up to the mic. She'd motioned for Gordon to take up his position as gate-keeper by the door. There was no more room at the inn.

'Thank you, Angus,' Maggie hissed as the chatter died down, cupping her hand over the mic. 'That means a lot. There's still time for me to fuck it up though.'

He shook his head and gave a thumbs up from where he was sitting beside her. They were an odd couple for sure: the mute boy and the franticly terrified woman old enough to have birthed him.

Maggie peered out across the sea of faces, only recognising Issy, Iona the waitress, Gordon, and of course, Roxie. People were standing at the back, some perched on stools, craning necks like meerkats. After the other acts, the expectation felt enormous. She gulped down a few mouthfuls of water.

'I'd like you to put your hands together for a very special guest all the way from London, accompanied by our very own, Angus MacMillan. Please give a warm Benlachie welcome to Maggie Pink.'

As clapping ruptured across the bar, a few whistles pierced the air.

'Hi. I'm, er... going to sing two songs, not written by me, I hasten to add. I'm very much a complete greenhorn, unlike Angus here, who's a consummate professional. I haven't... er, sung for donkey's years, so I apologise in advance if I sound a bit, er... rusty. I'm also very nervous... hence my babbling.'

The crowd cheered, instantly coddling her with their warmth.

She glanced over at Angus and nodded; the crowd hushed, bile burned her throat. The door of the pub swung open, and Gordon began to turn away the eager punter. Angus strummed the opening bars of 'Close to You' just as Roxie waved across the room at Gordon from her position up against the bar. Maggie lost focus, training her eyes on the pub's newest customer. Gordon opened the door wider as the customer raised his hands, and backed off, but Gordon beckoned him in and reached for his hand, shaking it. Adam sheepishly waved at Roxie and that's when Maggie realised she'd missed her intro.

26

Adam stared at his wife; the hackneyed saying, 'time stood still', might have been conceived for this moment. He could have been in Piano Bar Kensington in 2006 watching Maggie belt out 'I Will Survive' accompanied by the house band. He'd been instructed by his editor to investigate the upsurge of London's karaoke bars. Instead of the typical private booths, a backing track and words streamed across a screen, in Piano Bar, drunk punters sang with a real band while the audience sat around drinking and critiqued whomever was murdering the latest torch song. New York was considered the mothership for all piano bars and the template from which this one had been cut.

When Adam had sauntered in off the street on a Friday night after two casual pints with Eddie and Kev from the sports desk, he was expecting to scan the place, down a couple of expensed fancy cocktails, make a few wry observations on his Dictaphone, then shoot off to meet his flatmates over in Brixton at the new sushi place on Atlantic Road. Things didn't go according to plan. First off, the bar was actually pretty stylish and on his limited time slot was a lot to take in. The drinks were perfectly piquant, hitting the right notes of sweet and sour with the mule kick of rum, and the atmosphere trod an infallible line between rowdy and convivial. An older man, tie half-mast, was finishing up crooning a Frank Sinatra track, something so ubiquitous, with a big band showstopper chorus. He wasn't half bad and the crowd clapped in between sipping their mai tais. A gaggle of drunk women started chanting 'Maggie, Maggie' as soon as the man slunk off to his seat. Adam was just ordering his second drink, a margarita, when this Maggie replaced the Sinatra wannabe at the mic, whispering her song to the piano player. As the unmistakable opening chords of 'I Will Survive' ricocheted across the bar, Adam rolled his eyes, *how predictable*, and prepared himself for three minutes of a cat being skinned alive.

Very little surprised Adam. He'd interviewed Eminem when he'd been high on some substance and had to can the article because his people declared it unsavoury; he'd flown to NYC and back in a day to hook up with some rock band about to make it big, only for them to be a no-show (and ultimately crash and burn); he'd partied with the Red Hot Chili Peppers at the MTV Awards and woken up in a hot tub with two hench security men and a slobbering Rottweiler – the list of improbable situations was endless. But standing in Piano Bar watching Maggie knock out 'I Will Survive' trumped them all. There was undeniably more than one way to skin a cat and he immediately found himself ensnared. She owned the tune like a made-to-measure spangle-tastic silver-sequinned dress. It became part of her as she etched the lyrics with the pain of betrayal yet retained the diva sense of confidence that she would, indeed, move on. Her voice was strong enough to cradle the depths of all the emotions side by side, knitting together an unequivocally unique Piano Bar performance. And this was the thing – she had no idea how good she was. Second to all, she had striking red hair flying all over the place, a gap between her two front teeth that was surely a marketing team's dream, and her own sense of style pitched somewhere between rock goddess and indie girl. When she finished, the bar erupted into chaotic cheering and calls for one more tune. Maggie endearingly flushed red and refused the band's standing ovation and offer of another song. She appeared mortified by her own success and dived into her crowd of friends, disappearing among a sea of cackles and whooping.

Adam had downed his drink. He didn't know what to do with himself. He'd garnered enough information to finish his article by tomorrow when he had to send it in. He harboured a nagging feeling that if he walked out of this bar without saying hello to Maggie, he would regret it for ever. How had his life condensed down to such a cliché? Before he could answer, the gods of music indulged him: she was walking this way with her purse in hand, obviously about to buy a drink. She'd squeezed in next to him where he sat on his stool, the two hastily drunk cocktails imbuing him with a false confidence.

'Hi,' he'd opened with, inwardly wincing. He could do better. He'd managed to get Kylie to smile at one of his jokes... 'You survived then?'

Maggie had turned to him and he could tell she was drunk. Her eyes were glazed and she swayed ever so slightly on her feet.

'What?' Her brow dipped in concentration trying to focus. She had a few freckles sprinkled across the bridge of her nose and cheeks, and the trace of bright pink lipstick had melded with red wine, staining her teeth as well. She was perfect.

'I said... Oh, never mind. Do you want a drink?'

'I'm buying a whole round, but thank you anyway.'

'Let me buy it for you. I can expense it. It's not every day you meet a bona fide disco diva.' Actually, Adam *had* met Gloria Gaynor, well, he'd spoken to her on the phone, but he didn't want to boast.

'If you're sure. It's two bottles of Cristal champagne and five tequila shots.' She pursed her lips, trying not to laugh.

'Oh, OK. I just need to ring my broker, sell a few companies first. I won't be a minute...'

'Don't worry, a bottle of house red will be fine and a vodka and Coke.'

As Adam had made the order, he'd sneaked in a few cheeky glances at Maggie. In the course of time, her side profile would still set his heart racing. The way she slowly pushed her hair over her ears made him want to kiss her exposed neck, even during the mundanity of stacking the dishwasher or nagging him about the overflowing food waste bin. He knew he would never grow tired of her as he stood in such close proximity, her rose perfume provoking all sorts of morally questionable thoughts.

'So where can I see you perform again?' he'd asked, handing her the bottle and vodka.

She'd appraised him, as if noticing him for the first time and smiled lazily.

'In the bedroom. Thanks for these...' He watched her sashay back to her table, where she plonked the vodka in front of a mate and turned round to look at him, instantly bursting out laughing at his gawping.

The following morning, he'd woken up next to her asleep in her Clapham flatshare, his head exploding and his phone full of texts from the guys asking who the girl was he'd obviously ditched them for. There were five texts from Ollie, an old friend from uni. He opened one – it was a reply to a text he'd sent.

Wow, mate, who is she? You got any more footage?

Oh no, what did he do? He felt sick, surely not, he wasn't that kind of guy... All subsequent messages were in the vein of 'call me, I've already shown the exec, they want to meet her, mate call me!'

A heightened sense of panic had made his fingers fumble opening the sent message folder, where he found a video delivered to Ollie at 3 a.m. He opened it. It was of Maggie singing 'I Will Survive' in bed. The lighting was dreadful, the sound dubious, but you could tell she had an amazing voice even filtered through the basic video phone technology. The clip was about thirty seconds if that and in the text box he'd typed:

A future contestant???

Life had unwittingly come full circle as Adam stood in Maggie's direct eyeline in The Sea Shanty Tavern. He'd reaped what he'd sown, ending up in last chance saloon. The doorman had insisted he come in, even though Adam had a plunging sensation in his guts that it was the wrong thing to do. When Maggie stared at him from behind the microphone, her face a quizzical mess as she simultaneously noted his entrance and realised she'd missed her vocal cue, Adam felt guilty. He was supposed to have arrived an hour ago, slipped in quietly, not crashed her vocals, in a desperate attempt to try to sort this chaos out once and for all. But his flight from Berlin had been delayed.

Maggie looked to the young kid on guitar, who nodded and seamlessly played the intro again, leading her back to the beginning. No one noticed, it all happened so quickly, but he knew Maggie would now be on the hop, terrified of making more mistakes and it had all been his fault. Fuck. This did not bode well.

Instead of making his way over to Roxie, he stayed exactly where he was, his carry-on bag at his feet, the heat of the compressed bodies making his pores tingle.

Maggie sang the opening bar – her voice had changed over the years. Lack of practice and training finally taking its toll. He hadn't heard her sing since just before Louis had died, a long time ago, and that had been at a birthday party as a favour for friends. Her timbre was deeper, richer, like raw meat mixed with gravel, but the ability to hit the high notes was still present. Her range had remained the same and lent itself perfectly to 'Close to You'. The fact that she'd chosen it lit a tiny flame of hope. It was their song – well, their comedy sex song. Every time he heard it, it made him smile and envision her naked arse cheeks disappearing between the two beds. He couldn't remember the last time he'd seen her naked...

As Maggie wound up the song, he looked over at Roxie; she was enthralled and he could feel tears sting his eyes. Roxie was why he was here. He'd made a silent promise when she entered the world, that he wouldn't be a fair-weather father or husband like his own dad had been. He was here for the long haul and owed Roxie another stab at fixing it. But he couldn't fall apart yet; he needed to focus.

Maggie spun out the 'close to yous' with such gentle alacrity, he felt the crowd swaying either side of him as they got caught up in the emotion. The kid on guitar was excellent and he rounded off the song beautifully, bringing it to a satisfying close. The crowd exploded and all around him he heard chattering, whispers: 'She's Morag's daughter, you know...' 'Wasn't she like her mum, so beautiful...' 'It was like watching Morag...' 'I wish she could see her...'

While the crowd's applause battered the ceiling, he picked his way through to Roxie, who flung herself at him like he was the returning hero.

'Dad!'

''Tis I!'

'I can't believe you're here! Fiona, Issy, this is my dad!'

Adam poked his head above Roxie's and caught the puzzled

glance of an older woman who must have been the Aunty Fiona Roxie had mentioned, and Issy, the statuesque woman who ran the local shop that sold everything. He'd taken notes on his phone so he didn't forget, memorising everyone before he arrived. He had to have some advantage, he'd no idea what had been spilled about him. Not a lot, knowing Maggie.

His first observation was Roxie was talking to these grown-ups in a way she didn't at home, and the second thing, both women were horrified he was here. Before anyone could say a thing, Maggie spoke.

'I'd like to dedicate this next song to Morag, whom sadly I never met, but who I'm sure you all miss terribly.' A burst of clapping and 'hear, hear' rippled round the pub before Angus played the intro to 'Crazy'. It was Adam's favourite Patsy Cline song and he had no idea Maggie even knew who she was. Roxie had delivered a crash course on Morag's life over the phone. He'd googled her and downloaded her EPs, listening on the way here. He'd enjoyed the music and thought Morag's voice was stunning – Maggie's was similar, a little rough around the edges in comparison. It was a real shame Morag had never continued as country was now huge in the UK, in a way it hadn't been in the nineties.

Maggie's contralto delved into 'Crazy's' lyrics, plucking them apart, solidifying the mutual feelings of longing and regret and spinning them out into the pub, where the audience soaked them up.

The hairs stood to attention on the back of Adam's neck as he watched his wife bleed her heart into the audience. He wanted to scream he was sorry, sorry for everything, for not being good enough, for not understanding, for not listening, for royally fucking things up, for everything he felt he was and all the things he wasn't. Not a day went by when he didn't wish things were different. If Louis were alive, he truly believed they would have beaten the odds and remained a quotidian two-point-four nuclear family. He couldn't resurrect Louis, but there was an infinitesimal chance in hell he might be able to save his marriage. He understood he was expecting the moon on a stick, all Maggie had to do was give it a real chance...

27

One of the many benefits of singing live is that one can't commit murder at the same time as performing. It was the finest example of unadulterated mindfulness, something Maggie struggled with, having a ridiculous pinball brain. Singing didn't lend itself to multi-tasking unless you were also a dancer and built it into the show. Maggie was not a dancer, she was barely even a singer, she worked in fucking marketing for God's sake. Watching Adam walk into the pub during what was possibly the biggest deal for her in a million years, she could scarcely keep the words of 'Close to You' in her head. *Close to kicking your shitting head in...* She just wanted to let rip, scream: 'What the fuck are you doing here?' down the microphone. However, she expected the audience wouldn't have appreciated being part of a Jeremy Kyle-esque pastiche. *I Killed My Soon to be Ex-Husband at a Charity Event for My Dead Mother Whom I Never Met*. It had all the controversial elements for a juicy show right there. At least Adam had the grace to look shamefaced.

Singing was always an out-of-body experience for Maggie and it wasn't until she'd finished that she realised she'd been clenching her toes inside Issy's ankle boots that were two sizes too big. She'd found her flow in the end. 'Close to You' had been a warm-up, and by the time she reached her sweet spot with 'Crazy', really bedding down in the low notes so the higher ones could shine, it was over. She wanted to do something else, adrenaline coursed through every contour of her body, tingles danced across her scalp. The crowd held her and cheered like a rambunctious football coach pitch side. Then the chanting started. *One more song!*

Maggie looked across at Fiona and she shrugged. She only had one other set of lyrics burned into her larynx, but it wouldn't be as impactful with a guitar. She caught Adam's eye, not on purpose, in fact she'd been purposely avoiding looking, but something predetermined forced her hand. He clearly mouthed something at her.

Fiona fought her way over, the crowd were still chanting and clapping.

'Adam said you know the words for "I Will Survive". I think it'd go down really well. How do feel about playing with a four-piece?'

* * *

'Oh my God, that was pure fucking magic!' Issy screeched. 'Everyone went batshit, did you see them?'

'Mum, you were totally amazing!' Roxie cried, hugging her voluntarily. 'You need to start singing again!'

Maggie revelled in Roxie's praise, letting it cloak her like a warm blanket. Maybe things had finally started healing between them…? Good old Gloria Gaynor uniting everyone, reliably serving up four to the floor disco beats. Maggie had sung with the Southside Crew, Dillon McCrae gallantly stepping aside. They knew the song from the wedding circuit where they forged out their regular bread-and-butter income. She'd loved every second and had even managed a wiggle on stage, not a dance routine, but her own slimmed-down version of multitasking. After all these years, the lyrics had streamed across her tongue in the right order, totally astounding her. She didn't miss a beat. To be fair, it was her karaoke go-to and she'd always been able to recover the lyrics no matter what kind of pissed-up state she'd found herself in. They were filed away in her reptilian brain, imprinted in her DNA. She wouldn't be surprised if Roxie had inherited them in some kind of genetically mutated legacy.

Fiona was about to introduce the next artist, a young girl called Maeve Milstead, someone who'd also gone to school with Angus. On her way over to the bar, Maggie was stopped countless times by people wanting to talk about Morag, what she had meant to them, how they knew her, what a shame it was she'd never met her. But the funny thing was, standing out front, she felt like she *did* know her. Being in Benlachie, reading her diaries, mingling with her community, talking to her sister – her aunt – and Issy, her friend, Morag felt as alive to Maggie as anyone here. The difference was, she was ethereal and, in a way, maybe she always had been. There were traces of her everywhere, especially in her shrine-like flat. Maggie had fingered her eclectic collection of clothes hanging in the wardrobes, pulling out items that had caught her eye, holding them up against herself in the mirror, not quite having the gall to try them on. But, mostly, Morag was woven between hers and Roxie's cells. She'd gifted Maggie her voice, and Roxie's artistic vision. Her sensible side was most definitely thrust upon her by the Pinks, but all the impulsive, party-loving, karaoke-singing actions were undeniably Morag. She was evidently fifty per cent someone else too, but one thing at a time...

Adam hung back with Roxie, plainly cognisant some kind of retribution was heading his way, he just wasn't sure when. After two glasses of wine, Maggie couldn't be bothered to even talk about it, practicalities came first...

'So, have you got somewhere to stay?' she asked while also attempting to eat a packet of cheese and onion crisps.

'I thought I could crash on the sofa?'

'What if there isn't one?'

'Roxie said there was.'

Maggie knew better than to say no. One wrong move could send Roxie scuttling back into her sullen teenage shell.

'Can't we all just stay longer, Mum? Have one last holiday? I'm not gonna lie, I like it here.' Roxie's wide-eyed expression belied her potential wrath if Maggie didn't agree.

'Rox, I promised your mum I'd bring you back with me, remember? It was only a few days ago that you didn't want to come at all.'

'Yeah, well. Things have changed...'

'I'm not talking about this now,' Maggie said, quite fairly she thought, all things considered. 'Everything will be clearer in the morning.'

'Yeah, right,' Roxie huffed. Oh how quickly the worm turned.

As Fiona took to the mic, Issy grabbed Maggie's elbow and motioned with her head over to the back door. She followed, leaving Roxie with Adam. Angus was standing further down the bar watching the next singer. Maggie noticed the way he kept eyeing Roxie. Something had happened between those two...

Outside on the street, Issy produced a fat spliff out of her purse.

'Noooooooooooo!' Maggie laughed.

'I think now is the perfect time to have a toke.'

'Bloody hell, I can't face those two stoned.'

'I think that's exactly why you should have some. Adam's clearly here to win you back.'

'I think Roxie forced him to come with some mad idea about

not coping with her foot, then somehow engineer a family holiday out of it, hoping to fix it all.'

'That sounds like quite a cunning plan.' Issy lit the end of the spliff, waiting for the twisted tip to burn away before inhaling a few times. 'It's quite strong.' She passed it over with an impish grin.

'It smells potent. What is it?' Maggie inhaled deeply, spluttering on the exhale. 'Shit the bed! That's just burned my singing voice. Chances of *Britain's Got Talent* dashed for good.'

'It's grass I got from one of Angus's friend's parents. He grows it in his greenhouse. It's organic. I swapped it for some artisanal coffee and wine.'

They stood in silence, passing the glowing butt between them. Even at ten o'clock, dusk was still a good way off. Maggie leaned back against the wall of the pub and looked towards the heavens. It was hard to believe that they shared the same sky in London where insipid stars fought through a haze of orange light pollution. But here, when the sun finally set, the stars popped like fireworks across the truly black sky with nothing to curtail them.

'Let's go in, I need the loo before the finale. Fiona's going to announce the total from the ticket sales,' Maggie slurred. She couldn't seem to walk at the pace her body required, like the air itself was viscous treacle. 'I'm as high as a giraffe's nuts,' she mumbled as they each found an empty cubicle.

'Good. It will make dealing with what's going on less stressful.'

'Or more stressful if I can't focus.' Maggie bunched up her dress and pulled down her knickers, staggering – almost missing the toilet seat altogether. 'I can't talk about it today with them.'

'Is there a chance you would think about getting back with Adam?'

'Too much has gone on.'

'You never said what.' She could hear Issy peeing next to her.

'It doesn't matter. Just shit... I'm not making a go of it for Roxie's sake, that's what I've been doing for the last however many years. She'll get used to us being separated eventually.'

'Don't you miss how it was with him though? I miss Francis. We didn't have a perfect relationship, but I miss him being there. Someone to share things with. And they hold all the back-catalogue memories with you. No one else can share those intimate family moments...'

'To be honest, I think it's all rose-tinted. Nothing's been real for years. I was playacting.'

Maggie flushed the loo and rearranged her clothes before opening the door straight onto Roxie standing by the sink, a thunderous look across her face.

'Oh, shit, Roxie. I didn't know you were there.'

'You were *playacting*? No wonder you and Dad are fucked. He never stood a chance. Thanks for putting up with us for as long as you have.'

As Issy opened her cubicle, Roxie turned on her heels and ran out of door.

'What happened there?' Issy asked, her eyes like pee holes in snow, the whites burning red.

'I don't know how much she heard, but none of it would have sounded good to be honest. I'm going after her.' Maggie washed her hands, the cool water soothing on her wrists. 'Just when things had felt better between us.'

'But it's not all one person's fault when a relationship breaks down. Why is she blaming you?'

Maggie shook her head in defeat. The words lodged themselves deep in her ribcage, refusing to budge as the grass continued to derail her.

'I need to...' But Maggie wasn't sure what she needed any more.

'I always let Angus have his strops. There's no point in stopping them, intervening just makes things worse.'

Maggie knew this was more than a strop though, Roxie had heard her mother confess she'd been faking everything, but that wasn't the whole story. Maggie was in no state to process and followed Issy out into the pub, intent on finding Roxie, only for Adam to pounce on her.

'I was just about to look for you in there. Roxie said she's going to bed and just disappeared. I don't know where that is. She seemed upset.'

'It's upstairs.' Maggie pointed towards the back stairs with a wavering hand.

Adam squinted and peered inquisitively at her face. 'Are you... *stoned*?'

'Not that it's any of your business, but yes.' She giggled quite unexpectedly.

'Great. Would you mind showing me where "bed" is so I can talk to her?'

'Fine.' Maggie turned to Issy. 'I'll be back in a bit.'

Issy nodded and motioned she'd be at the bar.

'Roxie, can I come in?' Adam called through the closed door once they were inside the flat.

'No. I'm asleep.'

'You're clearly awake.'

'I one hundred per cent don't want to talk to anyone, especially *her*. Please leave me alone.'

'What have you done *now*?' Adam hissed accusingly.

'What have *I* done? That's rich. I haven't *done* anything.' Maggie stalked off to the living room and round to the kitchen to grab a glass of water with Adam tagging behind.

'Oh wow, this place is so eclectic. It's like a museum. It's Morag's place?'

Maggie nodded while gulping down water, trying to hastily chase away the weed.

Adam picked up some of the knick-knacks on one of kitchen shelves, examining them with the intensity of a gallery curator. Adam had always been nosy. When they'd visited people's houses, he would browse their shelves, sliding out books and opening them like he was in a library. Maggie remembered one school mum's fortieth they'd been forced to attend. While people were in the garden, Adam had been fiddling with a CD collection housed above a shelf of delicate ornaments and glass animals. He'd pulled out one too many and about four fell at once. He'd caught one, juggled another away from the menagerie, but two were direct hits, taking out a Mexican Day of the Dead figurine and an ironic crystal cat. They smashed on the floor, the Day of the Dead bride had lost her head. 'Fuck, fuck, fuck...' was all he could say, still holding the CDs (Jackson Browne and the Prodigy – varied taste). Maggie had swept up the broken carcasses and hid them all in her handbag wrapped in a napkin from the buffet. She wondered if whatsername ever missed them...

'Don't break anything,' she said now as he honed in on a row of trinkets. He turned away and looked at Maggie instead.

'What happened?'

'Adam, I can't talk about this now. My head's full of cotton wool.'

She got him a pillow from her bed and the extra blankets she'd shoved on Morag's wicker chair.

'Here, the sofa looks OK. I'll ask Fiona tomorrow if there's a spare mattress or bedding anywhere. Bathroom's near Roxie's room. I'm going back down in a bit. You do what you like. The door's on the latch.'

'Thanks. I might go for a walk.'

Maggie returned to the bedroom to examine her eyes in the mirror. They looked like she'd just escaped a burning building. Listening to the muffled thump of music reverberating through the floorboards as Maeve sang with her guitar, she lay on the bed, her body welcoming the duvet like a caress. Adam slammed the door and she deliberated making her way downstairs to find out the total. However, she awoke fully clothed at three fifteen to complete silence, damp hair and the overhead light blinding her. How had things nosedived from triumph to not quite tragedy in such a short space of time?

28

Roxie lay in bed seething. Her mum was a prize douche, her dad a pushover. Could it be possible she was the only normal person in this family? She heard the door bang. It was difficult to tell if the flat was empty because of the music downstairs. Roxie was frustrated with herself more than anyone else. She'd softened her shell, connected with her mum after a lifetime of her 'otherness'. She'd loved the last few days with the rehearsals, helping out with the tune selection, chatting with Fiona at the amazing chocolate cake café in Dingwall. She'd even managed something really grown-up – Ash, her moral sounding board, had forced her hand to be fair... After agonising for two hours over texting Angus, Roxie (Ash) eventually decided it was best to if he was accompanying her mum on guitar. After everything, she couldn't ghost him. Only complete twats did that. She apologised for wanting to escape the caves, for being so abrupt – she used the pain in her foot as her feeble excuse. When he didn't reply for what felt like a whole day (an hour and ten minutes), she thought she'd ruined what remained of their fragile friendship. 'He's probably working out the perfect reply to show he don't give a shit,' was Ash's verdict.

Finally he'd sent a very curt *Don't worry about it*, and she hoped that was it.

It was and it wasn't. When he'd been rehearsing in the flat, he wouldn't even look at her. However, she'd caught him unawares, staring a few times before ripping his eyes away. He was very cute, and still sent her gut flailing up to her chest whenever he played the guitar, but she was leaving Saturday, that was not in question now. There would be no family holiday, no chance for her machinations to unwind their way towards a happy-ever-after or a more realistic lukewarm reunion, but with her parents sleeping in separate beds. Her mum had made that perfectly clear. Did her dad know she'd been faking it all these years? He must have. But why did he stay? She found the workings of adult relationships confusing and also not representative of the supposedly 'real life' drama box sets she watched. Day to day, married life typically revolved around a series of questions about the bins, who ate the last bag of crisps, and homework, with simmering undertones of politeness masking a potential explosion. Oh yes, not forgetting muttering 'For fuck's sake' under your breath at every little thing, even the kettle.

Roxie wanted to scream, but didn't in case someone heard. Instead, she Snapchatted Ash, who was trapped at a family party with their parents and had to escape to the bathroom to reply. Their parents were fanatically strict about phones. If they were seen with it out when they were together 'as a family' they got it confiscated for two days. Trouble was, they did loads of things 'as a family'. Ash spent a lot of time going to the toilet...

'So, right, that all sounds mad! Your mum's been faking being married for ever? Do you think she's with someone else or something? What's Highland Boy doing now? Does he still want you? Was he eyeballing or giving you the side-eye? I wanna know about the gig. My bloody mum's shouting me. Can you hear her? (Imitating their mum's voice) *Where you, Aisha? Aunty Priti wants to*

measure you up for a bridesmaid dress – fucking bridesmaid dress. I
hate frills and all that shit. Can you imagine me? She's doing a
white wedding too and then a traditional one. I gotta do both!
Fuck's sake. Aunty did ask if I would prefer to be a page boy, I can't
even... I'd prefer not to do it at all! Anyway, I got about one minute,
shoot away and let me know what's going on.' It looked like Ash was
in a magazine spread reflected in the bathroom mirror. Patterned
tiles, those chunky candles that cost a hundred quid and gold
everywhere, super posh.

After updating Ash, Roxie lay back down and decided to watch
Pose on her iPad. Towards the end of the episode, the front door
slammed again and the floorboards creaked loudly as someone
walked past her room, stopping briefly, presumably listening at the
door. She'd already muted her iPad and found it depressing that
here she was on one side of the door listening to her dad doing the
same when she wanted to knock her parents' heads together for all
the miscommunication. She was envious of Ash and their strict
parents who constantly bickered and kept them on a short leash.
They weren't perfect by any stretch, but at least Ash knew where
they were with them. Bickering meant they were communicating! It
was better than painful civility.

The shadows were creeping high up the walls as the sun finally
began to sink. The music downstairs had given way to stifled mic
chat and cheering. Roxie plugged her AirPods in and drifted off to
sleep on a sea of ASMR Scottish whispering.

She woke with a jolt. One of her AirPods had dislodged and a
seagull was screeching right outside her window, no doubt
complaining about a lack of ice creams so early in the morning.
Roxie had slept in one of Issy's long thick winter dresses she'd
chosen for the charity event, now crushed from being used as a
sleeping bag. It wrapped around her with a dark navy and orange

plunging neckline exposing her midriff, having come loose in the night.

She checked her phone: nine ten in the morning. Her right nostril was throbbing. It could only mean a violent spot was brewing deep in her soul, an angry warning against sleeping with make-up on. She literally couldn't get away with anything. This needed urgent attention with Duac like a mitigation offering to Vesuvius.

'Sorry, skin gods. I won't do it again...'

Roxie slipped off the dress, letting it drop on the floor, and rammed a T-shirt over her head, then guided her cast into her shorts. She crept out of her room hoping to sneak to the bathroom without having to face either of her parents just yet. She hadn't worked out anything to say. It was beyond her capabilities thinking she could change her mum's mind. And just as she'd seen a different side to her over the last few days. Roxie had actually, shock horror, liked her. So if she liked her, surely that meant there was an awful lot of her she kept zipped up. Maybe meeting her Scottish family had exposed her mum's true self?

As Roxie turned the bathroom doorknob, voices in the kitchen chattered away. She hesitated when she heard her name. Well, if they were going to talk about her behind her back, she may as well have the privilege of listening. Careful not to step on the creakiest floorboards, she made it to the living-room door undetected. She could understand well enough without venturing further.

'So it was Roxie's idea?' she heard her mum ask.

'I think she just wants to know we gave it all we could.'

'I've been giving it everything for the last seven years, Adam. I can't give any more.'

Roxie growled under her breath. *Whatever...*

'When are you coming home then?' her dad asked.

'Femi said I don't have to come back until September...'

'You're going to stay here all that time? We didn't agree that.'

'No, but things are different now I'm here. I feel like I need to explore my roots. I've waited my whole life for this. I'll talk to Roxie and see if she wants to stay here with me for some of it.'

'I could stay too, get somewhere local...'

'Why would you do that?'

'To support you with Roxie. Help her get about while you go off and "discover your roots".' Roxie could hear the air quotes.

'Don't say it like that. My mum's just died *and* my real mum – this isn't a joke. It's my actual life, my family.'

'Sorry, I'm just upset. I know it's all shit. It just feels like we're not your family any more...'

'Don't make it about you, I know that's your speciality.'

Her dad *never* made it about him. He always gave and gave and gave! Roxie silently huffed.

'Anyway, I don't need support. We've got on fine until yesterday. You needn't have come early.'

'What happened?'

'She overheard me talking in the toilets with Issy.'

'About what?'

'About us.'

'You told Issy? Is that why Roxie wouldn't talk to me either?'

'About your fling? You're kidding me, right? She'll hate us both. Somehow I'll still be the baddie, it's always the way with her. You can't do anything wrong in her eyes.' Maggie spat her hurt right into Roxie's ear.

'It wasn't a fling.'

'A fucking two-night stand then. Fuck's sake, Adam, whatever way you dress it up, it was shit.'

'It *was* shit. Utterly shit. I'm shit. But everything was shit. We've never properly talked about it. You just shut down. All I want—'

'There you go, making it about you.'

'No, sorry, look... OK, it's over, I get it. But I need to say my piece if you won't come to Relate with me.'

'I don't want to hear it, is that why you came early?'

'No, I came to fight for us, Roxie needs us to be a family.'

'I *knew* it was her idea.'

Her dad had done this! He'd screwed it all up. Burning betrayal outstripped Roxie's rationale. Instead of red, she saw white when her legs moved of their own accord, her injury no barrier to hotfooting it to the kitchen doorway, where she hovered, shaking with indignation and rage.

'You liar! You lied,' she shrieked. 'You're the reason this is happening.'

'Roxie!' Adam looked stricken. 'I... errrr—'

'Roxie, it's not just one thing—' Maggie began.

'And you! You covered for him. I thought all you cared about was Louis, I thought you preferred him, that you didn't want us. You let me hate you when I should've hated him! *He's* the homewrecker.'

'No, it's not that simple—' Maggie tried in vain, walking towards Roxie.

'Don't touch me! Don't, just don't. I hate you both. How could you lie for so long? Don't worry – it's a *rhetorical question*.'

Roxie's rage consumed her, mutating so the urge to run was overwhelming, unhelpful with a painful foot. Anaesthetised by fury, she steamed out of the kitchen, ransacked her room, grabbing her bag, walking stick and hoodie, ramming her good foot into her trainer, only to stumble into her dad blocking the doorway.

'Let me go.'

'No. You're injured and there's literally nowhere to go here. I walked it in forty minutes last night. Let's talk.'

'Nope. I don't want to talk. I'm doing an Angus from now on.'

She zipped her lips and threw away an imaginary key over her shoulder. *Fuck you*, she thought.

'Well I can still talk. Sit down.'

She shook her head and clamped her hands over her ears.

'Roxie!' Adam shouted, something of a rarity.

'Adam! Leave her alone. Let her go out and get some air. Have you got money, Rox?'

Roxie blanked them both and pushed past Adam on her way to the front door. She turned the key in the door and limped down the stairs. The pub door was just being opened by Wayne, the sous chef, light spilling on the doormat. There was a bread delivery to get inside.

'Morning!'

Roxie raised her hand in brief greeting and stepped out into the misty morning, the gull cries now as familiar as sirens and horns. She walked towards the seafront like a tentative old lady escaping her carers for the first time. The sun was valiantly trying to burn off the brume, causing her to inexplicably cry from the sheer effort it was making. While the breeze cooled her tears, she wiped them away with the back of her hand, contemplating her rash exit. *Where was she going?* She needed some quiet space to mull it all over.

Pausing outside Trading Post, she peered in, catching Issy rearranging the fresh bread underneath the posh biscuit shelf. Issy looked up and waved, beckoning her inside. Roxie shook her head and walked off, dreading Issy would try to worm last night's details out of her. She didn't want to talk to anyone; Angus's retreat from conversation finally making complete sense.

She headed for another shop round the corner, one with less baked goods than Issy's but more crisps. Roxie just needed some fuel while she unpacked her head and examined her childhood. She'd been batting for the wrong parent all these years. Being an only child really stung her today of all days. If Louis were alive...

But if he were alive, she wouldn't be in this state. Things would be OK. Fucking dead Louis, screwing it all up for her yet again. When would his reign of terror end?

As she chose Pringles and a can of Coke, the perfect thinking place popped into her head. She was going to need a plastic bag.

29

Fiona's phone pinged just as she pulled away from the crossroads on Blackwood Rise. Then it started ringing on the front seat; she could see it was Maggie. She hadn't answered any texts last night after she'd disappeared. Issy said they'd smoked a spliff and Maggie had presumably passed out. Fiona had a hunch there was a gap in the narrative that she couldn't put her finger on. Maggie had known they were going to announce the total, so why had she completely vanished? Roxie, Maggie and Adam had all disappeared at the same time.

Fiona pulled into the car park five minutes later and read the text.

Has Roxie rang you? She's gone out upset, not worried just yet.

Fiona hurried down to the seafront just as the mist was burning off. It was going to be a glorious morning, but rain was forecast for later on in the day. She slipped in the back door of The Sea Shanty, signalling to Wayne that she was just popping upstairs to see Maggie.

'Hellooooo! Anyone in?' She ventured through the door and further down the hallway.

'In the kitchen!' Maggie called out.

Fiona found her still wearing her new dress, her hair piled in a topknot tied with a pair of what looked like knickers and last night's make-up still remarkably intact. She could have been a renaissance painting reimagined by Peter Blake, the knickers a comedic touch.

'You OK? What's happened?'

'Roxie stormed out earlier. I'm sure she'll come back soon – she left her phone here. Adam's gone to get us some breakfast and have a quick scout in the shops for her. She can't really go far, can she?'

'Not really. A gammy foot kind of holds you up. No teenager can survive without a phone for more than five minutes anyway.' Maggie looked like she'd been crying. 'Do you want to talk about it? Tea?'

Maggie nodded and Fiona busied herself with the kettle.

'Roxie overheard us talking this morning about something that happened a long time ago. It upset her.'

'Oh dear. Is that why you disappeared last night?'

'Kind of, but not really. They were two separate incidents. Did Issy not tell you?'

Fiona shook her head as the kettle reached boiling point.

'Last night Roxie walked into the loo just as I was telling Issy I was finally free of pretending to be married. Or some words to that effect. I was stoned – not my finest hour...'

'Ouch.'

'She was furious, wouldn't come out of her room. Turns out she'd asked Adam to come up and give it one last try with me. Try to persuade me into a family holiday up here...'

'Oh dear. That's hard for you to deal with... Are you sure you don't want to give it one last try?' This felt like a similar conversation Fiona had had with Morag over twenty years ago. *Casey won't hang around, you might regret it one day...*

'No, I'm done trying. I wanted to get to know everyone with just Roxie, find out more about Morag and her family. Not play happy families with Adam.'

Fiona handed Maggie her steaming tea in Morag's favourite cream china mug emblazoned with a giant blue M.

'What she overheard pushed her dad off his pedestal.'

'Och, that's not a bad thing though, surely? It's not healthy to have people on a pedestal because when they fall, it's a right old mess.'

Maggie blew on her tea and looked at Fiona.

'At the time, I couldn't talk to anyone about what happened. My parents wouldn't have understood. I eventually told my best friend, Nisha. She kind of understood why he'd done what he'd done because I'd treated her the same way as I'd treated Adam...'

Fiona sat down with her tea and patted her hand. Maggie appeared to be wrestling with telling Fiona too, opening her mouth three times, only to blow on her scalding tea.

'You know I visited Maw the other day before I met you in Dingwall? I didn't say, because I wasn't sure what I was walking into. She thought I was bringing you with me. She'd guessed you were Shona.'

'Oh God. How was it?'

'Not at all like I'd expected. I needed to keep what Maw and I had talked about to myself for a bit, let it digest. I think I felt overwhelmed without Morag here to hash over the details with. Of course, Morag knew most of what had happened in the past, but those diaries only told half a story.'

'And?'

'All these secrets, Maggie, these half-truths lingering in the shadows, breeding untruths of their own like an army growing out of control. If everyone was just honest in the first place, dealt with the truth, moved on from the truth, then none of the shit would hit the fan years later.... The truth always resurfaces, no matter how hard you try to hide it.'

'Are you talking about me or Maw in relation to that?'

'Maw, but you could apply the principle universally. All families have secrets and no family is perfect because they're made up of deeply flawed humans. Maw wasn't driven by guilt from the church, or what people thought, it turned out she was dogged by her own experience.'

Maybe they could both share their experiences, shake off whatever power they held, and stand back unattached. Fiona smiled to herself; she'd been listening to too many therapy podcasts.

'When you're ready, I know right now probably isn't the best time, you deserve to know how you really came to be adopted. I thought I knew the story until Maw told me her side... Just about everyone's involved... A cast of bloody thousands...'

Maggie bit her lip and stared out of the window beyond Morag's plants and Casey's dog-eared postcard, over the rooftops and towards the sand dunes. Morag used to chew her lip while ruminating. Fiona felt like a missing part of her had returned home to roost, Maggie's familiarity as comforting as Morag's clothes still hanging in the wardrobe and her half-squeezed toothpaste standing to attention next to her brush in the little blue glass in the bathroom.

'I think today is the perfect time to tell me. I need distracting. I don't know what to do about Roxie, whether to tell her what really happened. Maybe Maw's story will give me some insight. Secrets have got us all in trouble and I don't know how to untangle my one. I was just trying to protect Roxie... and myself.'

'Like Maw protecting Morag. Shielding people from the truth doesn't always work though... If you're sure...?'

'Yep, I'm sure. Hit me up. It can't be any more snarled than the mess I'm currently sitting in.'

'It'll give it a run for its money, I can tell you.'

Fiona shivered before she relayed the tale that linked all their futures together, including her own narrow escape from the knitting needles. Her mum's face had remained inscrutable as she'd finally surrendered her truth, her back ramrod straight in the chair, plummeting into her past like a deep-sea diver off a rig. She'd exposed some shocking truths in those murky depths and yet they'd still not fully sunk in...

30

Two days earlier, Agnes had stared at her only living daughter sitting opposite her on the settee. She'd looked tired, bags smudged beneath her eyes and the beginnings of jowls. Fiona had lost too much weight, something Maw didn't usually believe was possible, but she was seeing facial evidence that it didn't pay to be too thin.

'This part might also be hard to hear, Fiona,' Agnes had admitted. 'I want you to know... I'm glad I'm here...'

* * *

When Fiona had arrived into the world, she'd remained quiet for almost a week, and then she found her voice, bellyaching night and day until she was about four months old. Agnes had turned doolally from it. She'd almost thrown Fiona across the bedroom one evening when she'd been awake for what felt like eternity. Lachlan had slammed the door of their tiny estate cottage, kicking his boots off at the bottom of the stairs, and had clomped up the steps to find his wife and daughter. As he'd pushed open the bedroom door, Fiona had stopped screaming in shock, Agnes having just dropped her on the bed, not trusting herself another second. Lachlan had taken one look and instantly understood, it had been brewing for months.

'You need to get out, get some fresh air. Ma said she'd help any time. You know that. Yer own ma said the same.'

'Fiona hates me. All she does is greet. I hate—' Her words drifted away from her. Lachlan's mouth a straight line, holding his own thoughts to attention.

'Och, she doesn't hate you. Babies don't know what hate is. Ma said it's colic. Your own ma agreed, remember? It's nothing to do with you, it'll soon pass.'

He leaned down and scooped Fiona up into his arms, patting her back and kissing her head. She looked like a cough candy boiled sweet, shiny and red. The love came easy for him, but all Agnes felt was a nub of hot sticky anger in her belly, swirling and swooping up any nascent love. She'd read Doctor Spock in the end, Nancy had found it in the library for her. The doctor said babies might be able to pick up on frayed emotions. So really this *was* all her fault was what Agnes had gleaned from the close-set type. Fiona had absorbed her hatred of every waking moment and was broadcasting it to the world.

Agnes let herself out of the front door and walked through the dank woods until she reached the estate's west gate. Why couldn't they live in the town? But only having one child meant they got the small cottage. If they had another bairn, they'd been promised one of the places in Tain with a proper plumbed-in kitchen. Agnes didn't want another child, ever; she couldn't get along with the one she had. She faced a life condemned to the shack in the woods away from civilisation. If she'd never had any child, she'd be off at Glasgow now, smoking French cigarettes and drinking red wine while Keith visited at weekends, or not, depending on what she was doing. She felt like she was looking at her life from the wrong end of a telescope.

As she headed down to the back of the town, she realised she'd brought no money. She'd just grabbed a thin mac from the coat rack and wasn't wearing decent shoes, just her red indoor Dr Scholls. Did it matter? Where was she headed? Anywhere other than back to the cottage. Keith had come round with his new girl-friend last night. Lillian. She was bonnie, a secretary in one of the law firms in Inverness. Lillian had cooed over Fiona the entire evening, actually settling her for Agnes so she could lay her down in the basinet and have a few moments to herself.

'Ah, you're a natural!' Lachlan had proclaimed, making Lillian blush, Agnes's failures keenly clawing at her. When Lillian had disap-peared outside to the loo, Keith admitted he was going to propose to her that weekend. He appreciated it was very soon, but when you knew, you knew. He had his eye on a house in the city where they could settle, maybe start a family once he'd qualified. Agnes had had to run to the kitchen to vomit. Maybe the lamb stew hadn't agreed with her.

Keith hadn't looked at Agnes the entire evening and when it had been time for them to leave, he'd pecked her coldly on the cheek. It wasn't fair, Lillian was living *her* life. It should have been Agnes being proposed to, though, to be fair, she was ill prepared for marriage, even though she was already married! She'd had so many goals to achieve before settling down, and yet here she was, perpet-ually trapped, all choices snatched by a screaming bairn...

Agnes passed cagily down Tower Street, her Scholls echoing along the uneven paving slabs. She tried to avoid the cracks – old habits die hard. The shops were all shut for the night, most people in having their tea or rounding up wee ones for bed or bath. She briefly stopped and peeked longingly in Sheila's Dressmaker's window at a headless dummy flaunting a pink and orange halter-neck dress. Sheila copied the more modern styles in *Woman's Own*, with some local success. Nancy always scoffed she should branch out, try a racy *Vogue* pattern instead of outfits for all the wifies who smothered them in a housecoat. What was the point? Agnes swore she'd never wear a housecoat like her ma and Marion. So when her ma had bought her a blue and beige one from the back of *Woman's Own* just before her wedding, it was her personal nadir. How could things get any worse? Quite easily it would appear...

The few cars that trundled by didn't disturb the quietness on the street. The peace was comforting after Fiona's incessant screaming. Even if Fiona wasn't yelling, it was all Agnes could hear between her ears, like ringing following a bomb blast. Agnes kept her head down, not wishing to bump into an acquaintance or a family friend, acutely aware she looked a state. But, honestly, what did it matter? Nothing did any more...

She'd not eaten at all that day. She usually pushed what food she did make for her and Lachlan round her plate until he ate hers as well. Mince and tatties and tinned peas was the only meal she could confidently make without panic storming her scattered mind. Lamb stew had been her first foray into more complex cooking when Keith had visited. No one had complained, but all she could recall was fatty deposits floating like viscous islands amid a sea of watery gravy. Her ma had had to teach her how to cook before she'd married Lachlan. Not that her mother was renowned in the kitchen, but she could make the necessary meals to keep a family alive. Agnes hadn't realised how much time and effort it took to prepare just one proper meal, let alone doing it every day. She'd find herself staring at the kitchen wall while Fiona screamed in her basinet, wondering what else she could make with mince. She'd even started clipping out recipes in *Woman's Own* (slowly but surely turning into her ma) and saving them in the kitchen drawer with the knives and forks and spare elastic bands.

As she shuffled past the Royal, she glanced in through the low-lit windows, watching people at the bar, not a care in the world. No one was worrying about how many ounces of milk they'd got their baby to drink, or if that same baby would wake ten times in the night, turning you into a zombie that didn't know its arse from its elbow. What she wouldn't give for a carefree night listening to Radio Luxembourg with Nancy in her childhood bedroom, sneaking wee drams of Bucky from under the bed, dancing to the Everly Brothers or Elvis, while her parents watched the *White Heather Club* on the box downstairs, the volume turned up high because her da was going deaf. They'd smoke Woodbines out of the window while spraying Glade to mask the smell, though not at the same time in case they set themselves on fire. Nancy was at catering college now, not back from Edinburgh till Christmas. Agnes missed her and eagerly anticipated her letters filled with recipes (that she'd not attempted yet) and gossip about the other students. Agnes, in turn, wrote fictional notes about how wonderful it was being a mum and how much she loved being married. Agnes had no idea she was such an accomplished liar.

Agnes checked her watch. Six nineteen. Wasn't there a fast train to Wick at six thirty? It usually ripped through the station, the toilet signs creaking for at least five minutes in the wake of its departure. She headed down the hill, her mind blank, now following the pavement as it wound its way towards the wrought-iron gate.

She was the only person there when she reached the long platform. Wind whistled through the wires atop the telegraph poles planted along the entire length of the platform to the bridge at one end. The lights were out in the ticket office. She perched on a wooden bench underneath the portico away from the men's toilets. You could ride all the way to London from here should it take your fancy. She'd never been to London. She'd never been anywhere, apart from Inverness, and Ullapool when her parents had taken them camping once. They'd been eaten alive by midges hungry for human blood and sweat. She'd loved being able to roam where she wanted and her da had built the most amazing fort out of sand. However, the best part had been swimming in the sea every day. She'd felt free, floating on her back, the sea gently cradling her as she watched the sickle moon rise in the mid-summer sky... Aye, it had been grand apart from the constant itching.

Agnes leaned her head against a wall-mounted timetable behind and closed her eyes. Her body had turned to ashes, her heart had stopped beating and all she wanted to do was stay here and sleep until she regenerated. The bairn sucked the marrow from her bones, how was she ever going to recover?

She jumped suddenly, as if falling off a cliff. The rails were humming. She dragged herself up from the bench and stepped out of her Scholls, the stone cold underneath her bare feet, like she'd plunged them into the icy water on Dornoch beach. She couldn't remember which side of the track the train was travelling on. She listened intently to the buzzing, deciphering its exact proximity. Maybe it was this platform, the train heading to Wick. She waited, hedging her bets until it became obvious.

The stars were out above her head, white stones tossed across the inky sky. Her da had taught her all the formations when she'd been a wee girl. They'd searched them out on the camping trip all those years ago. The Plough, the Bear, Orion and his belt... Venus was blinking like a warning beacon this evening.

The train rounded the corner at speed, ruffling trees like a flat stone skimming a millpond, and Agnes stared into the headlights of the oncoming locomotive. Before she could take another breath, she flung herself forwards, only to be snatched back by a pair of strong arms. She screamed bloody murder as she was dragged back from the platform edge, the sharp blast of air flapping her untied mac around her like a bird's wings in flight.

'What are you doing? You're hurting me!' she screamed as Ted McMahon, the deputy stationmaster, grappled with her, grazing her heel on the hard stone.

The train shot past in a clackety-clack of machine gun fire, lit windows dancing before her eyes like a zoetrope. As the final carriage disappeared into the night, its lights diminishing along with the last vestiges of hope, Ted spoke.

'I could just tell…'

'What could you tell?' she raged, struggling to set herself free.

He let her go, immediate danger having passed.

'That you were going to jump. You left your clogs on the platform.'

31

Even gliding towards old age, the little girl inside Fiona had shattered that day in the front room. Maw had been right, she'd not been prepared to discover Agnes would rather have died or terminated her than suffer being her mother.

'No one knows about that night... I'd a taken it to my grave. Och, I never even told Morag in her dying days; it wouldn't have served a purpose.' Maw twisted her hands on her lap, her face deadpan, emotions under lock and key as usual.

'So you wanted to die because of me?' Fiona asked, her voice wobbling as she hurried away a tear. Apart from the funerals, she'd not cried as an adult in front of Maw...

'No. Not you. Everything. Fiona, there's not a day goes by that I don't think thank God young Ted caught me. It would have been a death by a thousand cuts... I was too young to be a wife and a mother married to a man I didn't really know or love. I'd wanted to go to Glasgow School of Art, not settle down. Your father was a good man. He understood what he was letting himself in for. That day when he sent me out for a walk, I think he was scared I wouldn't come back, but he knew it was what I needed. Ted dropped me home, told your da he'd found me wandering by the station. I'd made him promise to keep my secret. He made me promise to ring him if I thought I was going to do it again. We'd no phone, but I promised anyway.'

'I'm sorry you had to go through all that... Surely it was post-natal depression?'

'Aye, most likely, not helped by all the other factors. I still felt awful, but your father stepped up. He came home at lunch every day, helped with you, he was back at night on time, bathed you, sang to you, and he made a fuss of me. My ma and his ma also rallied round, even though Marion could be a right old boot at times, telling me I was doing everything wrong, which was why I'd never wanted her there in the first place... Your da asked me to go to the doctors', but in those days, no one did. I was lucky, I slowly recovered, your da insisting on a daily dose of malt extract like it was going to cure me.'

Fiona smiled. She and Morag had been subjected to the same treatment after every cough and cold when they'd been younger.

'And when Morag arrived, I didn't suffer like that. But my head and heart were in a right old mess... Before I got pregnant with you, your da and I... well, we dated. I wouldn't say we were going steady, we weren't in love, well, *I* wasn't, but he was decent. I was seventeen, what did I know? Your uncle was also sniffing round. And that was where the missing spark was, Keith held it.'

Fiona nodded. Her dad had been steady, reliable, a man of few words, kind and patient. Keith was turned up a notch or three: garrulous, charming, a great host, a wonderful raconteur and people warmed to him, some people obviously too much...

'Were you and Uncle Keith... together?' Fiona's body shifted away from her consciousness as the floor began to slope towards her mum. Not only had Maw admitted to contemplating abortion and a botched suicide, but they were going to dissect her sex life too? Her stomach gripped the Dundee cake in protest.

'On and off.' Maw heaved herself off the chair and pottered into the kitchen, returning with two glass tumblers and the Co-op entry-level whisky she used for lighting the Christmas pudding. 'We'll need this for the rest of the conversation.' She poured two snifters into the glasses. If Fiona ever needed a shot of whisky, it was now. Something had to shock her back into her body.

'Were you in love with him?'

'Madly.'

'Oh.' Fiona sipped her drink. It tasted like petrol after tea and cake, but the warmth slid down her throat, seeping into her bones, anchoring her. 'When did it begin?'

Maw squirmed in her chair, the truth a seemingly prickly concept.

'Soon after I met your father. You see, I'd no idea I'd end up marrying your da. He was just supposed to be... a, how do I put this... a practice man. Someone who'd—'

'Yep, I get the idea. Deflowering...'

Maw nodded. Fiona felt queasy.

'So when I met Keith, it was like jumping from sparklers to a full-blown firework display. Keith would mosey past school when he got off the bus from college early, meet me and walk me home, or take me to get a hot chocolate at Pringles. All very innocent, though I'm sure he never told Lachlan. I certainly didn't. Before long, we were kissing, but he never got past the stocking top. He said he loved me, but he couldn't betray Lachlan, even though he already was. I said I'd end it with his brother, but he said no, not yet, that I should wait till I went away to art college. You see, I didn't know Lachlan had already told Keith he wanted to get engaged. It was what people did in those days. A long engagement, tying someone in with a ring. I would've said no, of course. Meanwhile,

Keith and I would've picked up long distance if I'd made it to Glasgow; we'd have just concocted some story about it all happening a long time after. I was so young, marriage wasn't in my head, not even with Keith. As for babies...'

Fiona could have predicted Maw's thoughts on a family.

'I never played with dolls or fussed over wee bairns. I found them... dull. Sorry, Fiona, I know that's probably not what you want to hear... Och, I'm sure *none* of this is...'

'I did ask.'

'Aye, you did.'

Maw proffered the whisky bottle in her direction, but Fiona declined, she needed to drive to Dingwall after. Maw poured herself another dram and placed the half-empty bottle on the carpet.

'It was about five months later I found out I was pregnant with you... Obviously, Keith ran a mile. I was heartbroken, and everyone took that I was terrified of the future. It was both things. I thought Keith would be heartbroken too, but he either wasn't or he covered it up well. He had to, he was living in the same house as your da.'

'Uncle Keith ghosted you?'

'If that's acting like I was dead, then yes.'

'So I'm confused, there's something in Morag's diaries about her confronting you and Uncle Keith in his back garden? Thinking you were having an affair...'

Maw paused, cogitating on the past like a cow chewing a cud.

'Hold your horses, something else happened before that. My brain hurts trying to remember it all. It was so long ago now...' Another sip of whisky. 'It's very fuzzy. I think the gist of it is a few years after I'd just had Morag he'd come round for Sunday dinner in the new house. He and Lillian were living in Inverness by then, that big place, you remember?'

Fiona nodded.

'Lillian had given up work but still no baby. Keith wasn't

himself, I asked if he was OK and he just unburdened everything. How he'd married in haste, running from what had happened with us, but thought that at least if they could have a family it would knit them together. It turned out Lillian had, now what was it? The doctors called it something awful...' Maw drummed her fingers on the arm of the chair, summoning the phrase. 'Oh yes, an inhospitable womb, and he wasn't any better, low count or something. So they were completely doomed to be childless. Then Lillian's mum subsequently died and Lillian ended up having a breakdown and being committed to hospital for electric shock treatment after pills and whatnot didn't work. I suggested adoption, but they couldn't entertain it because of her breakdown.'

'Oh my God, this is more tragic than one of those clog and shawl novels. I'd no idea!'

'Aye, the truth often is, for sure.' Fiona couldn't remember ever talking with her mum like this. They'd circled at arm's length for years so that anything other than a 'how are you?' felt like being waterboarded by MI5.

'Anyway, there was always something between your Uncle Keith and I, but the timing was all to cock. Our feelings didn't die, but I'd also grown used to your dad and Keith remained loyal to Lillian. But any time we met up, the chemistry reignited, especially after a glass of wine or two. Then Morag's pregnancy dragged the past back with it... Keeping the baby felt like the wrong thing, she'd no idea what it involved. She'd her whole life ahead of her; I was certain a baby would ruin it all. But that wasn't the only thing to contend with... Keith started hassling your da about letting him and Lillian bring up Morag's baby as their own, like she was up for grabs to just anyone. He even talked to me about it, like a dog with a bone, saying it would be keeping the baby in the family and Morag could still have contact – he'd no idea. Shona wasn't one of Lillian's bloody show dogs. It was bad enough for Morag Shona going at all, but imagine her being dangled just out of reach...? I kyboshed the idea completely. We didn't talk for an age – they couldn't forgive me. They were just desperately clutching at straws, I think. Then we went for that Sunday lunch when you got engaged, had a chat in the garden, mostly about Shona, about how it was probably for the best they hadn't adopted her. It wouldn't have been fair. It'd taken him a long while to understand that. But Morag was earwigging and thought she heard something else. Thought we'd been together for years. I couldn't admit we'd been talking about Shona. If she'd known Uncle Keith had wanted her, she would have gone understandably crazy.'

Maw stared off out of the window, then turned to face Fiona.

'I know you both never forgave me for giving Shona away, and your da tried to talk me into keeping her. He'd assured me Morag wouldn't miss school, that we could help her, that what happened to me wouldn't happen to her. But he'd no idea about the real depths of my despair, of my failed platform jump or even running away from the abortion. I was terrified of history repeating itself and Morag actually killing herself if she ever started to feel like I had, so much of the situation was already eerily similar. I needed to keep her safe. I was thinking of Shona too – a better life away from here, maybe she wouldn't repeat the mistakes we'd obviously made. Have a better chance with two adult parents rather than a schoolgirl like I'd been, like Morag would have been...

'I'd cut my heart from the whole situation because all I could see was me standing on that platform waiting for the train. I thought Morag would come round and realise this way was the better option. But, over time, I wasn't so sure. It was too late to reverse the adoption, so I begged the agency to ask if Morag could have pictures, but I now realise that was probably a bad thing too, giving her false hope of a reunion. I didn't realise the magnitude of my mistake for quite a few years, or rather I refused to believe it.'

Maw stumbled towards her Damascene moment, sipping more whisky to bolster her on what was a torturous admission of fallibility.

'Fiona, I... I couldn't admit I was ... wrong. At least *believing* I'd done the right thing gave me some kind of protection, from what, I've no idea. Myself, probably. Of all the mistakes I'd made, giving Shona away had been the biggest. Keeping you and then having Morag had been the best things, but again, that didn't register for years... I'd felt trapped for so long, but watching you and Morag achieve so much made me realise I used having a family as an excuse... I was frightened of life.

'The past is so hard to recall fully, but I do remember feeling terrified when I got my interview for Glasgow School of Art. Frightened they'd see through me. My parents thought I was getting above my station, "no one like us goes to art college", and I'd taken it to heart, started to believe them, even if I didn't admit it. So really, were you an accident or the answer to my prayers?'

Maw looked at her hands round the glass, as if noticing them for the first time. Fiona wanted to grab them and offer solace, but they never did that.

'The life I'd anticipated compared to the one I ended up in were miles apart. And yet I blamed *everything* on having a family for years. I blamed not being maternal, for not bonding with you. I truly believed the only reason I saddled myself with another child was to escape the cramped cottage in the woods. I blamed the fact that I wasn't swept off my feet with romance because I married the wrong brother... But I'd always had choices. I just preferred not to see them... Morag taught me all that. She taught me everything was as it should be, and that even though we'd not talked for years, we could talk right then. She showed me it was never too late to do anything. That's why I started volunteering at the shop...'

Maw inhaled deeply, her hand grasping the tumbler so hard her delicate bones strained against her skin. Fiona realised she was gawping.

'Why did you never talk to me about any of this?' she asked eventually, her brain brimming with so many questions. 'I realise that's a stupid thing to say, but you never had to keep that all inside. I know I don't talk to my girls about every detail of their lives, but if I thought something was useful, I'd speak about it.'

'Morag wanted me to tell you about the past before she died, but you're always so busy. Not playing my wee violin, I understand I've pulled away, not been the gushy mum your friends had. That's not me anyway, you know that. But the truth is, I don't know your girls, or you really... I've only myself to blame, for everything...'

'No, Maw. Don't blame yourself. Wanting to jump in front of a train isn't your fault. Postnatal depression isn't your fault. Falling pregnant wasn't *just* your fault. But one thing I would still like to understand, you and Uncle Keith? What actually happened?'

'Ah, yes.' Agnes shook her head sadly. 'You know the thing with chocolate and cakes is that when you have them they're a treat, but you don't want them for every meal. *That's* your Uncle Keith. I realised all this too late. Timing never was my thing.'

'So what was Da if Uncle Keith was a treat?'

Maw smiled fondly. 'Your da was neeps and tatties, my true north.' Her voice quivered, a scintilla of emotion betraying her. 'When your da died, I was numb for weeks. I thought it meant that I'd been right, Keith was the man for me all along. Your da had only been gone about three months when Keith turned up to make sure I was OK. I felt depleted, but nothing more. He was down this way for a client, did I want to go out for dinner. I said yes, it felt like a date. I got all dressed up, he drove us out to the Morangie. It was exciting. At first, it felt like no time had passed at all from being that young girl having hot chocolate at Pringles. But he'd changed, or maybe he'd always been that way and I'd just chosen not to see it.

Throughout dinner all he could talk about was himself. Golf and
Majorca featured heavily and he complained about Lillian's obsession with the dogs. Och, those bloody Pomeranians, you would
have thought he'd be glad she had something to love. He said she
treated them like children.'

'You don't say!' Fiona butted in, rolling her eyes.

'Aye! He barely asked me how I was coping, maybe he didn't
want to know. And that was when I thought I saw your da sitting at
another table. I got in a right old flap, started wailing. To give Keith
his dues, he was brilliant. He got me out of there, drove me home
and sat with me till I'd calmed down. He suggested I come away
with him to Paris for a break. He'd a business trip coming up,
Lillian never wanted to leave the dogs. He wouldn't mention it to
her, of course, she might get the wrong idea. I was in shock after
seeing your da, so I agreed. Anything to get away from here.'

'We always thought it was strange that you went on your own. It
makes sense now!'

'Aye. We had separate rooms, and I wandered round the
museums and art galleries while he was in his conference or whatever it was. In the Musée D'Orsay, I just stared at the Impressionists,
wishing I could turn back the clock, find my spark. Everything felt
too late. Then I remembered your da had bought me a box of
watercolours for my birthday the year before, tried to encourage
me. Those watercolours stayed in the back of the wardrobe while I
took in sewing and mending for extra cash. I liked sewing – it kept
me busy and was easier than opening the watercolours. Painting
felt too out of reach, what if I'd lost the ability?

'Anyway, your uncle was hoping the flame was still there. But all
I wanted to do was see the art in Paris. The heart wants what it
wants when it can't have it, then if it's served on a silver platter...'
Maw raised her eyebrows. 'I realised we had nothing in common,
and the one link we did have had died. Your da would have come

round those Paris galleries with me. He did when we went to Edinburgh, he liked me explaining what everything was, who the artists were, what the paintings meant. It wasn't until he died and I was stuck in Paris with his brother that I realised Lachlan had been the love of my life. I couldn't have done any better if I'd tried. He supported me in his own quiet way, never forced anything on me, even when he suspected I might love another, he let it play out, let me hang myself by my own rope.

'I'd still been caught up in the whole magical chemistry between Keith and myself for a few years after Shona was adopted. It gave me something to look forward to, that butterfly belly whenever I saw him. I'd never had it with your da... That night in the garden when Morag was listening, I think we talked about the past, about how different things might have been had I not got pregnant, something along those lines – silly talk really because I *had* got pregnant. But that night, Keith had said he'd never leave Lillian, what if she did something stupid? I realised I was stuck with your da. I mean, I wasn't, it was the eighties, people divorced, but I was terrified of everything... And your da, he was a good husband. Would I ever have left him? Keith and the Glasgow School of Art were lumped together in the same category of "what should have happened".

'I took to my bed for a week, told your da I'd caught a bug. Stewed under the covers, accusing everything, everyone, for all the terrible things in my life. I think I was a bit mad to be honest... When I came round, Morag was seething. She'd guessed right I'd got pregnant before I could be with Keith. But we were never "together". The idea, the excitement of "us" was bigger than the thing itself. Then before I could make it right, Morag left. That was another blow, but again, one I'd brought on myself. You were married, living away, and it was just your da and me. But you know what, it was probably the best thing because we fell into a routine and got to know each other as people for the first time without a family constantly being there. It took years, because I'd built up a wall, had tunnel vision about Keith. But in the end, your da and I were happy, and then he died. It felt so unfair.

'After I returned from Paris, I didn't want to leave the house, couldn't talk to anyone. I couldn't explain that I'd only fallen in love with my husband twenty-five years after I'd met him, but didn't realise until he was dead. This was more than grief, it felt like my whole life had been for nothing. My relationships with you two had disintegrated and the man I thought I'd loved was at best a friend.'

'What happened after Paris?' Fiona probed further. 'Keith always asked after you whenever we visited, but only if Lillian was making the tea. I was never sure if you kept in touch, you always evaded the question if I asked, so I stopped.'

'Lillian found out about the trip, some secretary spilled the beans. She turned up at the house, roared at me in the street, the dogs barking in the back of the car. Every bleeding net was twitching. I thought she was going to batter me.'

'But nothing happened!'

'Aye, but she didn't know that, or believe it. Would you? Adultery doesn't have to be purely physical. Keith and I'd spent twenty-odd years circling each other with just a few gropes to our name.'

Fiona cringed. Just the thought of creaky Keith and her ma sent her stomach into spasm.

'The unspent passion was obvious. Lillian was furious. I didn't see them after that, then she died last year, as you know. I spoke to Keith on the phone, and he was at Morag's funeral of course, but I didn't know what to say.'

'You could be friends, finally?'

Maw shrugged. Fiona saw a proud old woman who had lived in fear her entire life but didn't want anyone to know or help her. Morag had been right: the sisters had both told themselves a story about her that wasn't even halfway true. How could they have known any of this? Morag at least had decided to find out some of it before she died.

'It's such a shame you pushed me away after Da died. I could have helped, visited more.' Fiona felt tears on her cheeks.

'I was scared, Fiona. I've spent so long running. It's easier to keep on than to stop.'

'Maybe we should all just unpack our pasts, have a family heart-to-heart?'

Maw stared at her, narrowing her eyes to a laser pinpoint. 'I can never tell when you're joking.'

'Kind of, not really.' Fiona inched forward on the settee, like she was contemplating getting up. 'It might help. Katie and Laura are staying at the weekend. And Maggie's here for another week. There's ample opportunity.'

'I think the past can stay where it belongs.'

Fiona was surprised at how crestfallen she felt.

'But I'm more than happy to live in the moment and plan for the future...'

'You sounded just like Morag then.'

Maw beamed, the sun catching her eyes as it peeped from behind a cloud, fighting its way through the bleached nets.

32

'Maw thought that adoption would save Morag's life? Stop her from possibly killing herself?' Maggie asked flabbergasted once Fiona ground to a halt.

'Aye. It sounds so dramatic out of context, but all things considered, I can finally understand her motives. This explanation feels more tenable than saying you would have both had better lives. There were no guarantees the Pinks weren't planning to keep you in a Harry Potter cupboard.'

Maggie had sat stunned as Fiona talked at length, a skin forming on her neglected tea. Maw's tale wound its way through her, the vignette uncannily similar but with different players. 'I never outran the mistakes Maw made.' A wave of anguish tumbled over Maggie. 'Nature versus nurture – nature wins every time. The mess I'm in was predetermined.'

'Oh, Maggie. I'm sorry. I shouldn't have said anything.'

'No, you should. I need to know where I'm from. Roxie needs to know *my* truth.'

'Is now the right time? Not that I'm judging – I've no idea what you're telling her. Just maybe wait till you get home, so she's in her safe space?'

Maggie considered that might be the best option. Roxie had lasted this long without knowing the ins and outs of why things were the way they were in her parents' marriage, but it had been to her detriment. Parents were supposed to protect their children, but Roxie had been cooped up in a glass menagerie that had just shattered around her.

'Adam had a fling after Louis died.'

'The wee shite!' Fiona's eyebrows shot into her hairline. 'The devilishly handsome ones always let you down.'

'The fling wasn't straight away, it happened almost three years later, when I still wasn't in a great place, but back at work... I can relate to Maw standing on that train platform. I've been there, not on a platform, but battling dark thoughts, so frightening that I never felt safe.'

'Oh, Maggie. I'm truly sorry. That must have been terrifying.'

Maggie had not visited this fragment of her past for a while, having shoved all sorts of stuff in front of it, like the fur coats guarding the entrance to Narnia. Maggie would be sitting on the loo and images would flash across the back of her mind like a cine film: sobbing in a hospital bed as her milk came in, her breasts leaking nutrients for Louis, her tiny Pied Piper, who'd slipped away, taking all future children with him. These flashbacks insisted on playing out to the end; she had no choice but to endure, whether she was in the queue at Sainsbury's or having a blow-dry at Tortoise and Hair. If she breathed properly, she could ride past them. But if ignored, they rode on her back, squashing the air from her lungs until she acknowledged them.

Once her physical scars had started to heal, she'd been sent home from hospital. Home where an empty room throbbed with the loss of her boy. Roxie's cot had been made up, her baby mobile hung expectantly above, tiny clothes in all colours were folded away in the upcycled drawers she'd found at a flea market in Crystal Palace, lovingly sanded down and painted in a Venetian green chalk paint. All Maggie could think was she'd have to empty the drawers so they could use it for something else... She'd not seen Roxie at all, and when she came back from school she clung to her mum's legs, but Maggie couldn't give her a hug. Her scars were too painful and the fear of something dreadful happening to her only child overwhelmed her, so she'd retreated instead of keeping Roxie close. Loving Roxie now felt like a future scar to guard against. There was no way Maggie could survive grief like this again...

As the months rolled by, Maggie couldn't rid herself of egregious thoughts. She'd never had depression in her life, but when faced with her own head, she'd have done anything to escape... Maggie remembered standing in the shower with the razor, the water pouring into her eyes as she popped the blade out of the head, holding it in her fingers, pressing it against her arm. She'd forgotten to lock the door and Roxie had wandered in to use the loo. Maggie had dropped the blade, the clattering when it hit the bath tub temporarily shocking her out of her shadow place. Roxie didn't see, but she'd felt ashamed...

Maggie blinked, snapping back to the here and now in the kitchen, Fiona waiting for her to speak.

'I pushed everyone away – my parents, Nisha, work friends, Adam. I shut up inside myself, waging war on my thoughts. In the end, the doctors worked out it was a perfect storm of postnatal depression, the menopause and post-traumatic stress disorder from Louis's stillbirth. I was experiencing post-partum psychosis on top of everything else. Once they realised, things slowly improved.'

'What a dreadful experience. Are you OK now?'

'Yes. Apart from the occasional flashback, as you've seen. If I play them down, they don't feel as scary.'

'But flashbacks are scary! The menopause *is* scary – I hate it. And all the suffering you've experienced is so much worse. No one my age talks about it – it's up to your lot to wave the flag, warn those coming up the lines what to expect. I don't think we *should* play everything down. That's half the problem!'

'Yes, you're right. I just find the whole menopause and PTSD situation... excruciating. After all that's happened, I just want to distance myself from anything whenever I feel affected by hormones or flashbacks. My reaction to them both and Adam's fling – all contributed to where we find ourselves now.'

'Whatever and however you responded to losing your son and your fertility is completely normal. Don't let anyone tell you otherwise. Giving birth is traumatic enough without a beautiful baby at the end of it... Have you had couples therapy?'

Maggie shook her head.

'Can I ask why not?'

'I can't face it.'

'But it might help?'

'It's been this way so long now. It feels too late.'

'Why did you stay?'

This was the question Maggie had asked herself more recently.

'I was frightened of being on my own still feeling like I did, and he begged, said it was a stupid one-off, which I still believe. His childhood had been so unhappy, he couldn't bear it for Roxie without trying to fix the family.'

'So you think his fling *was* stupidity?'

'More like desperation.' Maggie breathed deeply, recalling the events leading up to their protracted demise...

Her parents had travelled down from West Kirby to look after Roxie so Adam and Maggie could reconnect. They were adrift on separate life rafts, the wind blowing them further apart. Adam had failed to talk her into an overnight stay in a posh hotel in town, relive their past, cocktails, dinner... She hadn't wanted to go away, she was terrified of intimacy. Maggie hadn't let him touch her since the birth. She always wore a T-shirt in bed and got undressed in the bathroom, avoiding any kind of accidental misinterpretation of a sexual come-on. Instead, she insisted they just went to dinner locally in Peckham, a trendy new small plates restaurant where you never felt satiated but still got fleeced, gorging on toast later at home. She thought it would be a distraction and give them something to bitch about instead of acknowledging the elephant in the room.

Just as Maggie had hoped they'd talked all around the houses, the wine certainly lending a helping hand, and she'd almost let her guard down and enjoyed herself until, on the way home, Adam had asked her if she still loved him...

'I suppose so,' she'd eventually answered, terrified of admitting anything any more.

'That's it? *I suppose so*?'

'I don't know what else to say. No? Would that be better?'

'No! Is that the truth? You don't love me?'

'No, I don't *not* love you. I don't love anything any more.'

The truth was, she could barely love herself, let alone anyone else. Even after two and a half years, the numbness had calcified so that it felt natural to just feel bleugh. Not what Maggie would consider depression, this was more comparable to living life under a light grey filter that permeated every second of every day.

'I lost Louis too, I lost my son. And now I've lost you.' Adam had stopped and grabbed her hands in front of McNeil's Chicken and Pizza takeaway, the overpowering fried chicken aroma wafting out onto the street. Maggie recalled looking past his face like a sulky teenager so she didn't have to engage, instead silently reading the jazzy yellow and red menu on the back wall, noting down prices and portion sizes. How come pizzas were more expensive than chicken? They should have eaten here... 'When will you let me back in? Roxie misses her mum. I miss my wife. It feels like you don't want either of us any more. Like Louis was everything.'

'That's not true!' she'd cried, snatching her eyes away from a meal deal of medium chicken and fries with a large drink. 'Louis isn't even here.'

'But we are! We're here and we need you.'

'It looks like you're doing just fine on your own.'

'What's that supposed to mean?'

'Roxie and Daddy, Daddy and Roxie, Mummy's not coming, just Daddy.'

'She's just reacting to being pushed away. I can appreciate why you're emotionally unavailable, but Roxie doesn't understand...'

'As I said, Adam was now Roxie's main carer, and I'd pushed everyone else away as well,' Maggie explained to Fiona. 'Though Nisha, my best friend, kept visiting even when I didn't want her to. Adam continued sleeping in the same bed when I said I wanted to be on my own. But I didn't want to be alone either; I didn't know what I wanted. To not feel like the living dead. I was angry at everything, even him, because no one understood. Of course Roxie was going to gravitate towards her dad in that situation. I think I was very difficult to be around at home...'

'All this is understandable though. A marriage would have to be coated in Teflon to survive that kind of pressure. You were seriously unwell and traumatised.'

'When I suggested maybe we needed some time out, a break from trying, or rather, a break from Adam trying and me feeling like a rabbit in the headlights, he agreed. I never expected him to, so admittedly it stung. He went away to York with some friends. I hoped the break might help, throwing me in with Roxie so she had no choice but to attach to me again. Looking back, it was ridiculous. How was ten days going to mend two and a half years? She was at school for some of it, but I remember the dread of the weekend. She had swimming and a party, and she was cross the whole time. She kept asking when Daddy was coming home. I realised how much he did for her and for me; I missed him, and rang him, even though we'd said no contact. He didn't answer and I felt stupid leaving a message. I felt like his complete absence woke me out of the coma.

'When Adam came back, he was distant. I wanted to touch him but felt terrified, nervous of initiating anything, we'd not been intimate for years. I stupidly thought an evening out might help, cancel out the last woeful experience. But the whole night was stilted and awkward. Even when things were terrible, it had never felt like he wasn't there... I really need a tea. You want one?'

Fiona shook her head as Maggie flicked the kettle, rinsing her cold drink down the sink.

'I feel for you, I really do, but I feel for Adam too. None of this is easy on either of you or Roxie. People mess up, we're human after all. Something I think our own kids forget. I know I felt Maw's behaviour towards Morag was unquestionably black and white because I'd no idea about her own upsetting past and how that affected things.'

Maggie sat back down with her tea and sipped it, almost burning her tongue. She preferred it lava hot, no other temperature would do. The teaspoons were resting across each other, unsettling her. She uncrossed them, setting them a neat one centimetre apart, their tips in line.

'We can be very quick to judge. But if you don't know every person's past all you do is take behaviour at face value... Adam asked me on a date a week after he returned, took me to a place I'd never been before, some cool restaurant in Soho. We actually had a great time, and that night we finally... got together. We started to gel and I distinctly remember feeling hopeful and told him I loved him.

About two weeks later, his iPad was in the kitchen when a text pinged. I've never looked at his phone, but I looked at the message on the iPad – it said from Aoife. I'd no idea who she was. Then another pinged from her. I don't know what made me open them – now I wish I hadn't. There were two massive long paragraphs about what a shame she wouldn't see him, that she'd had a great time in York and she hoped he worked it out with me. But, if not, he knew where to find her.'

'Ooohhhh,' Fiona cried. 'What did you do?'

'Went mental. He tried to deny anything had happened, but I knew, because of how he'd acted when he'd returned home. She'd been a last-minute addition to the trip, someone's younger sister. He finally confessed he'd been very drunk two days before the end of the holiday, smoked weed and they'd ended up snogging, then woke up in bed together. How convenient. I asked if that was it, and he couldn't hide it. They'd shagged once more, but that was it, then he came home and had a total crisis. When he realised I'd snapped out of the darkness, he wanted to fix our marriage, but she kept texting him. I'd never have known if she'd not bothered. I googled her – she had bright red hair like me but was much younger...'

'Oh my God, textbook.' Fiona grimaced.

'He was beside himself. The whole time this was unfolding, Roxie had a friend for a sleepover and we were trying to not shout in the bedroom, hissing at each other. Looking back, it was comedic, but at the time, horrendous.'

'Well, you know what they say? Tragedy plus time equals comedy.'

Maggie smiled ruefully. 'In the end, we agreed to start again. I could tell he was devastated at the thought of us splitting up after we'd finally started healing. Only I couldn't get past the betrayal. Especially knowing his thoughts on divorce and after everything we'd been through and only just getting back on the horse myself. I know I'd suggested the break, but I'd not expected him to run off with someone else. I'd not known what to expect, but not that. He'd thought we were over when he went to York. To be fair, it was like it was…'

'Oh, Maggie. What an absolute Ross and Rachel tornado. How did it end up like this if you started again?'

'I kept trying and trying to ignore that he'd shagged someone else. But it ate away at me, picked me apart. I was too scared to admit I'd probably caused it by pushing him away.'

'No, he made that choice, but therapy would have helped.'

'I couldn't bring it all up again, so we just swept the whole thing under a giant carpet and concentrated on Roxie. I didn't want to be a single mum, especially after all that horror, and I'd initially worried he'd do it again even though he went to great lengths to prove he wouldn't. So I protected myself from caring by pulling away, only more subtly this time, until I realised I was indifferent and that felt awful, even when we tried romantic getaways or dinner out. I started resenting how close he and Roxie were, how I'd ended being outside the tent again and it materialised in different ways: grumpy with him, snappy at Roxie. Basically I was jealous, but we still limped on regardless, Adam as parent of the year and me as the pariah. Then, a few years ago, I called time on the marriage and almost immediately my mum was diagnosed with cancer, so he asked if we could just wait. I think he thought I would change my mind, get distracted by Mum's illness, and he went on a charm offensive. But it was too late, it felt like a force majeure and I'd already decided I was going to find Morag. That became my new focus after parenting Roxie, even though by now she and I weren't exactly getting on. And so here we are. I know I snapped at him about the fling earlier, it sometimes irks me still, even now.'

'If it irks you, doesn't that make you think there's still a chance you have feelings?'

'Nope.' Maggie sipped her tea before it leaked vital heat.

'How can you be sure? They reappeared when Adam went to York. Look at Maw. Years and years believing she loved Keith when, in fact, she loved Da. She hadn't realised that the greatest love of her life had been standing next to her the entire time. *And* they were married!'

The front door opened, stalling Maggie's standard well-rehearsed reply.

'Hello? Is she back yet?' Adam called hopefully from the hallway.

33

The sun had succeeded – the sky proudly blazed cyan, the wind guiding Roxie towards her contemplative sanctuary with her picnic of trashy salty snacks. She'd wrapped her foot in the plastic bag procured from said trashy snack shop, securing it with a few hair clips she'd dug out of her shorts pocket. A cortège of seagulls accompanied her along the rocky outcrop towards the caves, calling aggressive greetings, their eyes on the prize. She'd bolted from the flat over an hour ago, or so she guessed.

She reached into her bag to check her phone but could only find her purse. She bent down and searched more thoroughly, finally tipping out her make-up bag, hairbrush, lip balms, crusty tissues, creased Maoam wrappers, an empty packet of Wotsits, a spare pair of dubious knickers, sanitary towels and a postcard from Ash of Mickey Mouse smoking a massive bifta stuck to the plastic bag of snacks. It wasn't there, but she had thought she felt it earlier – it must have been the edge of the hairbrush. She stuffed the entrails back inside her bag and squashed down the mild panic. She never went anywhere without her phone, it felt like an extension of herself, her comfort blanket if faced with tricky situations or bitchy girls at a party. She could just dive into her screen and escape, wiping them all away like a magic trick. She'd wanted to take some photos of the cave to use in recreating a painting of the fairy land. She contemplated returning to the flat to grab it, but she was already a third of the way, and there was nothing like stealing your own thunder by sneaking in the back door and getting caught doing so. She would simply have to carry on and burn the scenery into her retina.

She tried to block out the intrusive thoughts that crept up on her while she limped along the stony walkway. Her dad whom she thought could do no wrong had behaved like a walking and talking box set cliché. Roxie trudged fiercely forward, ignoring the pain in her foot, leaning on her stick that bit too hard. When she reached the hefty boulder with the footholds, she threw her bag and walking stick on the top and pulled herself up with her hands, her feet barely gracing the well-worn footings, her arms doing all the work. She sat atop, out of breath, pleased with herself. See – she didn't need anyone, she could do this by herself.

After scrambling down the long way round rather than risking the jump, the rest of the trek was a breeze. As she rounded the edge of the bluff, the cave's craggy arch rose far above her as impressively *Lord of the Rings* as she'd remembered. She limped over to a flat rock next to a pool and sat down, resting her foot out in front of her, congratulating herself on her impeccably timed visit – deserted just as she'd hoped. The orchestral sounds of the waves tolled loudly today. The sea was definitely nearer than last time, but there didn't appear to be any immediate danger of being cut off.

Before Roxie had devised her underhand scheme, forcing her dad up here to win her mum round on holiday, the plan had been for him to arrive Saturday and fly her home. But now the very idea of existing with him in an aeroplane's confined space knowing he was a snake felt untenable. She wished she didn't know, she wished she'd treated her throbbing zit instead of entertaining her nosy side and listening at the door. Now she had a head full of unwelcome information and a zit threatening to cut off one airway. The more her thoughts boiled like a steaming kettle, the more she wanted to hurl things. She felt stupid. Roxie hated feeling stupid, probably more than fake pockets if she was honest. And orange Fruitellas. Why did anything orange-flavoured taste like a headache?

She picked up the largest stone she could reach and hurled it in front of her. It hit another rock and bounced pitifully into a limpid pool. She needed height to throw her weight behind her frustration. Other satisfying missiles were just out of reach, so she heaved herself up and crawled over to the edge and started hurling them on her knees like a stack of snowballs.

'Arghhhhh!' Another stone flew through the air, shattering on rocks before plopping into a pool, possibly alarming molluscs and other innocent sea creatures. 'Fucking twats!' her throat straining from the words' vigour. A more clichéd, 'I hate you!' followed the same trajectory as an excellently pitched stone shaped like a dog's head that she managed to land in the actual crashing wave some way out. If she could summon up this kind of rage in shotput at school, she'd make the Olympics.

Her arm started to ache and she looked around quickly to see if anyone had crept up on her. The caves were still disconcertingly empty now the wind had dropped. She screamed full pelt, ripping her tonsils, ears ringing as the cave amplified her rage, throwing down the gauntlet to the hovering gulls.

Did she feel better? Not really. Her throat throbbed and she needed a drink. She opened her Coke and drained the can, burping loudly several times. Next, she attacked the snacks – a giant bag of Walkers Thai Sweet Chilli Sensations and some BBQ Pringles. She sat back down and stared out to sea, hand to mouth crunching her contraband. What was she going to do? She knew deep down she didn't really hate her dad. What bugged her was all these years her mum had known something Roxie didn't and never said a word. Every time Roxie had thrown an insult, or made it obvious she didn't want her mum there, she'd sucked it up like poison. A freight train of recognition hit her: maybe her mum didn't love Louis more, maybe she'd just been hiding her feelings about everything. About Adam. Why were her parents such twats? Why hide things and pretend, making her think her mum was pining after Louis when in fact that wasn't the entire story? At least being here she'd managed to unravel her head, and she wanted to ask her mum what she'd meant when she'd said 'It's not just one thing.' What other things had happened apart from Louis dying and her mum never getting over it? Surely an affair was the end? One thing was concrete, her parents were splitting up and there wasn't anything she could do to stop it. Two homes, two bedrooms, maybe more kids for her dad one day? The horror of step-siblings after years of being an only child, of step-parents, sharing them with other people…

As Roxie catastrophised her future, the air shifted around her. She didn't notice at first, her eyes unseeing, locked somewhere else in a house she'd not yet visited with babies not yet conceived and arguments waiting to explode. The future wasn't looking bright. In fact, the future was clouding over rather rapidly. The sea had disappeared in less than five minutes. A thick bank of white mist moved steadily towards her, swirling like smoke, the bottom of the cloud greedily consuming the rock pools, while the top dawdled, engulfing gulls and the blue sky, unapologetically absorbing them whole until all that remained was white marshmallowy fluff.

Roxie hastily stuffed her crisps back into her bag and looked towards the way she had just come. The cloud was already rolling over the rocks, obscuring everything. She glanced over her shoulder, everything still intact, the cave mouth, the rocks, the cliff face, all visible like a theatre set, whilst standing front stage looking out over the orchestra pit all Roxie could see was a blank canvas. The cloud was going to catch her if she didn't run. Shit, she couldn't outrun a hedgehog, let alone some weird ghostly mist that ate up the sun, dropping the temperature to somewhere between February and March. This wasn't like the morning mist she'd thundered out in earlier, it was far more sinister.

Roxie pulled her hoodie over her head and hobbled down from the rock, heading as quickly as she could without slipping towards the back of the cave, using her walking stick to test the ground. Even the gulls' cries were muffled, but the crashing waves sounded as loud as ever. Hadn't Angus mentioned the tide got higher incrementally each day? Was this why no one had ventured out here today, because they knew it was about to be high tide?

Roxie turned round again as she stepped in a puddle; the fog seemed to be pursuing her, tendrils snaking forwards hovering over the rock she'd been sitting on a few minutes before. She shivered – it felt sentient, like it was trying hard to scare her shitless. She pulled her foot out of the water, at least it was her trainer and not the cast, but still, annoying. She squelched onward, a plan feverishly hatching as she recalled part of her conversation with Angus, something about the legend of the cave and where it might lead. Maybe it was time to discover if the legend was real, either that or get eaten by the flesh-melting fog in the horror movie projecting inside her head.

There wasn't time to feel actual fear, there was just action as Roxie slipped and slid over the stones in a futile attempt to reach a mythical escape route. The one time she hadn't got her phone. Typical! If that was the reason she was about to die, the world was indeed an unfair place. At least it would be some kind of vindication for all kids shouted at by adults about their obsession with phones. Perhaps her death wouldn't be in vain as parents everywhere realised one day a phone could save your life...

34

'The haars normally last a few hours, depending on the wind and how hot the sun is.' Fiona explained away the fog that had descended from the heavens blanketing the whole village in candy floss.

Maggie struggled to keep up with Adam – he was in full panic mode, striding ahead, his legs itching to cover more ground than they were capable of. Maggie could barely see him as they headed towards Issy's shop. She almost bumped into a man walking a white terrier like a teeny floating cloud on a lead and just as she recovered from stepping on the dog, a woman pushing a pram loomed out of the fog running her off the pavement.

'I've never experienced anything like it before,' she said as the woman apologised. 'I literally cannot see my hand in front of my face.'

'It's like city smog before the Clean Air Act, except the haar is natural. It comes in off the sea when the warm air meets the cold water. You can't drive in this, it's too dangerous.'

Just then a maverick delivery van materialised from nowhere, its headlights diminished to the glimmer of two tealights.

'Adam, you've walked past it!' Fiona called into the brume as they pulled up outside Trading Post, just the door and window visible. Maggie could hear gulls and the distant crash of waves, but it felt like an overlaid soundtrack of a mock-up hinting at a seaside reality.

'Keep the door shut!' Issy called from the counter as they pushed the door open. 'I don't want it in here.'

Once inside with the overhead lights on and the old-school funk playing, they almost forgot they were trapped in a pea-souper until someone looked outside.

'Are you OK? Angus is on his way over. He'll help with the search.'

'When you saw her, did you see which direction she headed off in?' Adam asked, wringing his hands.

'She disappeared round the corner. Maybe ask in one of the shops? There's another convenience store she may have popped into, not wanting to see me? Do you not think she'll just come back in this weather? Or hang out in a café? It's no fun when it's like this.'

'Aye, but she could have gone further afield,' Fiona replied. 'There's no way of knowing.'

'One of us should stay at the flat in case she turns up?' Adam suggested.

Fiona agreed to head back in case Roxie arrived like a Brontë heroine out of the mist.

Maggie was trying hard not to rehash the row. She didn't for one second think Roxie had run away, she wasn't that dramatic. She was just angry. But this sea haar had rammed its murky fingers into the machinery, ramping up the ante, dropping unsavoury scenarios inside her head. Maggie berated herself. She scarcely told her daughter she loved her. It sat on her lips most days, but faced with Roxie's derision, she always backed down. Maggie wished she told her more often. In Maggie's childhood, 'love yous' hadn't been bandied around in the same vein as 'tidy your room'. Her buttoned-up dad had told her he loved her on her wedding day and again when she was trapped in her own sea haar after Louis died. He thought the rarity of his utterance would somehow break the evil spell of her incarceration, wake her from slumber like true love's kiss. It didn't. Maggie believed the true meaning of 'I love you' came without any expectation. It couldn't heal someone, it couldn't make someone stay, it couldn't wipe away pain, it just was. Like the precept – you don't give to receive, but on most occasions, it was nice to hear. Maggie realised she should have said it more often, regardless, instead of thinking about her own loss handing it over. What was the worst that could happen...? The worst had already shown its face...

The bell above the door tinkled and Angus stood, filling the frame, mist swirling behind him. Maggie fully expected him to be wearing a cape.

'You'll find her. She's just flexing her muscles, they all do it,' Issy said, squeezing her hand before they left.

Outside, the obstinate haar showed no signs of shifting. Ghostly figures intermittently passed by, only to instantly vanish on their way. Adam decided they would try the convenience store then split up. They edged round the pavement until they reached Cosy Corner. Angus followed them inside. Adam flashed his phone at the middle-aged man behind the counter, showing him a picture of Roxie.

'Sorry to bother you, but has this girl been in here today?'

'Oh aye. She had a cast on her leg.'

'Yes! That's her. Can you tell me anything. We're trying to find her in this fog.'

'Well, she bought some snacks, crisps I think. She did ask for an extra plastic bag. I saw her wrap it over her cast before she headed towards the harbour.'

Angus started furiously scribbling on his pad and showed them. *She will have headed to the caves or the dunes if she's covered her foot.*

'I know where the dunes are,' Maggie said, eager to get going. 'Angus, will you go to the caves?'

More scribbling.

It's going to be high tide in the caves soon.

'Oh shit.' Panic rose into Maggie's throat. 'You shouldn't go there.'

'You've got about thirty to forty minutes,' the man behind the counter interrupted. 'If you run. It should be OK. The dunes will be fine.'

'I should go to the caves then,' Adam insisted.

Angus shook his head.

I can go. I know the way really well. You could take a wrong turn in this weather and end up trapped. I have my phone, I'll be OK.

'Let Angus go,' Maggie pleaded. 'We can go to the dunes. We won't get lost.'

She watched Angus's back fade into the fog in front of the sea wall, his shoulders hunched, waves breaking on the veiled shore. Maggie led Adam down the steps, sinking immediately into the yielding sand, and headed for the dunes. She wrapped her coat around herself, glasses already steaming up. *Please keep her safe. I promise to spend more time with her, tell her I love her, treat her to a whole day shopping, let her have as many sleepovers as she wants, even if I can't cope with the racket. She can have pizza every meal...* Maggie bargained her way across the beach to the more solid ground where last night's tide had carved methodical ridges, and tiny curlicues of sand disclosed life existing beneath their feet. Adam walked next to her, no doubt chasing similar thoughts.

'She'll be OK, won't she?' Maggie said into the fog.

'Of course. Come on, we can't think otherwise. She's headstrong and has just decided to show us who's boss.' Adam grabbed her hand and she didn't let go. 'How the fuck does she even know what rhetorical means?'

'She probably learned it from TikTok,' Maggie said smiling. 'It's where she gets all her information. That and YouTube.'

'This is all my fault,' Adam said quietly. 'She needs to know what happened, that you did nothing wrong.'

'Adam, it isn't! You were pushed to your limit living with a wife who didn't know if she was dead or alive. Doing everything without complaining.'

'Who does that, though? You'd birthed our dead son and I repaid you by shagging that girl. I can't even remember her name now. Something unpronounceable.'

'Aoife.'

He hung his head.

'Yeah. God, I'm such a dick.'

Maggie stopped walking, unlacing her fingers from his.

'What? We need to get to the dunes.'

'You are a dick... But so am I – our only daughter thinks I loved poor Louis more than her. We can't tell Roxie all the gory details of what happened in our marriage. Imagine being her age and your parents spilling their darkest secrets... You'd be sick in your mouth.'

Adam raised his eyebrows and looked right at her, his lips pursed in mock indignation, his shiny widow's peak creasing with hyperbolic overreaction.

'Oh yeah, I forgot you grew up like that. No skeletons in your closet.'

'Let's just concentrate on finding her. She might not even want to come with us. The main thing is we get her back to the flat safe and sound.'

'This is like that time when she got lost at Disneyland in Belle's

Kingdom. Remember?' Maggie smiled at the memory, not amusing at the time.

'Oh Christ, yes! You were just pregnant, kept puking in the bins, and she wandered off following that tall one, a dog, what's he called?'

'Goofy! She assumed he was the beast. Everyone thought we were terrible parents, that woman was so fucking judgy, thinking I was hung-over. How awful though. At least Roxie couldn't leave the park. This feels a lot worse...'

Maggie's phone rang, activating fight-or-flight mode. It was Fiona.

'I thought I should let you know I've called the coastguard as a precaution. If Roxie's near the caves, then they need to know and be prepared. We have to cover all bases. The tide's tricky round that part of the coast and can cut it off for hours. There's not much room for manoeuvre and very little high ground. I'm not trying to worry you, I just think it's for the best.'

'OK, thanks, bye.' Adam glanced at Maggie quizzically. 'Roxie!' she screamed frenziedly into the mist. 'It's Mum! We're sorry. Please. Let's go home.'

Nothing but incessant gull screeches and surf hissing on the sand answered back. Life carried on while Maggie hovered in freeze-frame once more...

35

Without a phone she could handily use as a torch (see, parents, phones are digital Swiss army knives), Roxie ground to a halt in the tunnel. She'd been inching up for about fifteen minutes, before sliding partway down and starting again. Progress was slow. The stale seaweed smell lay on an olfactory scale somewhere between sulphur and a really rancid fart. She was wasting time and it just wasn't worth risking even if the legend were actually true and the smugglers' pathway wound all the way to the top of the cliffs. It was still a steep incline that needed both feet to be in working order.

Roxie gave in, skidding gently on rocks towards the mouth of the tunnel, her bum landing in a puddle. Meanwhile, the mist had fully claimed the shore, grinding to a halt halfway under the cave's overhang, a ragged grey curtain draping across the menacing backdrop of the oncoming sea. There were precious few avenues back the way she had come, the mist masking the one approach she was certain she'd be able to manage confidently.

She spotted a rock lording it above the rest and limped towards it, the tide just beginning to touch it. She stood on top as a wave broke around her, spray splattering her legs. Behind her, the tide receded, but it wouldn't be long before she was an island, like Blake Lively in that shark film. Clueless about the exact height of the tide, Roxie was left with one tool in her Get Out of Here arsenal...

'HELP! HELP ME! I'M TRAPPED!'

The fog flattened her yells, absorbing her urgency.

She tried again, this time screaming, hysteria bubbling in her chest. 'PLEASE HELP, I'M IN THE CAVE BY THE TUNNEL! HELP!'

She repeated her plea until she grew hoarse, her words dwindling, along with her courage. Fear tightened its chokehold until she couldn't stop the tears. Not knowing what was in store was almost worse than a tidal wave rushing at her full pelt. She sat down, defeated, head in hands. As water swirled around her, Roxie was suddenly hit with a memory: her mum in bed ill after Louis had died. Roxie had taken her a biscuit to eat. She'd found her crying into a blue teddy bear with an L embroidered on its belly.

'Why you crying?'

Maggie had looked at her. Roxie remembered feeling frightened, her mum looked like she'd stepped out of her skin and an imposter had sneaked in her place.

'I'm scared, Roxie. I'm scared I'll lose you too.' Even her voice was wrong, wispy and strained, like the effort of speech was beyond her grasp.

'I'm here, Mummy.'

Her mum had pulled her into the bed for a cuddle, but it had felt like someone desperately clawing at life to stave off drowning. Roxie remembered crushing the biscuit in her hand and being worried she would get told off for dropping crumbs in the bed.

Was her life flashing before her because she was about to die? Isn't that what happened?

Another wave crashed around her – would she remain an island or would the tide take the rock too...? How had it reached her in such a short space of time? She shouldn't have left the bowels of the cave. As she looked back now, she was cut off. Not badly, but it meant getting soaked wading through the water to the slightly higher ground. She didn't know what was the best option...

'I'm sorry I'm such a grumpy fucker,' she whimpered into the fog. 'I'm sorry I've been so mean to Mum. Please, just make sure I can get home. Please. I'll be better. Don't make this my karma. I don't hate Dad. I-I... I just wish they wouldn't get divorced...'

Another wave crashed, this time the spray hitting as far as her arms. Panic surged.

'I'm sorry! I'm sorry! Please, let me get out of here...' She tried to control her breathing, sobs stifling the oxygen so she felt even more frightened. The rock wasn't going to submerge any time soon, but what if it did eventually? 'I'M SORRY!!!!! I PROMISE I'LL BE BETTER!'

'ROXIE! IS THAT YOU?!'

Roxie's adrenaline pumped, cutting off her sobs.

'YES! AT THE TUNNEL!'

'HANG ON, I'M COMING!'

Roxie waited for the disembodied voice to find her. It wasn't her dad, he sounded too young. Maybe one of the coastguards?

Splashing preceded the emergence of a shadowy figure ten metres in front of her, his jeans soaked up to his thighs, his hood pulled over his head. A wave sluiced towards him over his knees. The water was suddenly deep.

'Angus!? Was that you shouting?'

He nodded.

'You can shout but you won't speak?' she almost laughed, hysteria not far behind her sobs.

'God, you're annoying!'

Roxie's heart burst with gratitude and also something else.

'Sorry,' she replied chastened. 'Thank you for coming to get me.'

Angus peeled his hood off and stopped a few metres in front of her, pulling out his phone and typing a text before tucking it inside his T-shirt top pocket to try to keep dry. He sucked in his lips, as if forbidding more words.

Roxie gathered her bag up and waited for him at the edge of her rock. He climbed up and she threw herself at him, crying, laughing, not knowing what she was doing but just so glad she wasn't going to die alone. They would be like Leo and Kate on the door, only she wouldn't push Angus off into the icy sea; the rock was big enough for both of them.

Angus patted her back as she snotted on his T-shirt. She suddenly realised she was being overly dramatic and pulled back, self-conscious. She also hadn't brushed her teeth that morning...

'I like your accent.' Roxie wanted to smash her own face in for such a trite utterance when they might not get out of here alive. 'Sorry, I'm not gonna lie, I don't know what to say. Is the tide in as far as it comes? Can we get back?'

Angus scratched his cheek thoughtfully and glanced down at her injured foot encased in its blue plastic bag. 'Can you walk on that?'

Roxie stared at him in a daze, so unused to hearing his voice.

'Roxie!'

'Yes, I can walk, slowly though.'

'We're almost out of time here, but we can make it over there...' He pointed to the right. 'We should be able to paddle through. Your cast will have to suffer or you OK having a piggyback?'

For the second time that week, Roxie found herself grasping Angus's shoulders as he strode steadily through the water...

* * *

Angus was on high alert. He didn't want Roxie to know they needed to reach the boulder before the tide completely cut them off. The water had surged since his arrival and in places he was wading as far as his thighs, meaning he could barely give attention to a more pressing matter. He'd broken the silence. His mum was going to have a fit, everyone would make such a big deal about it. He wasn't sure he was ready to speak to the whole world. He'd shouted because it was the only way he was going to find Roxie in the haar. Admittedly, a life-and-death situation was allowed in the addendum he'd swiftly added to the rules in his head directly before breaking his vow. Previously, the rules had been silence whatever the weather. He was literally treading new ground. His nose sniffed out the boulder as he felt his way along the seabed, his internal satnav well acquainted with the vagaries underfoot as the water now almost reached his waist.

'You're going to have to climb if I lift you up here. The path's higher than the tide on the other side.' He clumsily shoved Roxie over his head, no time to worry about his hands on her bum as a wave hit him sideways, dragging him into another rock, smashing his arm.

'Angus!!!!!'

His head went under for a second as he inhaled a lungful of water, coughing to expel it. Another smaller wave hit, then he steadied himself, waded towards Roxie, but he felt like he was now striding in mud, his progress slow. His arm hurt – he'd better not have broken it.

'Are you OK?' She leaned down on her tummy and stretched out her hands. He grabbed her fingertips, holding on while the current tried to drag him into a slimy crevasse.

'I'll pull you in, I'm too heavy.'

When the swell dramatically receded, he knew he was in trouble. A breaker exploded over the rocks to his left, smashing his side, his fingers slipping out of Roxie's tenuous grip as the undertow drove him right into the crevasse this time.

'Angus!' He could just about hear Roxie's urgent cries underneath the smashing waves.

'I'm stuck!' Water sloshed into his mouth as yet another swell forced itself over him. 'My foot's trapped.'

'Pull it!'

'I am!' He glanced down but couldn't see anything apart from fronds of swaying brown egg wrack. He tugged harder, but his feet were tightly laced in his Jordan Maxs. Why today of all days had he tied them? He usually left them loose for easy access.

'Shit, Angus. Is it your whole foot?'

Another wave crashed over him.

'I'm gonna have to undo the laces,' he managed to spit out.

As he dipped under, he had no time to panic. His fingers fumbled as the current strove to tow him with it. He came up for air twice, unable to tease the knot free.

'I can't do it.' Now he started to panic. He was hindered by an injured girl who would take too long to get help...

'I have an idea!' Roxie yelled.

He watched her tip her bag upside down and grab hold of a smaller zip-up black bag. She rooted around, triumphantly drawing something out.

'Nail clippers!'

She leaned as far as she could out towards him, but they couldn't quite reach.

'I need a big wave!' he shouted.

Roxie rested, awaiting instruction.

They had two near misses where the clippers almost fell into the depths, then the swell receded optimistically.

'This is it!' As the water swilled over the rocks, Angus was buoyed up that vital few centimetres, allowing him to grab the clippers from Roxie's pincer grasp before he slipped back down in his bear trap.

'Hurry!' she pleaded, like he didn't already know he had to!

Angus clutched the clippers, spinning them round so the blades activated, and plunged underwater, snipping at his laces, managing to cut through one side, shredding it through the holes until the Jordans released his ankle and he joggled his foot out.

'I'm free!' But he didn't want to leave his Jordans behind. They'd been his birthday present from Morag. He slid under the surface and slipped his trainer up from the bottom of the crack to the wider gap at the top, yanking it out of the water. He waded over to the rock, chucking the trainer on top, the soggy missile almost hitting Roxie. She leaned down again, reaching out for him.

'I'm stronger than I look!' He seized her arms, pain shooting down his own and she moved backwards while he gripped the slope with his bare foot and one trainer, gradually heaving himself out of the swill.

He lay face down on the rock for a moment, his breath bubbling. 'Thanks for saving my life.'

'Thanks for saving mine. Angus, I thought you were a goner!'

He rolled onto his back and stared at her, shaking his head, testing his arm. He could move it OK, it was only bleeding. Roxie was trying hard not to cry. He extended his arm and grabbed her hand. To be fair, he wasn't far from blubbing himself. That was possibly the closest he'd come to death since the car crash, but he couldn't remember that, so it didn't count. He squeezed her fingers.

'I'm like a cat; take more than that to get me. My phone might be fucked though.'

They briefly rested, both gazing at the sky before Angus eased up to standing, ramming his foot into his sodden trainer. Offering his hand, he pulled her up, drawing her into a wet hug, her warmth delaying the inevitable shivers generating in his bones. He absently kissed the top of her head, and when he realised, he swiftly switched to business mode.

'Come on, our parents have probably shat themselves.'

The jump down wasn't as treacherous, but it was hard to ascertain with the fog blotting out their landing.

'I can walk the rest,' she said once Angus had set her down like a ballerina.

'Are you sure?' Angus fretted he was using up his emergency allowance on frivolous words.

'Yes, I'll be fine. You've just had a major trauma.' She smiled at him and his insides spun into a double helix despite everything. Even with globby eye make-up and hair like a rat's nest, she was still profoundly more interesting than other girls. He couldn't think of anyone else he'd rather have a near-death experience with.

They trudged the remainder of the way, both soaked and shivering, waves breaking just out of reach, a few teasing them with spray. Just before the rocky outcrop dissolved into sand, Angus was forced to speak.

'Roxie, can you keep my secret?'

She turned to look at him quizzically.

'Oh, right. You're not going to talk any more?' She sounded so disappointed.

'I... I don't... No, not yet.'

'So you will at some point?'

'I don't know.'

'But you broke the seal.'

'It was an emergency.'

She nodded.

'Look, I'm not saying never. I just want to keep it to myself for a bit... until I'm ready.'

'I'll zip my lips.'

He smiled.

'One thing, will you never talk to me again?'

'I don't know, I'll see. You can take the secret with you when you leave.'

She saluted him just as a voice called out through the fog some distance away.

'Roxie! Are you there? Are you OK?'

'Mum! I'm fine.'

Maggie suddenly appeared, running gawkily towards them across the sand like a slow-mo nana about to tumble arse over tit. She threw herself at Roxie, squashing her in her arms, making her cry at the same time.

'I'm sorry we're shit. I've been so worried. I couldn't lose you. I'm sorry you think I love Louis more than you. Nothing could be further from the truth. I'm no good... at talking, at a lot of things, it seems...' She hugged a sobbing Roxie even harder.

'Well, I guess my work here is done,' Angus said before he could stop himself. 'Fuck!'

'Angus! You spoke!' Maggie squawked. 'What happened, you're both soaked? Angus, you're shaking.'

'Mum, you can't tell anyone. It's a secret.'

'Can't tell anyone what?!' Issy emerged from the mist with Adam in tow. She strode over the sand in a more glacial manner, while Adam headed in a straight line for Roxie, enveloping her and Maggie in a hug.

'Fuck's sake!' Angus groaned again, his teeth chattering.

'Bloody hell, you spoke!' Issy shouted.

He shook his head and zipped his lips, his whole body shaking now.

'No, oh no! You spoke, I heard you! Don't throw away the key now, not after all this time!' Issy tramped over to him and hugged him despite his waterlogged clothes. 'I want to hear my boy's voice.

You don't know how much I've missed it.' And then she promptly burst into tears.

Angus squirmed, unacquainted with such excessive emotional leakage.

'Mum, stop. Fuck's sake.'

'Angus, you've made me so happy,' Issy cried. 'Just one thing, couldn't the first thing you say to me not be "fuck"?'

A phone started ringing.

'It's mine, sorry.' Maggie answered it. 'Fiona!'

Everyone tried hard not to eavesdrop on Fiona's tinny reply.

'Bloody hell, really? What timing. OK, she's with us and seems all right. We'll be back in a bit. I think we'll have to go to hospital at some point to get a new cast.'

'Everything OK?' Issy asked.

'I don't know. Fiona's mum's just turned up at the flat. Apparently she wants to meet me and Roxie.'

36

What had prompted Agnes to order an extravagant taxi after her morning shift at the Cancer Research charity shop? There wasn't a stand-alone reason, the last week had swept in an accretion of instances, driving open the crack in the door. Agnes had never subscribed to the dictum, it's good to talk. Why would anyone want to listen to the contents of your head? Surely it would just upset everyone (and you) to rehash the past – so emotionally chaotic! But ever since Fiona had released her floodgates, well, Agnes just wanted to keep on talking. The earth hadn't swallowed her up and she realised she'd missed so much. Knowing her long-lost grand-daughter and great-granddaughter were heading home without her saying hello didn't sit well. Morag would be raging at her mother's hesitation, but, more importantly, Agnes would be cross with herself if she let them go without at least a proper introduction.

As she washed her hands in the bathroom, Morag's toothbrush stared at her from the glass next to the cold tap. She swallowed the lump in her throat and inspected her face in the mirror. She was old. It didn't matter how much she told herself age was a state of mind, the wrinkles and the bags had other ideas. Still, anyone over twenty was old to a teenager, so she wasn't alone.

Nerves urged another pee, but she ignored it. How could you be nervous of a child? Children were different these days. They spoke their mind, didn't wait for something to happen, they *made* it happen. Look at that Greta Thunberg. Agnes found it intimidating. Life was easier without all that. But not necessarily better.

When she was waiting in the living room with Fiona, her foot tapping, she thought of all the times she could have been here, if she'd just been honest, if she'd not buried her own story. She'd no idea what her mother's story was, no one in her family had ever talked about anything. Shame wielded its hand easily. Truths were woven into lies and life was a charade. She idly wondered how many generations that went back? Maybe she could change it.

'Has Maggie read the diaries?'

'Aye, and Roxie before you ask.'

Agnes was shocked. The child had read *that*? Before she could digest the information properly, the flat door opened and voices and feet clattered into the hallway.

'Dad, I'm fine, I don't need to go to the hospital right now. Just leave it!'

'We're in here,' Fiona called from the living room.

Agnes stood, clasping her hands in front of her expectantly. A tall dark man with a widow's peak and intense eyes walked in, followed by Maggie, who could have been Morag at the same age, though Agnes wouldn't honestly know, Morag had cut her off by then. The girl looked a fright. Well, she *had* almost drowned in the cave, so she was forgiven that. She had a plastic bag on her foot. Was that a strange London trend?

'Hello...?' Maggie looked stricken.

'Agnes,' Fiona said. 'Sorry, I should've said. Maggie just knows you as my mum.'

'Hi, Agnes,' Maggie said. 'I'm afraid we're a bit of a state. I'm sure Fiona's told you what happened.'

Fiona had mentioned something about an argument, and Roxie running away. Things didn't change that much then. Morag was always running away...

'Aye, briefly. How are you now, Roxie?'

'Fine thanks.' She didn't look fine. She looked like she needed a good scrub and a hairbrush. 'I'm just going to get changed...'

'I'm Adam,' the husband said and walked over to shake her hand, almost crushing it.

'Would everyone like tea?' Fiona said rather brightly, jumping up from the sofa.

'I'll help,' Adam offered.

It was confusing, Fiona had said Adam and Maggie weren't together, but the way he'd just looked at Maggie, well, Agnes knew what *that* look meant...

* * *

Adam opened cupboards looking for mugs. This was possibly one of the most surreal moments in his life. His daughter had almost drowned in a cave and now he was making tea with his estranged aunty-in-law in a kind of Pinter-esque farce. What the actual fuck.

'Are you OK?' Fiona asked quietly. 'This must feel all a bit much after what's just happened. I didn't feel I could tell her to go away. She never visits of her own accord.'

Adam shut the cupboard he was aimlessly staring into (rice and pasta bows in Kilner jars) and turned round, unable to stymie his verbal diarrhoea. 'You know what, it is. But this is a big deal for Maggie. Roxie is actually OK. It's just strange seeing Maggie with people who look like her, and *are* her. Not that her parents weren't her parents, they were. But I can see you look like her, and Agnes does too, a bit. I think this is what she needs right now.'

Fiona remained strangely silent, seemingly struggling for words while she opened the right cupboard for mugs. When her back was turned, she spoke.

'Please don't think I'm speaking out of turn, but Maggie told me everything.'

'Everything?' No one knew 'everything'. Well, apart from a few friends. But they didn't judge, or at least he hoped they didn't. Oh, and Nisha. But Nisha inexplicably didn't judge either. She'd been their cheerleader. Just a shame Maggie didn't listen...

'Aye, the whole shebang.' Fiona nailed him with a gimlet stare, laying the mugs on the table. 'I think it's terrible what happened, losing your son like that, but Maggie lost herself as well. Hard to come back from that.'

'I know. We're over, she's made it clear.'

'Aye, so she says. And I'm not interfering with a cosy fireside chat about the easy way to win her back. I'm not sure you can, but I do think this isn't as black and white as she believes. Sometimes distance can fuel the missing links, reattach them. What she might need is real space, not you possibly running off and hitching your wagon to the next available horse.'

Adam laughed out loud, mortified. Fiona had covered more ground in a few sentences than any of his friends had in seven years...

'Sorry, I think I've got myself all het up about it. From the outside, I can see how you fit together. I obviously can't see inside her head, but her mum went through something similar.'

'Morag?'

Fiona nodded, filling the kettle from the tap. 'Aye. She'd been with this guy for years. Lovely man, adored her; they met travelling and formed the band. Had some success. Anyway, long story short,

Morag contracted breast cancer the first time, became infertile, it was a real blow. She pushed Casey away, didn't want to saddle him with her infertility. He would have moved to Benlachie, he loved Scotland – he was Canadian – but she wouldn't have it. She loved him, but she couldn't handle being beholden to his wishes to have a family. She set him free.'

Fiona leaned over towards the windowsill, where a menagerie of plants thrived amongst knick-knacks and picked out a card resting against a plant pot.

'She kept a card he sent her when he was touring and she'd returned here to see if Maggie was going to contact her. He sent it over twenty years ago, yet she never threw it away. The torch for him burned bright. He married, had kids, but he was bawling his eyes out at the back of her funeral service. She never met anyone else like him.'

'What do you suggest?'

'Walk away.'

Adam thought he'd misheard her.

'You have nothing to lose. It may well remain as it is, but I think trying to win her round could make it worse. If she's like her mother, she needs to hoist herself by her own petard but have a way back in. Casey believed it was the end and moved on, but his heart was always hers...'

'Bloody hell, this all sounds like one of those tragic country songs.'

'Aye, it does. Shall we make the tea before they send the lifeboats for us? We actually need biscuits...'

* * *

Roxie walked into the living room just as the pleasantries between her mum and Agnes dried up. They both stared at her, desperately expecting a lifeline, evidently skirting round the mountainous pretext of Maggie's visit to Benlachie. The entire day had become a surreal out-of-body experience, and an involuntary audience with her great-granny who'd ruined everyone's lives was the cherry on top. Her mum had briefly tried to explain Maw's motives on the way back to the flat.

'Maw isn't who you think she is. She isn't a bad person. She had her reasons...' But Roxie was too exhausted to give a toss, no one in her family appeared to be who they said they were... She had more exhilarating things to contemplate: Angus had kissed her head and was speaking, but she'd screwed everything up by dismissing him before the final curtain. She was convinced the kiss had been a post-near-death accident. She was leaving tomorrow, she'd not see him until... who knew? Boys at home were ten-year-olds laughing at YouTube videos of farting cats in comparison. She just wished she could stay longer, leave Dad to go home on his own. He deserved it after all that shit he'd just shovelled into her life.

'So you're the one who ran away,' Maw said, looking her in the eye.

And here she was wasting her last day being belittled when she could have been hanging with Angus. Angus who had risked his life for her...

'Actually, I didn't run away,' she snapped. 'I just got trapped in the caves, but Angus found me. He nearly drowned.'

'The mute boy?'

Rude.

'He's not mute! He chooses not to speak.' Roxie could feel the air almost crackling.

'I stand corrected,' Maw replied, her eyebrows arched.

Her mum stepped in with her small talk flash cards. 'Roxie, Maw's into art like you. She got in to the Glasgow School of Art in the sixties.'

'Aye, I did, but I never took the place.' Roxie's ears pricked up. 'I got pregnant with Fiona.'

'How old were you?' Roxie's nosiness undermined her ambivalence. She still wasn't sure though; the old witch could be playing her.

'Seventeen.'

'And you're an artist?' she asked in disbelief, almost laughing at this crisp of a woman who looked like she couldn't paint her way out of a paper bag.

'Naw, I wish I was though.' Roxie could tell this wasn't bluff. 'Too old now...'

'You can still do it, be an artist you know. Age doesn't matter.'

Maw smiled wryly. 'So you're studying art, are you?'

'Oh, Roxie is very talented,' her mum proudly butted in. 'You should see some of her stuff on her iPad.'

Roxie hated when her mum paraded her like a golden goose. She glanced at Agnes, who conspiratorially rolled her eyes.

'I'm sure Roxie wouldn't want my opinion on her talent.' Maybe Maw wasn't as evil as she'd been painted, though she'd have to prove it. 'Unless she wants to show me herself.'

Half an hour later, after tea and some red velvet cake foraged from the pub kitchen, Roxie sat with Maw on the sofa scrolling through her iPad.

'So you use this wee pen thingy as a brush? But it changes on screen, not on the pen.'

'The pen's just an avatar,' Roxie said.

'An ava-what?'

'A stand-in,' Fiona explained.

'Och, I don't know about this. You say you did that with just the iPad?' Maw pointed to the beautiful portrait Roxie had done of Ash in class.

'No, that's a photo of a massive painting I did with acrylics. But these ones are drawn on the iPad.'

Maw stopped her on one of a mythical creature in an aubergine-coloured woodland, ethereal faces secreted in the shadows. 'I like that.'

'Thank you, that's done with Procreate on the iPad.'

'I can't believe that. I've a load of paints at home – I've never even used them – they'll all be dried up by now.' She glanced quickly at Roxie. 'Anyway, it'd be a waste of paper.'

'Try on here, you don't waste anything! That allows more freedom...' Roxie offered her the iPad, but Maw flinched like she'd been stung.

'Nooo, I couldn't. I'll break it.'

'You won't.'

'No, no...' Maw eyed it suspiciously.

'Have a go, Maw. I've said before you should get an iPad,' Fiona encouraged.

'Och, and I've always said what do I need one of them things for?'

Roxie placed it gently on her lap, a fresh page waiting to be filled. She handed Maw the pen. 'Look, click on that for colour, then that for brush or pen size.'

'I feel silly,' Maw protested, waving the pen like a wand.

'We won't look,' Roxie said, pretending to turn away.

Maw tentatively chose black and a medium-tipped nib. She swirled the pen over the screen.

'Would you look at that!' she cried in delight as if she'd just painted a Picasso. 'How do I rub it out?'

Maw settled down with the iPad while Fiona collected up the mugs with help from Adam.

'After everything, I forgot to say, the total was one thousand two hundred pounds last night,' Fiona called from the kitchen.

'What total?' Maw asked, looking up from her drawing.

'Open mic night downstairs. Maggie sang.' Fiona returned to collect the plates.

'You sing too?' Maw sounded surprised. 'I wish I'd seen that.'

'Not usually. I haven't sung for years. I came out of retirement for Fiona.'

'I'm sure we can find footage somewhere. So many people recorded it. I've not looked on the Facebook page yet. We can show you later...'

'A shame Morag never got to meet you, Maggie...' Roxie watched Maw's face – it creased with obvious effort as she prepared to excavate the truth like a painful tooth. 'For that I'm truly... sorry.'

Roxie held her breath. Fiona hovered with a pile of plates and Adam retracted his hand from gathering the unused forks. Maggie shrugged, magnanimously underplaying it.

'I had no right to play God. I didn't feel there was a choice though, not for Morag. And I felt you... well. It doesn't matter what I felt. It was the wrong decision...'

'You did what you thought was best.'

Maw nodded gratefully.

'I may not have met Morag, but I'm here now. I feel like there's something, a connection to her.'

'If I'd known what... how it would affect *everyone*, we could have kept you. I'd do it differently if I could.'

'They were different times, Agnes, and Morag was so young. I know you didn't make the decision lightly. I might never have met Adam and had Roxie if I'd lived up here. I wouldn't be who I am today. I had a nice life. Mum and Dad gave me everything I needed, and they loved me... It's just good to fill in the blanks, know where I'm from.'

'I'm glad. They were kind people, allowing Morag the pictures...'

Roxie felt like she was watching a stilted piss-take of those Mexican soaps on TikTok. But instead of screaming theatrically about the harsh reality of life, everyone was so uptight and British. *I'm sorry I forced your mum to give you away. No, I'm sorry you felt you had to. No, I'm sorry I ruined your life. No, I'm sorry I was born...* Just fucking say it how it is. But no one ever did; she still had no idea what was going on with her own parents. Sometime in the future if she ever had children (highly unlikely, if they were anything like her), she would make the effort to communicate, even if her own skin wanted to pucker up in a cringe-fest. Clearly, burying secrets helped no one.

As the lengthy silence split into more than a pregnant pause, Roxie couldn't bear it. *Someone say something!* She looked hopefully at the iPad.

'Oh wow, Agnes, that's amazing,' she cried gratefully, no fibs necessary.

'Och, no, it's just a wee sketch,' Maw said bashfully, pulling it towards her chest.

'Let's see, Maw,' Fiona asked. 'Hold it up.'

'Fiona, it's not show-and-tell!' Roxie laughed in relief as Maw held it up, pleased the tension had dissolved. Maw had sketched a quick pencil drawing of Maggie outlined against the windows, and standing behind her was Morag. It was beautiful in its simplicity, capturing the essence of them, sparing the details rendering it observational without being mawkish. Roxie glanced nervously at her mum.

'It's wonderful, Agnes,' her mum said, clearly moved. 'Do you mind if I keep it?'

'Of course! It's just a wee doodle.'

'Maw, where have you been hiding *that*?' Fiona cried in surprise. 'You need to carry it on. You've a gift.'

'Naw, don't be silly. I haven't done anything for years. No point starting now...'

'There is!' Roxie backed up Fiona. 'I'm not gonna lie, the fact that you haven't done anything since you were a teenager is impressive. You should go on TikTok and showcase your sketches. I can help you create an account. You're like Bob Ross.'

'Bob who?'

'Never mind. You should draw though. You're really good.'

'Well, I do like the galleries and whatnot. Not been to one since just after Lachlan died, mind you. He always humoured me with my visits.'

'We could take you, couldn't we?' Roxie said excitedly, peeking at her mum again.

'If you want to go to galleries, that's easily arranged,' Fiona agreed.

'Aye. I want young Roxie to take me though. She knows what's what...'

'Looks like I'm going home on my own tomorrow then...' her dad piped up, glancing over at her mum.

'What do *you* want to do, Roxie?' her mum asked.

Roxie didn't even hesitate. 'I'd like to stay, if you don't mind. I've got a job at Help the Aged.'

'Cheek of you!' Maw cried in mock indignation. 'You'll get a clip round the lugs with your bloody tablet if you don't respect your elders.'

'Sorry, Great-granny.'

* * *

Later that evening after they'd all eaten downstairs in the pub, Fiona drove Maw home and Roxie, Adam and Maggie retired upstairs to the flat. Roxie had just brushed her teeth and finished her evening ablutions when she opened the bathroom door to find her dad leaning against the wall.

'I need to explain something,' he began.

'I don't want to hear it, Dad. It's too weird.'

'Tough. It needs to be said.'

Roxie walked into her room trying to ignore him, but he followed her.

'Look, I made a massive mistake, and I'm paying for it, have been paying for it ever since—'

'Good!'

'OK, I get it, you're angry. Don't take it out on your mum, OK? She's done nothing wrong.'

Roxie couldn't find the right words, everything she wanted to say felt jumbled up and would only come out wrong, so she slammed her washbag on the desk, defiantly grabbed her phone and shoved her AirPods in her ears.

'I'll say bye in the morning. I love you. Sleep well.'

But she couldn't sleep. Ash wasn't answering their phone. She Snapchatted Angus instead, deleting the message four times before finally posting.

Thanks for rescuing me today. Hope your phone survived. Wondered if you're around tomorrow?

Roxie sat back and tried to listen to Yo La Tengo, but couldn't. She was too busy waiting. Only ten minutes as it happened.

No problem. What time you leaving?

I'm not going now. I'm staying with Mum for a bit.

How long?

Dunno, the summer?

She immediately sent another, closed her eyes and squirmed to her core.

Wanna hang out?

She couldn't even identify the tracks, it was just dissonance accompanying her beating heart at the base of her throat. After three tunes, a message popped up.

Yaldi. Sure thing. 😊

And just like that, everything stopped feeling so shit.

Maggie walked past the dunes down towards the shoreline, the wind failing to nudge her in a different direction. She'd read the final extracts of Morag's diaries in the few days since Adam's departure almost two weeks ago. There had been a lot of minutiae to skim over, funny stories of life on the road. However, after leafing through journals, she'd uncovered some gold.

* * *

April 23rd 1997

Today is Shona's (Margaret's) eighteenth birthday. I bought a cake from Dingwall and plunged eighteen candles into the chocolate icing. I've decided Shona likes chocolate best. Who doesn't? I sang her happy birthday, but it's also <u>my</u> day. ('My' was underlined three times.) The day I became a mum, but wasn't allowed. I ate a slice of cake for breakfast, it was really gooey, just what the doctor ordered. I've got the day off and Fiona's taking me out later, we're going for a swim in the sea – first one this year, then having a bottle of champagne to toast Shona and warm us up. I will not be sad. Now she's an adult, she can come and find me. I know it's not guaranteed, but the fact that I've had pictures all these years gives me some vestiges of hope.

I wonder what she's doing today on her big day? Does she ever think about me? I hope to be able tell her I've never stopped thinking about her, she's in my heart and head every day. That if I'd had a choice, she would be here now and we'd be celebrating in style, having the best party with all her friends, and dance the night away under the stars. I'd give anything to wish her happy birthday.

In other news, Casey rang to make sure I was OK. He's flying over at the end of June. I miss him, we won't have seen each other for three months.

Bitter regret stung Maggie's tongue, Morag's words threading round her neck like links in a chain. How had Maggie ever thought she'd just thrown her away without a second thought? Maybe that version of events had been easier to stomach than the unalloyed truth. She thought of Louis most days. On waking, he greeted her at the age he would be had he lived. In so many ways, her connections to Morag were ancestral. The patterns had repeated in triplicate: they had both lost a baby at birth; they were respectively left infertile facing early menopause; and finally after all that trauma, each of their romantic relationships had imploded. It felt sewn into their matrilineal DNA, a Rubicon having been crossed the night Maw's platform jump had been intercepted, setting the predetermined domino run into action.

Roxie and Maggie were driving to Glasgow tomorrow, staying overnight in a hotel and taking Maw on an art tour. Roxie had scoped it all out; they were collecting her later that afternoon. Apparently Maw was very taken with Roxie, recognised in her a kindred spirit. She'd even bought an iPad and had googled all the places she wanted to visit. She'd FaceTimed Roxie two nights ago. Maggie had hovered outside the bedroom door listening to them cackle, hyperaware eavesdropping never led anywhere pleasant...

'Roxie, be cross at your da, but don't take a bath in it. Grown-ups are eejits just like children. Some of us just have more money and better vocab, so we look like we're getting away with it. I've spent too long hiding and not living, too busy feeling terrible about my mistakes, and what good's it done anyone? Och, your dad'll be reliving and regretting his mistake every day. But you've only heard the one side. Don't jump in too quick to judge.' Maggie had crept away before the final instalment.

Maggie had also been drafted in on a dinner service one evening when Iona had an eighteenth birthday to attend. Fiona asked if there was any way Maggie would consider another open mic night before leaving – people had been asking. Maggie had been ploughing her way through Morag's vinyl, starting with Lonestar's. She'd unearthed some tunes that resonated, and Angus said he'd rehearse them with her. He'd been spending time in the flat, when Issy was there and also when she wasn't. He was still a brooding presence but appeared to be finding his footing with speaking, still reticent to throw himself into conversations, choosing his words carefully.

Meanwhile, Maggie could feel the neglected parts of her clamouring to be heard. She mourned all those times when music had engendered a wound so visceral she'd had to shut it down, rather than risk digging over old bones. But the old bones had been aired and hung out to dry. Taking comfort in her mother's struggle helped Maggie feel closer to her. Yet there was still a whole half of her unchartered.

As she shimmied out of her tracksuit bottoms, stuffing them inside her rucksack, along with her hoodie, glasses and phone, the wind almost carried her resolve with it back towards the dunes. Maggie was determined to get into the sea; she couldn't believe she'd been here now for weeks and hadn't yet ventured in. She was no fan of communal swimming pools with their screaming kids and slippy changing rooms. However, she always dived into a hotel pool when abroad where the sun forced your hand with its incessant heat. Swimming in the sea was different though whatever country she happened to be in. She considered it an act of self-care, like a bracing walk to clear one's head. Sea water was healing, carrying with it the support of the earth from the seabed below, along with all the ancient history and wisdom circumscribed within its unfathomable depths. The sea had seen everything.

Maggie launched herself into the waves before the cold could disarm her. The temperature difference slapped her skin, her scalp tingling as she dived beneath the surface, coming up for air to swim out where her feet couldn't reach the sand below. Her skin buzzed as she lay on her back floating on the chameleon sea, ruled not by itself but the premature crescent already suspended between the clouds. What would happen if the moon decided to take a day off? Would the sea know what to do? Would it have to slap on a moon replacement patch, like Maggie? Even with all the upheaval, she felt more grounded than ever, especially within the sea's briny embrace. Nevertheless, her story still didn't feel complete.

'You asked about your father at the beginning,' Fiona had said last night. 'How do you feel now?'

Maggie understood that by asking pertinent questions, other people's lives would be substantially ruffled. *No one likes change*, she told herself, *especially out of the blue*. Isla Ross was Maggie's first point of contact. She had her number scribbled down on a yellow Post-it note inside her bag. She'd waited too long to find Morag:

three parents dead, one unknown, and so floated awaiting clarity from the heavens, her eyes fixed upon the ghost moon. After five minutes of bobbing gently up and down, the cold began to grate, and she swam towards the shore still uncertain when to make the call. As she waded out of the water, her teeth chattering, two incongruous magpies swooped down landing on the sand, scaring off the gulls: two for joy. It was all the permission she needed.

Maggie delved into her rucksack, pulled out her hoodie and rammed it over her head. She found the crumpled Post-it and retrieved her phone. Heart galloping in her chest, she pressed Isla's number into the keypad and hit call before chickening out. With only three rings before she answered, Maggie had no time to even practise her opening gambit.

'Hello? Frank?'

'Er, hello... No, I'm not Frank... You don't know me, but I'm Fiona Stewart's niece.'

'Fiona Stewart...? Sounds so familiar...'

'Her dad used to be a ghillie for your father, Lachlan MacDowell...'

'Oh, I remember, yes, Lachlan. Sorry, I was waiting for a call. How is Fiona? And her mother? I heard Morag died recently. Very sad.' The onus of dropping a bomb into Isla's life overwhelmed her.

'She did... Look, this is er... massively awkward and I wondered if you were free at all to talk in person?'

* * *

An hour later, Roxie and Maggie were driving over to Tain on the A9, a journey they had to undertake anyway. The car radio smothered the expectant silence and, for once, Roxie wasn't plugged into her phone, AirPods blocking out her mum's presence.

Maggie worried that Isla wouldn't tell her where William was. What if she thought Maggie was after her estate, wanted to contest the inheritance?

'Remember he was cut off,' Fiona had reassured her. 'So you wouldn't have a claim anyway...'

The estate's main entrance just outside Tain dwarfed Maggie's tiny Micra hire car, like storming a castle in a shoebox. Roxie jumped out and rang the buzzer. The gates slowly juddered apart and they drove through, winding up a potholed road, through a dense pine forest, past a few squat grey stone houses with washing hanging outside and white plastic garden furniture stained by the elements. The house surprised them on the other side of the trees. They'd been expecting an historic pile like Downton Abbey.

'We've been short-changed!' Roxie laughed, the wheels crunching their way round the turning circle as the Micra pulled up by the stables.

The faded glory sandstone manor was partially concealed by tenacious wisteria but was no grand stately home. Maggie didn't know why she'd picture it as such. It looked like the original blue-print for all those aspirational housing estates in Caldy modelled on imperious farmhouses with Georgian pillars and sentinel bay windows.

The battered black front door opened and a woman walked out onto the front step eyeing them apprehensively.

'I thought we could chat in here,' she said, after shaking hands. Her greying blonde hair tamed into a long plait, ruddy sun-damaged cheeks, and shabby but expensive clothes exemplified her lady of the manor air. Her frayed salmon pink shirt collar was the only sliver of vivacity in her utilitarian navy palette.

She led them to a drawing room at the front of the house over-looking the drive. It was heavily papered with port red damask, dusty gilded portraits graced the walls. Shelves of leather-bound books and fringed standard lamps were arranged much like a stage set authentically depicting a fictitious down-at-heel country pile. Even the sheepdog asleep on a threadbare bed under the window had seen better days. The house felt weary and a heavy musty smell hung in the air.

'So, I think I can guess what this is about.' They sat on opposite lumpy sofas, Maggie shuffling to avoid a spring.

'You can?'

'Aye. Would you like tea first?'

'No, we're OK, thank you.'

'I'm assuming it's about the rent rise on Agnes's house. I know she's on a long lease that my father agreed for Lachlan's death in service, but all the utilities have skyrocketed. We're not managing to heat this place in the winter.'

'No, sorry, we're not here about that.'

Isla's face dropped, expression blank now.

'I'm Morag MacDowell's daughter; I was adopted in 1979. I've only very recently found out she died, which was a massive blow. Unfortunately, I'd left it until now before contacting her. Fiona has been amazing and I've been staying with my daughter in Morag's home in Benlachie. During a clear-out, we found letters and journals naming William as my father...'

Isla opened her mouth and sighed, then started shaking her head, her eyes pinching together like she was trying to crack a tricky crossword. 'But William was... *is* gay.'

'Yes, Fiona thought that was the case. Morag insisted he was my father. She fell pregnant just before he went to London.'

A flinty spark in the woman's eyes set light to any gold-digging qualms.

'Let me assure you, I just want to speak to him, nothing more...'

'I haven't spoken to him for a good couple of years. He keeps himself to himself.'

'Do you know where he is at least.'

'Aye.'

'Is it true he lives in Canada?'

'Look, forgive me, but how do I know you are who you say you are? I'm not handing anything over.'

'You can ring my family to check, of course. I can also do a DNA test. I just want to find my dad, that's it. All my known parents are dead and this is my last chance at finding a connection...'

'What if he doesn't want to be contacted? He ran away to Canada to escape the Highlands. You'll just be another thing he might want to run from.'

'He won't know until I give him the choice, will he?' Maggie could feel frustration snapping in her belly. She hadn't realised until this very moment just how much she really wanted to meet her father.

'Excuse me, but do you mind if I use the toilet?' Roxie piped up.

Isla directed her down the hallway.

'How old is your daughter?' Isla boldly tried averting Maggie's line of questioning.

'Fifteen, the same age Morag was when she had me.' Maggie wanted to hammer home that she sought contact, nothing more. 'Morag said in her letter she thought William would be pleased to know he had a daughter.'

Isla smiled thinly and Maggie couldn't tell if she disapproved of her or William. After all, Isla was also related to her, the bastard child of her errant unapologetically gay brother.

'Look, I admire you for coming here, that can't have been easy. But we don't want any trouble.'

'I'm not here to cause trouble or make a claim—'

'William was disinherited.' She played her trump card.

Awkward silence settled while Maggie contemplated her next move.

Isla wasn't going to acquiesce, clearly viewing her as some kind of carpetbagger. 'He and my father had a massive quarrel, after which he left for good. Father decided I should take on the estate after his death, and Lachlan had shown me the ropes from a wee girl. I'd always been more interested in the law of the land than William. He was ... more creative, airy-fairy. Not very traditional at all. He'd wanted to use the outhouses for musical weekends, and stop all the hunting...' She made it sound like he'd committed a crime not following the conventional route expected of him. 'My eldest is currently in training, showing huge commitment to the land and our traditions. William would never have carried that on. In the end, he made his choice. Nothing's fairer than that...'

Maggie wanted to point out he'd probably made no such choice and that his own father had apparently thrown him out on his ear for being gay. How was that fair? But she knew Isla was operating within her own blinkered boundaries. Inspecting them further, like Maggie's presence happened to be doing, would only open up a can of worms. She was doing what any good Tiger mum would do – protecting her progeny and their life's plan from any interlopers, whether they were genetically linked or not...

'Here's my number, if you change your mind, or manage to talk to Agnes or Fiona, you'll find out I'm genuine. All I want is to talk to my dad, if he so wishes.' Maggie placed a business card on the coffee table just as Roxie reappeared and sat on the very tip of the sofa, poised to leave any second. Maggie took her cue from her. 'Thank you for seeing us, I really appreciate it. I know how it looks, but it isn't like that. This can't have been easy on you and I'm sorry to have caused any distress.'

Isla nodded curtly, willingly accepting victimhood. Maggie

stood at the same time, Roxie practically springing to her feet, eager to escape.

As they drove off, Maggie glanced towards the drawing-room window and caught Isla watching their departure as the white Micra wobbled across the pane of glass.

'I guess it's up to me to track him down, she's never going to give me his details.' Disappointment pressed heavily on her shoulders. William's own flesh and blood was blocking him from meeting his daughter, Maggie's motives not understood in the slightest. The gates were already opening as the car approached them.

'You could email him,' Roxie said casually as Maggie steered out of the entrance and headed to Maw's.

'How? I suppose I could google his name, see if he's on social media. People his age are more likely to be on Facebook than anything else...'

'Or you could use this.' Roxie flashed her phone screen at her mum.

'What's that?'

'His email address and telephone number.'

Maggie slammed on the brakes, skidding to a halt at the side of the road. A Highland cow looked up from its grass and winked at her from the adjacent field.

'How'd you get that?' She grabbed the phone and inspected the photo. A neatly scripted postal address in Vancouver and an email address and telephone number stared back at her.

'I looked in her address book next to the telephone in the hall. It was by the loo on one of those fancy tiny tables. I'm not gonna lie – I was going to try to find her office and have a snoop, but that was there like a sitting duck.'

Maggie kissed Roxie before she could protest. 'You little star! I can't believe you did that.'

'I could one hundred per cent tell the old cow wasn't going to crack, and thought she'd have an address book somewhere, like Nana used to. It was worth a shot.'

'What would you have done if you'd been caught?'

'Said I got lost looking for the loo!'

'Genius!'

'Not just a pretty face, eh?' And Roxie pulled her best pouty photo pose, her lightness sweeping away the cobwebs.

EPILOGUE

Margaret Pink, Maggie for short, sat with her back to the kitchen window, hunched over her laptop. It had been five days since she'd returned from Glasgow. She'd taken a back seat while Roxie and Maw had taken charge round Kelvingrove, bathing in Dalí and other more traditional pieces, whilst finding herself completely puzzled by some of the exhibits in the Gallery of Modern Art. 'I could have made that!' she'd said about a 'sculpture' of a white Anglepoise lamp set on a box. 'Ah, but you didn't, did you?' Maw had replied, making Roxie laugh.

They'd had a lovely time, Roxie enthralled with Maw's enthusiasm for even the most outlandish of visual concoctions. When they had dropped her home, Maggie found herself inviting Maw to come and stay and visit the London galleries, but only once she'd sorted a new flat after the house sale. Maw had eyed her closely and patted her hand. 'Don't jump the gun, hen. You mightn't move yet.' Maggie hadn't known how to respond and the furtive look that passed between Roxie and Maw obviously hung on the back of a conversation Maggie hadn't been party to. She hoped Maw hadn't been filling Roxie's head with hopeful nonsense...

Maggie stared at her inbox. She'd sent a business-style email to an ancient AOL address on the other side of the North Atlantic on the day of her return. She'd checked for a reply at least ten times a day, mostly when she went to the loo, but still nothing. Her thoughts were being drawn more and more towards the fathers in her life. Her dad, Jonathan, a kind and patient man for whom nothing had ever been too much trouble. Emotional he was not, but reliable and steadfast were decent qualities. She'd rung Nisha with an update on everything, and talk had turned to the other father in her life: Adam.

'Wow, so Roxie knows the truth?' Nisha had exclaimed. 'The entire truth?'

'What do you mean?'

'How Adam thought he was Ross and you were Rachel and you were on a break, permanently...'

'I can't tell her that. One day, but not now.'

'Why not? You don't have to go into details.'

'He was still unfaithful.'

'I thought you were over it now?'

'I am.'

That's the thing with old friends that know everything, have seen your face open with love and joy, they've invested in you too. Maggie and Adam had been aspirational paragons of true romance, a benchmark for all other relationships around them. Being with them had made friends like Nisha feel she always had a home in their presence. So when they suffered the inconsolable loss, their friends felt it too. And when their relationship floundered, others looked inward at their own connections, and some found them lacking. If Adam and Maggie were screwed, they all were. It sent out a ripple of insecurity.

'Anyway, I like being on my own. I get the bed all to myself.'

'That can't be the only benefit?'

'It's a major one! Don't you like it when Lisa's away and you get to stick your leg into the cold part of the bed?'

'Jesus, if you're measuring your quality of life on your obsession with the cold side of the pillow and bed sheets, then there's no hope for you.'

'I can't remember what good sex is like. This is the next best thing...'

'How will you feel when Adam meets someone else? When he marries someone else?' Nisha wasn't above shock tactics in a fight to the death. But those thoughts were something Maggie had pushed so far back, she couldn't locate them among her daily reflections that consisted of such aperçus as would Louis have had red hair?; are Tena Ladies the same as sanitary pads?; will I ever have pant-ripping sex again?; what's the point of those paper flaps under margarine lids?; would I die of malnutrition if all I ate was crisp sandwiches?; how do untouched wires get so tangled?; was Mum ever scared Morag would turn up at our house?; how many people will come to my funeral? The one thought she never *ever* entertained was: what would've happened if I hadn't snooped on Adam's iPad? If she contemplated that, she'd have to closely inspect all the evidence instead of clamping down on the one clear-cut fact: he was unfaithful. But it wasn't an unrelated fact...

'I'm sure I'll cope,' she replied to Nisha. What if he was swinging from the chandeliers right now though? While the divorce was still in the dry dock? Nothing she could do if he was. She ignored the scintilla of fear that flickered in her belly. Divorce was hard no matter what side of the launchpad you were on; no one got out unscathed.

She popped in to see Issy at lunchtime. Angus and Roxie were watching a film and she needed distraction. Rain sluiced down the hill, but nothing deterred the gulls. They couldn't be accused of being fair-weather friends.

'Any news?' Issy asked.

'No,' Maggie sighed. 'Maybe it's an old address and he hasn't bothered to tell his sister he has a new one?'

'Aye. Or maybe he's scared shitless. He mightn't realise you know he's gay and he'll have to come out all over again. He could be worried about being a disappointment. You've no idea what's going through his head...'

'Yes, I know. Can I have a coffee please?'

'I'll bring you over my latest treat too. They're pure dead brilliant. I found a small bakery in Inverness that's perfected them.'

Maggie sat staring aimlessly out of the rain-streaked window as tourists browsed the exotic shells and holiday tat Issy insisted they loved. Adam persistently flitted across the back of her mind. She pushed him away. Today was a divorce-free zone. She had no idea what divorce entailed, apart from being costly, fighting over who got to keep the onion goggles and separating everything into his and hers piles. Who would get custody of Roxie's box of baby teeth? Would they have to divide them up? She only wanted the incisors... As for the CDs, Adam had digitised them years ago and all the vinyl was his, apart from some of her Five Star albums and a couple of her Mariah Careys from years ago. He wouldn't want them; he'd actively mocked her teenage musical taste.

'We can't all have been born with *NME* in our mouth,' she'd retorted. 'Rain or Shine' was a pop classic, not timeless enough to ever receive radio play though...

Issy plonked her coffee in front of her, along with a majestic swirl of sugary doughy delight. 'It's a bona fide Danish Cinnabun.'

Maggie burst into tears, startling Issy, who grabbed a paper napkin from the steel dispenser and thrust it at her.

'Och shit, what have I done?'

'Nothing, it's nothing.'

'It must be something.'

Maggie shook her head.

'Shall I take away the bun?'

'No! I want it, thanks. I just need a minute.'

Issy pulled out the opposite chair and sat down. 'I don't want you to leave and go back to London. Neither does Fiona. There, I've said it!'

'I know, she's already mentioned it. Keeps making noises about me visiting the festival, about singing at it... Anyway, I'm not going yet.'

'Aye. I know. You'd bring the house down... if you sang. Think about it...? I also know you'd be brilliant at organising the festival, but that's a long shot...'

Maggie grinned and picked up the bun, biting into it, transporting herself back to Copenhagen March 2008. They'd had a family city break before she finished maternity leave, Roxie had come along for the ride. It had been one of the happiest times in her life, and that memory exploded in her mouth as her teeth cut through the crust and tore into the sweet squidgy cinnamon centre... Adam had popped out from the rental apartment to get breakfast, leaving her in bed with Roxie. When he returned, he'd clumsily kept dropping cutlery as he made them both tea before appearing in the doorway with a tray holding two mugs and the largest cinnamon swirl Maggie had ever seen.

'For my love.' And he'd bowed, lowering the tray onto the bed at the same time.

Maggie had squealed at the sight of the sugary treat, making Roxie laugh, and she'd swooped it off the plate towards her mouth. As she broke off a corner for Roxie, a giant crystal of twinkling sugar caught her eye in the centre. On closer inspection, she noticed it was a diamond attached to a platinum ring. She looked up and found Adam on one knee, a flustered look on his face...

'What's going on?' Issy asked. Maggie's eyes were leaking again.

'I don't know. I keep trying to block things out, but they won't.'

'Won't?'

'Go away. Things I've not looked at keep ambushing me...'

'Maybe you need to allow them... Maybe being here has opened a portal?'

Maggie nodded in agreement. From the instant she'd sung 'I Will Survive' in The Sea Shanty, things had taken a weird turn. Actually, before that. From the moment she'd landed on Scottish soil, returning to her roots, it felt like the shell she'd spun around herself had slowly fractured until the entire thing had fallen away, leaving her exposed like a new-born chick.

'I need to go. I want to send another email telling William everything, that I know he's gay, that I don't care, that I just want to meet him. He needs to know he's my dad and that's all that matters. How much for the coffee and bun?'

'It's on the house. You go and sort your head out. I'll be over later with some new wine made from grapes grown by fairies in a French valley under a pink full moon. It was free, so bottoms up!' Issy leaned over and kissed her friend's cheek.

* * *

Maggie made a big deal about shutting the door to the flat, a warning klaxon for herself more than anything. She didn't want to walk into a teenage grope-fest.

'It's me!' she called down the corridor over the blaring TV. She slipped into her room and picked up her laptop on Morag's dressing table. She clicked on mail and there waiting was an email from William Munro. She stared at it for at least a minute before she opened it, her pulse beating in her ears.

Dear Maggie,

Wow, how lovely to hear from you. What a huge surprise. You say you're my daughter? I did always wonder, but Morag never said a word. I don't really know what to say to you other than I'm in shock. Not in a bad way. Just surprised, at my age, to discover I have a long-lost daughter. Here's one thing you need to know, I'm gay. Morag was one of the only women I connected with in that way. She was a belter, and I'm so sad to hear that she's passed. What an absolute shame she never got to meet you because I know she never wanted to give you up. Life has a funny way of turning out. I hope you're happy, you said you also have a daughter called Roxie, my granddaughter. So not only am I a father, I'm a granda too. I think my life's complete. I'm happy to carry on corresponding in this way, or we can try FaceTime or one of those other video calls. I'm not so old that it fazes me. In fact, it's how I keep in touch with friends across the world as well as the music community. I'd love to see a picture of you. I've attached a recent one of me taken by my partner, Andrew. Please excuse the bad hair and unshaven face. It hides a multitude of sins. I look forward to your reply. Thank you so much for finding me. You have no idea how happy this has made me.
Yours truly, William

Maggie's phone beeped right at that moment with a text from Adam.

I think some paperwork has arrived for you from the estate agents. Do you want me to open it later?

'Oh, hello. I didn't mean you had to ring.' Adam sounded startled.

'It's OK. Yes please do open it. How are you?' Maggie's tummy didn't feel right.

'I'm OK. I'm at work, about to go for lunchtime drinks. Someone's leaving.'

JANET HOGGARTH

'Where you off out to?'

'Same old, same old, Crown and Two Chairmen. Other pubs are available...' Maggie smiled. 'What are you doing? How's Roxie?'

'Roxie's good, she and Angus seem to be very close. I don't ask, you know what she's like. But she seems happy.'

Maggie paused. She wanted to tell Adam, but ... *but what*?

'I got an email today. From my dad.'

'What? Your *real* dad? I didn't think you knew who he was.'

'Yes, Morag left a note. William Munro. He lives in Canada.'

'Do you know anything about him?'

'He lives in Vancouver...' Silence from Adam. 'Are you googling him right now?'

'You know me so well!'

'It's Munro with a u and no e on the end.' Maggie chuckled. 'I have a picture here.' She opened it and gazed at her dad, his eyes crinkling at the camera, his salt-and-pepper beard adding a distinguished touch to a strong face. Roxie had his nose.

'Wow, so there are a few. A lawyer, a paediatric nurse, a constructional engineer, a gardener, a guitar teacher, a—'

'That's him! Possibly. I know he played guitar at one time. Worth a punt.'

'He has a beard, here, I'll send you the link for his website...'

* * *

When Roxie knocked on Maggie's door half an hour later before pushing it open, she found her mum roaring with laughter with someone on the phone.

'Mum, oh, sorry. We're going to get some ice cream. It's stopped raining.'

Maggie nodded and smiled.

'Is that Nisha?'

'No, your dad. He says hi by the way.'

Roxie almost choked, but didn't say a word. Instead, she quietly closed the door and walked down the hallway to meet Angus.

'What flavour you trying today?' he asked.

'What the actual fuck flavour.'

'Me too.' He kissed her forehead and they pulled the front door shut, Maggie's laughter still audible behind them.

ACKNOWLEDGMENTS

I would like to thank my mum for all the small adoption details that make this story a living breathing tale. Thank you to my dad, Paul, for the 1960s minutiae. Special thanks to Joanna Hoggarth, Katie Hoggarth and Andrew Watson for all the Scottish vernacular. And also to Susie Hoggarth, Sharon Boxall and Rachel Johnson for the eighties trip down memory lane. I'm too young to remember... Thank you to Heather Jane James for reading a very rough draft and inspiring me. I'm very grateful to Lindsey Shaw for her insight into the life of a professional singer. Thanks as always to my agent, Charlie Viney, and my editor, Sarah Ritherdon, for believing in Maggie Pink. Thanks to all at Boldwood, especially Jade Craddock, Sue Lamprell, and Sandra Ferguson for polishing my story. I am also very grateful to friends who have shared distressing experiences of losing their babies. Thank you. And finally, thank you to all the mothers and children who shared their forced adoption experiences in the press. All the articles shored up my mum's adoption experience and subsequent reunion with her birth mother, Mair. No mother should have to go through that trauma. So many lives were damaged. My mum was lucky, she had a happy childhood, but so many children didn't. Gladys and Hector MacDonald were kind people and for that, I will be eternally grateful. Even though I was not related to my nana by blood, we were alike in many ways. Nature vs nurture – I still don't know what side of the fence I stand on.

MORE FROM JANET HOGGARTH

We hope you enjoyed reading *Who Do You Think You Are, Maggie Pink?* If you did, please leave a review.

If you'd like to gift a copy, this book is also available as an ebook, digital audio download and audiobook CD.

Sign up to Janet Hoggarth's mailing list for news, competitions and updates on future books.

https://bit.ly/JanetHoggarthnews

ABOUT THE AUTHOR

Janet Hoggarth is the number one bestselling author of *The Single Mums' Mansion* and the highly successful *Single Mums'* subsequent series. She has worked on a chicken farm, as a bookseller, a children's book editor, a children's author, and as a DJ (under the name of Whitney and Britney!). She lives with her family in East Dulwich, London. Her first book for Boldwood will be published in 2022.

Follow Janet on social media:

 facebook.com/JanetHoggarthAuthor
twitter.com/Janethauthor

Boldwood

Boldwood Books is an award-winning fiction publishing company seeking out the best stories from around the world.

Find out more at www.boldwoodbooks.com

Join our reader community for brilliant books, competitions and offers!

Follow us
@BoldwoodBooks
@BookandTonic

Sign up to our weekly deals newsletter

https://bit.ly/BoldwoodBNewsletter

Printed in Great Britain
by Amazon

84655165R00203